)ead Man Walking

1 *Spy Amongst Us*

By

Toby Oliver

Cover Design: CreateSpace

Published April 2015

Republished January 2017

Copyright 2015 Toby Oliver

This is a work of fiction. Names, characters, places and incidents are either the products of the author's imagination or are used fictitiously, and any resemblances to actual persons, business establishments, events or locales are entirely coincidental.

ISBN: 978-1508476948
ISBN:-10-1508476942

With grateful thanks to David Morris and Jill Langley for their patience and support.

"Do you realise that by the time you wake up in the morning, 20,000 men may have been killed?"

Winston Churchill to his wife, the night before D-Day

Chapter 1

The Blackout was in full force, and London was shrouded in darkness, save only for the soft, pale moonlight reflecting on the rain-soaked streets. The moonlight shadows crept from behind the trees on either side of the road, and a biting wind rustled softly through their branches. A green Jaguar Roadster drew up in Lord North Street, turning off the Embankment near Westminster Abbey. Being only four minutes from the heart of government, the exquisite Georgian Street was much favoured by parliamentarians. Inside the elegant, softly-lit drawing rooms, deals were cut, power was brokered, and careers were either ruthlessly made, or destroyed, in equal measure.

Outside one of the imposing, five-storey townhouses, was a discreet police presence; Special Branch had no wish to arouse the interest of the great and good of Lord North Street, at least not just yet. The body of Lord Oakways, a prominent member of Churchill's coalition government, had been discovered by Mary Green, his housekeeper, on her return from a visit to her sister in Dulwich, across the river in south London. The poor woman had found Oakways in the library, slumped in an armchair, with a knife embedded deeply in his neck. In a state of near hysteria, Mary had contacted the local police, who then promptly handed the matter over to Scotland Yard's Special Branch. Potential criminal investigations involving either National Security or members of Parliament were, without exception, conducted by officers from Special Branch.

After arriving at the crime scene, DCI Harry Mackenzie decided to place a call to an ex-colleague and close friend, Luke Garvan, who'd been on secondment to MI5 from the beginning of 1941. Garvan had recently been promoted to the rank of Superintendent, with the blessing of the

Commissioner, in recognition of his work for the security services.

During a routine search of the house, Mackenzie had stumbled across a letter in Lord Oakways' study, which he knew would be of particular interest to British Intelligence.

Out of the Jaguar Roadster stepped Garvan and an MI5 officer, Major Spencer Hall. Mackenzie was awaiting their arrival with a young plain-clothed constable on the doorstep of Oakways' house. He stepped toward the kerb, and extended his hand in greeting.

'Guv'nor,' he said, addressing Garvan, 'I wasn't sure if you could make it at such short notice.'

'You were lucky we were both still at the office.'

'What have you got for us?' Spencer asked with undisguised curiosity.

'Follow me,' he said, heading the way into the house, and across a cavernous tiled hallway, through into the tawny panelled study overlooking Lord North Street.

On entering, the first thing which struck them were the blood splattered walls and a hideously large crimson stain on the Persian carpet. It was only then they noticed the body of Lord Oakways, seated in a dark green high-backed leather chair, which was angled slightly toward a marble fireplace. It wasn't a particularly pleasant sight. A small bladed knife was embedded up to the hilt on the left side of his neck, and judging by the horrific amount of blood loss, the blade had presumably severed the jugular vein.

'Well, someone certainly didn't like the poor old bugger, did they?' Spencer mused, moving in to take a closer look at the body.

Oakways was in his late sixties. Behind the scenes, he had been something of a political wheeler-dealer, and, more recently, had held a series of ministerial roles within the current wartime coalition.

'By the look of it, His Lordship had evidently made one or two enemies in his time,' Spencer continued breezily. He took a step back from Oakways' body, and studied him thoughtfully. 'He looks vaguely familiar.'

'You've probably seen his photo in the newspapers,' Mackenzie said. 'He's been a member of the Cabinet for at least four years, or more.'

'Why call us?' Garvan asked.

'I thought you might be interested in this,' Mackenzie said, picking up a diary from the desk. 'I found it in the drawer; check out the entry for Tuesday, 20th of June.'

Garvan opened the diary, and found the indicated entry. His gaze glided over the neatly written scrawl. "Lunch – Tuesday, 12.30, Claridge's." The entry was circled with two exclamation marks in red ink. Obviously important. As his gaze drifted further down the page, his face suddenly registered surprise recognising the name of Oakways lunch date. 'Take a look at this,' he said handing it over to Spencer.

Seeing the name Toniolo, Hall's expression hardened immediately. He looked back at Mackenzie questioningly. 'Has anyone else seen this?'

'No, I thought I'd better hold off forensics, until you had both had a chance to look round.'

'I suppose that's something,' Spencer said. 'Just make sure they don't get their hands on the diary!'

Mackenzie nodded.

Toniolo was the codename of a suspected spy operating at the heart of the British establishment, who was believed to be covertly working on behalf of Stalin's security service, the NKVD. Since Hitler's invasion of Russia back in 1940, Britain and the USSR had become allies. It was an alliance driven by necessity, rather than by any great overriding political desire. While some intelligence regularly passed between the two countries and the USA, dissemination was on a severely restricted basis; neither the Allies nor the

6

Soviets being quite able to trust the other. The identity of Agent Toniolo remained still very much a mystery to the British security service.

The investigation into tracking him down had, until now, provided few tangible results, and for several months, had scarcely got off the ground. Some senior members of the intelligence community had cast grave doubts about the veracity of the information, and felt it could have been nothing more than a red herring to deflect their attention. The trouble was, the main thrust of the intelligence had derived from George Rowlands, a disgraced MI6 spy, who had, at one point, severely compromised Allied secrets by passing the Abwehr high-grade classified intelligence. Understandably, there had remained a certain amount of reluctance to treat the allegation that seriously, and many suspected Rowlands might well have only been playing for time.

The fact Mackenzie had stumbled across Toniolo's name was significant, and finally provided British Intelligence with confirmation Toniolo had contacts within government circles. In essence, it was the first step in providing proof of the traitor's existence, and that they had a Soviet spy operating under their noses.

'Check the entry for lunch on the 27th,' Mackenzie said, pointing toward the diary.

Spencer turned the page over, and read it aloud, 'Len Dunmore, the Savoy, 1.30pm.'

Dunmore was a renowned Fleet Street journalist, who had his finger on the pulse of Whitehall thinking. Long before the War, he'd already developed a reputation for cultivating political contacts, but had skilfully avoided abusing his position as a journalist. It had been a fine balancing act, but his investigative journalism had led to some spectacular editorial scoops and front page headlines. At the end of the day, he'd never lost sight of a good story, and perhaps, more importantly, he'd never lost the trust of his well-connected contacts.

Garvan knew Dunmore of old, but at the moment, he was more interested in Oakways; he was a new name to him.

'So what, do we have on Oakways?' he asked.

Mackenzie gave a shrug. 'I'm not quite sure where to begin,' he offered. 'A few months ago, the Commissioner asked me to pull his security files.'

'Why?'

'Apparently, the Home Secretary tipped him the wink Oakways' behaviour was becoming a bit irrational.'

'What's that to do with Special Branch?'

'Oakways believed he was being threatened.'

'Did you check it out?'

'Not really, the boss just told me to keep a weather eye on the situation, but not to bust a gut, as most people seemed convinced Oakways' alcoholism was the real problem.'

'So, was there anything interesting on his file?'

'Before the War, he was known for being on the extreme right.'

That wasn't the answer Garvan had been expecting. 'You mean, a Fascist?'

He pulled a face. 'I wouldn't go so far as to say *that*. Since the War, he's certainly kept his head down.'

'That doesn't mean to say he isn't a Fascist.'

'I really can't see it myself.'

'What have we got to go on?' Garvan continued, 'There has to be a connection.'

'More to the point,' Spencer said, 'what exactly was he doing in the government?'

'He was a Minister at the Foreign Office.'

Spencer smirked. 'I guess that covers a multitude of sins.'

Mackenzie laughed. 'Oakways seemingly had political responsibility for the Iberian desk.'

'Did he? Then, he was in it up to his neck, working alongside MI6.'

'I believe so.'

The Iberian desk covered Spain, Portugal, Gibraltar, and Africa. It was a pivotal role for any politician, and would have brought Oakways into daily contact with British Intelligence.

'Was he married?' Spencer asked.

To Mackenzie's mind, the question seemed quite random. 'No, he divorced his wife, Laura, before the War. By all accounts it was quite a pretty high profile court case, and she ended up losing custody of the children.'

'Why was that?'

'The judge considered Laura to be the guilty party; she'd had an affair, and wanted out of the marriage. At the time, the Press reports nicknamed her "the Bolter." From what I can gather, she'd been pressured by her family into the marriage. Oakways was rolling in old money, and they saw it as a way of advancing their standing in society. It doesn't ever seem to have been a marriage made in heaven, but whatever the rights or wrongs of the case, Laura ended up crucified in the Press for supposedly abandoning her children.'

'And did she abandon them?' Spencer queried.

'No, not at all. She fought for their custody, but as the guilty party, she didn't have a cat in hell's chance of winning, or, at least, that's how the court viewed it.'

'How long ago did they divorce?'

'Don't quote me, but I think I read on file somewhere it must have been at least eight to ten years ago now.'

'Do we have anything on the housekeeper, Mary Green?'

'Nothing of note. She's worked for him for twenty-odd years. He'd given her the night off; he was supposedly working late at the office, so she wasn't expecting him home. When Mary returned from visiting her sister in Dulwich, she noticed the light was on in the study. The poor woman went to check on him, opened the door, and found his body slumped in the chair.'

'It must have given her quite a fright,' Spencer said sympathetically.

'It's enough to give anyone a fright. Mary seems a genuine enough sort, but the trouble is, she's as deaf as a bloody post. If the entire Household Cavalry had charged through the house, she wouldn't have heard anything.'

'Was there anything in the diary for this evening?'

Mackenzie shook his head. 'No nothing at all.'

Garvan suddenly noticed the display cabinet to the right of the fireplace showcasing a broad array of Staffordshire figures. He decided to take a closer look. 'Was Oakways a collector?'

'No, they're not his. According to Mary Green, they belong to his wife,' he said by way of explanation. 'Apparently, he hated the ruddy stuff, but when they were still together, she loved to show the collection to their dinner guests. Mary reckons some of the pieces are worth a small fortune.'

'Why didn't she take them with her after the divorce?'

'I've no idea.'

Garvan nodded, and moved slowly around the tawny panelled study. He couldn't help noticing that there was a fine film of dust coating the surfaces of the furniture. Mary Green was obviously not that diligent in her housekeeping duties. On the mantelpiece was an opened letter, Garvan picked it up, it was an invoice from a removal company. He waved the letter in Mackenzie's direction.

'What's this all about was he moving house?'

'Yes, the dining room is stacked out with packing-cases, according to Mary he was due to move house next week.'

Garvan's face registered surprise. 'Why would he want to leave? I'd bite my ruddy hand off to live in a place like this.'

'Mary wasn't a hundred percent sure why, but thought it was all down to Oakways convincing himself that the house was bugged.'

Garvan instinctively looked toward Spencer, who seemed on the surface, at least, to be as genuinely taken aback as he was. 'Bugged,' Garvan repeated.

'Yes, he thought the place was wired.'

'Not by us,' Spencer ventured uncertainly, 'or at least not to my knowledge, his name certainly hasn't come across my desk, but I'll have to check when we get back to the office.'

'What about MI6?' Garvan suggested.

Mackenzie gave an indifferent shrug. 'If they are responsible, I doubt if they'll own up to it.'

'What made him think he was under surveillance?'

'God only knows. I can only believe he started to get a bit twitchy after George Rowlands was exposed as a double agent. Being in charge of the Iberian desk, he received regular updates from Lisbon, and in particular from Rowlands. I guess he was afraid it was a case of guilt by association.'

'What did he do before the war?' Spencer asked.

'Before becoming an MP, he joined the Civil Service, and spent a few years on the diplomatic circuit.'

'Did he work anywhere of interest?'

A slow smile crossed Mackenzie's face. 'He spent six years in Portugal, and after the outbreak of the War, he was an obvious candidate for the FO.'

'Who did he work for?'

'Jeremy Haining.'

'I've heard of him,' Spencer said.

'Rumour has it, he's something of a rough diamond, a dyed in the wool Labour MP for Southwark in South London.'

'What else do we know about him?'

'He's apparently a local grammar school boy made good. His headmaster had wanted him to stay on and complete his education, but his family was pretty poor, so Haining decided he'd better start earning a living, and help his parents out financially. Give Haining his due, he carried on with his education at evening classes.'

'What did he do to earn his keep?'

'He started work as a junior clerk in a legal firm. It was there he decided to drop his London accent.'

'Why?'

'He thought it would probably appeal to the firm's society customers.'

'How in the hell did he end up becoming an MP?' Spencer asked.

'After his marriage to a local girl. Maria Bell, Haining secured himself employment as a ledger clerk for the Transport and General Workers Union. His activity within the Labour Party and their youth movement sealed the deal. He was academically gifted, and had become an astute operator. All in all, I guess it was probably only a matter of time before he got himself noticed as a prospective Parliamentary candidate.'

'How did he end up at the Foreign Office?'

'Churchill rates him it's as simple as that; he wasn't particularly interested in the colour or persuasion of his politics. All that mattered was whether he could deliver the goods. Haining's an adept communicator and understands the political issues; he also happens to be popular on both sides of the House.' Mackenzie hesitated; it wasn't strictly true. The far left of the Labour Party had often accused him of not only playing to the gallery but of betraying their socialist roots.

'Is there anyone else of note who worked with Oakways we should perhaps take a look at?'

'You might want to interview Jamie Burdis.'

'The name seems vaguely familiar.'

'He's not exactly your typical rich Tory MP, don't get me wrong he has all the right credentials. He went to Eton and graduated from Cambridge with a second-rate degree, but he's always been a bit of a wild card. Intelligent enough, but arrogant with it. By all accounts, he's a nasty piece of work. He worked alongside Oakways for a while at the Foreign Office, but fell out with Jeremy Haining, and was eventually demoted to the backbenches after Churchill grew tired of his behaviour. I think you'll find there are an awful lot of people, even in his own party, who were rubbing their hands that it was about time he got his comeuppance.'

'Has Special Branch ever been interested him?'

'Once or twice. He's had some narrow scrapes, mainly with women. In fact, amongst his fellow MPs he's known as the "Loins of Westminster".'

Spencer smiled. 'Has he ever been blackmailed?'

'Not to our knowledge, although he's certainly paid off a few people to keep things out of the Press. There have also been a couple of successful paternity suits against him, and the odd libel case. Let's just say, he's one of our more colourful customers.'

'How long have we got to take a look round?' Spencer asked.

'Maybe an hour or so before the pathologist and the forensic team arrive.'

'They're the least of our problems.'

Mackenzie assumed he was referring to MI6.

'We'll need to make a clean sweep of the house.'

Mackenzie looked at him speculatively. 'How long do you need?'

'If MI6 have been trailing Oakways, it's only a matter of time before they start pulling strings. They'll try to outgun you.'

Mackenzie couldn't fault his logic. If Oakways had been placed under official surveillance, then he would be ordered to back off immediately.

'It'll take MI5 the best part of the night to make a full sweep of the house. Does that give you enough time?'

'It won't be easy.'

'Who else knows what's happened?' Spencer pressed him.

'Mary Green phoned the local police station.'

'In which case, you really ought to think about battening down the pathologist and forensics until tomorrow morning.'

'That's all well and good, but how the hell am I supposed to do that?'

'Give them the usual excuse.'

'You mean national security?'

Spencer nodded.

Mackenzie hesitated, and looked toward Garvan, as if for support.

'We don't have a choice,' he responded bleakly.

*

Later that evening, at MI5's HQ in St. James's, Spencer placed a call to Deb Gander at Bletchley Park, and asked her to check for any intercepted signals either from Lisbon or Berlin regarding Toniolo over the last few months. The Abwehr were occasionally guilty of being slapdash in some of their communications; there'd been incidences where their agents' full names had been signalled inadvertently to

Berlin. It was also worth another shot to see whether German Intelligence believed George Rowlands, or Agent Schornsteinfeger as they knew him, was still active.

From MI5's standpoint, the general opinion was, since his enforced return from Portugal, they'd successfully managed to close down his activities as a double agent, but he needed to reassure himself. Up until now, Rowlands had been their only, if somewhat unreliable, source about Toniolo being a Soviet spy. It was a long shot, but he needed to re-visit every possible avenue of enquiry.

Four days later, Spencer received a call back from Deb Gander; her cryptographers had intercepted a message. It was short on detail, but important all the same.

Chapter 2

George Rowlands had once been the subject of admiration at MI6, something of a high flyer, destined to become a leading figure in their ranks. But, those days had long since passed. He was now little more than a social pariah, an outcast, a double agent, who was caught red-handed by Spencer Hall and Garvan in Lisbon. It was during this time Rowlands had covertly managed to gain access to the personal safe of his boss, Frank Lucern, and photograph top secret documents at the MI6 Station. He had then passed the negatives on to the Abwehr. By default, he had also stumbled across a stream of intelligence about British and US intentions in the near and Middle East, which proved at the time a veritable godsend to Nazi intelligence. In hindsight, perhaps Lucern's greatest failing in Lisbon was he had blindly stood by his staff, beyond the call of duty, and, as a consequence, had then found himself blindsided by Rowlands's treachery.

Almost a year had passed since then, Rowlands was still under house arrest, monitored twenty-four hours a day by Special Branch. However much MI5 had wished to press formal charges against him, the Government had eventually come to the conclusion it could not risk compromising National Security. At least not for the sake of punishing a single traitor, like Rowlands. It was not a decision they had made lightly, far from it, but there was much more at stake than prosecuting one treacherous double agent.

Throughout the proceedings, Rowlands had failed to show the slightest sign of remorse, even though he had knowingly sent many agents to their deaths, including at least one close friend, an agent called Pete Starling. Both Spencer and Garvan had long harboured suspicions he was still holding out on them, and the drip feed of intelligence he'd parted with was probably just the tip of the iceberg.

*

A sleek black Wolsey headed along a bomb-damaged street in north London. Rowlands was seated in the back, and casually glanced out of the window toward a gang of steeplejacks demolishing what remained of the surrounding houses on either side of the road, before the buildings collapsed of their own accord. Most of the terraced houses appeared to have already been totally destroyed; their bricks pulverised to a pulp by the sheer force of the explosions.

Further along, the street, the auxiliary services had formed a series of chain gangs to clear the rubble, and were loading up several trucks with any salvageable wood and surviving bricks. The devastation appeared so great it momentarily crossed Rowlands's mind a V-1 rocket might well have been responsible for the decimation of what had once been a quiet residential street. Since D-Day, it had been inevitable Hitler would seek revenge, and order the rockets to be launched against civilian targets in London. The Führer had wanted to both demoralise and to decimate the population to such an extent the British Government's hand would be forced into negotiating an early end to the war. Nazi Germany was fast running out of options. This was their last real viable hope of regaining some ground, and to try and stem the increasingly unstoppable Allied invasion of Europe.

The Special Branch driver pulled over outside a rather forlorn-looking house; it was one of the few still standing in what had obviously been a neat Victorian terrace. Rowlands took his cue from the driver, and stepped somewhat uncertainly out of the car, glancing almost questioningly toward the plain-clothes police officer.

'This way, Mr. Rowlands,' he said curtly, and escorted him inside.

It struck Rowlands as a particularly odd choice of venue, and for the first time in many months, he started to feel slightly ill at ease. Since being outed as a double agent, there had been countless interviews, and formal interrogations lasting long into the dead of the night, but why this place, and why now?

The officer quietly closed the door on Rowlands, leaving him alone with his thoughts. He was left, he felt, quite deliberately, entirely on his own, for at least a quarter of an hour. It was standard practice to keep the accused on edge. Counter-intelligence was after all about psychological tactics, mind games, and retaining the upper hand.

He puffed out his cheeks, his gaze gliding slowly round the room. The bare floorboards were uneven, and the ceiling yellowed with nicotine stains. The room was empty, save only for a single light bulb and five, rather shabby Windsor chairs.

A flicker of irritation crossed his face, as he suddenly noticed the turn-ups of his Savile Row suit flecked with dust. He was about to brush himself down, when he heard the door click open. He swung round and saw Spencer, smart as always, dressed in khaki. Some months ago, one of his Special Branch guards had inadvertently let slip Spencer had moved up into the higher echelons of the Service. It was hardly surprising. In his experience, his erstwhile colleague was as hard as nails, powerfully built like most Commandos, and if there was ever any trouble in the field, he was usually his Section Head, Colonel Robertson's, first choice to go in and clear up the mess. While he was not in the least bit surprised to see Spencer, he was surprised to find him accompanied by Superintendent Luke Garvan. For some reason, Rowlands had assumed that he had probably returned to Scotland Yard by now.

'Is this how it's going to be?' he queried addressing Spencer.

'What do you mean by that?'

18

'Every so often, you'll have me picked up, and hauled in for questioning.'

'I'll do what I bloody like!' Spencer answered dismissively.

Garvan looked through Rowlands rather than at him; there was no acknowledgement in his eyes as he set his briefcase down on one of the chairs. It was a heavy brown leather affair, with a crown and GR, oriented just above the lock, printed on it in faded large gold lettering. He retrieved a small notebook with lined paper from the case, and a pen from the inside pocket of his suit jacket, before placing the briefcase on the floor beside the chair.

'Do you mind if I smoke?' Rowlands asked, producing a slim silver cigarette case.

'Feel free,' Spencer said.

'Thank you.'

'Take a seat.'

The chairs were scattered randomly around the room. 'Do you want me anywhere in particular?'

A flicker of amusement crossed Spencer's face. 'Don't worry. The place isn't wired, if that's what you think.'

'Not wired?' Rowlands said curiously. 'That's got to be a first.'

'Bring a chair over here,' Spencer said pointing to where Garvan had sat himself down.

Rowlands complied. There was still a certain arrogant poise about him Spencer found particularly irritating, although he suspected much of it was probably just bravado, and inside, Rowlands was probably not quite as relaxed as he outwardly appeared.

'Why the hell are we meeting in this godforsaken dump?'

Spencer smiled tautly. 'Actually, I thought it was quite an inspired choice.'

'Really, why's that?' Rowlands said, taking his time opening the cigarette case, before slipping one casually between his lips.

'The street was destroyed by a V-1 rocket.'

Rowlands flicked on his lighter. 'That's very sad,' he said mechanically, without a shred of compassion.

Spencer shot him a look. To his mind, Rowlands was driven by nothing more than an addictive love of deceit itself, rather than any deep-rooted sense of conviction. But, whatever his critics might level at him now, no-one could ever take away the fact Rowlands, in his day, had been a renowned expert in counter-espionage. For Spencer, it had been one thing to suspect he was spying for the Nazis, but it was quite another actually to hear him confess his treachery.

Since the 13th of June 1944, a week or so after the allies had invaded France, as the Third Reich attempted to bring Britain to its knees, there'd been a marked increase in the strange sounding V-1s clattering noisily across the skies of southern England. People had half-jokingly called it the Doodlebug Summer. But, it hadn't taken them long to realise if the noisy pulse jet engine powering the missiles suddenly cut out overhead, then, at best, they probably had about fifteen seconds, before the deadly missile came crashing down to earth.

Rowlands gave the impression of having no particular moral qualms about his having betrayed his colleagues during his time in Portugal. Or the fact he'd revealed the whereabouts of a brilliant French scientist, who'd managed to escape from Germany with a blueprint holding the key to the design of the rockets now soaring across the English Channel. However, for all his faults, and there were many, he remained an easy mix of charm coupled with an underlying sense of duplicity.

Rowlands drew on his freshly lit cigarette; his expression appeared remote and somewhat withdrawn. 'Let's cut to the chase, shall we?' he suggested.

'Our cousins across the water need answers about Agent Toniolo,' Garvan said.

He looked faintly bored. 'I've already told you everything I know.'

'I think that's probably a moot point, don't you?'

'I don't know why you're still so concerned about me, dear boy. Right now, I'd have thought you'd have had your work cut out with the Nazis.'

'Aren't you forgetting one thing?' Garvan shot back at him.

'What's that?'

'You are a *Nazi*!'

Rowlands appeared genuinely affronted by the accusation. 'I was the victim of a honey trap; I was blackmailed!'

'Blackmailed into betraying, not only your country, but your Service colleagues as well. As far as I'm concerned, that makes you a traitor in anyone's book.'

Rowlands was always terrified his sexuality would be exposed; it was one of the reasons why he'd been so careful to keep his nose clean in Lisbon, until he was set up by a good-looking Portuguese young man, in the pay of German Intelligence. Rowlands knew he'd been a fool, a bloody fool, not to have seen it coming.

His past relationships had not exclusively been with men; he'd always been popular with women, but his most intense and loving relationships were invariably with men. During his time with the Service, he'd not only been good at his job, but had also commanded the respect of his colleagues. He was generous in his praise, a great raconteur and hugely understanding with everyone he met. Coupled with his innate suave and sophistication, he'd easily managed to smooth his path on the diplomatic circuit, both at home and abroad.

Rowlands admitted privately the Abwehr's honey trap was practically straight out of the textbook, and he, of all people, should have known better. Regardless of his sexuality, as Deputy Head of the Lisbon Station, right from the start, he'd been a prime target; it had come with the territory. He knew all that, but had stupidly ended up leaving himself wide open to blackmail. The Abwehr had compromised him completely. He could have handled it differently, of course, to have come clean with London, but a heady mixture of pride and fear panicked him into an endless spiral of double-dealing.

All his training and ingrained sixth sense for trouble had let him down, overpowered by flattery, the prospect of companionship, and the fleeting hope of love. But, that short-lived moment had cost him dear; not only his career and the trust of his peers, but it had also ended in a deadly trail of death and destruction, including that of a colleague under his command.

'The thing is, George, why bother telling the truth, when any lie will do?' Spencer mused, breaking his train of thought.

'I know if you'd had your way, I'd have been strung up from the nearest lamp-post.'

'I wouldn't have wasted a bullet on you, that's for sure.'

Rowlands heard the door click open. He glanced over his shoulder to see a well-built, smartly dressed man in army uniform join them. His complexion was pale, and his silvery blonde hair was thinning on top. Rowlands's poise immediately began to falter. Major General Sir Stewart Menzies, or C, as he was known, was the Head of MI6. *What in god's name was going on?* All of a sudden, his mouth had dried, and the palms of his hands began to feel sweaty; this was becoming serious, *deadly* serious.

Rowlands thoughts began to spiral into freefall as he recalled his first sighting of C in the ancient lift serving the eight floors of MI6's HQ in Broadway. At the time, he'd been new to the Service, and a complete non-entity. He remembered asking the liftman who the rather distinguished looking gentleman was. On discovering he was C, he recalled feeling somewhat overawed. Their paths had crossed infrequently; the next time had been a year or so later, in the great man's office, accompanied by his boss, Frank Lucern. It was all still very much of a blur; the only thing he recalled with any degree of clarity was Menzies's stationery was vivid blue, and he only ever wrote in green ink.

'I'm running late,' Menzies said, almost by way of apology.

'I guess that's my fault, sir,' Spencer said.

'No, no, not at all. My secretary double booked my diary.' On seeing Garvan, Menzies's face suddenly relaxed into a smile. 'Good to see you again, Superintendent.' His eyes then rested fleetingly on Rowlands, his expression at once intense and quite unforgiving. 'Shall we get down to business, gentlemen?'

'Yes, of course, sir,' Spencer said.

C glanced swiftly round the room, and without further ado, pulled up a chair and sat himself down.

General Menzies was renowned for his skill at negotiating his way through Westminster's mazy and occasionally treacherous corridors of power; also, he faced the constant threat of a midnight summons from Churchill to his subterranean bunker at the Cabinet War Rooms.

Rowlands believed Menzies was primarily an administrator, whereas Colonel Tar Robertson, Spencer's immediate MI5 boss, had always struck him as the ultimate spymaster. C was a stickler for correct procedure, and he didn't possess Robertson's flare of a dyed-in-the-wool counter-espionage expert. Despite this, he was still a hugely formidable figure in British Intelligence circles.

Menzies apparent outward sanguinity masked a deep personal worry as to how far MI6 had been infiltrated. Privately, he'd admitted to Tar, and his MI5 counterpart, Sir David Petrie, he was beginning to feel a little like King Canute, vainly holding back a relentless tide of treachery. Petrie had assured him he was unduly pessimistic, but it was a genuine concern all the same. It was also a matter of profound professional embarrassment its sister organisation, MI5, was investigating his department. His initial overriding fear was any infiltration of the Service might compromise the preparation for D-Day, but as it turned out, his concerns proved to be unfounded. However, he believed there remained a very real and on-going constant threat to security.

'Have I missed much?' he asked.

'No, sir, you haven't,' Spencer said.

'Good, good,' Menzies replied, lighting a cigarette. 'Please continue.'

Under C's watchful, steady gaze, Rowlands didn't appear to be quite as relaxed and seemingly unflappable as he had before.

'When did you first meet Lord Oakways?' Garvan asked.

The question took Rowlands by surprise; it showed on his face. 'Oakways … doesn't he work at the Foreign Office? Or, at least, he did,' he said, rather vaguely.

'That's right,' Garvan said. 'He cut his teeth on the diplomatic circuit.'

'Did he,' Rowlands said disinterestedly.

'He ended up spending six years at the Embassy in Lisbon, before entering Parliament.'

He still looked faintly bored. 'That's right, I'd completely forgotten. Rumour had it, at the time, Neville Chamberlain gave him a peerage just to get him out of the

Commons. By all accounts, he wasn't exactly a great success as a Tory MP.'

'Didn't you work with him?'

The merest hint of a smile traversed Rowlands's face. 'You know that I did,' he smirked, waving his hand in the air, wafting a stream of smoke in its trail.

'What did you think of him?'

'To be brutally honest with you, I don't think I thought about him at all. He was just there in the background. He always struck me as a rather grey figure, a yes man, blowing in the political wind, trying to please everyone, and ending up pleasing no-one.'

'I take it, then, you didn't exactly like him?'

'He wasn't important enough to form an opinion about. On a day-to-day basis, we had very little contact. He occasionally attended a meeting with MI6, but that's about as far as it went.' Rowlands eyed Garvan warily. 'Why the sudden interest in Oakways?'

Garvan looked up from his notes. 'He was found dead yesterday evening at his home in Lord North Street.'

Rowlands held his cigarette poised lightly between his fingers. 'I presume we wouldn't be having this conversation, if the old boy died of natural causes?'

'No, we wouldn't.'

'To be honest with you, I barely knew the man, so I'm not sure why you've dragged me halfway across London to talk about him.' He shot a sharp look toward Menzies. Just as he remembered, his former boss had a rather unnerving habit of clearing his throat, and shifting his buttocks on the chair. In fact, it had been something of a running joke at MI6. He looked almost grey, at times, reflective and somewhat world-weary. The strain and responsibility of command were perhaps beginning to tell on him, he decided, or maybe he was just having an off-day. If truth be told, sitting in Rowlands's company certainly wasn't helping his demeanour any.

'We found an interesting entry in Lord Oakways's diary,' Spencer cut in.

Rowlands arched his brows speculatively.

'He was booked to have lunch at Claridges's on Tuesday, the 20th of June. The entry was circled in red ink, with two exclamation marks. So, it was obviously pretty important to him.'

'I'm sure you're about to enlighten me. Who was it with?'

'It was with Toniolo.'

Rowlands's expression didn't falter, but having Toniolo's name thrown into the mix certainly went a long way to explaining Menzies's presence. The old boy was naturally worried about the possibility of having another highly-placed mole. Rowlands knew he was under scrutiny; a slight glance toward the window, or even a twiddling of his thumbs always, without exception, merited another note in the notepad. Garvan began to toy with his fountain pen, twisting it deftly between his fingers, waiting for a response. Rowlands began to find it vaguely annoying, but he guessed that was probably the whole idea.

'Well?' Garvan pressed him. 'Was Agent Toniolo perhaps a mutual friend of yours from the Foreign Office?'

'Oh, for Christ's sake, we've been through this so many times before. I've no more idea who Toniolo is than you do.'

'And I'm telling you it wasn't just a coincidence Oakways was meeting Toniolo for lunch?'

Rowlands's eyes narrowed, as he tried to read his face.

'From my experience, George, if it doesn't make sense, then it's usually not true.'

He wasn't entirely sure how to counter him.

'I think the Superintendent has a point, don't you?' Menzies pointed out the obvious.

Rowlands folded his arms and smiled almost indulgently. 'I'm not quite so sure about that, but I do think you're missing something.'

Menzies's temper was slow to rise, but an air of indignant bewilderment shrouded his face. 'Are we?'

'If the Abwehr has got it right Toniolo is a Soviet spy, then, whatever I may, or may not, have personally thought of the old boy, Oakways never exactly struck me as a covert Soviet agent. Quite the reverse, in fact. He was a staunch, land-owning Tory from the Shires.'

Garvan interjected sharply, 'I didn't exactly have you marked down as a double agent, either, so where does that leave us?'

'I'm not sure; you're the sharp, no-nonsense detective you tell me!'

'I guess it leaves us back at square one.'

'Precisely,' Rowlands said, looking at him with wary curiosity. 'Maybe Oakways thought the diary entry was a kind of insurance policy.'

'Go on.'

'If he'd entered his real name, we'd be none the wiser; perhaps he was afraid his life was on the line.'

'Or, maybe, he was protecting Toniolo's identity.'

'It's possible,' Rowlands conceded.

Garvan slowly eased himself back into his chair. 'I'm curious about something. You haven't bothered to ask how Oakways died.'

'I didn't think it was that important,' he said, indifferently.

As Garvan scribbled something on his notepad, the smile came off Rowlands's face, as he caught the unnerving, dead-eyed threat in Hall's expression.

Garvan looked up and continued, 'It's just it's usually one of the first questions people ask. You know, they're naturally curious, unless, of course, they already know what happened.'

Rowlands rolled his eyes. 'For God's sake, I'm under surveillance twenty-four hours a sodding day! Do you know what I think, Superintendent?'

'No, you tell me.'

'I think you haven't got a effing clue what's going on.'

Garvan shot Spencer a look. 'Do you want to tell him, or shall I?'

'Do you remember Deb Gander?' Spencer asked.

'The name doesn't ring a bell.'

'It doesn't matter either way; after Oakways was murdered, I called Deb at the Park.'

In Government circles, it was known as GC&CS, short for the Government Code & Cypher School, and had been based at Bletchley Park in Buckinghamshire since the Munich Crisis in the autumn of 1938. Rowlands's apparent smugness began to wane; he was intrigued, if not a little hesitant.

'I asked Deb to recheck the Park's intercepted messages over the last four months. With the increase in recent signals traffic, I guessed they might have missed something. Anyway, it was worth a punt.'

'Missed what, exactly?'

'Whether the Abwehr had been a bit slapdash in their communications. Let's face it, it wouldn't have been the first time, would it?'

Rowlands couldn't argue the point. 'Did you find anything on Toniolo?'

'No, we didn't.'

'What did you find?'

'Deb's cryptographers' came across an intercepted message. Although it was pretty short on detail, it was important all the same.'

28

Rowlands tossed his cigarette butt on the bare floorboards, and stubbed it out with his foot. 'Go on. Put me out of my misery. What did it say?'

'The intercept was from Nikolaus Ritter.'

Rowlands stared at him in a state of barely concealed panic. Ritter was a highly-placed Abwehr spymaster, based in Hamburg, and, in effect, was Tar Robertson's opposite number in German Intelligence.

Spencer took his time, and lit himself a cigarette, before continuing. 'Deb's cryptographers apparently thought it was completely innocuous at the time, but, in hindsight, it wasn't that unimportant. Ritter sent a message to Berlin stating Schornsteinfeger was dead, but not yet buried. I'm not sure why they didn't pick up on it, but that's really neither here nor there.' Spencer sucked on his newly lit cigarette. 'In my shoes, George, what would you be thinking right now?'

It was a fait accompli; Schornsteinfeger had been his Abwehr codename, but no matter how much he wanted to protest his innocence, they had assumed he'd found a means of communicating with German Intelligence.

Throughout the proceedings, General Menzies had been unusually reticent. Rowlands wasn't entirely ungrateful, but C suddenly rose to his feet, indicating the interview was over. He'd heard more than enough, and announced sharply, 'I've ordered your imprisonment at Latchmere House for the remainder of the War.' He breathed deeply, adding, 'And I hope to God they throw away the ruddy key!'

Latchmere was a sparse detention and interrogation centre, known as Camp 020; it was a fortress, surrounded by huge interlocking piles of barbed wire. Incarcerated within the forbidding complex were enemy agents captured by MI5 and members of the British Union of Fascists. The regime was spartan, and knowing how much Rowlands loved the finer things in life, Menzies knew being locked up at Latchmere would be a complete anathema to him.

'Whatever we do now,' Menzies said sourly, 'it's far too late for those who you betrayed.' He moved over to the door. 'I wouldn't normally say this, but right now, George, I really can't help thinking I ought to turn a blind eye to the legal niceties, and allow Major Hall here to beat the ruddy truth out of you!' He opened the door, but turned around; he hadn't quite finished with him. 'From the moment we were first introduced, I always thought you were an irritating bastard, but I completely underestimated you.' He looked to Spencer, and added, 'Let me know how you get on.'

'Yes, sir.'

'I'd appreciate it if you could have a word with Jeremy Haining, as soon as possible.'

'It's all in hand, sir.'

As Menzies paused, his expression appeared remote and withdrawn. 'If I find out you've been meddling again, so help me, George, I'll put a bullet in you myself!'

With that, he stalked out of the room, and noisily slammed the door behind him.

Chapter 3

As a respected parliamentarian, it probably wasn't surprising that Jeremy Haining lived a few doors down in the same street as Lord Oakways. By the time Spencer and Garvan arrived at the impressive Georgian terraced house, it was a typical London night. A thick blanket of dense fog had descended over much of the capital, a pea-souper, a killer fog, thick and strangely yellowish in appearance.

Inside Haining's elegant London townhouse, a red dispatch box lay on a long wooden table in his immaculate library. Within parliamentary circles, he was a man with a reputation for being flamboyant, and for knowing every nut and bolt of the political system. Dispensing whisky to his guests, he sat in his favourite chair with his back to the three, rather tall, narrow sash windows overlooking the street. He told them he viewed the library as his bolt hole, his sanctuary from the hurly-burly of Westminster, and, with a conspiratorial wink, he also added, his wife.

Haining had served notably alongside Oakways in the Foreign Office since 1940. The security files recorded that, before the War, he had represented the Transport and General Workers Union as a Branch Secretary. In his early days, he was known to have held Communist leanings, but since becoming an MP, was generally viewed as being on the right-wing of the Labour Party, and had subsequently proved himself an efficient election campaigner.

He told them how Oakways had suffered a couple of burglaries while living in Lord North Street, and he'd always insisted the break-ins were part of some shady plot to discredit him. He claimed, or at least convinced himself, elements of British Intelligence had a personal vendetta against him.

'To be perfectly honest with you,' Haining said, taking a sip of his whisky, and then slowly swirling the amber

31

liquid in the glass, 'the trouble with you lot is it's all wheels within wheels, isn't it?'

'That's the general conception.' Spencer smiled. 'But, the burglaries, well, that's another matter altogether.'

'What do you mean?'

'If the Service had burgled him, it would have required top cover authority.'

'Quite so. You have access to the files, Major?'

'The trouble is, sir, there's nothing recorded in the files.'

Haining seemed unconvinced. 'Or, at least, nothing in the files you're willing to share.'

'No, I assure you, there's nothing on the files.'

Haining thoughtfully played with his whisky glass, rolling it between the palms of his hands. 'Tell me, Major, do you have full access to MI6 files?'

It was an astutely loaded question, and one Spencer was unable to answer unequivocally.

Haining passed him a smile. While not quite smug, it was near enough. 'No, I thought not. Oakways wasn't a fool; he had his moments, of course, but so does half the Cabinet. Lord knows if it was true, or not, whether he was being bugged, but that's the way he was. I do remember him becoming paranoid the gent's toilet at the Foreign Office was bugged; he once pointed at the light fitting, while standing alongside me at the urinal, but God only knows why you lot would want to bug the ruddy loo. It's beyond me!'

Garvan smirked. 'I'm not sure, either.'

'I'm not saying he couldn't be a silly old bugger, at times, but we got along really well. After his divorce, I think he became quite lonely, and was always popping along the street of an evening to have dinner with us.'

'Your political differences didn't get in the way?'

'No, not at all. I suppose, to the outside world, it might all have seemed rather strange Oakways, the grand Tory grandee, and his boss, the Labour MP, who was born and bred on a Peabody Estate in South London, were surprisingly close friends. On the surface of it, I'll be the first to admit we didn't appear to have much in common, but we enjoyed each other's company, and got on like a house on fire.' Haining retrieved a guillotine cutter from the desk drawer, and snipped the end of a cigar. He struck a match, and placed a large Havana, in his mouth, rotating it slowly in such a way just the tip touched the flame of the match. After taking a few slow puffs, the surface started to catch and glow bright red in places.

'Forgive me,' he said, between puffs, 'but the War has got an awful lot to answer for.'

Garvan looked at him quizzically.

'The only reason I started smoking these bloody things is because of the PM.'

'Why's that?'

'He has a habit of handing them round at Cabinet meetings, almost as generously as Boodles's gin,' he said, puffing contentedly. 'It's become something of a ritual after a hard day's slog at the office. It's my one guilty pleasure.' He chuckled. 'And Churchill has been kind enough to ensure I always have a steady supply.'

As an opening gambit, his name dropping was pretty impressive, there again Garvan assumed that it was meant to be.

'So, gentlemen,' Haining continued smoothly, 'shall we get down to business? I understand that you're here to discuss my old friend Lord Oakways.'

'Yes, sir, we are. It must have come as a terrible shock to you, sir.'

'I still can't quite believe he's dead. You hear about these things happening, of course, but you never actually think it's ever going to happen to someone you know. It just brings it all home,' he said, shaking his head.

'I'm so sorry we couldn't delay our interview.'

'There's no need to apologise, Superintendent; I know you're both only doing your job.'

'Thank you, sir.'

Haining took a sharp intake of breath. 'Then, can we just get this over and done with.'

'Did you ever give any credence Lord Oakways was under surveillance?'

Haining's expression closed down. 'I think you're probably in a far better position to answer that than I am, Superintendent.'

His question was met by a wall of empty silence.

'No, I didn't think you'd commit yourself to answering that one,' he smiled dully. 'To be perfectly honest with you, I didn't think it was that surprising. In my book, we were both fair game. No-one can or should automatically assume they're above suspicion. In the end, the trouble was, it came to a point where he started to make himself look slightly ridiculous; people just didn't believe him anymore.' Haining appeared momentarily lost in some distant thought. 'Sadly, it all became something of an obsession with him, almost to the point of paranoia. What is sad is, when I first met him, he was at the top of his game, but the booze eventually began to take its toll. It was just more and more people were becoming aware of his alcoholism.'

'Did you raise it with the PM?' Garvan queried.

Haining looked genuinely surprised. 'Why the hell should I?'

'Weren't you afraid he might crack under the pressure of working at the FO?'

Haining pulled a face. 'Oakways had always been a hard drinker, but where do you draw the line?'

'You tell me.'

'It's a difficult call, Superintendent, when half of your bloody colleagues are borderline alcoholics.' He shot Garvan a tight smile. 'Besides, he was a friend, and a close one, at that.' He blew out a cloud of blue-grey cigar smoke in his direction. 'And, before you ask, let's just say, the PM was fully aware of the situation.'

Garvan was unconvinced. 'Friend, or not, he was vulnerable. He needed protection, and moved out of harm's way.'

'That's a matter of opinion; it just doesn't happen to be *mine*. You have to understand, Oakways was a high-performing alcoholic.'

'Is there such a thing?

'In his case, yes, he was.'

'He was a train crash waiting to happen; you know he was. Did your loyalty to him overcome common sense?'

Haining wouldn't be drawn.

'Did you think by standing by him, you were doing the right thing? You must have known he was a significant liability.'

'All I can say is, he still put in the hours at the Foreign Office. I won't deny he had his enemies, but then again, so do I.'

'But, I take it you're not an alcoholic?' Spencer queried.

'Maybe not, Major, but I guess, not unlike the Intelligence Service, it's very much a case of dog eat dog, and the survival of the fittest.' He pulled on his cigar, and said wearily, 'God knows half the Labour Party, my own colleagues, hate my guts. The Left view me as an intellectual traitor.' Haining let out a rasping chuckle. 'I suppose, all things considered, it's rather flattering anyone could ever view *me* as an intellectual, but, at the end of the day, mud sticks.'

'Does it bother you?' Spencer asked.

'No, why should it?' he said easily.

However much Haining might play down his standing within the Labour Party, Spencer knew that he was reportedly a leading player, and was more than adept at holding his own in the rarefied Westminster hothouse. Apart from Labour's left-wing faction, he was generally popular, not only within his own Party, but right across the Parliamentary divide, as his close friendship with Oakways and his inclusion in the coalition government confirmed.

'Word has it *the Daily Express* was on the point of running an article about him,' Spencer said.

'Were they?'

They were playing cat and mouse with one another, they both knew that. For legal reasons, the paper would never publish the entire truth about Oakways's alcoholism. But, reading between the lines of the intended article, it described him as being somewhat tired and emotional. To those in-the-know, it was a euphemism for his being drunk, but it was worded in such a way even the general public would have picked up on its meaning.

Haining stuck to the script and denied all knowledge.

'You didn't hear anything on the grapevine?' Garvan asked.

'I'm sure you know how it is,' Haining replied glibly. 'Rumours circulate Whitehall all the time. Most of them are, just that, rumours.'

'Nothing at all?'

'No, I didn't, Superintendent,' he maintained.

'And, I take it, you can't think of any reason anyone would have wanted him dead?'

'Lord only knows.'

Garvan held his gaze. 'Maybe he wasn't quite so paranoid after all.'

Haining conceded thoughtfully. 'You might have a valid point; perhaps we were all just a little guilty of dismissing him too readily. In hindsight, I should have probably listened to him more closely.' He took a long-considered gulp of his Jameson's. 'The trouble is, gentlemen, so many of my colleagues in Parliament drink and womanise to excess. It's become almost second nature to them. But, I'll give Oakways his due, there was never so much as a whisper about his sex-life. He remained utterly devoted to his wife, Laura, divorced or not; he simply didn't want anyone else.'

'Did you know why the marriage broke down?' Garvan asked.

'No, I've no idea what happened between them, but my wife and I always loved Laura. She was great company.' He paused, thoughtfully swirling the amber-coloured Jameson's in the glass, before taking a large gulp. 'You have to understand,' Haining explained at length, 'Oakways, after his divorce, was in a very dark place.' He set the glass down, and absentmindedly puffed on his cigar. 'In fact, I don't think he ever truly recovered from it. I remember him saying to me once, shortly after Laura upped sticks and left the family home, he was having a shave one morning, and found himself staring at his reflection in the mirror. The face seemed strangely familiar, but much older than he cared to remember or admit to. It suddenly dawned on him, maybe that's why Laura had decided to walk away from their marriage. He was no longer passably handsome, just a rather sad, grey-haired old man, with nothing much to offer an attractive younger wife.'

Haining smiled slightly, and said with a sigh, 'But, with the best will in the world, they were never a match made in heaven. Laura was always so full of fun and so vibrant.' He paused, his thoughts tumbling back to happier times, of long evenings setting the world to rights, and of the laughter and warmth of their friendship. Haining admitted he still couldn't quite get it into his head Oakways was dead.

'I understand Jamie Burdis also worked alongside you at the FO,' Spencer said.

Haining gave him a slow, half-hearted smile. 'Major Hall, you know full well he did.'

'We'll be contacting him shortly.'

'Then, heaven help you. If you ask my opinion, the man's an utter arse. I'll be perfectly honest with you, earlier this year, I asked the Prime Minister to have him removed from the Foreign Office.'

'Why was that?'

'Mainly because he's an insufferable little shit!' he said, with feeling.

Spencer was beginning to warm toward Haining. He was a man after his own heart. There was no side with him, like himself. He might not be the world's greatest diplomat, but he guessed Churchill valued his opinion. Rough edges or not, Haining was a leading member of the coalition government, because he was not only smart, but could cut through the dross, and the minutiae of the day-to-day red tape.

'I guess being an insufferable little shit was reason enough, but how did you manage to persuade Churchill?' Spencer asked.

'It wasn't easy.'

'I don't suppose it was.'

'There's no denying there was a time when he believed Burdis had the makings of an astute politician, we all did, but his increasing carelessness and loose mouth ultimately led to his downfall. At the end of the day, he was his own worst enemy.'

Garvan looked up from his notebook. 'What happened?'

'You have to understand. While Burdis is an ambitious, arrogant bastard, and, what's more, a loose cannon, with an eye to the future, he's never quite understood the game.'

'What game?'

'In a wartime coalition government, there's very little room for personal ambition. There were a couple of occasions when Churchill was forced to rap him across the knuckles, until he finally lost patience, and sent him scurrying off to the backbenches. Ever since, he's become increasingly bitter at being left out of the loop, but it'll be a cold day in hell before that bastard betters me. I know Burdis still harbours a personal grudge against me,' Haining said, drawing heavily on his cigar. 'But, I had to act, for the sake of the Department.'

'Why didn't you report Oakways? Was it out of loyalty?'

'No, it was a different kettle of fish.'

Garvan looked at him searchingly. 'I don't see how?'

'He wasn't exactly threatening the war effort,' Haining said, draining his Jameson's. 'Paranoid, or not, in my opinion, Oakways was loyal to the core. On the other hand, Burdis was an entirely unknown quantity. Once the War's over, of course it'll be open season again, and we'll be at each other's throats, but until then, all bets are off. There's simply no place for the likes of Burdis, riding roughshod over his colleagues.' He looked across the desk, and fixed Spencer with a hard-eyed stare. 'Tell me, Major, do you seriously believe Oakways's death is connected to his work at the Foreign Office?'

'It's far too early to say.'

'Oh, don't start trying to fob me off, Major Hall. I know how things stand with you *lot*.'

'I'm sure you do sir,' Spencer said smoothly.

'While I understand you have to investigate his murder, I think it's also fair to say you can't deny your own Service isn't entirely squeaky clean, is it?'

'I never said it was,' Spencer said bluntly.

'No, no, you didn't.'

'Tell me,' Spencer suggested, with an easy offhand calm, 'at one point, didn't George Rowlands work for you on a project about the Iberian Peninsula?'

'Was that a question or a statement, Major?'

'Whatever you'd like it to be.'

'Then, it was a statement. You know full well he did.' Haining eyed him curiously. 'After all, he was one of your people.'

'Only in a manner of speaking. He was MI6.'

'Well,' Haining said, with a wave of his hand, 'it's something of a technicality. You people are all the same, when it comes down to it.'

'That's like saying all politicians are tarred with the same brush.'

'Touché, Major,' he said, puffing on his cigar, as his eyes thoughtfully set on Garvan. 'You must have found it a baptism of fire working alongside this lot, Superintendent.'

'No more than I have working alongside politicians and civil servants. You're all a rather strange breed to me, sir.'

Haining gave him a rueful smile. 'Yes, I suppose we are.'

'I carry out my orders and keep my opinions to myself; I find it tends to be safer that way.'

'You're very well versed Superintendent perhaps you should have been a politician I think you'd have done very well for yourself.

'With due respect, sir, I'd rather pull out my own teeth than play politics!'

Haining threw his head back, and let out a chesty laugh. 'I admire your honesty; we don't see enough of it around here at Westminster.' He set his cigar in the ashtray. 'Now, gentlemen, how are we going to play this from here on in?'

'We'll make a start by interviewing Jamie Burdis,' Spencer said, pushing back his chair.

Haining nodded.

'Thank you for your time, sir,' Spencer said.

'You'll keep me abreast of the investigation.'

'It goes without saying.'

'By the way,' Haining smiled, 'good luck with Burdis; you'll certainly need it. He sees himself as an ideas man. Amusingly, no-one agrees with his bloody ideas!'

'We'll remember that,' Spencer laughed.

From the available intelligence reports, Jeremy Haining was often guilty of being brutal in his dealings with colleagues, and also of making snap, impromptu decisions. He certainly had no time to allow emotions to get in the way of work. One way or another, he made for a deadly enemy, and Burdis had not only irritated him by his heavy-handed approach to the FO, but had also stymied his ambitions for what he wanted to achieve, not only for the coalition government, but the country at large. Politics was all about power and how to navigate it, and Haining was a past master. Burdis had never stood a chance.

Chapter 4

It had already been a long day, but after their meeting with Jeremy Haining, Garvan and Spencer headed straight over to the MI6 HQ in Broadway. They specifically wanted to catch up with Frank Lucern, Rowlands's erstwhile boss from his days at the intelligence station in Lisbon. In comparison to the MI5 offices in St James's Street, Broadway was a rather unprepossessing dingy building, all frosted glass and a veritable warren of wooden partitions, which formed various cramped offices resembling something akin to a collection of makeshift rabbit hutches.

Despite Lucern's apparent shortcomings as a former Head of Station, and the perception he'd lost control of an already difficult situation in Portugal, C had insisted on retaining his services, despite some serious misgivings amongst his colleagues. In hindsight, he'd always been more of a desk man, a good operator, but didn't want to tackle issues head on, without someone else's okay. At heart, he remained a much-valued desk officer and analyst, a skill MI6 desperately needed both before Operation Overload and the subsequent battle for control of occupied Europe. Lucern's ability to assess intelligence reports, which landed on his desk, was acknowledged widely as being second to none. Although, at times, his control of the Lisbon mission had been somewhat vaguely administered, having been posted back to London, he had successfully managed to regain a measure of his former reputation within the intelligence community.

On first impressions, he appeared to be deceptively mild-mannered, a fact which had, in the past, resulted in his being foolishly underestimated by both his colleagues and hostile intelligence agencies alike. But, beneath the apparently outward happy-go-lucky persona, lurked a stubborn, steely character, whose inherent skills as a counter-intelligence analyst could not be faulted.

Lucern had cut his teeth at the beginning of the War, as a member of Tar Robertson's MI5 team in London. Ever since he'd remained totally loyal to him, and was one of his men to the core, and like Spencer had been a founding member of the double-cross system, turning German Abwehr agents into spying for the Allies. As the War progressed, Robertson had appeared increasingly reluctant to part company with Frank, especially to his old adversary MI6. It didn't initially sit at all easily with him, or at least, that's the way he wanted it to appear to his colleagues in Whitehall. Tar was often to be heard sounding off, to anyone who was willing to listen, all his best people were poached, but the reality was somewhat different. In effect, all his agents had remained good and loyal to him. However, their first allegiance lay firmly with Tar, and, in fact, acted as plants, and were a way of his being able to retain a finger on the pulse of the various conflicting strands within British Intelligence.

The workload was monstrous; Lucern had always maintained MI6 was understaffed, unlike its sister organisation, MI5. In appearance, Lucern was lean and rangy, and possessed a slightly unruly shock of thick salt and pepper-coloured hair and watchful pale grey eyes. Before the War, he'd been a somewhat seriously-minded aero engineer; word had it he was considered accomplished in his field. Spencer had always assumed that was how he'd probably come to the attention of the shadowy men in grey suits. The Intelligence Service required people with a variety of skill sets. As an ex-aero engineer, his initial work had been in the evaluation of technical information stolen from the Nazis. Eventually, he'd fallen into Robertson's hands, and had ended up working alongside Spencer.

He showed them into a slightly larger office than most of his colleagues possessed, although it still seemed quite cramped, almost to the point of being claustrophobic. A bank of battered green filing cabinets. There was barely enough room to swing a cat, but he'd somehow managed to squeeze two small chairs in front of his desk for them.

'How are things going?' Spencer asked, taking a seat.

Lucern winked conspiratorially. 'So-so. I've volunteered to be a firewatcher on the roof during bombing raids.'

Spencer looked at him askance. 'Why?'

'It's all about timing.'

He knew Lucern of old; he was up to something, but couldn't quite work out what, and said as much.

'The night shift at Broadway picks up all the latest British Military Missions intelligence traffic sent across via SIS channels.'

A slow smile dawned on Spencer's face. 'And Tar wants to know?'

Lucern nodded. 'I have to say, I've put in a lot of bloody effort.'

'Have you found anything important?'

'If only,' he sniffed. 'All I've managed to produce is a ruddy forest of waste paper.'

'Then, you're groping in the dark.'

'Don't we always? The bottom line is, for us to win, others have to fail. Would either of you like a cup of tea?' he asked.

They both declined the offer.

'Why were we having Oakways watched?' Spencer asked, coming straight to the point.

Lucern gave him a long hard stare. 'I'd have thought that was rather more your department, than mine.'

'Why's that?'

'To my knowledge, we didn't have any particular interest in him.'

Spencer looked into his eyes. 'I would have thought by being at the Foreign Office, and rubbing shoulders with your MI6 brethren would have placed him on your radar?'

'Well, only loosely.'

'What does his file say?' Spencer pressed him.

'That he was a bit eccentric, if that's what you're angling at,' Lucern said, removing a pipe from the desk drawer, and packing it with tobacco from an engraved silver tobacco box bearing his initials. 'But, in all honesty, he hadn't seriously crossed our radar; in fact, for the most part, he seemed nothing more than a harmless old duffer, with a drinking problem.

Spencer pressed him further. 'Are you trying to tell me MI6 weren't particularly bothered he had sight of top secret material on a daily basis?'

'Not especially.'

'Why ever not? Surely he was a potential security risk.'

'He was being monitored.'

'Are you saying his house in Lord North Street was *bugged*?'

'Christ, you know how things are, Spence. Besides, I can't imagine you didn't order a clean sweep of the place after the poor bugger was murdered. You must have found the equipment by now.'

Spencer didn't deny it. 'You know I did.'

'Precisely, you'd have been a bloody fool, if you hadn't swept the place.'

'Why did he suspect we were bugging him?' Garvan said, less of a question than a demand.

'God only knows.'

'Was it after Rowlands?'

'From our perspective, it was all pretty routine stuff. He didn't exactly stand out from the crowd.'

'And what about the break-ins? We understand nothing was stolen. Were they just meant to scare the poor old sod?' Garvan queried.

'Ah, now, that wasn't down to us,' Frank insisted. 'Besides, let's not forget MI5 also had their sticky little fingers in the pie, as well.'

'Only in a manner of speaking,' Spencer owned up. 'We certainly weren't responsible for the black bag jobs.'

Garvan shot his colleague a cold, hard look; he had been involved with the Service long enough to know a black bag job was intelligence slang for a secret entry into a home or office to steal or copy documents. 'I thought you said Oakways's name hadn't dropped on your desk before.'

'Not mine specifically, why would it? Thankfully, dodgy politicians aren't usually on my agenda.'

'But, his name obviously landed on someone else's desk, then?'

'Of course, it did,' Spencer said, with a touch if impatience.

'MI5 have been spying on him?'

'They wanted to test the waters, to see if MI6 had set up their own surveillance.'

Garvan shook his head almost in despair. In effect, the sister arms of British Intelligence were spying on one another.

'At least MI5,' Spencer continued, 'considered him to be in a high-risk category. We had the Watchers on his case.'

Garvan knew only too well the so-called Watchers Branch, or A4, as it was officially titled, was an MI5 surveillance unit, mainly staffed by former Special Branch Officers. A flicker of irritation crossed his face. By not being pre-warned, he found himself placed in an embarrassing position. It was regrettable, but as Spencer explained to him later, there'd been no underlying motive on his part; it had simply slipped his mind.

'How close was your surveillance?' Garvan asked Lucern.

'It certainly wasn't around the clock, by any means.'

'It was a bit wishy-washy, then?'

'We didn't think it necessary.'

'Then, I guess you underestimated the problem, didn't you!'

Although Garvan hadn't said it maliciously, it was a barbed comment all the same. Under Lucern's watch as the Head of the Lisbon Station, he'd managed to underestimate the Abwehr's successful intrusion into the MI6 operation completely.

Lucern thoughtfully placed the pipe between his lips, and slowly took a test draw, to see if he'd packed the tobacco too tight. It was fine, so he struck a match, and let it burn for a few seconds to get the sulphur off. He then gently drew on the pipe, and moved the match in a circular movement over the surface of the tobacco, until it was evenly lit. Lucern had always struck Garvan as something of a nervous smoker, who was always fidgeting, either toying with a match box or dottling with the unburned and partially burned tobacco in the bowl of a pipe.

'Part of the problem, Superintendent,' he puffed, 'is when two sister organisations are working on the same subject, it tends to become fraught with danger, and somewhat messy. What do you really want from me?'

'Your thoughts on who might have a motive for wanting Oakways dead,' Garvan said.

'He'd certainly made a few enemies, in his time.'

'What politician hasn't?'

'I presume you're looking to those closest to him?'

'We've got to start somewhere.'

'Well, there's Jeremy Haining, of course; he's an interesting character. He's on record as having denounced the Bolsheviks, and everything they stand for. The trouble was, by doing so, he ended up alienating half the left-wing of his own

Party. If you're looking for an NKVD angle, he doesn't automatically fit the bill as a covert Soviet spy.'

'But, isn't that the general idea?'

Lucern arched his brows curiously.

'Maybe he's playing a game; perhaps it's all just rhetoric,' Spencer suggested. 'If he is a Soviet spy, he's unlikely to draw attention to the fact, and what better way than by publicly denouncing Communism, in all its shapes and forms.'

Lucern coolly met his gaze, and said a little testily, 'Yes, maybe you have a point; Haining doesn't give a damn about anyone, or anything. He tends to shoot from the hip, and doesn't take any prisoners. Haining might occasionally be obnoxious, but my gut feeling is he's as straight as a die. All the reports indicate what you see is what you get, and there are no hidden agendas. It's just his mouth runs away with him, sometimes.'

'The trouble is, Frank, we all know reports can be wrong. Are *you* ruling him out of the equation?'

It was a loaded question. 'Christ, Spence, as you are aware, I've been wrong before. I could have misread the situation entirely. Haining is a wily old sod, but I wouldn't go so far as cancelling him out altogether as a potential suspect. He may have had his reasons for wanting Oakways dead, but they're just not that obvious. There again that doesn't mean to say there isn't a hidden agenda.'

'So, who else worked with him at the FO?'

'Jamie Burdis.'

'What do we know about him?'

'I suppose he could best be described as a Tory toff.'

'I'd imagine the NKVD wouldn't normally consider Tories as recruitment fodder, or do they?'

Lucern puffed on his pipe, and blew out a swirl of smoke. 'During the late twenties and thirties, you have to remember many middle and upper-class Oxbridge students toyed with Communism, especially during the Spanish Civil War. So, it's probably not quite as strange as it sounds.'

'Did Burdis join the Communist party?' Spencer asked.

'Some of his friends dabbled while they were at Cambridge, but we've nothing too much on Burdis himself; at least, nothing on record. He might be well worth taking a close look at, though.'

Spencer eyed Lucern inquisitively. 'Something tells me you've heard a whisper on the grapevine.'

Lucern smiled, and gently rested his pipe down in the ashtray on the desk. 'I've never quite understood why Churchill put Haining and Burdis together at the FO. If you ask me, it was always going to be a disaster in the making.'

'Isn't that what happens in a coalition government?'

Lucern creased up his face, and said speculatively, 'It happens all the time, of course, it does, whatever their persuasion MPs and members of the Lords are appointed on merit rather than their political allegiances. The Home Secretary, Herbert Morrison, is a staunch Labour MP, but all bets are off, and Churchill knows he's the right man for the job.'

'What's your problem with Haining and Burdis?' Spencer queried.

'It just seems such an unlikely pairing.'

'Superficially,' Spencer agreed with him, 'but, surely, you have to read between the lines.'

Lucern observed him warily. 'You've read the reports. You tell me,' he shot back at him.

'From all I've seen, Haining is an accomplished politician, but a wild card. Even his own party have trouble controlling him.'

Lucern couldn't disagree.

'And Burdis is very much in the same boat on the Tory side of the House. I could have misread the PM's motives. But, I'd have thought, at the back of his mind, by throwing them together, he hoped to cause something of a political stalemate, in so much as neither of them could cause too much trouble behind the scenes, and they'd end up cancelling each out. It was a rather smart move.'

Lucern looked at him curiously. 'Initially, that might have been his plan, but for a variety of reasons, it didn't work out, otherwise Burdis wouldn't have found himself languishing in the background.'

'What prompted the PM to have him removed from the Foreign Office?' Garvan asked.

'It seems there were one too many occasions when he sinned by not returning confidential and secret papers to the registry. The junior staff correctly reported him, but for whatever reason, he wasn't reprimanded in-house. It could be all or nothing, but looking at the report, the papers might be of some significance.'

'Were they connected to the Iberian Desk?' Garvan pressed him.

Lucern narrowed his eyes. 'Not exclusively.'

'What other documents did he sign out from the registry?'

'Nothing too toxic, but some of the files were outside his remit. He was either just being nosey, and taking advantage of his position, perhaps with an eye to stirring up trouble in the future, or he may have been on a genuine fishing trip for information. There's no way of telling for certain. As far as I can tell, there was nothing overtly of interest to the Soviets. But, I might have missed something, or, at least, it didn't instantly jump off the page.' He drew on his pipe, before cupping it in his hand. 'But, we all know how these things work. Little snippets of intelligence can help build up the wider picture. There were perhaps one, or two, things of value to the Russians in the files about our planning, but, to be honest, it would have been of far more value to the Nazis.'

'Who else worked closely with Oakways?' Garvan queried.

'Civil servants and politicians right across Whitehall. It's quite a mixed bag really.' He paused, and added, with a taut smile, 'You have to include George Rowlands and me. We both worked alongside the old boy.'

'On a day-to-day basis, George suggested he had little contact with him, and Oakways only occasionally attended meetings with MI6, but that's about as far as it went.'

'Dear George,' Lucern sighed wearily. 'Since he was outed as being a double agent, he's developed a somewhat selective memory. Treat it with a pinch of salt, Superintendent. When we were languishing at the FO, before our posting to Lisbon, we were in daily contact with Oakways. Don't get me wrong, his Lordship was never considered a part of the inner sanctum of the intelligence community. But, he had a liaison role with the Cabinet Office. Access to top secret material was on a need-to-know basis. He was never granted a free hand, or, at least, he hadn't during my time.'

'And did that change at a later date?'

'There's nothing on file to indicate his role changed at all. In fact, quite the reverse; he became increasingly side-lined, because of his rumoured excessive drinking.'

Spencer let out a heartfelt chuckle. 'Christ almighty, the old boy must have had a pretty terrible drink problem for anyone in MI6 to notice!'

In spite of himself, even Lucern smiled slightly. Like most of his MI6 colleagues, he was a formidable drinker. 'I think you'll find it was Haining who initially raised the issue, certainly not anyone within British Intelligence.'

'I thought not,' Spencer smirked. 'Do you have any ideas about Toniolo's name appearing in Oakways's diary for lunch at Claridge's?'

'We've drawn a complete blank so far,' Lucern said.

'Who made the appointment?'

'Oakways. Apparently, he was a regular at the hotel.'

'But, if Toniolo is a codename, why would he openly use it in his diary? That's what I don't understand.'

'The trouble is, dear boy, at this stage of the game, it's all sheer speculation. Maybe he simply didn't know the significance.'

Spencer seemed unconvinced.

Lucern rested his pipe in the ashtray, and linked his fingers behind his head. 'Part of the problem was Oakways's enemies played on his paranoia, and made political capital out of it. Personally, I had a great deal of time for him. He seemed a genuine enough sort.' A slow ironic smile began to cross Lucern's face. 'However, I thought much the same about George Rowlands.'

Chapter 5

Len Dunmore, the renowned Fleet Street political journalist, was waiting outside the Garrick Club. He had been there a little while, and instinctively glanced at his watch. Garvan was running late, but it didn't matter one iota. He stood riveted to the spot, as several waves of Allied fighter and bomber planes flew overhead. Weeks earlier, the sky had become blackened by the ominous droning shapes, flying relentlessly toward the south coast. While this was not quite on the same scale as D-Day, he still found himself fascinated by the deadly, on-going Allied air offensive.

In the run-up to the invasion, Garvan had found himself increasingly based in a large office in St. James's, which Tar Robertson had dubbed the War Room. Both MI5 and MI6 officers, with a contingent from the American OSS Intelligence Agency, staffed the office. Until the War was over, their work would continue, without a break, twenty-four hours a day. In a smoke-filled environment of clattering teleprinters carrying enciphered messages, Bakelite phones ringing constantly, and the noisy clatter of Imperial typewriters conveying the latest intelligence reports to the various Allied Commanders. Within the War Room itself, there was a palpable sense of urgency, mingled with a frisson of anxiety. They knew the coming days and weeks would inevitably become increasingly crucial.

Garvan had wanted to cancel his meeting with Dunmore, but had come under increasing pressure from Spencer to keep it.

Spencer had sat in a swivel chair, with his hands clasped behind his head, swaying slowly from side-to-side, a cigarette resting in the corner of his mouth. 'We can spare you for an hour,' he assured Garvan. 'Whatever happens here we still need to track Toniolo down.'

Garvan had reluctantly slipped on his suit jacket. 'I can still cancel,' he'd said, glancing around the office. 'If it's all the same to you, I'd rather stay here, and feel as if I'm at least doing something useful.'

'*You* are doing something useful.'

He looked at him doubtfully.

'The Colonel wants you to keep the appointment with Dunmore. Besides,' he added, with a rueful smile, 'we'll still be here when you get back.' Spencer had eased himself upright, and reached forward for his phone. 'Have a good lunch,' he said, almost dismissively.

Garvan's gaze again glided around the office; he was still reluctant to leave, but Robertson had obviously made the decision, and he was scarcely in a position to counter his boss's orders.

*

'So, Garvie, I guess things are still going okay?' Dunmore said, as he joined him outside the Garrick.

Garvan followed the direction of his gaze toward the Allied planes heading toward the coast. 'We've nothing else left in the bag, Len. It's a case of do or die.'

'Makes the hairs on the back of your neck stand on end, doesn't it?' he whispered, tears beginning to well in his eyes. 'God help them. God help them all.'

Garvan gently patted his shoulder. 'I'm sorry, Len, but I don't have long,' he explained. 'We can have a quick bite to eat, and then, I'll have to start making tracks back to the office.'

'I daresay you have. I'm just surprised they let you come out to play. It must be something quite important,' Dunmore said, shooting him a quizzical look.

'You could say that,' Garvan said, distractedly following him inside the Club.

54

'Do you know I still don't understand?'

'What's that, Len?'

'Why the hell you, of all people, accepted a secondment to MI5.'

'Sometimes the reasons you do things in your career aren't always clear cut. In my case, MI5 wasn't only a challenge, it was more like a poison chalice.'

'Why *did* you do it?'

He gave a slight shrug, but wouldn't be drawn.

Len supposed the fact Garvan was still unquestionably at the top of his game, and was, without a doubt, an even bigger name at Scotland Yard than he had ever been, was perhaps validation enough of his decision. They'd been friends for some ten years now, and Dunmore sensed something was troubling him.

In the main foyer, the Garrick's porter greeted Dunmore warmly; he was obviously a regular visitor to the Club. Busts of the great and good of the theatrical and literary world lined the corridors. Portraits of previous illustrious members filled in the gaps. The Club was named after the great eighteenth-century actor, David Garrick, and many of the leading literary personalities of the nineteenth century had been members. In essence, it was a well-run dining and social club.

On being escorted into a small select dining room, Garvan couldn't help himself from blurting out, 'Bit out of your league, Len, isn't it?'

'You cheeky bastard!' he said.

'How did you become a member?'

'It's all about contacts, me old darling. That's how.'

'Even so, I thought they were pretty picky.'

'I think you forget something, Garvie.'

'What's that?'

'I'm considered to be a man of letters,' he added rather grandly.

55

Garvan laughed. 'Well, that's one description, but it's not the first one that came to mind.'

'Did you know Charles Dickens was a member of the Club?'

'Not making comparisons, are *you*?' Garvan smirked.

'He was a man of letters.'

'You're a third-rate political hack,' Garvan laughed again, but not unkindly.

'If I were a third-rate hack, me old darling, we wouldn't be sitting here now, would we?'

'I guess we wouldn't. But, all jokes aside, Len, who proposed you for membership?'

Dunmore screwed up his face. 'I wish you hadn't asked me that one.'

'Why?'

'You won't like the answer.'

'Try me.'

'It was George Rowlands.'

'Rowlands,' he repeated in surprise. 'How do you know him?'

'The second Mrs. Dunmore was an actress.'

To Garvan's knowledge, there had been three ex-Mrs. Dunmores.

'Joan was quite a good actress, in her day; George was her agent for a while, until she managed to cross him. As you know, our George was a successful theatrical agent, before this lot started, and MI5 recruited him. Mind you, even at the best of times, Joan could be bloody neurotic. In the end, he completely washed his hands of her, dropped her like a stone. There was never any ill feeling between us; God knows he tried his best for her, but Joan was pig-headed. Thought she knew best, and, in the end, he slapped her down to size.'

Their conversation lulled, as the waiter presented them with the menu and a bottle of wine; they both chose the salmon en croute.

'What's this all about Garvie?' Dunmore asked closing the menu.

'I thought you might have guessed.'

He shot him a look. 'If I were of a betting persuasion I'd presume it might have something to do with my old friend Lord Oakways?' he ventured.

Garvan smiled. 'There are two particular entries in his diary that we're interested in.'

'Go on.'

'The first was for lunch last Tuesday at Claridge's, with someone called Toniolo, have you ever heard of him?'

'No, I can't say I have,' Dunmore pondered, 'do you mind if I smoke?'

'Feel free. There were two circled exclamation marks next to Toniolo's name, so we're assuming it must have been pretty important to him.'

'I'm sorry, me old darling. I really can't help you there,' he said, opening up a packet of Players cigarettes.

'There was another entry for lunch the following week.'

Dunmore coughed wheezily. 'Yes, that's right. It was with me.'

'What happened?'

'He never turned up.'

Garvan smiled. 'We kind of worked that one out for ourselves. The poor bugger was already dead. But, didn't you think it strange he never turned up?'

Dunmore blew out a plume of smoke. 'All politicians tend to be strange, me old darling; it comes with the territory.'

'Did you try contacting him?'

'I called his number at the Foreign Office.'

'And what happened?'

'They stonewalled me, and said he wasn't available.'

'Did you have his home telephone number?'

'Yes, there was no answer.'

'Wasn't his housekeeper there?'

There was a flicker of amusement on Dunmore's face. 'Have you met Mary Green?'

'Not personally.'

'Lovely old girl, salt of the earth, but as deaf as a bloody post. She probably didn't even hear the phone ringing.' Dunmore puffed contentedly on his cigarette. 'But, I guess you already know that much.'

Garvan held his gaze. 'Why were you having lunch with Oakways?'

'Ah, now, me old darling, he promised me a scoop.'

'What kind of a scoop?'

'Well, that's the rub, isn't it; he was hardly likely to discuss it over the phone. I take it you know how things were with him?'

Garvan nodded. 'Weren't you a bit wary?'

'You mean about him being viewed as paranoid.'

'Yes, I do.'

'Whatever you may think, paranoid or not, I've no doubt whatsoever that he was under surveillance.'

'What makes you say that?'

Dunmore shot him a rather bemused smile. 'He'd had a few well-publicised problems, so I daresay the men in grey suits would have deemed him a potential security risk.' He exhaled the cigarette smoke slowly through his lips and nostrils. 'You're playing with me, Garvie, aren't you?'

Garvan's expression was deadpan; he was giving nothing away.

'Your MI5 mob and your other friends in MI6 were presumably both bugging him?'

Garvan allowed a slow smile to cross his face.

Dunmore knew how the system worked; Garvan was interested in what he had to say. 'You have to ask yourself, me old darling, who had the greater vested interest in keeping tabs on his lordship?'

Garvan considered his reply. 'Ostensibly, it was MI6.'

'But, was that the case?'

'Enlighten me,' Garvan said.

'Let's just say, Jeremy Haining isn't one who scatters his venom at long range.'

'What the hell is that supposed to mean?'

'He always prefers to tackle a problem head on, face-to-face, and take the bull by its horns, rather than waste his time on writing letters, or venting his frustration over the telephone.'

'I still don't get your drift. Haining told us they got along really well, and Oakways often popped along the street of an evening to have a bite to eat with his family. There's nothing on record to suggest there was any animosity between them, far from it, and he certainly didn't report Oakways's drink problem to the Cabinet Office *that* I do know.'

Dunmore continued to puff on the cigarette, as the waiter returned with their lunch. They thanked him.

'Before the War, Oakways was rumoured to have held extreme right-wing views,' Garvan said. 'Is that true?'

Dunmore raised his wine glass to his lips, and gulped it back. 'Not to my knowledge. I guess, like most of us, he'd probably mellowed in old age, but he was never associated with the likes of Oswald Mosley's Fascist Party, if that's what you're hinting at?'

'You tell me.'

'Oakways didn't always conform to Party politics. In a small way, he was just as much a rebel as Jeremy Haining ever is. Maybe that's why they formed such a close friendship. In their own way, they were both mavericks and bloody-minded.' Dunmore reached across the table for the bottle of wine, and refilled his glass. 'I know Haining didn't report him to the Cabinet Office,' Dunmore continued. 'But, I think it very likely he probably let it slip to your friends in MI6

Oakways was becoming a liability. Whatever Haining may or may not have told you, he is very much a part of the intelligence community, or, at least, from a Foreign Office perspective.'

Garvan didn't let it show on his face, but he was surprised Lucern hadn't told them about Haining's involvement with MI6. He also began to wonder whether Tar Robertson had suspected Lucern probably wasn't dealing him an entirely even hand. It would certainly go a long way in explaining why Spencer had also given him the okay not to cancel his meeting with Dunmore.

Dunmore knew his way around the Whitehall system. Garvan couldn't fault him for playing things cagily, but he needed answers.

'Word has it *the Daily Express* was on the verge of running an article that Oakways was experiencing certain, how shall I say, personal problems, is that correct?'

The hard edge to Garvan's voice spoke volumes. Len sat back in his chair, and regarded him thoughtfully.

'Did he really offer you a scoop, or was it perhaps more to do with his trying to suppress your editorial about his drink problem?' Garvan said.

'We'd planned to run an article.' Len confessed.

'It would have destroyed his career?'

Len pulled a face. 'That's probably a moot point; we had our lawyers go through it with a fine-tooth comb. I never once mentioned he was an alcoholic; we'd certainly never have gone that far. Besides, we'd have ended up in Court, Oakways would certainly have taken it to the wire.'

'But, reading between the lines, his being tired and emotional in public was nothing more than a euphemism he was pissed out of his brain.'

'We never ran the article,' Dunmore said defensively.

'No, you didn't. The poor old sod was murdered before you had the chance to.'

Dunmore shrugged indifferently. 'I was only doing my job.'

'So, what prompted you to run the story?'

Dunmore poured himself another glass of wine. 'He was fair game,' he said dismissively. 'I'm sure you know how it is. Rumours abound Whitehall, all the time. Most of them are just that, rumours, but Oakways's alcoholism wasn't just a rumour, we had proof.'

'So, he was a piss head, but why would anyone want to kill him?

'He'd made more than a few enemies in his time,' Len said, tucking into his lunch. 'But, who hasn't. I'm not sure why anyone would want to bump him off, unless he was onto something, something really important, but it's only a guess.'

'Did you ever meet up with him in Lord North Street?'

'Yes, that's how I met his housekeeper.'

'How long had you known him?'

Dunmore puffed out his cheeks. 'Christ knows. He was on the diplomatic circuit when we first met. It must have been back in the twenties, I really couldn't give you a date. All I know is it was years before he ever thought of standing for Parliament.'

'I take it you've met his wife?'

'Lord, yes. Dear old Laura,' Dunmore guffawed wheezily. 'The Bolter.'

'Didn't you coin the phrase?' Garvan said accusingly.

The smile slowly died off his face. 'Much to my shame, yes, I did. For what it's worth, I liked Laura. She was a lovely girl. The trouble was, she married far too young, and it didn't work out. There was a large age gap between them. Let's just say Oakways had never exactly been the life and soul of the party, whereas Laura was always full of life. She deserved better, and certainly didn't deserve to lose custody of the children. In my opinion, he'd have been much better off staying with her.'

'Where's Laura now?'

'She's a volunteer ambulance driver. Laura's moved on with her life, whereas Oakways never quite recovered after their divorce. I understand she's engaged to an American Naval Officer.'

'Was she still in contact with Oakways?'

'Not on a personal level. If there was ever an issue with the children, they only communicated via a third party, usually through their solicitors, or occasionally through their in-laws, but never face-to-face.'

'How well did you know him?'

'Well enough,' he said. 'You have to understand Oakways was prone to melodramatic gestures. The promise of a scoop, or not, a meeting in his diary for lunch was pretty standard fare. It was always along the usual lines.'

Garvan narrowed his eyes curiously.

'It was about the dark forces.'

'What forces?'

'Ah, now, Garvie, not the obvious ones, like you and I know. In fact, we scarcely touched on the War at all. He was far more concerned about the dark forces within the British Establishment.'

'Begs a question...'

'Does it?'

'Why call you?'

'He wanted my help to investigate them.'

Garvan looked doubtful.

'Bless him; he seemed to think I might be able to help him expose a spy who was risking National Security.'

'And could you?'

Dunmore set his knife and fork down on the plate. 'You know me, Garvie. I try not to court disaster.'

'That's not what I asked. Presumably he gave you names?'

'It wasn't quite like that.'

'Then, what was it like?'

'He tended to be quite woolly about his accusations. It was all of a piece, really.' Dunmore cradled the wine glass thoughtfully between his hands. 'The sad part is, because of the booze, everyone started to view him as a bit of a joke.'

'And was he a joke?'

'What do you think?' Len shot back at him.

'You knew the man; I trust your judgment. You tell me.'

'Jokes don't usually end up being murdered, do they?'

Dunmore was right; he couldn't argue the point.

'But, was his offer of a scoop simply a way of delaying the publication of your editorial?'

'I've no idea.'

'Don't play with me, Len.'

'Genuinely, I've no idea.'

'Something doesn't make sense.'

'What's that?'

'You said you liked the man.'

'Yes, I did.'

'Why write an editorial that would have destroyed his career?'

'You know how it is.'

'No, I don't.'

'Journalists are like whores, Garvie. They're only ever as good as their last trick.'

It was an effort to keep the contempt off his face, but he did so.

Dunmore shrugged; it was a slight shrug, but spoke volumes. 'Well, me old darling, you know how it is. Business is business. I've never allowed personal relationships to get in

63

the way of a good story. Besides,' he added reflectively, 'there was a certain amount of *outside* pressure.'

The penny had finally dropped. Dunmore had been leaned upon to write the editorial. In the past, Scotland Yard had also used his services for their own ends, but he'd always assumed somehow his old friend had skilfully avoided falling into the trap of working for the Service. They'd both thrown their hat into the security ring, but under very different circumstances. Garvan's decision had been his, and his alone, whereas he suspected some underhand dealing probably mired Len's reasons. Perhaps he'd overstepped the line, and fallen foul of a member of the Service, or maybe he'd ended up as a pawn, and a bit-part player in some dark establishment game.

'Who asked you to write the article about Oakways?'

Dunmore breathed deeply. 'Who do you think?'

'MI6?'

'Ah, now, *that* would be telling, me old darling. In my experience, I've always avoided answering direct questions.'

Garvan looked at him speculatively. 'Why's that?'

'If you do, you're apt to get an evasive answer, or, at best, a downright effing lie.'

'Which are you going to give me?'

Dunmore knew he was seriously batting out of his league, and he wasn't prepared to come clean and offer up a name. It was more than his life was worth. At length, he said, 'I guess the art of being a first-rate journalist is a little like being a top-notch detective. It's all about drawing your victim into your confidence.'

'Is it?'

'You know how it is, me old darling. I'm talking to the converted. You get the drift of your opponent's thinking, or, at least, an idea about their views.' Dunmore smiled at Garvan; it was a slight one, but by the look on Garvan's face, he understood his drift.

'Oakways trusted you, but all the while MI6 was pulling your strings?'

Dunmore tightened his lips and confessed, 'It was something along those lines, but nothing is ever quite what it seems.'

'But, you've missed something.'

'Have I?'

'If Oakways was right all along, that someone was out to destroy him, and I'm sure they were, you had a helping hand in destroying him. Whoever asked you to write the scoop not only wanted to humiliate him, but to close him down for good.' A look of disappointment crossed Garvan's face. 'I'd have thought you'd have seen the broader picture, Len.' He looked at him questioningly. 'Unless, whoever ordered you to write the article had something on you as well?'

'No, no me old darling it was nothing like that at all.'

'Then what was is like?'

There was a shrewd glint in his eye. 'I didn't have a choice.'

'If you didn't have a choice, you were under orders. So, who asked you to do it? Why did you agree?'

Dunmore's expression closed down.

'If you hold out on me, I can't help you.'

'I know that,' he said, with a brittle smile.

Garvan looked at him searchingly. Up until now, he'd always valued Len's opinion, but something had happened, something or someone had got to him. He tossed his napkin down on the table in exasperation. 'I hope to God, Len, that you know what you're doing.'

Dunmore's face remained impassive; he made no attempt to reply.

'If you can't meet me halfway, then you know how it stands. I can't provide you with top cover. You'll be entirely on your own.'

Dunmore stared thoughtfully into the contents of his wine glass. 'I know how things stand,' he murmured.

'You do realise whoever killed Oakways will now have an entirely free hand.' He looked across the table at him.

'I'm not a fool, Garvie.'

'But, you still have a choice!'

'Do I?' he queried glumly.

'Who ordered you to write the scoop? Why not give me a name?'

Whatever, or whoever had put the fear of God into him, had won the day; he could do no more, Dunmore wasn't about to budge.

Chapter 6

By the time he pulled up in John Adam Street, close to the Strand, it was already dark, and had started to rain. Len Dunmore had a strange feeling something wasn't quite right. Taking a quick glance through the windscreen, he decided to stay put, and keep the engine ticking over, until his contact arrived.

He owed Garvan a favour, and had decided to follow up on a lead about Toniolo; he'd heard a whisper that certain elements within MI6 were becoming decidedly twitchy, and that MI5's investigation was starting to stir up a hornet's nest. Certain members had apparently made a formal approach to C, and requested, under the circumstances, he might consider having the investigation scaled down. They were overloaded already with intelligence work, and with Allied troops currently battling their way across occupied territory, they argued concerns over an alleged Soviet mole was the least of their problems, and taking up an inordinate amount of manpower from the main task at hand. General Menzies had swiftly drawn a line under the protests, explaining Toniolo wasn't just an in-house British matter. Washington was expecting results, Churchill was expecting results, and, therefore, so was he. Nonetheless, the rumblings of discontent within MI6 ranks had continued unabated. There remained a deep-rooted resentment their sister organisation was investigating them, which had upset their somewhat fragile professional sensitivities.

Sitting in his old Morris 10, with the rain hammering down on the windscreen, Dunmore was beginning to think maybe he ought to have simply let sleeping dogs lie. He started to drum nervously on the steering wheel; he needed a cigarette, but he always needed one. He began rummaging through his jacket pockets, dug out a lighter, and reached forward for the pack of cigarettes on the console.

His contact, an MP, had suggested meeting for a drink at the Schooner pub at the end of the road. The offices on either side of the pub had long since shut up shop, and at this time of night, there was very little through traffic, unless, of course, you were on foot, heading down toward Embankment Station.

Dunmore blew out a column of smoke. His contact was running late; he'd give it another five minutes but no more. He'd only just finished the editorial for the morning edition. He was tired, and wanted nothing more than to scurry off home, have a quiet drink, relax, and listen to the radio, before collapsing into bed.

Something caught his eye. It was someone, walking along the road, with a small pencil torch aimed toward the pavement. The Blackout was in full force, and the dimmed headlamps of the Morris were pretty ineffectual. Dunmore flicked on the windscreen wipers, and leaned forward to get a better look. Squinting through the misted glass, it started to run through his mind he really ought to think about having his eyes tested; vanity in a man of his age was just plain stupid.

He could just make out the figure of a man wrapped up in a belted raincoat, and a trilby hat pulled down to keep the rain out of his face. Dunmore relaxed slightly. This wasn't his contact. He was about four stone lighter, for one thing, and not overly tall. He puffed on his cigarette, and watched him cross the road no more than twenty yards in front of his car. Maybe he was heading off to the Strand; there any number of hotels or bars to choose from along the main road.

Drawing level with the car, he crouched down and knocked on the driver's window, Dunmore's face registered surprise. After a moment's hesitation, he wound the window down, and to his horror, found himself confronted by the barrel of a revolver. It certainly wasn't his contact, but he did recognise the face beneath the trilby hat. *Christ almighty, why hadn't he decided to keep his head below the parapet? Was it perhaps misguided loyalty to Garvan?* Whatever it was, he'd sailed pretty close to the wind before, but nothing like this. The only given was Dunmore knew he'd been betrayed by his contact. His heart was racing; it wasn't in good nick, anyway. With any luck, he'd keel over from a heart attack before the bugger had a chance to pull the trigger.

'What the hell are you doing here?' he asked, his mouth set in a rictus smile. He wanted to play for time, but guessed it was running out fast.

'Get in the back of the car.'

'What's going on?' Dunmore stumbled.

'Just get in the back of the sodding car!'

Dunmore shakily stuck the cigarette between his lips. *Realistically, what were his chances?* He could smack the bastard in the mouth, and make a run for it down the road, but it wouldn't give him much time. Either way, he was going to die. It was a choice of a bullet in the back, or look the bastard in the eyes. His life was over, but he needed to do something. His thoughts were in freefall; he'd never get the chance to see his children again, he'd never walk Meg, his Labrador, again. Whatever mess Garvan had embroiled him in, it certainly wasn't worth all this.

'Get in the back of the sodding car!' he repeated.

Dunmore heaved himself out of his beloved old Morris10, then pulled the driver's seat forward, shakily clambered into the rear, and collapsed wheezily onto the back seat. As his killer leaned into the car, he met his eyes; knowing he was about to die, the only thing he hoped for was, God willing, he wouldn't feel any pain.

'Whatever you do to me, you're living on borrowed time, you know that,' he said.

There was no response.

'However long it takes, you know the Service will eventually track you down.' He met his killer's eyes; there was a bright flash, and the force of the bullet shot Dunmore's head violently against the seat.

*

In the morning, when Dunmore failed to attend a crucial meeting in Fleet Street, his editor, Frank Tredget, had eventually become so concerned he decided to take matters into his own hands by driving over to his flat in Wigmore Street. Outside, there was no sign of his familiar battered old blue Morris, and being unable to raise any answer, Tredget reluctantly decided to call in the local police. After a bit of persuasion, they eventually agreed to break down the door. Inside, everything was neat and tidy, just as Dunmore had left it. There was certainly no sign of a burglary, or that anything untoward had happened.

As Dunmore's name appeared routinely on a Special Branch list circulated to local police stations as being someone of potential interest, West End Central contacted Scotland Yard. After an hour, or so, a message ended up landing on Harry Mackenzie's desk saying, Dunmore had gone missing. Harry had then immediately placed an all-points bulletin across the Met to track down Dunmore's car, before finally picking up the phone to Garvan.

'What do you mean, gone missing?' he'd asked him.

'Len's editor, Frank Tredget, initially raised the alert,' Mac explained.

'When did he report it?'

There was a pause, as he checked his notes. 'Not until lunchtime.'

'Give me a call, if there's any news,' Garvan said, slamming down the receiver.

The afternoon had stretched into the evening, before Mackenzie called back. He had just emerged from a long meeting with Tar Robertson, and was on the point of wolfing down a much-needed sandwich at his desk, when the phone rang.

'We've found his car,' Mackenzie told him.

'Where is it?'

'It's parked up in John Adam Street, outside the Adelphi Building.'

'Is there any sign of Dunmore?'

'The message was a bit sketchy. The local beat copper phoned in to report it. Apparently, there's a body on the back seat. I thought I'd better give you a call, before I shoot down there.'

'Give me ten minutes, and I'll meet you there.'

By the time Garvan drove along the Thames Embankment, it was still raining, and a slow swirling grey mist clung tenaciously to the ebbing tide. Mackenzie was already there, with two junior Special Branch officers and a clutch of local uniformed coppers from nearby Charing Cross Station, all gathered around Dunmore's ancient Morris. The light was beginning to fade, and the fine drizzle was the kind that really soaked through your clothes. Garvan pulled up nearby, and Mackenzie instantly recognised the green Jaguar Roadster.

As Garvan headed down the street to join them, his tall, loose-limbed figure dressed in a smart pinstriped suit and unbuttoned raincoat, drew their attention. There was an inherent commanding physical presence about him and as one, the officers around Mackenzie suddenly recognised the Guv'nor. It was something of an open secret he was currently on secondment to British Intelligence, but even so, his reputation as a detective was second to none.

Until his arrival, the atmosphere on the scene had been professional but almost light-hearted. The ribbing between the officers had rolled back and forth, despite the obvious seriousness of the situation. But, Garvan commanded respect, and, as one, they withdrew seamlessly back across the road, leaving Mackenzie alone beside Dunmore's car.

'Guv'nor,' Mac said, extending his hand in greeting.

Garvan's attention roamed slowly over the scene, his gaze idly resting on the officers who had respectfully retreated, before returning his attention back toward the Morris 10.

'What have we got?' he asked.

'Take a look,' Mac said, gesturing toward the car.

The front passenger door was wide open. Garvan leaned inside, took a quick look round, and saw Dunmore slumped on the back seat; his eyes were closed, almost as if he'd fallen asleep. Only the dark staining on his shirt gave any hint he'd been murdered. Garvan climbed inside the car, and slipped out the torch from the pocket of his raincoat. The light was drawing in; he needed to take a closer look at the body. He shone the torch, probing the beam directly on Dunmore's blood-splattered face, before playing it across the back seat. He flicked it off, as he climbed back out of the car.

'What do you think?' Mackenzie asked.

Garvan took a sharp intake of breath. 'We met for lunch yesterday at the Garrick Club to discuss Oakways's murder.'

'How did he seem?'

Garvan shrugged. 'Cagey.'

'Did he come up with anything?'

'Nothing much. He claimed that he'd never heard of Toniolo.'

Mackenzie pulled a face. 'I know Len had made a few enemies in his time, but who would have wanted him dead?'

'Exactly. Someone had leaned upon him to write an article about Oakways, that much he did confess. Had it gone to print, his political career would have been destroyed, but something happened to force Toniolo's hand, before it ever went to print.'

'So, who was pressuring Dunmore?'

'He was too bloody scared to say.'

'Mackenzie looked at him searchingly. 'From what I understand, Oakways's career was already a busted flush so why bother going to the effort of killing the poor old bugger?'

'Maybe Toniolo started to have second thoughts, and to get a bit twitchy that, once the article became public knowledge, and with nothing else to lose, Oakways might seriously begin to blab. He might have been a busted flush, but mud sticks, and if he named enough names, then he'd probably manage to bring down a few other people. Maybe, he knew Toniolo's identity. In Oakways's shoes, I'd have gone down fighting. Let me know what forensics and the pathologist come up with.'

'Yes, Guv'nor.'

As Garvan started to head back toward Spencer's Jaguar, he inclined his head in acknowledgement, and smiled briefly at the officers huddled across the street.

Although Dunmore had denied hearing of Toniolo, whoever ordered him to write the article about Oakways had apparently wanted to silence his lordship for good, and for whatever reason, he guessed, was also responsible for murdering Dunmore as well. The dark forces within the British Establishment Oakways had alluded to were, perhaps, not just a figment of his imagination after all. Whatever the truth, Dunmore had obviously been too scared to come clean with him at the Garrick Club.

*

After reporting back to St. James's with news of Dunmore's murder, Spencer and Garvan arranged to meet Jamie Burdis at his Parliamentary office.

73

His in-tray was full, as were the two large glass ashtrays; the desk was covered with a plethora of files and loose papers, while his out-tray was, perhaps tellingly, entirely empty. He offered them drinks; they accepted. Macallan was his whisky of choice, but by all accounts, he wasn't that selective with what liquor he poured down his throat. His opening gambit was to reminisce about his experience as a relatively junior Member of Parliament, when he'd cut his teeth at the Cabinet Office, and had also spent time working at No10. According to the files, it had been a somewhat short-lived experience, but he was full of himself, and loved to brag. Fortunately, they'd been well-briefed, and knew exactly what to expect of him.

'I'd arrive in the bloody office,' he explained expansively, 'and wonder which effing rabbit had leaped out of the hat overnight.' His voice carried loudly through the room, the Oxbridge accent sharp, and peremptory. He came across to both of them as being overbearingly arrogant. 'After doing my bit at No10, I qualified for lunch with the PM.' He looked to each of them in turn, hoping they'd be impressed; the trouble was, neither of them seemed particularly interested in what he had to say, and judging by the look on Spencer's face, he appeared markedly underwhelmed. He couldn't quite decide whether Burdis was bragging for the sake of doing so, or was hoping to impress them. Either way, it didn't matter much, as he hadn't succeeded on either count.

From what Garvan knew of him, in the early days, Burdis had managed to steadily climb the slippery slope by detaching himself from the political epicentre, and apart from his personal peccadilloes, his career had remained largely untainted, until his promotion to the Foreign Office. After that, he'd found himself with no place left to hide, or any wriggle room to sidestep the issues. Burdis had finally been forced to face the fact, he was out on a limb to prove himself as a first-rate politician, or die on his sword. Haining was not the man to give him any quarter, for his Labour Party boss was not only astute, but quietly ruthless.

Garvan caught the cynical smile on Spencer's face, but managed not to react as Burdis continued, unabated, to bore them with tales of his apparent successes. If they hadn't known any better, they'd have thought he was destined one day to step into Churchill's shoes. Maybe he'd spun the story so many times, which he might have, and begun to believe his own rhetoric.

But, what wasn't in doubt, was his ability as a gifted linguist. On paper, he was always destined for a spell at the Foreign Office. However, buried beneath the inherent, inbred upper-class arrogance, lurked a somewhat vain misfit. Although Burdis openly admitted he'd toyed with the idea of Communism during his time at Cambridge, he dismissed it as a fleeting generational thing. It was fashionable and the thing to do, but it had been no more than that.

'At the time, we felt a sense of obligation,' he explained, disarmingly, 'or maybe it was sheer bloody stupidity on our part we were somehow combating Fascism.' He lit himself a cigarette, and added, with a twinkly smile, 'In hindsight, it was all baloney, but we were young and idealistic. We thought we could make a difference. It was crap, of course, but it was *idealistic* crap!'

'Did you join the Communist Party?' Spencer queried.

'Major Hall, I rather suspect you already know the answer to that one. Besides, my father was horrified when he discovered I was attending left-wing meetings at Cambridge. Let's just say, things became quite tricky between us, to the point where he was threatening to disinherit me.'

Spencer held his gaze, and said cuttingly, 'At which point, I guess you probably rediscovered your Tory roots?'

In fairness, Burdis laughed at his own expense. 'It wasn't quite like that, but I like your style, Major.'

'What was it like, then?'

'Oh God, to be perfectly honest with you. I had developed an almost pathological hatred of my father's old school tie kind of snobbery. In some ways, you could say my entire youth was spent rebelling against my father, the establishment, and everything they stood for.'

Try as he might, Spencer couldn't help from looking faintly bored; fortunately, Burdis seemed not to notice. He had a captive audience, and that's all that mattered to him, but, more importantly, he liked the sound of his own voice.

'It's an open secret I joined the Cambridge University Socialist Society. As I said, you must have read the files, gentlemen? It's all on record.'

Garvan had indeed read the files, but, all the same, decided to play devil's advocate. 'I'm sorry, what exactly was the Cambridge University Socialist Society?

Almost immediately he began to regret asking, as Burdis launched into yet another long diatribe about how the Society was formed as a protest against the coalition government between Ramsey MacDonald's Labour Party and the Tories. His patience was beginning to wear thin, and it began to show.

'You have to understand, Superintendent, I believed the Soviets had got it right. They had the right values, and perhaps, naively, I jumped on the bandwagon, but that's all in the past now.'

There was an undisguised look of condescension on Garvan's face.

'What's wrong?'

'What the hell would you of all people *really* know about social justice?'

'I'm sorry?' Burdis looked genuinely surprised.

'Your father was an academic, I believe, and a brilliant politician, in his time.'

'Yes, he was.'

'And your family have always lived a comfortable life in North London, and on your estate in Kent. So, you've no real idea what it's like to be at the bottom of the ladder, to fight for survival, or worry where the money is coming from to pay the rent, or put the food on the table.'

'No, I haven't,' he confessed readily. 'But, that doesn't mean to say I can't believe in social justice.'

'Perhaps not, but I look at you, and can't help thinking your fight for so-called social justice is nothing more than some outlandish utopian ideal.'

Burdis looked genuinely hurt.

'It's just your views are so far removed from my own.'

As he returned Garvan's steady gaze, the blue eyes were hostile. Spencer decided to change track.

'I believe Jeremy Haining was your boss at the Foreign Office?'

'I'm sure you know he was.'

'Did you like him?'

Burdis was not one to hide his light under a bushel. 'Like him? He wasn't there to be liked. He was a force of nature.' He folded his arms. 'There's no point in denying I couldn't stand the ruddy man. As far as I'm concerned, he's an utter arse. He doesn't give an effing damn about anyone, or anything.'

A brief, if somewhat ironic, smile flickered across Spencer's face. 'Then, you would appear to have a great deal in common.'

'That's a matter of opinion, Major, but it just doesn't happen to be mine. The trouble is, with Haining,' Burdis continued expansively, 'is I never personally found overloaded with mental gifts, far from it, in fact. He's a rough diamond, and, by his own admission, a bit of a bruiser, but, on no account, is he a political heavyweight.' He lit himself a cigarette, and snapped the lighter shut. 'Personally, I've always believed it's one thing to achieve power, but quite another to hold onto it,' he added pompously.

'That's as maybe,' Garvan said, 'but gifted or not, Haining still managed to oust you to the backbenches, didn't he?'

A look of acid crept across Burdis face; he didn't respond, or know how. Garvan was certainly beginning to understand why his Parliamentary colleagues universally despised Burdis. He couldn't help thinking, in spite of his brashness and arrogance, it probably masked a myriad of deep-rooted insecurities. The contrast with Haining could not have been more marked. The rough diamond of the Labour Party was totally at ease and comfortable in his own skin, and was, Garvan decided, by far the deadlier of the two.

After a protracted pause, Burdis admitted, in a rare display of openness, being ousted to the backbenches hadn't come easily to him, quite the reverse, in fact.

'You have to understand, Superintendent,' he added, 'I was the victim of a bureaucratic intrigue.'

'You were sacked,' Garvan said directly.

'There was rather more to it than that,' he said off-handily. 'Haining was the instigator behind my downfall and demotion!'

'But, didn't the PM side with him?'

Burdis sucked on his cigarette. 'He did, but only after Haining plotted behind my back.'

'You're beginning to sound as if you're a victim,' Spencer suggested.

'Am I?'

Whatever actually lay behind the decision, Spencer speculated Churchill was unlikely to have been impressed by his self-serving arrogance.

Burdis shot him a cold hard look, but suspected it was entirely lost on this Major from British Intelligence, who appeared to radiate a certain inner menace.

78

'I take it you've heard Len Dunmore is dead?' Garvan cut in.

'Yes, I have.'

'Did you know him well?'

'We'd met socially, and at the occasional formal get-together. If I'm honest, I didn't particularly like the man.'

Garvan arched his brows in surprise. 'I'm sorry, maybe I've got the wrong end of the stick, but I was under the impression you both met regularly at the Red Lion in Whitehall and the Damaris Bar for a drink?'

'I can't deny it. Yes, we did.'

'But, if you couldn't stand the man, why did you bother socialising with him?'

'It was business, strictly business, old chap. He was a necessary evil. As a politician, it always paid not to get on the wrong side of Len Dunmore. He was a force on Fleet Street, and could either make or break careers.'

It was an honest answer. 'You worked alongside Lord Oakways for quite a while. What did you make of him?'

'I won't lie to you; I thought he was a sanctimonious little shit!'

'And it's rumoured he viewed you as a dangerous maverick?'

Burdis rolled his eyes. 'For Christ's sake, Oakways was so far up himself, he was in danger of disappearing up his own sodding arse.'

'What do you mean by that?'

'He once denounced me as a free-thinking intellectual.'

Garvan's face remained devoid of expression, but he couldn't quite see the connection to Burdis. 'And what, precisely, is a free-thinking intellectual?'

Burdis looked mildly irritated. 'Oakways was old school. If you didn't conform to traditional Tory values, or at least as he saw them, then he viewed MPs' like me as being subversive. It was all poppycock, but that's the way he was, and then the booze took hold. He was starting to lose the plot, and making a laughing stock of himself.'

'I thought that was more to do with his paranoia the security services were bugging him.'

'It was part and parcel of it all, but by no means the only reason.'

'Word has it, he also disapproved of your social life?'

'I can only describe Oakways as being repressed. We all knew that's why his wife Laura took flight. God only knows how the marriage lasted as long as it did. No-one blamed her when she finally upped sticks and left; the only downside was she eventually lost custody of the children. At the time, I remember it became very messy between them. My wife and I are still in contact with Laura; she deserved better than Oakways, but that's the price you sometimes pay for marrying too young.'

Garvan couldn't help thinking it was a case of the pot calling the kettle black. Burdis had also married someone much younger than himself, and, by all accounts, had even cheated on his wife on their wedding day. However, it was just that, rumour. Yet, Garvan suspected there was more than a grain of truth to it. His reputation as a philanderer had long since been the talk of Westminster, and it was acknowledged widely he had never been faithful throughout their marriage. But, despite his constant and sometimes outrageous infidelities, Jenny Burdis had remained blindly loyal to her husband.

Spencer and Garvan exchanged glances; it was time to call an end to their meeting.

'Thank you for your time,' Spencer said, coming to his feet, 'and thank you for the Macallan's. We'll be in touch.'

'Yes,' Burdis said resignedly. 'I had a feeling you would.'

Chapter 7

MI5 was housed in the former MGM building in St. James's. Its nondescript identity was camouflaged by a large "To Let" sign outside the main entrance. Colonel Robertson had called a meeting to discuss the way forward. The report into Dunmore's murder had confirmed the cause of death as being a single bullet wound to the chest. In the pathologist's opinion, death had been instantaneous.

Robertson swivelled around in his chair toward a large brown metal cupboard behind his desk. He twirled the tumbler lock carefully five times to the right, then to the left four, and so on, decreasing the number of turns each time, until it clicked open and released the combination to his not-so-secret stash of alcohol on the second shelf of the cupboard. There was a moment's indecision. It was something of a tradition their meetings began with a large dram either of whisky or Drambuie.

'So, gentlemen, I take it you've both read the Pathology Report?'

'Yes, sir,' Spencer said.

Tar handed them each a generous tot of Drambuie. 'Our cousins across the Atlantic are becoming increasingly twitchy about our apparent inability to track Toniolo down.' He leaned back in his chair, savouring the sweet tasting amber liqueur. 'The PM is also demanding results, and Dunmore's death hasn't exactly helped ease his mood any. In fact, he's spitting rivets. He's convinced himself Toniolo is starting to run rings around the Service.' Tar tapped the cold grey-white contents of his pipe into a large onyx ashtray, before re-filling it with a fresh supply of tobacco. 'While I don't entirely share Churchill's take on the situation, I'm finding it increasingly difficult to defend my corner.' He reached into his desk drawer for a box of matches. 'So, gentlemen, I'd appreciate your views. Have either of you managed to come up with anything new?'

Initially, his question was met with a wall of silence; it wasn't the most promising of starts.

'May I ask a question,' Garvan said.

'Go ahead Superintendent.'

'It was quite obvious when I met up with Dunmore at the Garrick Club, someone had leaned on him to write a critical article about Lord Oakways.'

'Yes, so you told me.'

'Someone, or something, had put the fear of God up him, so much so he was scared to reveal who wanted to destroy Oakways. I was just wondering, sir, whether you'd heard a whisper on the grapevine about the editorial.'

Robertson took his time answering. 'I'd always assumed MI6 might have been behind it.'

'Are you surmising, sir, or do you know they were?

A slight smile played around Robertson's mouth. 'I didn't have any concrete proof. That is, until this morning.'

'May I ask who tipped you off, sir?'

'The Director General,' he said flatly.

'So, they were out to destroy him?'

He gave a shrug. 'Let's just say, I think they wanted to ensure he was removed permanently from the Foreign Office. He'd become not only a laughing stock, but also a serious security risk.'

'Then, why was MI5 having Oakways watched as well?' Garvan continued.

Robertson's eyes briefly flicked toward Spencer. 'I thought it had already been explained to you.'

'It has, but I'd still prefer to hear it from the horse's mouth, so to speak.'

'As you're well aware, Superintendent, there were a number of issues placing Oakways in a high-risk category. As a precaution, we ordered our Watchers to put him under surveillance. It was a matter of routine, there wasn't any hidden agenda, far from it, at least not on our part, if that's what you're getting at.'

'And what about MI6, did they have their own hidden agenda?'

Robertson puffed heavily on his pipe. For some reason, he was struggling to keep it alight. 'I can only assume their motives were much the same as our own, but certainly, from our perspective, he wasn't our section's highest priority. In fact, he wasn't considered a priority at all. Oakways's work involved MI6's side of the house at the Foreign Office. As you're well aware, MI5 looks after homeland security for the UK, whereas MI6 is responsible for overseas security affecting the UK or any of its overseas territories. Oakways's ministerial role was therefore of far greater interest to MI6, rather than us. But, that's not to say that our interests don't occasionally overlap.' Robertson sucked on his pipe. 'You could say Oakways straddled both sides of the security fence.'

'Which I guess brings us neatly to Frank Lucern,' Spencer said in a deadpan voice.

'Does it?' Robertson queried.

'Come on, Colonel. He wasn't exactly forthcoming about MI6 priming Len Dunmore to do their dirty work for them by writing an editorial crucifying Oakways.'

'No, no, he wasn't,' Tar conceded, thoughtfully drawing on his briar. 'The trouble is, after his problems in Lisbon with George Rowlands, Frank has found himself between something of a rock and a hard place, trying to claw his way back into the fold. It hasn't been easy for him. Let's just say, there was a certain amount of resentment within MI6, that C had eventually agreed to keep him on the books.'

'But, Frank hinted that he was still in touch with you.'

"Being in touch" was a euphemism for Lucern supplying him with under-the-counter information from MI5's sister organisation.

'Yes,' Robertson said, 'yes, he is.'

'Why did he hold back about Dunmore?'

'I could probably give you any number of possible reasons why he didn't, but at this stage of the game, it would be sheer speculation on my part.' He leaned forward, and rested his pipe in the large onyx ashtray on his desk. 'But, that's not why I called you here. Gentlemen, we need to start sorting the wheat from the chaff.' A smile played about his mouth. 'I have a little job for you both.'

Spencer eyed his boss warily; he was up to something.

'I want you to break into Jamie Burdis's flat.'

Garvan looked at him askance. 'I hope you're not expecting me to play along, sir?'

Robertson arched his brows in surprise. 'Why shouldn't I?'

'Well, for a start, it's illegal.'

There was mild reproof in his eyes. 'My dear boy, you should know by now MI5 simply doesn't have a *legal* status.'

'Meaning what, exactly?'

'We operate on the 11th Commandment, thou shalt not get caught,' he said airily. 'I think you're forgetting, Superintendent, since the outbreak of the War, we've routinely burgled and bugged our way across the entire length and breadth of the country, on the State's behalf. As long as we get results, it pays for our worthy, law-abiding politicians to turn a blind eye to the legality of our operations.'

'I'm sure it does.'

Robertson smiled disarmingly, 'You know full well the Double Cross certainly wouldn't have been successful without specialising in bugging our opponents.' He despairingly placed the briar back between his lips. 'We already have enough on our plates with the Nazis, let alone having to track down traitors crawling out of the woodwork spying for Stalin's intelligence service.'

'We could request a Home Office warrant to search the place,' Garvan suggested.

'My dear boy, there's a time and place for red tape. Obtaining government sanction to tap a telephone is one thing, but getting a bunch of civil servants and the Home Secretary to sing off the same hymn sheet, and agree to a specific breach of the law, is quite another thing altogether.' Robertson could see Garvan was still uneasy. 'In my experience, Superintendent, matters of the highest possible importance and delicacy are best handled at the lowest possible level.'

Garvan returned his gaze questioningly.

'What I mean is, unless it's absolutely necessary to involve politicians and government departments from the off, it tends to end up muddying the waters. You really must learn to trust my judgement. Besides, I constantly have to watch my back, working for a former copper.'

Garvan knew Tar was taking a side swipe at Sir David Petrie, Head of MI5, who had, at one time, worked for the Indian Police, before going on to hold down a variety of intelligence roles, the pinnacle being his appointment by the Home Secretary as the Director General.

'Why are we specifically targeting Burdis and not Haining?' Garvan pressed him.

'We need to start somewhere, and if we get lucky, you never know we might be able to discount him altogether.' Robertson cast him a rather rueful smile. 'It also won't hurt to ruffle Burdis's feathers a little.'

'Hasn't he already been wired?'

'Not to my knowledge. During his time at the Foreign Office, he wasn't considered to be of any great interest to us.'

'But, what are we meant to be looking for?'

'I just need you both to have a general sniff round that's all. We already have full access to his diary, so there isn't an issue about tracking his movements. His secretary, Caro Tait, once worked for the Service,' he added, by way of explanation.

'Is he currently under surveillance?'

Robertson nodded his confirmation. 'Well, he is now, or at least, he has been for the last week, or so.'

'What about Jeremy Haining?' Spencer asked.

Robertson shot him a quizzical look. 'What about him?'

'By all accounts, he's quite cosy with MI6.'

'Yes, he is.'

'Exactly, so we can't rule him out of the equation.'

'No-one is out of the frame!' he said sharply. Tar leaned forward, and began rifling through his in-tray, searching for a memo. He found it, and smiled slightly. 'That brings me to another matter. We've received confirmation Burdis has accepted an invitation to attend a dinner party at Phil Simpson's house tomorrow evening.'

Spencer knew Simpson to be an old school friend of Tar's, and he had served as a Liberal Member of Parliament for many years. Tar had apparently managed to orchestrate the invite, leaving them a free hand to take a quiet look round Burdis's flat. He knew Burdis's wife, Jenny, rarely ventured into London, preferring to spend her time on their large sprawling estate in Kent.

However, Robertson had something else up his sleeve.

'I've also secured an invite for Joyce Leader.'

Garvan met the suggestion of Leader's invite to Phil Simpson's dinner party with undisguised horror. Even Spencer seemed taken aback by the announcement. As her Desk Officer, Spencer controlled every facet of his double agents lives, but for whatever reason, Robertson hadn't consulted him first about the invitation. In fairness to him, maybe he simply hadn't had time, but it certainly wasn't standard practice. Spencer felt justifiably annoyed he hadn't been involved, not that he allowed his feelings to show. Besides, it wouldn't have got him anywhere.

It was also an open secret in the Department Spencer admired Leader's skills as a spy. She was tough-minded and sharp-tongued. In fact, in many ways, Joyce was a woman after his own heart, and would, in different circumstances, have made a deadly enemy. She had been a member of Robertson's Double Cross team for several years now, and possessed a somewhat chequered past. She was a tall, blonde, attractive woman, whose recruitment to the Nazi cause had come about, or so she claimed, almost by default; neither she, nor her family, had been ardent members of Hitler's Nationalist Party. Her father was of Anglo-Austrian origins, and was born into an extremely successful family, whose political allegiance, or lack of it, to the Reich had frequently brought him into conflict, but despite his ambivalence, the family had continued to prosper, supplying armoured vehicles to the regime.

Joyce had always maintained her recruitment to the German Intelligence Service had stemmed from nothing more than a desire to protect her family from the Nazi regime. Whatever the truth, she'd proved herself time and again as a double agent, and her importance had increased steadily, not only in the eyes of British Intelligence and the SOE, but perhaps, more importantly, the Abwehr, who had never once doubted her integrity, or the quality of her work. She was quite simply a godsend to MI5, and had played a key role with other leading double agents in helping to persuade the Germans the main area of attack of the Allied invasion had been an area around Calais, and not the Normandy beaches. The disinformation had paid major dividends, not only aiding the successful outcome of D-Day, but, in the process, it had also helped to save countless lives.

Since the invasion MI5's Double Cross agents had continued to operate and flourish, despite initial fears their deliberate failure to alert their German spymasters of the truth about the impending Allied invasion would ultimately lead to the entire system being shut down, and thereby cutting off a valuable strand of communication to the heart of the Third Reich.

In order to assess Hitler's future plans, it was vital to keep open communications with Berlin after the invasion. It was decided their agents's best form of defence was to apologise and admit, in Leader's case, she had been misled by her "entirely fictitious" Royal Navy boyfriend. Her only real hope of weathering the storm was, prior to the invasion, she'd previously reported visiting Portsmouth to see him. She had reported there were American troops in the area, and preparations were under way for an armada, but she had mistakenly believed the invasion wasn't necessarily imminent. She had messaged her Abwehr controller, Bernard Drescher, that she had no reason whatsoever to doubt her boyfriend's supposed indiscretion that the main thrust of the Allied invasion would be in the area of the Pas de Calais. Joyce skilfully protested her innocence; she'd been duped, and in her own way, was as much a victim as the German High Command had been. Like them, she was totally unaware the intended Allied strike would be centred on the Normandy coast.

There followed an uneasy twenty-four-hour delay, before her German controller in Hamburg, Bernard Drescher, finally responded to the transmission. The main fear had been Drescher might not fall for the story; it was also uppermost in Spencer's mind as well. It was a pivotal moment, and much had depended on his reply. When it did arrive, his continued support far exceeded their initial expectations. In fact,

Drescher went out of his way to reassure Joyce he recognised the value of her work, and begged her to continue aiding the Third Reich in its on-going struggle for the control of Europe against its enemies. Drescher had ended his response, that, God willing, in the end, justice would be served, and the Third Reich would yet be victorious in the face of the enemy forces.

But, as the war progressed, and the Allied advance began to seem almost unstoppable, Spencer had instructed Joyce to write a formal letter to Bernard Drescher. He told her Tar Robertson had felt the content would be better served by writing than by her sending a wireless transmission. In it, Joyce had expressed her fears the war was probably now lost, and the advancing Allied forces would eventually discover evidence of her work for the Third Reich. She, therefore, assumed her safety would inevitably be compromised. The letter was no more than a fishing trip for information, but Drescher hadn't read between the lines, and replied in writing, assuring her the Abwehr's records would be destroyed, long before the Allies ever gained control of Germany itself.

In spite of her worth to MI5, Garvan remained dubious about Joyce Leader's invite to Phil Simpson's dinner party; Robertson obviously had something up his sleeve. Simpson was a Liberal Member of Parliament, so he couldn't quite understand why Burdis, a Tory, would be so keen to accept Simpson's invitation. It didn't add up, or, at least, not to him. Robertson elbaorated by explaining Simpson was a Member of the War Cabinet, and therefore, as far as Burdis was concerned, he was a political lifeline to help re-ingratiate him back into the political fold.

It seemed reasonable; Garvan couldn't fault his logic, but, all the same, he found himself saying, almost involuntarily, 'But, why do you want Joyce Leader at Simpson's dinner party?'

'What do we know about Burdis?' Robertson shot back at him sharply.

89

Garvan considered his response.

'Come on,' Robertson pressed him. 'As a detective, what's the first thing you start to look for in a suspect?'

'I guess their weakest link.'

'Which is, in Burdis's case?'

Garvan pulled a face. 'Well,' he conceded, 'I know he apparently can't keep his trousers zipped.'

'Quite, Superintendent. Our Jamie's a philanderer of epic proportions; he's always had a weakness for a pretty face.' Robertson took his time. He was curious; the last thing he'd expected was for him to question his decision. 'But, that weakness plays into our hands.' Robertson held Garvan's eyes. 'And I really can't think of anyone better equipped than Joyce Leader to reel Burdis into our net, can you?'

'It's just I thought the Director General had recently given Leader a clean sheet.'

'Has he, Superintendent?' Robertson said, with a characteristic quiet smile. 'I may well have missed something.'

'I think you'll find there was a directive, sir, stating she has been officially pardoned.'

'You really can't expect me to read everything on my desk.' He smiled. Sensing something was wrong, he looked at Garvan searchingly; it was equally obvious to Garvan Tar knew all about the Director General's proposed directive. 'I think you'll find the DG's decision,' he explained coldly, 'is very much on hold, until after the war. Leader's still a valuable asset to us; we're certainly not going to loosen the noose that quickly.'

Garvan had been put firmly in his place; he'd overstepped the mark, and he knew it. It would have been far better to have kept his mouth shut. By talking out of turn, he had inadvertently placed himself in the firing line.

'I think *you'll* find,' Robertson said evenly, 'Any proposed pardon from the DG was always non-negotiable.

Besides, we mustn't lose sight of the fact Joyce has always been good at hunting men down. It was one of the main reasons why the Abwehr recruited her.'

Garvan couldn't refute that.

Tar bestowed a rather watchful smile on him. 'You have to remember, Superintendent, I'll use any means at my disposal to get to the truth, including using Joyce Leader, or any of my other agents. As far as I'm concerned, they're nothing more than disposable assets!'

'Yes, sir, I know that,' he said dully.

'The only given is, we know Toniolo is a plant, but are we looking for a member of the intelligence community, or perhaps, more obviously, a well-briefed politician?' Robertson tugged thoughtfully on his pipe. 'Either way, gentlemen, we mustn't lose sight of the fact, nothing in our world is ever quite what it seems.'

*

In the corridor outside Robertson's office, Spencer rounded angrily on Garvan. 'What was that all about?'

'I don't know what you're on about?' he said defensively.

'Don't bullshit me, Garvie. What's going on?'

'Did you know Leader *had* an invite to Phil Simpson's dinner party?'

'No, I didn't,' was his clipped response.

'You're her Desk Officer, so why didn't Tar think to run it by you?'

'Right now, that's not what's bothering me.'

'So, what is?'

'All that bloody crap about Joyce Leader being given a clean sheet by the DG! What the hell were you playing at?'

Garvan shrugged indifferently, and continued down the corridor to the operations room. On reaching the door,

Spencer stepped in front of him, barring his way. 'Up until now, you've never given a sod about how we've used any of our agents, so what's different?' Spencer narrowed his eyes suspiciously. 'It's Joyce, isn't it?'

The look on Garvan's face spoke volumes.

'Christ almighty, you've slept with her, haven't you!'

A look of resignation crossed Garvan's face; he hesitated before saying, 'I don't suppose there's any point in denying it, at least not from *you,* anyway. What are you going to do?'

'What the hell do you think I'm going to do?'

'Tell Robertson.'

'I think it's probably a bit late for that!'

'That obvious, was it?'

'He'd have to be deaf, dumb, and blind not to have picked up on it. So, how long has this been going on?'

'A few weeks, no more,' he assured him. 'We'd been working late one night in the run-up to the D-Day landings.'

'Go on.'

'And one thing led to another.'

'And you ended up in bed?'

Garvan held his gaze. 'It was something like that.'

'How serious is it between you?'

He shrugged. 'On my part, serious enough. As for Joyce, well, you'll have to ask her about that.' Garvan knew he'd more than overstepped the line, and by doing so had recklessly, compromised his position. He could also see that Spencer was disappointed, rather than angry, with him, but, he felt obliged to say, 'It might be better all-around if I hand in my resignation.'

To his surprise, Spencer said, 'If you do, it'll be over my dead body.'

Garvan didn't quite know how to respond. But, then again, he didn't get a chance. Spencer abruptly headed off down the corridor. He called after him, 'Where are you going?'

'I need to have a word with Joyce.'

'Go easy on her, *will you*?'

Spencer did not bother replying.

Garvan had thought that he had weighed up all the facts, but, up until now, a small part of him had closed his mind to them. *What the hell had he been thinking?* That one impetuous kiss had spiralled out of control. He had not only compromised himself, but also, Joyce Leader's tentative position as a double agent.

Chapter 8

Spencer flung open the office door. Joyce Leader was at her desk, looking at him with her trademark sultry gaze, peering through her long lashes. Her ice-blue eyes and long smouldering stare possessed an almost other-worldly quality about them. But, Spencer had always been entirely immune to her smouldering glacial beauty, bone structure, and formidable personality; it didn't matter to him, in fact, the only thing which mattered was Leader's importance as a member of MI5's Double Cross system. She had obviously been in the middle of writing something, but he wasn't particularly interested in what she was doing.

Her look was intense, and occasionally soulful; the trouble was he'd seen it all before.

'What's wrong?' she asked dubiously.

'It's Garvan.'

'What about him?'

'Stop playing cat and mouse with me, Jo, do I have to spell it out?'

When Spencer was in full flight, she'd long since learnt to come clean with him, and there was simply no point in prevaricating. It was obvious he'd managed to find out about them.

'You know, don't you?' she said warily.

'Yes, I do.'

'What's happened?'

'He's just bloody told me,' he shot back at her.

Joyce didn't quite know how to respond; she was fast running out of options, but decided to play it cool. On her part, there had been no real all-consuming attraction, but over a long period of time, that had all changed. Gradually, she came to realise, behind the taciturn and occasionally off-hand exterior, lay a terrifically kind man, who, in spite of her background as a double agent, had treated her with the utmost respect. She guessed right from the start he'd found her attractive, but had always rebuffed her sometimes clumsy come-on's, and was not even remotely a flirt, far from it. He had been the consummate professional, and up until recently, had never fooled around with women at work, more especially with anyone who might have compromised his integrity.

Spencer had completely wrong-footed her, and, for once, Joyce didn't know how to react, but the one thing she *did know* was he wouldn't relent. That both she and Garvan had overstepped the line, was a given, and their fate lay in his hands. Her eyes swept over Spencer angrily, but in doing so, he caught a glint of the uncertainty behind them.

He started to pace the office, angrily laying down the law, reminding her, in spite of her valuable work for the Double Cross, as far as MI5 was concerned, she was still an enemy agent, and subject to British law. His gaze was implacable, and it set Leader's thoughts into freefall. What happened between them had developed almost imperceptibly over a long period of time. Spencer knew Joyce had long wanted a relationship to develop, but had always believed, as far as Garvan was concerned, it was a step way too far.

But, that had all recently changed when Garvan had been standing behind her in the office, and, quite unexpectedly, he'd leaned over and gently spun her chair around, and placed his hand under her chin and kissed her. It was an impulsive gesture, and had completely taken Joyce off-guard. Only later did she realise his kiss hadn't been quite as spontaneous as she had assumed. Looking to the future, MI5 had, in principle, agreed to give their double agents a clean sheet after the defeat of Nazi Germany, and Garvan had just been made aware of this fact.

After that first kiss in the office, things had progressed cautiously between them, Joyce hadn't rushed things, sensing Garvan was still tussling with the morality of forming a relationship with an enemy agent, albeit one who had become pivotal in the intricate war against the Nazi regime. He was in an awkward position, and also in serious risk of jeopardising his career, not only with British Intelligence but with Scotland Yard, too.

But, for Joyce, that first spontaneous gesture, that first kiss, still resonated deeply. She'd smiled into his eyes, and for the first time in her adult life, she felt totally safe, so protected, cherished, and adored, as if she were a child in her father's arms. She knew Garvan's love, like her father's, was unconditional, and that was rare; she couldn't let him go without a fight.

Since then, they had occasionally met. For Joyce, his physical proximity became ever more important to her, but Garvan was obviously still wary of taking things further, and to the next level. She understood his reticence; he'd already taken an enormous gamble. He never called her flat, knowing that the phone was tapped. Neither of them told anyone, how could they, but Joyce was beginning to feel afraid anyone with half an eye would see there was something tangible between them. It must have preyed on Garvan's mind; he'd never said anything to her, of course, but she knew that it did.

As Spencer read the riot act to her, her stare was not so much icy, as one which could turn the recipient to stone. But, he'd seen it all before, and knew she was scared witless. Joyce had always successfully given off the appearance of being invulnerable, with a particularly tough, no-nonsense attitude, but it struck him perhaps Garvan had become her Achilles Heel. If she did love him, then she was probably terrified their relationship would not only potentially ruin his career, but could also lead to her ending up in an internment camp for the remainder of the war.

As a defence mechanism, and a means of survival, Joyce had long since built up a barrier against men, and, more importantly, her feelings. Spencer had often said Joyce didn't do vulnerability, but he knew somewhere beneath the withdrawal, there was still a small strand of her old self, a fun-loving woman, unfettered by being a double agent, and caught in the crossfire between the Abwehr and British Intelligence. But, at the back of his mind lurked a nagging doubt. Were her feelings truly genuine, or was she playing with fire just for the hell of it.

Since becoming her Desk Officer, Spencer knew Joyce had always imagined herself to be in love. There had been countless men, and she was always on the edge of love. It was one endless infatuation after another; the next was always going to be the love of her life, but they never were. Coupled with her ability to shut down her feelings and manipulate her many previous conquests at the behest of German Intelligence, it wasn't surprising Spencer was suspicious of her ultimate motives of falling for Garvan.

At heart, it was perhaps ironic Garvan abhorred deceit of any kind, and having a secret relationship, especially with Joyce, played heavily on his mind. But, she suspected he would never have made a move, if the DG had not let it be known their double agents were to be given a clean sheet after the cessation of hostilities. In hindsight, he'd jumped the gun a little too early, but by his admission, he had never known such depth of feeling before.

For her part, Joyce was certainly no innocent, and she suspected Spencer doubted her motives and sincerity, but this was different. She was experiencing so many new feelings, and Garvan had finally made her realise what it meant to be truly in love. A simple word or gesture would bring on a gut reaction; it was all strangely erotic and romantic, at the time. She had long known about his failed marriage, and as a consequence, Joyce desperately wanted to give him everything he hadn't experienced in a relationship before. For no-one had ever made her feel so wanted, and so loved.

In some ways, they had a great deal in common. Both had troubled personal lives, and had been afraid of the commitment involved with falling in love again. On the few snatched occasions when they had managed to have a moment of real intimacy, Joyce found herself so happy that maybe finally the fears and seemingly endless torment of the war was beginning to fade, there was a real hope and prospect of a life together. But, right now, it was entirely in Spencer's power to destroy that hope and their relationship for good.

Joyce opened her clutch bag, retrieved an ebony holder, and slowly tapped a cigarette into it. He was standing in front of the desk now, looking down at her, his expression entirely unreadable.

'What are you going to do?' she asked him, flicking on her lighter.

'Garvan's offered to resign,' he said flatly.

She hesitated. Spencer owed her a great deal, not least his life. A year ago, in Portugal, without her outstanding bravery providing cover for him against two Gestapo officers and a leading member of the Abwehr, he would never have survived to tell the tale. For his part, he knew only too well when faced with extreme danger, she lost not one iota of her coolness, but when all was said and done, she remained a double agent. Spencer always maintained if Joyce had been in a team of one, she'd probably end up having a fight with herself, but all the same, she was a cool-headed and skilful operator, and one St. James's could ill-afford to lose.

Spencer would never have admitted it, but he was torn between his loyalty not only to the Service but also his friendship with Garvan.

'Did you accept his resignation?' Joyce asked, somewhat stiltedly.

'No, I did not.'

Her usually impenetrable expression registered a palpable sense of relief. 'Are you going to report us to the Colonel?'

'I should do.'

She looked at him expectantly. 'And will you?'

'I figured if I did report you, it'd be a bit like cutting my own throat.'

Joyce met his gaze questioningly.

'As things stand, we still need to continue feeding disinformation to the Abwehr and the German High Command. You're good at what you do, Jo, I've never denied that, and realistically, finding someone who possesses your devious abilities and flair at short notice would be near nigh impossible. As for Garvan, he's not only a good friend, but an integral member of the team. So, in answer to your question, I'm not going to report either of you to the Colonel. But, that doesn't mean to say I'm going to give you carte blanche to do as you please.'

She studied him warily. 'You want me to break it off, don't you?'

Joyce had never been able to read Spencer, and right now was no different. His eyes were cool and watchful.

'Officially,' he said, 'I'm not aware of anything between you. Therefore, I can't exactly order you to end the relationship, can I?'

There was always a certain quiet mental discipline about him, he gave her a tight smile, and closed the door to the office, leaving Joyce with an expression of incomprehension on her face, still not quite able to believe Spencer, of all people, had given them a lifeline.

After the meeting, Joyce's defences were up, and whenever she saw Garvan at MI5, it became increasingly difficult to know where she stood. Maybe their relationship was just too complicated to continue, but, she couldn't just let it go; it was worth fighting for. The only unknown, was whether Garvan felt the same way.

Chapter 9

Phil Simpson owned a large five-storey townhouse in Manchester Square near Oxford Street. Joyce Leader had first met Simpson through her work for the Double Cross. She'd met him subsequently in a somewhat desultory fashion. His being an acquaintance of Jamie Burdis had meant Robertson's old school friendship was a means of paying dividends again, by allowing them direct access to Burdis, without arousing his suspicions.

Joyce made an immediate impact on the assembled guests. She was not only tall, but there was something imperious with each step she took. More to the point, she knew everyone had their eyes on her. It was a lavish political party, which was living up to Burdis's expectations. While it was important in terms of his career, what had started out as a potentially dull, but necessary, social event, had now suddenly gone up a notch on being introduced to the strikingly attractive woman who had just arrived.

'Do you know Joyce?' Simpson asked, knowing full well he didn't.

His eyes practically devoured the tall, statuesque figure before him. 'No,' he said, admiringly, 'I only wish to God I did. Where on Earth have you been hiding her, you old goat!' he rasped at Simpson.

Joyce had met his type before; he was like a dog in heat, with an ingrained self-belief he was God's gift to any woman who happened to be breathing. The bone-crushing handshake only served to add to her instinctive dislike of the man.

Within half an hour of their meeting, Joyce realised Burdis liked to talk a great deal, and loved nothing more than the sound of his own clipped Oxbridge voice. Although, the steady flow of pre-dinner cocktails helped a little in pacifying her growing antipathy toward him. While the evening meal was excellent, the same couldn't be said of Burdis's company. He was boorish and loudly boastful about his love of dining at the Ritz, where the staff apparently treated him with feigning deference. God only knew if it was true, or was just another facetious exaggeration. He also spoke at considerable length about his time at the Foreign Office; he over-egged his importance, and to the uninitiated, they'd have thought he was practically running the entire show. The trouble was, their fellow guests were either too polite or disinterested to correct his bragging.

Burdis was not particularly good looking, and only passably tall at five eleven, looking considerably older than his fifty-four years, possibly the result of his renowned over indulgence and hard living. His hairline was receding slightly and greying at the temples, and the light blue eyes twinkled mischievously throughout the entire evening. Leader began to realise, albeit somewhat reluctantly, beneath the obnoxious flamboyance and the irreverent outspokenness, he possessed a certain innate charm, which she assumed many women would possibly find attractive, but she certainly wasn't one of their number, far from it.

She continued to listen with half a mind to his often-banal chatter, as he let both his mouth and thoughts run free. In many ways, she was surprised by his candour, especially as this evening was meant to be all about trying to ingratiate himself back into the political fold. But, for whatever reason, he seemed not to possess either the wit or the wisdom to realise, even before the end of the first course, he had successfully managed to alienate most of his fellow guests.

Joyce played it coolly throughout, never once allowing her irritation to surface; she appeared to hang on his every word. In turn, he was flattered, and charmed by her apparent attention. To show she was attracted to him, she occasionally leaned forward, and fixed him with a radiant smile. It was all a game, of course, but no-one seated around

101

the table, least of all Burdis, would have guessed her real feelings.

'What does your father do?' he asked in his expansive manner.

Her glacial features broke into a smile. 'Actually, he doesn't do that much at all.'

'Really?' he quizzed her, his eyes narrowing curiously.

'He owns an estate in Sussex called Coppinhold.'

'Where about in Sussex is it?'

'Near a small village called Dragons Green.'

She was saying no more than the truth; her father had inherited the property from his English grandparents before the war, although he'd rarely visited the place, preferring to spend his time steadily gambling his way across pre-war Europe. For all its merits, Coppinhold scarcely registered in size or importance to his many hunting estates, both in Austria and Germany, where his real wealth derived.

'I've never heard of it!' Burdis said dismissively.

She looked at him flirtatiously. 'Well, in which case, I guess that makes us just about even, then.'

'How's that, my dear?' he asked.

'I'd never heard of you either, until this evening.'

Burdis threw back his head and laughed. He liked her style. She possessed an almost cat-like grace and a sharp, no-nonsense attitude. Although Joyce appeared to be interested in him, there was a certain haughty reserve about her he couldn't quite read. But, in his own imitable way, he managed to convince himself the attraction between them was mutual. She was very engaging, easy to talk to, with a self-effacing charm. Burdis was curious about her; she apparently knew Phil Simpson quite well, but for some reason, the wily old bugger had kept her under wraps. He'd also noticed Joyce wasn't wearing either an engagement or wedding ring, and surprised someone hadn't snapped her up by now.

'How do you know Phil and Sue Simpson?'

'Our families go back a long way,' she replied glibly.

From the head of the dining room table, Simpson caught her eye. 'What was that?'

'Jamie was just wondering how we know one another.'

'It's a long story,' Simpson said dismissively, and skilfully cut the conversation dead, returning his attention back to the rather attractive brunette seated on his left.

Burdis thought no more of it. 'Tell me,' he asked Joyce, 'what kind of war work do you do?'

Without hesitation, she said coolly, 'I spray paint RAF bicycles.'

A look of incredulity crossed his face. Her reply was so obscure he had no reason to disbelieve her, but the expensive clothes and jewellery didn't quite match the image of Joyce toiling away on some godforsaken factory line.

'It was either that, or be called up to do my bit in the armed services,' she explained.

'But, surely, my dear, that would have been the lesser of the two evils?'

Joyce pulled a face. 'I'm not very good at taking orders.' She winked at him, and added with a giggle, 'At least this way, I still get to have a decent social life in London.'

'Yes, I am sure you do.'

She began to finger the pearl necklace around her throat absent-mindedly before shooting him a meaningful look. 'Besides, I'd never have met you, would I?'

He looked up into her eyes. There was a hint of amusement, or was it possibly condescension. It didn't matter. He liked her, and he liked a challenge.

As the evening wore on, Joyce had him wrapped around her little finger. He willingly fell for her spiel; however, he had no reason to doubt her sincerity. The slight smile on her lips faded, her expression almost impassive. After taking an instant dislike to the man, there was something particularly satisfying in being able to reel him in so easily. She had met many men of Burdis's calibre before; pandering to their egos, and setting a trap, was ultimately nothing more than child's play.

In Burdis's eyes, the evening was indeed looking up. He'd never been a close friend of Phil Simpson, far from it. It was true they'd had the odd political scrape over the years, nothing too serious, but more importantly, Simpson was renowned for his influential contacts within the hothouse of Westminster. Receiving an invite from Simpson was something of an achievement in itself. Burdis had felt flattered, after his demotion to the backbenches, Simpson still considered him influential enough to warrant an invite to his supper party. It was an accolade, or so he hoped. The reality was somewhat different, but the invite at Colonel Robertson's request had served a purpose, and had also helped to massage Burdis's political ambitions. He viewed the invite as the first rung on the ladder in his bid to claw his way steadily back into favour.

When the evening was drawing to a close, Joyce checked her watch. A few of the guests had already started to drift away from the table and head off home. It was obvious Burdis wanted to take things a step further. She had successfully wound him up and led him on, throughout the evening.

He leaned conspiratorially toward her, and whispered, 'It's still quite early. Would you care to have a nightcap somewhere?'

She flashed him a flirtatious smile. 'I thought you'd never ask.'

He looked as pleased as punch and hurriedly threw down his crumpled napkin on the table. 'I know a nice little bar around the corner from here.'

'I'm sure you do.'

104

'Shall we make our excuses?' he suggested eagerly.

Burdis clearly wanted to make a move, but playing for time, she tapped her wine glass. 'Can you give me a couple of minutes until I've finished.'

'Yes, yes, of course, my dear.'

Burdis suggested they could perhaps have a nightcap at the Damaris Bar in nearby Wigmore Street. Across the dining room table from them, sat the drunken blonde, forty-something wife of the local Tory Member of Parliament, Johnny Horne. She seemed to be an old friend of Burdis, and having overheard their conversation, she decided to invite herself along as well.

'What do you think?' Marian Horne said, nudging her husband sharply in the ribs.

He looked startled. 'Think about what, old girl?'

'Jamie is having a night cap at the Damaris.'

Judging by his enthusiasm, it probably wasn't the first time they had decamped to the bar. A flicker of annoyance crossed Burdis's face, but neither of the Hornes appeared to notice, or perhaps they were simply past caring. Burdis had rather different plans on his mind, but as far as Joyce was concerned, there was safety in numbers, and leapt at the idea. In the interim, she wanted to avoid being placed in a potentially compromising situation.

'What a great idea,' she announced enthusiastically.

Seeing he had very little room to manoeuvre, Burdis swiftly, if somewhat reluctantly, came around to the idea.

They said their goodbyes, and thanked Phil and Sue Simpson for such an enjoyable evening, the food and the wine had been excellent. Burdis was gratingly over-effusive in his thanks. He also made a rather unnecessary point of thanking his hosts for seating him next to such a stunningly attractive guest. Although he had enjoyed himself, Joyce couldn't help wondering if sincerity sat easily with him. There always seemed to be an element of doubt whether he was sending up his fellow diners with his flattery and occasional supercilious remarks. Either way, Simpson, and his wife appeared to be outwardly, at least, charmed by his company.

'I had a feeling you'd get on well together,' Phil said.

'Yes, yes, that's why we've decided to go for a nightcap at the Damaris,' Burdis announced enthusiastically.

The remaining guests glanced in their direction; he'd wanted to attract their attention, and make a show of leaving the party, with Joyce in tow. Her expression remained dead-pan. If this evening hadn't been strictly business, then nothing would have given her greater satisfaction than to give him a short, sharp set down he wouldn't forget in a hurry.

Simpson cupped her hands briefly in his own, and out of earshot of Burdis, whispered, 'Good luck, Jo. You'll need it.'

The heavens had opened. Whipped up by an increasingly strong wind, the rain was sweeping across the Square in biblical proportions. Phil Simpson had thoughtfully ordered them a taxi. Although the Damaris Bar was within walking distance, it was far enough away for them to become drenched by the time they arrived.

Being a little awkward on their feet both Johnny Horne and his wife needed a steadying hand into the cab. Burdis then dashed back to the hallway with an umbrella to escort Joyce out of the house.

'We could always ditch going to the Damaris,' he whispered conspiratorially, 'and send the buggers off. Nip back to my place instead.'

Joyce smiled sweetly but cut him dead. 'I don't think so.'

The Damaris was a discreet basement bar in what had probably once been an impressive London townhouse. An insurance firm occupied the upper floors. As they arrived, it crossed Joyce's mind the Damaris was just a stone's throw away from Len Dunmore's old flat. The staff greeted them warmly. It was obviously a favourite watering hole of both Burdis and the Hornes. She guessed it was far enough away from the environs of Whitehall to afford a degree of anonymity.

Inside, the bar was secluded, lit with shaded lamps on the tables and a selection of discreet seating areas, surrounding a large well-stocked bar. Leader's first impressions were not entirely favourable. In spite of its location, the Damaris seemed a little seedy to her taste, faded flock wallpaper and carpets, along with rather distressed-looking Chesterfield furniture that had once seen better days. The place was a heady mix of tobacco smoke and alcohol. By the look of it, the bar's clientele was a pretty mixed bunch; there were punters off the street escaping the downpour, and those, like Burdis, who no doubt wined and dined there with his under-the-counter liaisons.

'So, what are we going to drink?' Horne asked, sprawling himself down on a sofa.

By now, a waiter had appeared at their forlornly lit alcove. Without hesitation Joyce ordered a double gin and tonic.

'But, go easy on the tonic, will you, sweetie.'

Burdis smiled almost to himself. 'Make that two, will you.'

'I'll have vodka on the rocks,' John slurred.

'What about Marian?' Joyce queried.

On their arrival at the Damaris Bar, Marian had immediately, if somewhat unsteadily, weaved her way off in the direction of the lady's toilet.

John seemed disinterested about Marian's order, but felt almost obliged to say something. 'Make it a pink gin.'

Leader's gaze travelled thoughtfully around the bar. 'How on Earth did you find this place?'

Sensing it wasn't quite to her taste, Horne said defensively, 'We were both introduced by an old acquaintance of ours.'

She smiled slightly. 'Judging by our welcome just now, you must both come here quite often.'

Horne chuckled. 'Chance would be a fine thing.'

'I think you'll find,' Burdis explained, 'Johnny's commitments at the War Office don't allow him much free time, these days.'

'Too bloody true,' he chuntered, as Marian joined them.

The waiter returned with their drinks; they thanked him.

Johnny grinned indulgently at her. 'You have to admit, Jamie, my Marian always lights up a room.'

'Yes,' Burdis said waspishly, 'but only usually when she leaves it!'

There was an awkward moment between them, but Marian was too far gone to have heard the slight, and, fortunately, her husband decided to let it ride.

Joyce picked out four cigarettes from a slender gold case, and handed them round. She gently patted her own into the elegant ebony holder, before lighting it. 'Was this acquaintance you mentioned a work colleague?'

'What are we talking about?' Marian slurred.

'Keep up, woman!' Johnny snapped at her.

They started to snipe at one another; it was a pity, really, before sinking one too many drinks. They had both been easy companions, speaking endlessly, but interestingly, on all manner of subjects.

Burdis rolled his eyes, and gave Joyce a half-smile. 'I'm sorry,' he apologised. 'It isn't always like this.'

'I'm sure it isn't,' she said, returning his smile.

'We used to meet up here regularly, with a journalist friend of ours,' he explained. 'You might have heard of him, Len Dunmore?'

She looked at him blankly.

'He was a Fleet Street hack,' he said, taking a large gulp of his drink. 'God knows if it's true, or not, but the duty rumour is he's been murdered.'

Always the consummate actress, her features registered surprise. 'Oh my god. Murdered? That's dreadful. What happened to the poor man?'

Hearing the word murder, Marian briefly stopped arguing with her increasingly irritated husband. 'Are you talking about Dunmore?'

Her rather nasal voice carried loudly across the muted tones of the bar; several people turned around to look at them.

'For Christ's sake,' Johnny spat at her in embarrassment, 'stop screeching like some bloody banshee, will you!'

'I wasn't screeching,' she shouted.

Burdis was fast losing his patience with them. 'Why don't you ruddy pipe down. You're both making a spectacle of yourselves.'

'I think that's a bit harsh,' Johnny snorted into his vodka.

Joyce smiled understandingly toward Burdis, and repeated her question. 'So, what happened to this journalist, do you know?'

'I'm not sure,' he said tensely. 'It hasn't been made public as yet. At one point, he worked for the *Daily Sketch*, but more recently he was with the *Express*.'

She held his gaze coolly. 'His name doesn't ring a bell with me, but what I don't understand is, why anyone would have wanted to kill him?'

Keeping his cigarette on the go, Burdis considered his reply. 'We live in strange times, Joyce. Who knows why, I have a feeling we'll probably never get to the bottom of it.'

'He was good at what he did!' Johnny snorted drunkenly.

Burdis glanced in Marian's direction; she was beginning to nod off, with the pink gin still firmly clasped between her cupped hands. It was something of a running joke with her friends, no matter how inebriated, Marian rarely, if ever, spilt her drink.

Johnny said to Joyce, 'Dunmore wasn't your average political hack. He had social ties on either side of the House. He didn't only know where the skeletons were buried, he'd helped to bury them!'

'He had his finger on the political pulse,' Burdis told her. 'These days, my dear, it's all cloak and dagger. If there's anything underhand, all you have to do is quote the Official Secrets Act or National Security, and that's an end to the matter. But, I'll give him his due, Dunmore always trod a fine line, and somehow managed to get away with it.'

Joyce looked at him with wide-eyed curiosity. 'You mean there's a possibility the authorities murdered this friend of yours, is that what you're saying?'

He smiled at her indulgently, as one might a child. 'Yes, my dear, that's precisely what I'm saying.'

Her eyebrows rose in shock. 'But, Jamie, aren't you worried?'

'Why should I be?' he answered, flattered by her apparent concern.

'If it could happen to a journalist, then, aren't you afraid?'

He raised his hand to silence her. 'Being a Member of Parliament affords me, us,' he said gesturing toward Johnny, 'a certain degree of immunity. Besides, you have to understand, Dunmore lived his life on the edge, and had made more than a few enemies in his time, not just in politics, but also within the intelligence community. In the long run, he was asking for trouble, and unfortunately, somewhere along the line, I can only guess he overstepped the mark, and made one enemy too far.' He sucked heavily on his cigarette. 'Personally, I'll miss the old rogue. We spent many a happy hour here, at the Damaris, putting the world to rights.'

'So we did,' Johnny mused draining his glass. 'It really won't seem quite the same without the old bugger,' he agreed.

Joyce shot Burdis a look, and said tentatively, 'Someone mentioned your wife earlier this evening.'

'I think it must have been me,' Johnny announced cheerily. 'Lovely woman, Jenny. She's a veritable bloody saint, putting up with Jamie; not many women would.'

He described Burdis's dalliances as being like an endless revolving door of girlfriends. He passed Marian a meaningful look. 'She bloody well wouldn't put up with it, for a start. Marian's always said if I ever played away, I'd be out on my ear.'

Joyce smiled. Marian was still fast asleep, otherwise she doubted whether dear old Johnny would have been brave enough to speak so openly about his formidable wife.

Burdis found himself glancing in Joyce's direction. The cold expression on her face spoke volumes. Somehow, he decided the remainder of the evening wouldn't quite pan out as he'd initially hoped, and Johnny's endless prattling wasn't exactly helping his cause. He was still talking about Jenny, and how they all loved her. Burdis needed to silence him, and quickly; he'd already done more than enough damage.

'I'm not quite sure you can describe Jenny as a saint,' he said sharply. 'I won't deny things have been quite tricky between us lately, but the only saving grace is we have two adorable boys, and we both love them to bits.'

'It's her way of fighting back,' Johnny announced unhelpfully.

'That's as may be,' was Burdis's withering response.

'So, how long have you been married?' Joyce asked.

Johnny threw back his head and laughed. 'If you ask me, it's been too bloody long.'

Burdis rounded on him. 'Isn't that like the pot calling the kettle black? I'd rather have a dozen Jennys, than someone like Marian. Look at her. She's a ruddy nightmare, man!'

Horne peered at his wife, and couldn't bring himself to disagree, ordering more vodka.

Joyce brushed her fingers gently over the back of Burdis's hand. 'So, how long *have* you been married?' she probed gently.

'The trouble is, my dear, Johnny has a point. Maybe it's been too long.'

'That's not what I asked.'

He let out an easy chuckle. 'I know it isn't. If you must know, our relationship died a long time ago; we, I mean, I fell out of love maybe five or ten years after we married.'

Joyce initially wondered if it was no more than a standard response, but then had a gut feeling, for once, he was probably telling the truth. 'Why on Earth have you stayed together?'

'Probably out of a misguided sense of loyalty I suppose. To be honest with you, I'm not sure, but Johnny here would tell you I fell out of love years ago. Perhaps I did,' he added reflectively. 'There's also a certain stigma attached to getting divorced. The Chief Whips and the Party bigwigs frown upon it, and in the blink of an eye, you find yourself de-selected, and cast out onto the social scrapheap.'

Burdis's reasons for not divorcing Jenny seemed valid enough at face value, but Oakways divorced his wife, without any apparent political consequences, and had remained at the heart of the government, whereas Burdis divorced or not, had found himself languishing on the backbenches and the fringes of power. Maybe it had simply been down to the fact, unlike Oakways, he had only ever held a mid-ranking ministerial post without portfolio, with no particular responsibility within the Foreign Office. By contrast, having served in several other government departments, Oakways was by far the more pre-eminent, and was very much at the heart of the Westminster hierarchy. Although Burdis remained ferociously ambitious, unlike Oakways, he never had quite managed to break through to the inner sanctum of the Tory Party.

Spencer had described Burdis to her as something of a vain, overpowering misfit, which had, in part, contributed to his eventual downfall with not only Jeremy Haining, but more importantly, with the Prime Minister. His political career had appeared scuppered beyond redemption. Phil Simpson's invite to dinner had been nothing more than a lifeline, a confirmation his political career was perhaps not quite yet dead and buried.

Joyce had Burdis where she wanted; in her company, he relaxed, and the steady supply of cocktails and gin had also helped to loosen his tongue. Both he and Johnny began reminiscing about their time at Cambridge University, and how, back then, their politics had swung almost as wildly as they had partied; getting a first-class degree was not exactly of the utmost importance, but having a good time was.

'I wasn't in your league,' Johnny said cheerfully. 'I never had as much luck with the ladies, and I certainly couldn't keep pace with you in the drinking department.'

Burdis freely admitted to being something of a social gadfly, and had persistently challenged people in power; men like his own father, a Tory grandee, but without ever having formed any personal, deep-rooted ideological belief.

Joyce remained sceptical. 'What did you believe in?'

'I certainly wasn't a Tory back then, far from it!'

'Were you a Liberal?'

113

Johnny threw back his head and laughed. 'Good lord, no. He's never liked the buggers; in fact, he can't stand them.'

She smiled slightly.

'Back in our days, it was fashionable to join the Communist party,' Johnny explained.

'And did you?'

'I didn't,' Burdis cut in, 'but Johnny was a member for a while.'

'Yes, good lord, so I did. What was I thinking of?' He guffawed.

'During the Spanish Civil War,' Burdis told her, 'politically, we were all over the place; nothing was cut and dried. We were either in one camp or the other, and with everything happening in Nazi Germany, I sided with the Communists.'

Joyce looked at him almost sympathetically. 'Where do you stand now?'

At first, it struck Burdis as a rather odd question; he was a good and loyal Tory MP. It was, in many ways, a loaded question, but even so, he seemed incredibly self-assured. 'I certainly believe in democracy and free speech.'

Her eyes glistened mischievously. 'Your politics are no longer swayed by how much booze you've consumed?'

Johnny chuckled. 'Good point. Well made, my dear.'

Even Burdis managed to raise a smile. 'I'm no longer an angry young man, if that's what you mean, quite the reverse, in fact. I've long since accepted the status quo, and if you want to change the system, then the best form of attack is to join, and do so from a point of strength. It's far easier to fight for change, without compromising your beliefs, if you jump on the bandwagon and play the establishment game.'

'What *do* you believe in?'

Sharp as a whip, he shot back at her. 'I believe in social justice.'

Like most politicians worth their salt, he had the ability to answer in depth any question put to him, except the one of any real relevance. He was, despite his reputation as an outspoken rebel, a consummate politician. His real ideological beliefs remained a mystery to her, and probably even to his own Party. But, since becoming a Member of Parliament, like his former boss, Jeremy Haining, he'd played an even hand, by vehemently opposing the Nazi regime, and at the same time attacking the potential threat of Soviet communism in the free world.

Joyce finished off her gin and tonic. Burdis asked if she'd care for another.

'It's getting late, and I really ought to be making a move,' she replied, shooting a meaningful look at his friends.

He perfectly understood her reluctance to stay, and he was also astute enough not to force the issue, especially in front of the Hornes. He assumed any invite would be greeted with a polite, but non-negotiable rebuttal.

Burdis desperately wanted to see her again; it was what Joyce had bargained on, and he didn't disappoint, asking for her telephone number. She smiled at him, and readily scribbled it down on a crumpled piece of paper he retrieved from his jacket pocket.

Joyce had slowly wound him up like a coiled spring. She seemed interested, and he wanted to get the right result, but now wasn't the right time or place. The Hornes had effectively scuppered any chance of intimacy between them, but there would be other evenings, a different venue and just the two of them.

Burdis clicked his fingers at the waiter, and asked him to order a taxi for her. Johnny gave his wife a nudge to wake her up.

'Time we were going, old thing!' he barked.

She awoke with a start still clutching the pink gin. 'What do you mean going?'

'You've been asleep with your mouth open, dribbling. Not a pretty sight, old thing, especially for Joyce here, never ruddy met you before.'

'I wasn't asleep!' she snapped.

Johnny adopted a look of weary resignation. 'Just finish your bloody drink, will you!'

She didn't demur.

'Jamie's just ordered me a taxi,' Joyce said. 'Would you like to share it with me? Where do you live?'

'That's sweet of you,' Marian said, draining her glass. 'We live in Great Peter Street.'

'That's fine; it's on my way home.' She then shot Burdis a speculative look. 'Are you staying?'

'Yes, I'll probably sink another couple before making a move home. If it's all right by you, I'll give you a call tomorrow evening.'

'I should be around.' She smiled warmly.

Watching the Hornes propping each up through the bar, Burdis began to kick himself he'd been so wrapped up talking about himself he hadn't bothered asking Joyce much about her personal life. He knew her family owned an estate in Sussex, and she was carrying out war work at some factory or other. Initially, he hadn't been that interested, but now, he was beginning to regret not being more attentive. She intrigued him; Joyce was in a different league to most of the other women he knew. There was something mysterious, enigmatic about her. She exuded charm and confidence in her physicality. In many ways, he had met his match. They had spent the entire evening flirting and talking. Intriguingly, he still knew nothing about her, but he guessed that was probably exactly the way she had wanted to play it.

Chapter 10

With Jamie Burdis safely occupied at the dinner party in Manchester Square, Spencer and Garvan made their way to his palatial flat in Sloane Street. They pulled up in nearby Chesham Place, with the intention of walking the rest of the way on foot. The main entrance of the purpose built red bricked block remained unlocked at this time of night. They made their way up unhindered to the second floor.

'This is it,' Spencer said, pointing to No12, and calmly produced a set of skeleton keys from the inside pocket of his jacket.

'What exactly did *you* do before the war?'

'You probably don't want to know,' he answered skilfully, opening the door.

Once safely inside, Spencer opened the doors on either side of the passageway until they reached Burdis's study. He entered and moved over to the window, closing the heavily lined curtains. Garvan then turned on the light, and shut the study door. Running the length of one wall was a collection of leather bound volumes, reflecting his wide-ranging interests from ancient history, ornithology to politics. He was a voracious reader and devoured books with almost as much relish as he loved female company.

Above the fireplace sat a large portrait of a rather austere bewigged figure, resplendent in naval uniform, no doubt of some long lost illustrious ancestor of the Burdis clan.

Slipping a Moroccan bound volume off one of the bookcases, Spencer said, 'Where do you want to start?'

Garvan's gaze glided slowly around the room, and hit on the rather impressive desk facing the door. 'I'll make a start over here,' he said.

On top of the desk sat a large mahogany box, with a family crest inlaid on the lid. He opened the box, but found nothing of any great interest, other than a rather untidy assortment of pens and a broken pencil sharpener. He then checked the pedestal on the right-hand side. It contained four drawers; the first was locked, and the other three possessed a plain brass button that sprang open to his touch, each of them crammed with embossed House of Commons headed notepaper.

'Can you open this one for me?' he asked, pointing to the top drawer of the desk.

Spencer wandered over and knelt down in front of the pedestal, and once more retrieved the set of skeleton keys from his jacket pocket. He took his time selecting the right one, before deftly opening the drawer. Inside was a pile of neatly folded letters; some had been replaced in their original envelopes. Fortunately, with Burdis safely occupied at Phil Simpson's dinner party, they had time on their hands. They rifled through the letters, and Garvan carefully photographed anything which looked remotely interesting.

They also took the opportunity to check Burdis's personal diary; it was sitting on a pile of papers in a battered, ink-stained wooden tray. Once they were satisfied, they then carefully returned the contents to the desk, and Spencer re-locked the top drawer. He then gestured toward the door. Beside it, was an ancient brown tumbler lock safe. Garvan arched his brows questioningly.

Spencer cast him a smile. 'Just give me a couple of minutes.'

Seeing the rather bemused look on his colleague's face, he thought it was probably an opportune moment to explain, as a former member of 30 Assault Unit, an elite team of commandos who specialised in targeting enemy headquarters in occupied Europe, their mission had invariably involved stealing either pieces of equipment or classified documents from the enemy. As a consequence, their unorthodox training had been an unholy mix of unarmed combat, coupled with lessons from ex-convicts on the finer art of burglary, be it bank heists, or straight forward breaking and entering.

Spencer chatted on seamlessly, as he slickly unscrambled the safe; the heavy door clicked open, revealing an untidy stack of paperwork. They again photographed anything remotely promising. Spencer spun the tumbler to re-lock the safe, before taking a look at the remainder of the flat. Once they were satisfied, they decided to call it a day. After leaving, they headed down the embankment in one of MI5's pool cars and parked up in Great College Street, a turning adjacent to Westminster Abbey.

Robertson had asked them to take a nose around the office of Burdis's secretary, Caro Tait. She was based in the nearby Cloisters in Dean's Yard. As Tait had once worked for the Service, they had already called in a few favours, and had full access to Burdis's work and social diary. Even so, Robertson decided it wouldn't do any harm taking a closer look. They'd already gone through Burdis's office at the Commons with a fine-tooth comb, and drawn a complete blank.

Robertson was also aware Caro was reportedly very close to her boss, and had long harboured suspicions she may well have ended up as another notch on his bedpost. In which case, her loyalty to British Intelligence could have been compromised by a fling with Burdis, and might be motivated into concealing potentially damaging documentation. Robertson fully accepted he might well be doing Caro a severe injustice, but until they could prove otherwise, he couldn't afford to leave any stone unturned.

Garvan and Spencer slipped through a small unlocked wrought iron gateway from Great College Street, which led directly to Dean's Yard, or the Green, as locals more popularly knew it, and the pupils of Westminster School, situated within the hallowed precincts of the ancient Abbey grounds. As they strolled past the Green, a Church Warden

119

dressed in his robes warmly bade them goodnight with a cheery wave, before disappearing into the gloom.

Spencer produced a pocket torch from his jacket, and led the way up an uneven flight of stone steps, before being confronted by a large medieval oak door.

'What now?' Garvan asked.

'Even you could do this one.' He smirked. 'It's not locked.'

'You're joking?'

'They've never bothered. Besides, the Abbey wouldn't allow a Yale lock to be drilled into the door; there's a bolt on the inside, though, a ruddy great thing.'

Spencer clicked open the heavy door, and sprayed his torch against the wall to search for the light switch.

'There it is,' Garvan said, pointing to their right.

Spencer flicked it on.

Once inside, the air was pervaded by a distinct smell of stale tobacco smoke, and Garvan's expression registered surprise. Office space was obviously at a premium, and many MP's secretaries had found themselves spread around Whitehall. It was nothing more than a dismal large open plan room, crammed with desks. Caro Tait's workspace was situated between that of two Labour MP's secretaries. Spencer explained the desks were allotted on a first come, first served basis, and the staff were not segregated along party political lines, but, by all accounts, they appeared to be relatively relaxed about the situation.

Admittedly, there were times during the day when everyone was in the office and either on the telephone or talking at cross-purposes to one another. Caro had once described it as being a little like sitting in the middle of Billingsgate Fish Market. Privacy, she had said to Spencer, was not a particular priority. Although they accepted the situation was far from ideal, but for some bizarre reason it seemed to work, and many MPs and their staff had grown to love being situated beyond the stiflingly cramped confines of Parliament itself.

Caro confessed however much the staff got along together, there were times when they needed privacy to discuss a particular issue out of earshot of their political opponents. This was easily remedied by popping across the road to the Commons, or having a quiet cup of tea or a drink at the nearby Red Lion in Whitehall, a favourite watering hole of both politicians and civil servants alike.

Garvan sat himself down at Caro Tait's desk, and gently ran his hands over a large square blotting pad; covered by ink stains interspersed with hastily written telephone numbers, and the smudged brown ring stains of tea cups, which had soaked into the green blotting paper. Spencer perched himself on the neighbouring desk; he needed Garvan's experience as a detective to cast his eye over Tait's workspace.

There were three trays set neatly to the right-hand side; the in-tray contained an assortment of letters and files. It struck him security appeared not to be an issue, practically non-existent. He could see at least one of the files had a confidential caveat marked on the front cover. The pending tray was entirely empty, and the out-tray possessed nothing more than a pile of torn pieces of paper. Beside the telephone, to the left-hand side, was a nondescript, Government Issue metal box, with GR VI printed in matching black ink with a crown over the royal cipher. It was locked, so he passed it over to Spencer to sort out.

'I take it Caro is left-handed,' Garvan observed.

'Lord knows is she, what makes you say that?'

The telephone cord was twisted, curled up and knotted; being left-handed himself, it was easy to explain. Her pens were in an old wooden pot on the top left-hand side of the blotting paper. Garvan's theory was as she picked the receiver up in her left hand, she then immediately placed it in

121

her right hand to make notes, imparting a half twist. When the call finished, she automatically hung up with her left hand, completing a full twist, which resulted in a mangled knot. It sounded feasible to Spencer, and he certainly didn't argue the point.

Spencer made short work of picking the lock, leaving Garvan free to relieve the box of its contents, and place them on the desktop. Spencer began sorting through a pile of typed and handwritten letters and documents from the in-tray.

Finding nothing of interest, Garvan looked up from the desk, and thoughtfully glanced around the large office.

'Surely, to God, she has more storage space than this?'

Spencer inclined his head toward a row of cupboards banked against the far wall. 'If you take a look in the cupboard in the right-hand corner, it's not all hers, but the last time I was here, she shared it with two other secretaries. I think you'll find Caro's stuff on the middle shelf.'

By the look of it, none of the cupboards were locked.

'Apart from the Iberian desk at the Foreign Office, do our contenders have anything else in common?' Garvan asked him.

Spencer wasn't entirely sure what was going through Garvan's mind. 'Well, apart from Haining, of course, the only other connection I can think off the top of my head is they all went to Cambridge University.'

'Did they go to the same college?'

'I wouldn't have a clue without checking the files, but Burdis and Oakways would have graduated years before Rowlands was there.' He looked at Garvan appraisingly. 'What's on your mind?'

'What about Frank Lucern?'

'What about him?'

'Wasn't he an accomplished aero engineer before the war?'

122

'Yes, yes, he was.'

'Presumably, he went to University. Do you know where?'

Spencer eyed him thoughtfully. 'I'm not sure where you're going with this, Garvie, but what the hell's this to do with Frank? You can't honestly believe he's our mole.'

'I never believed George Rowlands was capable of being a traitor, either. But, the fact remains, he managed to dupe British Intelligence, and it was Rowlands who tipped us off about Agent Toniolo.'

'I still think you're barking up the wrong tree with Frank Lucern, I really do!'

'Where *did* Frank go to University?' Garvan persisted.

Spencer sucked in his lower lip. 'Cambridge,' he said, almost reluctantly. 'But, let's face it. Half the ruddy intelligence service and the Cabinet went to Oxbridge. I just don't think there's any point having a scattergun approach in the hope of coming up with something, that's all.'

Garvan held his gaze. 'Right now, I have a foot in both camps.'

'Meaning what, exactly?'

'I've stepped into your world, where nothing is ever quite what it seems, but at heart, I'm still a copper, and until we flush someone out of the woodwork, as far as I'm concerned, no-one, not even Frank, is out of the frame!'

Spencer looked at him curiously. 'Does that include me?'

'What do you think?' he said tensely.

He laughed. 'Then I think, I'd better start watching my back, but my only defence is, like Haining, I've dragged myself up by my bootstraps. I'm not exactly Oxbridge material.'

'I've noticed,' Garvan said drily.

Spencer gave him a half-hearted smile. 'Lucern and Rowlands would have been at Cambridge, at least, ten or so years after Burdis, let alone Oakways, who was there in nineteen hundred and frozen to death. What we need is something tangible to go on, a clue to the identity of Toniolo, and sorting through this dross,' he said, clutching a fistful of papers, 'is our best bet.'

Garvan leaned forward on the desk, and clasped his hands together. 'I'm not disputing that, but if there's one thing I learned at Scotland Yard, it is the more reference points you build up on a case, the more chance you have of making a connection to the guilty party, and the easier it is to pick up on the clues.'

Spencer was almost on the point of countering him, but realised he was probably out of his depth, almost as much as Garvan was in the cloak and dagger world of counter-espionage. Tar Robertson had seconded Garvan to MI5 for one reason, and one reason only; he needed someone of his stature and expertise, and his acute detective's analytical mind. So far, he hadn't let them down.

'What do you want to do now?' Spencer asked.

Garvan glanced at his watch, it was only nine forty-five. 'We've still got time on our hands.'

'More than enough,' Spencer agreed with him.

Garvan searched through Caro's cupboard. There was little in the way of interest, other than a few expense bills, a couple of invites to various social events, and a pile of mundane constituency correspondence. He left the door ajar, just as he'd found it, and weaved his way back across the office to her desk, where Spencer was finishing off photographing a couple of potentially interesting documents, and carefully replaced the contents either in the trays or the metal box, bar one document.

Garvan shot him a questioning look. 'What's with the letter?'

'It's from the Chief Whip's office. Burdis is apparently trying to crawl his way back into favour with the Tory Party. The Whip, Simon Harrison, has agreed to have lunch with him on Friday.'

As Spencer placed the folded letter in his jacket pocket, he noticed the speculative expression on Garvan's face. 'Caro hasn't made a note in the diary.'

'And your point is?'

'It's probably the one document she'll miss in the morning,' he replied smoothly, while making no attempt to relock the metal box. 'Don't you remember Tar saying he wanted to ruffle Burdis's feathers?'

Garvan did. It was a valid point, but he needed to qualify something. 'Is that why Oakways's house was burgled? Was that to make a point, to give *him* a warning?'

'MI5 had nothing to do with the break-ins; I've already told you that.'

'That's not what I was getting at, but did someone in MI6 have a grudge against him?'

'You tell me,' Spencer said, 'maybe he was getting too close to Toniolo, who knows? Maybe he was on the point of outing them. My gut feeling is he was, and that's why someone killed the poor old bugger. What we haven't yet found is a connection to Len Dunmore's murder, but both you and I know there is a link.'

'You're right. There has to be.'

'Burdis might not be our man, but that doesn't matter, Caro will start to flap when she can't find the Chief Whip's letter. In itself, it isn't particularly significant, but Caro's an old hand at the job. She'll probably suspect we've had a sniff around the office, and left a deliberate calling card. Now, how she takes it forward, is another matter. If she's still loyal to the Service, then it'll go no further, but if she has slept with Burdis, then it's anyone's guess how she'll react.'

125

They switched off the light and retraced their steps back to Great College Street.

Chapter 11

A green light flashed on Colonel Robertson's intercom; he picked up the black phone from a bank of three.

'Superintendent Garvan is here to see you, sir,' his secretary explained.

'Thank you, send him in.'

He sat back in his chair, and reached for his pipe, as the door opened, and Garvan appeared.

'Come in. Take a seat.'

Robertson placed the pipe between his lips, and set a match to it. Garvan sat down on the other side of the desk. Robertson put the box of matches back in the desk drawer.

The summons had been unexpected, and although not quite out of the ordinary, Garvan suspected something was amiss. Behind his boss's shrewd, watchful eyes, was a mind as sharp as a razor, and very little passed him by.

'We've had a bite from Caro Tait,' he announced breezily.

Garvan thought it a little quick, but wondered what was coming next.

'Caro is well-versed at our game; she turned up to work this morning, and knew something wasn't quite right.'

'Did she call you?'

'No,' he smiled quickly. 'Typical of Caro, she pulled a few strings, and placed a direct call to General Menzies. He then called me, demanding to know what the hell was going on, and why I hadn't kept him in the loop.'

'And, why didn't you?' Garvan asked him pointedly.

'As you know, Caro once worked for Menzies.' He smiled faintly. 'I guess you might say I feared there could be a conflict of interest.'

Garvan shot him a look of incredulity. 'Surely to God you don't doubt Menzies's creditability. If you do, then we're all buggered!'

Acid seeped into Robertson's voice. 'You've never met Caro, have you?'

'No, sir.'

'She's an attractive woman. Don't get me wrong, I'm not suggesting any impropriety, far from it, just personal loyalties can sometimes get in the way, and cloud the issue.'

'What did she say to Menzies?'

'Someone had been snooping around her office, and it was either a botched job or a deliberate ploy.'

'Presumably Menzies denied all knowledge?'

'Yes, of course, he did, and then, he called me.'

'Why didn't he call the Director General?'

'Because he knows I'm in direct charge of the investigation, and Burdis is in the firing line.'

'Do you think this Tait woman has said anything to Burdis?'

He laughed, and rapped the desk with the flat of his hand. 'To be honest, I'd be disappointed if she hadn't. Spencer was spot-on; the one thing she'd have missed this morning was the letter from the Chief Whip's office. From what I can gather, she wasn't only angry but incandescent the Service might suspect her of any wrongdoing.'

Garvan pulled a face. 'Isn't that a natural reaction?'

'In part, yes,' Tar conceded. 'But, Caro lost the plot, and handled it all wrong. She bypassed her regular contacts within the Service, and went straight for the jugular by phoning Menzies. As I said, Caro is pretty switched on, which makes me suspect there is, or was, something between her and Burdis.'

'In which case, it's probably a given she's already discussed it with her boss.'

'Yes, I'm sure she has.'

'What do you want us to do now?'

'I've sent Spencer to see her.'

128

Garvan expressed surprise; in his experience, Spencer was the very last person he would have sent, let alone to Caro Tait, who was obviously more than capable of kicking up a stink.

'They've known each other for years,' Robertson explained. 'If anyone can pour oil on troubled waters, he can.'

'Well, let's hope so,' Garvan said dubiously.

'Caro trusts him,' Tar said, before letting out an easy chuckle. 'But, God only knows why. She must be more of a fool than I am!'

'And what about Haining? How are you going to ruffle his feathers? He's a whole different kettle of fish, altogether.'

Robertson gave him a slightly bitter smile. 'You mean, because he's hand-in-glove with MI6?'

Garvan nodded.

'To be honest with you, I don't think we'll have to do anything.'

'Why's that?'

'Because, by now, he'll certainly have heard all about Caro's rant at Menzies. Haining's nobody's fool. He knows the score, and will have already assumed he's under suspicion.'

'Even so, it might be worth taking a closer look.'

Robertson started to toy with his pipe. 'All in good time, Superintendent.' He leaned forward on the desk. 'That brings me to another point. Have you had a chance to check any of the photographic stuff from Burdis's flat?

'I'm still waiting for the lab to produce copies; they promised to have them on my desk by ten this morning. I understand Burdis is practically estranged from his wife,' Garvan said, taking out a cigarette, and lighting it.

'Yes, it's common enough knowledge.'

'I was just wondering if it might not be worth having a nose around the family pile in Kent.'

129

'Let's just see how things pan out first with the information from the flat, and Caro's office. I certainly haven't entirely discounted the idea, but there's no point in sniffing around until we have to.'

'How did Joyce get on with Burdis?' Garvan asked, trying to sound casual.

'Very well, by all accounts. Then again, she has a natural gift for exploiting male weaknesses.' He paused, allowing his words to sink in. 'Simpson told me she had Burdis wrapped around her little finger. She passed the old rogue her telephone number, so I should imagine he'll be pretty quick in giving her a bell.' Tar took his time drawing on his pipe. 'Burdis certainly didn't get his nickname as the "Loins of Westminster" without some justification.'

Robertson's barbed comments certainly didn't miss their mark; Garvan covered it well, but was beginning to feel distinctly uneasy. It was obvious Tar had sussed something was going on between them.

'You should have the report about the dinner party on your desk shortly,' Tar continued smoothly, before shooting Garvan a penetrating look. 'Spencer tells me you think there might be a connection to Cambridge University.'

'Not specifically,' he replied cagily.

'Interesting,' Tar mused, drawing slowly on his pipe, but surprisingly, let the matter rest.

His attitude was, as usual, business-like and pleasant enough, but Garvan sensed there was a certain undertone.

'Have you anything else to tell me, Superintendent?'

'No, sir.'

Tar raised his brows speculatively. 'Are you quite sure?'

His words lingered, almost menacingly, in the air. Garvan appeared nonplussed, and the merest flicker of irritation appeared on Robertson's face.

130

'For Christ's sake, Superintendent, whatever you do, don't ever try pulling the wool over my eyes. I know something is going on between you and Leader!'

He decided there was no point beating about the bush. What was done, was done, and reluctantly, he had fatally compromised his position. 'It shouldn't have happened, sir,' he confessed.

'No, it shouldn't!'

'I blame myself.'

Robertson's voice was modulated, but there was no disguising the hardness in his eyes. 'You somewhat gave the game away the other day, when I mentioned we needed Leader to get close to Burdis.' He paused for effect. 'The look on your face said it all.'

Garvan assumed Spencer had also let the cat out of the bag. 'I've offered my resignation to Major Hall.'

'Have you, indeed,' he replied thoughtfully, puffing on his briar. 'That's interesting.'

At that moment, Garvan knew he'd managed to score yet another own goal, and had also unwittingly involved Spencer. Judging by the expression on Tar's face, it was obvious he felt that Garvan had let him down. He couldn't afford to carry passengers, operators he couldn't trust implicitly. MI5's work was an unremitting grind of stress and responsibility. Countless lives depended upon their deception of the German High Command, and he needed not only commitment from his team, but also total loyalty.

There was a moment's silence between them, and it was Robertson who broke it. 'I think you should be aware I had Leader hauled into my office earlier, and told her I'd heard a whisper something was going on between you.'

Garvan held his gaze.

'She admitted everything, of course,' Robertson continued, and set the pipe down in the onyx ashtray on the desk. 'But, I need to know how serious this is, Superintendent.'

He answered honestly, 'I'm not sure, sir.'

Robertson looked at him askance. 'Come on, man! Stop pussy footing around. You must have some idea?'

'It's all blown up over the last few weeks.'

'You know how things stand with us, Garvan. We can't afford to play fast and loose, especially not with the agents under our command.' Robertson's voice remained controlled. 'I'll be honest with you, the first thing that crossed my mind was to have you removed from the Service! Had this happened a year or so ago, I wouldn't have hesitated, but now, well.' His words slowly trailed off.

Robertson was always even-handed, but if the situation demanded, he was more than capable of being utterly ruthless. From what Garvan knew of him, he certainly didn't relish getting himself embroiled in the personal, day-to-day problems of his staff. It was an unwelcome distraction from the job. He already had more than enough on his plate.

Tar considered his words carefully. He admired Garvan's abilities as a first-rate Scotland Yard detective. He had come up trumps, time and again, with an insightful analysis of their intelligence transmissions, and had also been involved heavily in the interrogation of German agents. However great his transgression with Joyce Leader might be, things had reached such a pitch with Operation Overlord it was all hands on deck. He couldn't afford to lose him from the team at such a critical moment. Even so, Garvan needed a sharp rap over the knuckles, a reminder he had stepped way over the line, and at any other time, MI5 would have given him no quarter.

'As things stand,' Roberson said coldly, 'I can't afford to relieve Leader from her duties. Right now, she's too valuable to pull the plug. But, I guess you already knew that, didn't you?' He gave Garvan a thin smile, and snorted. 'I presume Spencer spun you much the same line?'

'Yes, sir, he did.'

Robertson leaned forward, his eyes narrowing as he looked across the desk into Garvan's eyes. 'The fact Spencer didn't come to me about all this, is a measure not only of his respect for you as a colleague, but also as a friend.' He allowed a silence to fall between them, before adding, 'I also know he would never allow his personal feelings to cloud his professional judgement, so you can consider yourself lucky, Superintendent. Had he raised any concerns to me about your integrity, I wouldn't have hesitated in sending you back to Scotland Yard.'

Had Robertson done so, his career would have been over in all but name. He reached forward, and retrieved a file from his pending tray flicking it open, signalling the meeting was at an end; he'd been dismissed. As Garvan opened the door, Robertson glanced up from the file.

'A word of warning, Superintendent. Cool it. For both your sakes.'

Chapter 12

As Garvan headed back to his office, he bumped into Joyce Leader, who seemed unusually nervous.

'My report from last night's dinner party is on your desk,' she said.

'Thank you.'

'I'm sorry,' Joyce whispered, lowering her voice as someone passed them in the corridor.

Garvan looked carefully into her anxious grey-blue eyes. 'Why?'

'I take it you know the Colonel called me into his office this morning.' It was obvious he did. 'Maybe,' she added reflectively, 'I shouldn't have spilled the beans about us.'

'You didn't have a choice,' he said stiffly.

'But, even so.'

Garvan silenced her. 'There's no point beating yourself up about it. What's done is done.'

She attempted a smile. 'He hasn't sacked you, then?'

He returned her smile. 'Not yet.'

She looked palpably relieved he hadn't been given his marching orders. 'Thank God,' she whispered.

'Just put it this way, I'm not exactly holding my breath he won't change his mind,' he added ruefully.

'Was it that bad?'

'I'll speak to you later,' he answered, his tone softening slightly.

She reached out, and gently brushed her hand against his arm. 'When will I see you?'

'When the time's right,' he smiled tautly, and carried on down the corridor to his office.

*

Half an hour later, Garvan was entering a rather seedy bar near the Aldwych. Waiting for him was Michelle Rookwood, one of Robertson's double agents. She was already nursing a large gin and tonic, so Garvan headed straight for the bar, and ordered himself a pint of bitter.

Seeing him enter the bar, Michelle smiled, almost as if she was pleased to see him, but she wasn't. Truth be told, only a summons from Spencer Hall would have filled her with even more dread than she was feeling right now. Her standing within the Double Cross system had been damaged severely during her last posting to Portugal. The seeds of doubt about her effectiveness as a field agent were initially sown by George Rowlands, during his time at the MI6 Station in Lisbon.

In the course of events, it turned out his criticism was unfounded, and was nothing more than a means of masking his own treachery. However, quite separately from Rowlands's bogus reports to London, there were also rumours at the time she had become too close to the Abwehr's second-in-command, Gustav von Bertele. It was all in the past now, and although Rowlands had long since been outed as a traitor, the fact remained that mud sticks, and her reputation had been tarnished severely within the Service by the persistent rumours her relationship with Bertele had gone way beyond the call of duty. It was an open secret, even amongst the Abwehr, he had fallen deeply in love with her. Since her return to England, she had been nothing more than a bit part player on the periphery of the Double Cross system, and in Robertson's eyes, she was of little current use to the team's counter-espionage battle against German Intelligence.

Garvan took the seat across the table from her. She was smartly dressed, and was, as usual, overly made up, with heavily applied black mascara, red painted lips and hair bleached to within an inch of its life. It had to be said Rookwood did not go for an understated look.

135

She appeared drawn, with dark circles under her blue-grey eyes, and looked as if the weight of the world was on her shoulders. She had probably had a hard time of it, lately; many of the problems that followed Michelle back to London were not entirely all of her own making. But, sometimes, she could also be her own worst enemy, taking offence where none was intended, and arguing furiously with her MI5 controllers. Rookwood's volatility and emotional vulnerability had only served to heighten Robertson's concerns about her continued effectiveness as a double agent.

In fairness to Rookwood, her posting to Lisbon had been fraught with danger, and the ensuing trauma of her experiences had left her both physically and emotionally scarred. No matter how hard she tried, she'd never quite managed to drive the phantoms away. Robertson had granted her a certain amount of leeway and time to recover from the ordeal, but the Double Cross couldn't carry potentially unreliable Abwehr agents. Although he had decided against closing her files, Michelle knew full well it was probably only a matter of time.

'What's this all about?' she said, sucking on a freshly lit cigarette.

'I want to pick your brains.'

Michelle tossed back her head, and laughed. 'Jesus, that's got to be a first. It won't take too long, then, will it!' she said, without any hint of pretence.

'You might be right.' He grinned.

Her eyes examined him fiercely. 'Come on. Why did you call me?'

'How much contact did you have with George Rowlands and Frank Lucern in Portugal?'

Michelle considered her response carefully. She was still desperately trying to forget her experiences in Portugal. Just when she was beginning to believe MI5 had finally drawn a line under the whole sorry saga, Garvan was raking it all up again.

'I met them, of course.' She gave a slight shrug. 'But, as a Double Cross agent, I reported direct to London, and not to the MI6 Station.'

Garvan knew all that, so why was he asking? What had come up to resurrect their mission to Lisbon? The only thing Rookwood knew, with any degree of certainty, was Garvan was not about to tell her. Michelle had been left in limbo for so long she had begun to doubt her worth as a spy. She was nothing more than a dispensable commodity, caught in the deadly crossfire between British and German Intelligence, and, in Robertson's eyes, she was very much a spent force.

'You were very close to Gustav von Bertele,' he said, almost as a throwaway line.

She looked at him guardedly. After her arrival in Portugal, Colonel Robertson had ordered Michelle to ingratiate herself with von Bertele. It was easier said than done, but she worked hard, and produced results far beyond Robertson's initial expectations. In a classic honey trap, she managed to seduce von Bertele. Back then, only a year or so ago, she was highly regarded, and supplied London with a stream of high-grade intelligence, but agents were only ever as good as their last report. Her previous successes could not save her from punishment for a single failure. It was not only competitive, but ruthless. It was the game British Intelligence had to play. The stakes were simply too high to afford any mistakes.

'Does the Colonel know you're here?' she asked curiously.

He leaned across the table toward her. 'Just answer the question.'

Michelle thoughtfully stroked the rim of her glass. 'You know what happened with von Bertele. It's all on record.

137

I was under orders from London, and did as I was told, end of!'

'It's just I've always felt you knew far more than you were willing to let on.' Garvan said, lighting a cigarette.

She looked at him archly. 'What the hell is that supposed to mean?'

'That someone, or something, put the fear of God into you,' he said, snapping his gold lighter shut. 'I don't blame you, far from it; in your shoes, I'd probably have done much the same thing.'

Michelle's eyes were calm and watchful; she was giving nothing away. She needed to keep her wits about her. Her life as a spy was already in freefall, and it was difficult to know who to trust. Garvan might only be on secondment from Scotland Yard, but he was close to Spencer Hall. Nor was she quite sure how close he was to the inner circle of British Intelligence.

He kept his cigarette on the go. 'Von Bertele trusted you,' he continued.

She pulled a face. 'Well, only up to a point.'

'But, you knew a mole was working out of the MI6 Station.'

'Yes, but at the time, I didn't know it was Rowlands,' she replied indifferently.

As Garvan exhaled a plume of cigarette smoke slowly through his lips and nostrils, he examined her pensive expression. 'Did you ever hear of an agent called Toniolo?'

'Toniolo?' she repeated blankly.

Garvan could tell she was lying; it was a gut instinct. There was something about the eyes it was always a giveaway. 'Listen, Chelle, you're already treading water with MI5. If you want to come out of the war with a clean sheet, and more importantly still breathing, you'd better start giving me some straight answers.'

'There was *one* time,' she confessed.

'When was that?'

'It was at a restaurant,' she explained. 'I overheard a conversation between von Bertele and his boss, Colonel von Gruber. They were discussing an agent they suspected was working for the Soviets. I couldn't hear that much, but the codename sounded like Toniolo.' She pursed her lips. 'Or it was something like it.'

Rowlands had already told a similar story about overhearing a snatched conversation between von Gruber and a Gestapo officer.

He looked at her speculatively. 'Is that it?'

Rookwood's heart was starting to race. Something was wrong, and she was scared.

'Why didn't you report the conversation to London?'

'At the time, it didn't seem that important,' she said defensively. 'I mean, Toniolo was a Soviet agent. I was under orders to infiltrate the Abwehr. I already had enough on my plate with von Bertele, let alone worrying about some NKVD spy.' She paused, drawing heavily on her cigarette. 'Let's face it. We were all operating under the nose of the Portuguese authorities.'

'That's really beside the point.'

'Is it?'

'Since when were you given permission to cherry-pick intelligence?'

'What do you mean?' she asked tremulously.

'You were under orders to report everything, and anything, you picked up back to St. James's, not just the things you felt were important!'

Michelle had no defence; she should have reported the conversation to London. 'What's so important about this Toniolo, anyway?' she queried.

Garvan decided to come clean, and see how she reacted. He told her how Rowlands had first dropped

Toniolo's name into the mix during an interrogation, after being brought back to London in disgrace from Portugal.

Rookwood looked at him searchingly. 'What happened?'

He told her about the entry in Oakways's diary, and how they'd found it after his murder.

'I've never heard of him,' she said blankly.

'There's no reason you would have; he'd held a number of ministerial posts.'

'Anything of interest to us?' she quizzed him.

'His last was at the FO.'

'That covers a multitude of sins.'

'He worked on the Iberian Desk.'

She let out a low whistle. 'You think Toniolo murdered him?'

'It was either Toniolo, or someone connected to them, yes.' He took a puff from his cigarette. 'I need you to do something for me.'

She met his gaze warily. 'Christ, you must be scraping the barrel if you want *me* to do something?'

He let it ride. 'I'd like you to meet Joyce Leader this evening at the Savoy.'

'Joyce?' Michelle repeated warily.

'Yes, she'll be there about seven-thirty.'

'Why?'

'She's been ordered to meet an MP called Jamie Burdis.'

'Which bar at the Savoy?' she queried, knowing there were multiple ones at the location.

'They're meeting at the American Bar.'

'I recognise his name,' Michelle chanced.

Garvan smiled tautly, and explained Burdis was a former Tory Minister, whose ambitions were, by common consensus, way beyond his political capabilities. Sadly, the only thing which had marked him out for recognition was is his womanising, having reached almost legendary status amongst his colleagues.

'At the moment, he's kicking his heels on the backbenches.'

'Why has Joyce been ordered to meet him?'

'For a while, he worked alongside Oakways at the Foreign Office.'

Garvan didn't have to explain MI5 believed there was a possible link to Toniolo.

Michelle looked at him curiously. 'Knowing Joyce, as I do, I can't imagine she needs any help from me with some randy MP.'

Garvan picked up his cigarette lighter off the table, and slipped it into his hip pocket. 'Maybe not,' he said evenly.

Michelle nursed her glass between her hands. 'I don't suppose I have a choice?'

His expression said it all.

'There's one other thing,' he added.

'What's that?'

'Joyce doesn't know you'll be there.'

Michelle's eyes narrowed, as she scanned his face. 'Does Colonel Robertson know you called me?'

Garvan met Michelle's gaze. 'I'm not interested in what you think, or don't think,' he said dismissively. 'Right now, Chelle, the only thing you need to take on board is I'm throwing you a lifeline.'

'Meaning what, exactly?'

'Work your charms on Burdis this evening, and you might just manage to salvage something from the God almighty mess you've stirred up for yourself.'

There was a hidden agenda there, but Garvan had her over a barrel.

'If Robertson knew that you overheard Gruber and von Bertele discussing Toniolo in Portugal your feet wouldn't touch the ground.' He pushed his chair back and stood up.

141

'One more chance, Chelle, and that's it, screw up again and they'll not only close your file, but they'll throw away the bloody key!'

Chapter 13

As Joyce held a Martini glass to her lips, Burdis demanded, 'Where were you last night?'

'I'm sorry,' she apologised. 'I left a message with your secretary that I couldn't make dinner.'

He looked childishly petulant; her gaze was withering, but he seemed not to notice.

'I had a problem, a domestic one.'

'Really?' he snarled across the table.

'My boyfriend turned up,' she lied smoothly. 'I thought he was in the middle of the Atlantic somewhere,' she added, with a shrug.

The real reason for the cancellation was St. James's had needed her to make an urgent transmission to the Abwehr. Burdis was ordered to be kept on hold for the night.

'Is your boyfriend still in town?' he asked uneasily.

She smiled mischievously. 'No, he should be safely on-board his ship in Portsmouth by now.'

'Good,' he chuckled, with undisguised relief; he'd no wish to encounter some jealous muscle bound matelot half his age.

Burdis began to relax. His sulk was over, life was good again, and he was on a promise. If the evening panned as he wanted, he might just be able to sweet talk Joyce into bed. All was going well, until he noticed her gaze drift across the bar, and set upon a striking woman, who seemed to be hell bent on heading in their direction. She was perhaps a little overly heavily made up, but her pale blue dress showed off her stunning figure to perfection.

There had never been any great love lost between the two women. Leader's reaction was difficult to gauge. The fact she'd taken her old colleague and rival by surprise had set Michelle on edge, but she covered it well.

'Hello, Jo,' she said breezily. 'I thought I saw you earlier.' She gestured back across the bar, and added, with a sigh, 'I've been waiting for ages, but it looks as if I've been stood up.' Michelle flashed Burdis a smile. 'Knowing my luck, he's probably had a better offer.'

'Nonsense,' he said expansively. 'Why don't you join us for a drink, I'm sure Joyce won't mind.'

'Of course not,' Joyce answered mechanically, before making the necessary introductions.

All the while, she kept wondering what the hell Rookwood was up to. For all her faults, she'd never have interrupted a fellow agent without authorisation, without top cover. Besides, if she had been sitting on the other side of the bar, there was no way Joyce wouldn't have picked up on her by now.

'So, you're an MP. How exciting,' Rookwood cooed, all of a flutter.

'I'm afraid it sounds rather more exciting than it is,' he lamented. 'What would you like to drink, my dear?'

'I'd kill for a gin and tonic.'

Burdis laughed, clicked his fingers, and ordered another round, even though Joyce was still nursing a martini. Burdis seemed as pleased as punch by Rookwood's unexpected appearance; he loved nothing more than a captive audience, especially an attractive female audience. It was more than he'd bargained for, but old habits die hard, the more, the merrier.

'Have you two known each other long?' he asked.

'A while,' Joyce said, in a deadpan voice.

'Don't you remember we met at a place near Richmond,' Rookwood said merrily.

Joyce allowed the merest flicker of amusement to cross her face; Rookwood was obviously referring to their first encounter. At the time, they were both incarcerated at

Latchmere House near Richmond, MI5's enemy alien interrogation centre.

'I remember it well,' she replied drily.

Rookwood directed her attention back to Burdis. 'How long have you been a Member of Parliament?'

It was the opening gambit Burdis had been waiting for, a chance to talk about his favourite subject, *himself*. With each telling, his stories became ever more embellished to such an extent, Joyce began to wonder whether he remembered what was true, and what parts were down to a bid to please his audience. With the return of the waiter, Burdis was momentarily forced to draw breath. He was soon in full flight again, bragging about his time at the Foreign Office, and his growing influence in the corridors of power. Burdis had an opinion on anything, and everyone, in the political world. Never one to mince his words, he described Jeremy Haining as incredibly hard working, but an utterly disloyal little shit. Considering how Haining had been instrumental in his removal to the backbenches, it was probably fair to say it was not an entirely unbiased opinion.

Joyce reluctantly conceded Michelle was playing it rather well, all wide-eyed and hung on his every word. By degrees, Burdis started to neglect her, perhaps Michelle seemed a far safer bet, and less likely to brush off his advances. From somewhere in her mind, Joyce felt a frisson of relief she'd been let off the hook. But, was starting to worry her. Something must have happened. *Why had MI5 reactivated Michelle's file?* Up until now, she'd been placed on the back burner, kicking her heels around London with nothing much to do. She'd been instructed to keep in contact with her Abwehr handlers, but most of the information had been maintained at a low grade just enough to keep her ticking over.

It was getting late, but Burdis was still on good form, and reluctant to call it a day. He suggested moving on to his flat for a nightcap. Joyce quietly shot Michelle a questioning look, but it was obvious her colleague was eager to take up his offer. Joyce knew she had to play along.

Burdis excused himself and disappeared over to the bar, presumably to settle the bill. Joyce hissed at her colleague. 'What's going on?'

Michelle coolly drained her glass. 'I'm not here by choice!'

'Who sent you?'

'Garvan did.'

Leader met her eyes in an expressionless way.

'But, don't ask me why, I haven't a clue.'

'What did he say?'

She shrugged indifferently. 'Nothing much, other than I was to meet up with you here.'

'What about Burdis?'

Michelle shot her a smile. 'You both know why we're here.'

If Garvan had ordered Michelle to the Savoy, he was playing with fire, and she could only assume he had probably taken the decision without either Spencer or the Colonel's consent. Things were already difficult enough for them at St. James's, without risking rocking the boat any further. Michelle was persona non-grata at MI5; it was a high-risk strategy, and one that could seriously backfire on both of them. She had to play it calmly, and couldn't afford to allow her sense of growing unease to cloud her judgment.

Burdis re-joined them at the table, and offered to drive them to his flat. Leader looked at him archly, and questioned whether he was sober enough.

'Don't be silly, darling. I'm just getting into my stride,' he answered expansively.

Somewhat reluctantly, they both agreed. His driving, like the man himself, was erratic, but even sober it would probably not have made that much difference to his style behind the wheel.

Back at his flat, Michelle was still on a roll, and playing to Burdis's weaknesses, his love of flattery and a pretty face. In the space of an hour, he'd smoked seven cigarettes, and downed several more glasses of straight Scotch.

As Michelle drained her glass, he asked from behind a cloud of cigarette smoke, 'Would you like another?'

'Yes, yes, please,' she said, eagerly.

'And what about you, my dear, would you like a top up?'

'If it's all the same to you, I think that I'll call it a day.' Joyce smiled back at him.

There wasn't any point in prolonging the agony. Garvan had passed the baton to Michelle, and it was now up to her to produce the goods, and bed the old roué, gleaning what she could from him. Of course, he might be as clean as a whistle, but they still had to go through the motions in the hope of cancelling him out altogether. Burdis seemed genuinely disappointed by her decision to leave, and solicitously showed her to the front door.

'Have I upset you?'

'No, not at all,' she answered easily.

'Shall I call you a taxi? It's getting late.'

'There's no need. I'll walk. The tube station's only up the road.'

'Even so,' he protested.

She gently placed her right index finger to his lips to silence him. 'I'm not a fool, Jamie, I *know* how things stand with you.'

He looked at her curiously. 'My darling, what do you mean?'

'You're an attractive man and great company, but,' her words trailed off. 'Besides, you seem to be getting along just fine with Michelle, and it's becoming a little crowded in there, with the three of us,' she said, inclining her head toward the drawing room.

147

'Oh my God, I didn't mean to offend you.'

'You haven't,' she said quietly.

Burdis begged her to stay. Although Joyce was a challenge, blowing hot and cold by turns, right now, he'd have loved nothing more than to take her in his arms, but there was something about her that tempered his usual impulsiveness. It occurred to him Joyce was in complete control of her sexuality, and knew full well how to use it to her advantage. At face value, she appeared willingly to let people into her life, but the more time he spent in her company, Burdis began to realise it was only on a superficial level, and he didn't know her at all. The only thing he knew, with any degree of certainty, was he'd have to work damned hard to make any headway with her. Even then, he seriously doubted whether she'd lose a smidgen of her coolness.

'May I call you tomorrow?

Joyce returned his smile. 'Yes, of course, you can, and thank you for a lovely evening.'

She leaned forward, and gently brushed her lips gently against his cheek. Christ, Burdis wished she hadn't, but it had the desired effect, and he wanted her more than ever. But, yet again she'd slipped tantalizingly out of his grasp. Reluctantly, he closed the front door, and took a sharp intake of breath; the bloody woman was a complete enigma. It was rare, or so he imagined, for a woman to get the better of him, but Joyce had his measure, and that was dangerous. While his wife, Jenny, tolerated or turned a blind eye to his many affairs, anything of a more serious nature would bring his world crashing to the ground. As things stood, Jenny knew he'd always return to the family fold, and, more importantly, to her. It was all about perceived status in Burdis's mind, and he knew if anyone came between them, Jenny wouldn't hesitate to pull the plug, not only on their marriage, but his political career as well. It would be her ultimate revenge to ruin him completely.

Maybe it had been for the best Joyce had decided to leave. She might have slipped through his clutches, but he hadn't given up all hope. There'd be other opportunities, but all was not lost. Michelle was an attractive woman, all provocative pouts with large, inviting smouldering grey-blue eyes. Yet, if he knew anything about women, she seemed unlikely to turn him down. Michelle seemed like a free spirit after his own heart, who wouldn't think twice about defying convention. He liked that; it made life so much easier. She didn't disappoint.

He offered her another drink. She accepted, and wandered over to the window, pulling back the blackout curtains. In the soft pale moonlight, she could just make out the figure of Joyce Leader heading off in the direction of Sloane Square. He passed the drink to her, and stood back admiring her figure.

'I hope that I haven't caused any problem between you two?' he asked.

'You mean with Joyce?' she quizzed him.

'I think she was beginning to feel a little awkward.'

Michelle pulled a face. 'I wouldn't go troubling yourself too much on Jo's account. We're friends, of course, but she can be, how shall I say, a little straight-laced at times.'

'And you're not?'

She threw back her head, and laughed. 'Why don't we find out?'

This was going better than Burdis had anticipated; he didn't even have to make the first move. Rookwood promptly set her glass down on a side table, turned around, and kissed him passionately. After his dealings with Joyce Leader, this was so uncomplicated and so refreshing. In fact, it ran through his mind he couldn't remember the last time when he hadn't been forced to do all the running. Michelle skilfully undid his belt and let his trousers fall to the floor. He responded to her, and slipped off the pretty pale blue dress, revealing smooth

149

pale skin. His fingers gently undid the bra to reveal her large breasts. Burdis was momentarily mesmerized by the sight of her naked body; Michelle eagerly responded to his touch, and let out an eager gasp, as he reached out to touch her. She seemed as excited as he was, without the slightest hint of inhibition or remorse. So, he hadn't been wrong after all. She was a free spirit after his own heart; live for today and to hell with tomorrow.

'You're beautiful,' he found himself saying.

He gently guided Michelle toward the bedroom, and held her body close to his. She was good, very good, and knew how to please him; he never wanted it to end. When they were spent, they lay together in each other's arms, with Burdis drifting into a contented sleep. Rookwood smiled to herself.

Michelle slowly propped herself up on the pillows beside him, and glanced down, as he lay on his back, snoring slightly in fits and starts. She took a sharp intake of breath, for Burdis had been surprisingly gentle; it certainly hadn't been nearly as bad as she'd feared, far from it. If only he'd realised he had been the first man she'd slept with, since her return from Portugal.

She closed her eyes briefly reliving the moment; there'd been an incident which had left her not only traumatised, but mentally scarred. It was all in the past now. As strange as it might sound, Burdis had helped her feel wanted again, that she was still an attractive woman, but what's more, she could start to live again, free from the ghosts which had followed her back from Portugal.

Michelle slipped out of bed, and wrapped Burdis's discarded shirt around her shoulders; he was still fast asleep. She needed to get to work, and fast. Retracing her steps back to the drawing room, she flicked on a table lamp, and picked up his discarded trousers, systematically searching through the pockets. There was some loose change, a crumpled handkerchief and a wallet. She opened the catch of the wallet,

150

and rifled through its contents; there was a wad of pound notes inside, a folded receipt for a diamond ring, probably not for his wife, Michelle decided, and a bar bill. She carefully returned the wallet to the hip pocket of the trousers, and glanced around the room; this wasn't going to be easy, where the hell should she look next. In the gloom, something caught her eye, a smart, leather bound attaché case propped up behind the door. It was worth taking a look inside, it wasn't particularly promising, but she guessed it might contain something work related. She carried it over toward the table lamp, and skilfully rummaged through the contents. Much of it was dross, constituency correspondence in the main and the usual banal memos between fellow MPs, but something eventually stood out. It looked different from the other letters. Firstly, it was on expensive-looking blue-headed paper. There was a crest, or something very like a crest, in the shape of a pentagon in black embossed ink.

Her heart began to race. With any luck, Burdis was hopefully still asleep. She hurriedly scanned the page.

Dear Brethren,

Although the hyenas are circling around us, we must continue to stand firm together and not weaken; we cannot afford to let our guard down.

Yours always,

Signed T

Michelle puffed out her cheeks, *was T perhaps short for Toniolo?* It might be all or nothing. However, she moved over to her handbag, and retrieved a miniature camera, she briefly turned on the main light, and took a snapshot of the letter, then a second just to make sure she'd captured the image.

She was starting to lose her nerve, and daren't risk anymore, in case he woke up. She retreated to the bedroom and hesitated in the doorway. Burdis turned over in the bed, snorted a little, and instinctively reached over to nestle into her

151

body. He roused slightly, and called out her name. Michelle slipped in beside him; in his half sleep, he seemed not to notice she'd just sneaked back into bed.

Rookwood's heart was pounding out of control as he wrapped his arm around her waist; she waited, listening intently, until his breathing settled into a slow rhythmic movement, as he once again lapsed into a deep, untroubled sleep.

Chapter 14

Joyce Leader had been itching for an opportunity to seek Garvan out all day; she desperately needed to know why he'd sent Michelle Rookwood to the Savoy. Seeing him disappear into the office tea room, she seized the moment to confront him.

'What the hell's going on?' she demanded, following behind.

He swung away from the sink to face her. 'I don't know what you mean,' he said, rinsing his cup.

'What were you thinking about?' she seethed. 'Why the hell did you send Michelle to the Savoy, I'll have you know I'm more than capable of dealing with cretins like Jamie Burdis. Besides, we've already got enough on our plates, without your going out on a limb like that!'

Joyce nearly leaped out of her skin, as the door quietly closed behind her. In her anger, she'd failed to notice Spencer was already in the tea room, standing with his arm resting on an old filing cabinet used for storing crockery. She spun around sharply. His eyes were cool and watchful, a faint smile of contempt playing about his lips.

'There's no point in shooting the messenger,' he said, in a deadpan voice. 'It wasn't entirely Garvan's decision to involve Rookwood.'

Joyce was renowned for having a short fuse, but what mattered right now was why they'd doubted her abilities, and had passed her over for some failed double agent, who was no longer considered to be a top-flight operator.

'But, why Rookwood,' she hissed angrily. 'Talk about insulting!'

Someone tried to enter the tea room; Spencer had his foot pressed against the door.

'What's going on?' a disembodied voice called from the other side.

'Give us a couple of minutes,' Spencer called out, keeping his foot very firmly against the door.

Joyce looked at each of them in turn; it was Garvan who spoke up first.

'If you must know, Jo, my feelings for you didn't even remotely come into the equation,' he said dispassionately. 'Far from it.'

'Why then,' she bristled.

'We needed results, and we needed them fast. To put it bluntly, you simply weren't delivering the goods.'

A sudden red mist of blind rage clouded her expression. 'And you decided to call upon Rookwood. What in God's name, did you do that for? That's the part I don't understand.'

Well,' Spencer smiled smoothly, 'I think you'll find that was probably down to me, ultimately. It was my decision, and mine alone, to involve her.'

'*Why?*'

'We had some discussions about how the investigation into Burdis was going.' He paused, and flashed her, a taut, brief smile. 'As a matter of fact, we discussed you, as well.'

Her gaze drifted briefly toward Garvan; he was giving nothing away. It slowly started to dawn on Joyce somewhere along the line, she had completely underestimated him, had got it all wrong his feelings for her had somehow blinded his professional judgement. She'd been afraid his rashness had not only potentially risked her role as an MI5 double agent, but had also risked his career within the Service, and, in the longer term, with Scotland Yard. They needed to keep a low profile; he'd said as much. Perhaps, more than anything, Joyce had been afraid his actions might have been the final nail in the coffin for their budding relationship.

In hindsight, she ought to have known better. But, it was early days, and although she had worked alongside

Garvan for a couple of years, their relationship had always been somewhat standoffish. There had always been a sharp dividing line, and no matter how much St. James's valued her, she was still a double agent, and ultimately, an enemy of the State. All the promises of being given a clean sheet were still very much on hold, until after the cessation of the war. In many ways, Joyce was still getting to know him, but, on this occasion, he'd completely wrong-footed her. She'd finally began to realise, however intense their relationship might appear, he remained the same calculating, hard-headed detective she'd first met back in 1941. Perhaps she'd been so swept up in the strangely erotic romance of their forbidden love affair, she'd automatically assumed Garvan had felt the same way. But, looking at him now, an element of doubt began to creep into her mind. Maybe, his feelings were cooling, or he was having second thoughts.

Outwardly Joyce's expression remained completely impenetrable; the last thing she wanted, or needed, was to make a fool of herself in front of them. Involving Rookwood was a slight which didn't sit comfortably with her, but she decided to play it carefully.

Spencer could see how angry she was. 'It's nothing to do with your transmissions to Germany,' he assured her.

That was something at least.

'If we'd asked you, six months ago, to bag Jamie Burdis, what would you have done?'

She held his gaze, and knew what he was getting at.

Six months ago, she'd have bagged Burdis, and spat him out without a second thought; it was one of the reasons MI5 had taken her on in the first place. Even her German Intelligence controller, Bernard Drescher, had expected her to sleep with society contacts, with a view to either compromise or elicit information from them.

Spencer lit a cigarette. 'You wouldn't have blinked twice about sleeping with Burdis; you'd have found out what you could, and moved on, without even drawing breath.' He placed the cigarette casually in the corner of his mouth. 'The trouble is, Jo, I have a nagging suspicion your affair with Garvie has changed things, perhaps irrevocably.' He shot her a piercing look. 'You were dragging your heels, and we couldn't afford to hang around any longer. That's why we decided to reactivate Rookwood.'

She cast Garvan a pointed look; it was almost pleading. Surely to God he wasn't so callous he'd actually wanted her to fall into bed with Burdis. *Could he really be that cold-hearted?* Spencer knew her well enough to pick up on the signals; he certainly didn't want her having a full blown row with Garvan, nor could he afford to have one of his most valued agents cracking over an illicit affair with a member of the team. He needed to keep her head straight, and mind on the game.

'You know how things are,' he said, slightly softening his tone.

'Do I?' she queried belligerently.

'We live in this twilight world, where nothing is ever quite what it seems. You've been at the forefront of our intelligence operations for – for…' he hesitated, deliberately, she felt. 'Well it doesn't matter for how long. In the end, it's only natural something's got to give.'

Joyce didn't understand what he meant.

Spencer thrust his hands into the hip pockets of his trousers, and leaned his full weight against the door. 'It's an observation, but one which needs a straight answer from you.'

She narrowed her eyes questioningly.

'I need to hear it from you, Jo. Was I wrong about Burdis?'

He had a point. Joyce conceded she'd been so wrapped up in how Garvan was reacting to her assignment, she'd somehow lost sight of her own role, and what was expected of her. Even at the beginning of the year, she

156

wouldn't have thought twice about taking Burdis; men like him were two a penny, to be used and abused in the blink of an eye. It was what had made her good at her job. The Abwehr expected it, and, in turn, so had MI5. However, things had changed over the last few weeks. Her feelings for Garvan were strong, they always had been, and yet, he'd continually held her at arm's length. She'd been strictly off limits, but that first impulsive kiss in the office had not only taken her off guard, but had sent her world into freefall.

'I would have gone through with it,' she said bleakly.

'Maybe you would have, but we couldn't be sure.'

She gave Spencer a rather doleful look. 'Where does that leave us?'

He pulled a face. 'You carry on, as usual.'

'Tell me something,' she said, rather awkwardly. 'Did Rookwood manage to come up with anything?'

'Yes, in his attaché case was a typed letter, with an embossed header from the Lilburne Club. It was signed off with a "T." We've passed the photo down to Central Registry to see if they can come up with something on the Club.'

She thoughtfully sucked in her bottom lip. Being trounced by Rookwood didn't sit comfortably with her. She had always outclassed her colleague, had always produced high-grade intelligence elicited from the Abwehr. Whereas Rookwood, although good in her day, had a question mark hanging over her mental stability. It wasn't entirely her fault. They had all been to hell and back in Portugal, but Rookwood had suffered a raw deal, both mentally and physically; she accepted all that. Yet, it still niggled, still rankled her that she'd been side-lined for someone Colonel Robertson considered to be in the second eleven.

Still, they needed her. Whatever Rookwood may, or may not, have turned up at Burdis's flat might be significant, but at the end of the day, it didn't have a direct impact on the end game of defeating Nazi Germany. Right from the start,

Joyce had been implicit in helping the Double Cross build up an ambitious deception, to create and feed an entirely fake intelligence plan of the Allied invasion. The risks had not only been enormous, but many thousands of lives had depended on their success in duping the Germans into believing the main thrust would be centred on Calais, and not the sweeping sandy beaches of Normandy.

Spencer went over old ground in an attempt to calm things down, and tried to reassure Joyce she was still very much at the heart of their plans. The last thing he needed right now was an embittered double agent, capable of blowing the lid on the entire deception plan to her Abwehr controller. He knew Joyce had no real political allegiance to the Nazi Party, and the regime had victimised her family, but, to his mind, there'd always be a nagging doubt of uncertainty. Robertson had often described Leader as feisty and tough; he couldn't fault the description. In Spencer's opinion, she'd always moved from breezy self-confidence to darkness swiftly, but no-one could ever doubt her skill at counter-intelligence. Quite simply she'd been a godsend to British Intelligence.

Garvan had quite wisely taken a back seat; there was no point in adding fuel to the fire. Whatever he said, Joyce would probably have taken exception to it. Although judging by the sour expression on Leader's face, she'd hoped he might take a somewhat different stance and defend her corner.

Joyce knew Spencer had predicted their relationship would end in tears. She couldn't fault his logic. But, for all his astuteness, somewhere along the line, she suspected he had underestimated her feelings. Joyce needed, rather than wanted, Garvan, and for all his initial reticence, she hoped and prayed Garvan felt the same way about her. He'd already placed his career on the line by getting involved, and yet, she feared maybe her past was simply too much for him, too much of an obstacle to overcome. Realistically, perhaps there was no hope of a happy ever after for them, but right now, Joyce needed to

158

cling to the hope and belief, somehow, they could see it through to the end, and, God willing, they had a future together.

Joyce knew that Spencer was entirely sceptical about their relationship, but, in fairness, he'd played an even hand with her, he could so easily have destroyed both their lives and yet for whatever reason he'd chosen not to. At the end of the day, Spencer had decided to draw a line; there was simply more at stake than petty personal squabbles.

For all her flaws, and there were many, Spencer and the Double Cross openly acknowledged Joyce was playing a key role; she was not only smart, but a successful woman, operating in a man's world.

Chapter 15

Caro Tait had enjoyed a night out with her girlfriends. They were first and foremost work colleagues; traditionally, political allegiances to them were a secondary issue. Outside office hours, they enjoyed each other's company, and once free from the constraints of parliamentary politics, they let their hair down, and socialised on a regular basis.

Caro considered herself to be quite lucky. Many of the girls were living in shared accommodation, but her uncle, Hugo Tait, who was a leading barrister, had generously allowed her to live rent-free in the apartment above his chambers in Lincoln Inn Fields, which was reputedly the largest public square in London.

Caro pulled out a pencil torch from her handbag, and started to walk along Kingsway toward the flat. There were still a few people around. Like herself, they were mainly making their way back home after a night out. The moonlight cast a strange, almost eerie, pale light on the unlit streets; its glow glistening on pavements still damp from an earlier downpour of rain. She turned off Kingsway and into Court Lane. She was in a good mood, admittedly lightened by a couple of drinks after a rather fraught day at the office.

A run-in with Jamie Burdis about a missed appointment had caused a full-blown row between them. He blamed her for not entering it in the diary. "It might well have bloody helped if you'd bothered to tell me about it in the first place!" she'd snapped back at him. He'd defended his corner, but Caro was having none of it. She was increasingly becoming irritated by his cavalier attitude to work. It was always someone else's fault, and never his own. Burdis had a knack of wearing people down. Everyone had warned her against working for him, but she was only just beginning to see the light, and was no longer prepared to gloss over his failings, and to excuse his bad behaviour.

As she continued walking down the street, it ran through Caro's mind she'd made a dreadful mistake by turning her back on MI6. But, then again, no-one ever entirely left the Service. It was a little like being divorced, you might end up cutting the familial ties, but there remained an irrevocable link to the past. It could never be completely severed.

Caro had only walked a few yards, when a sudden sixth sense kicked in, as she realised she was being followed. She could hear the sound of footsteps behind her, whoever it was, was walking quickly. She had no evidence, other than intuition, so she crossed the narrow road. The footsteps followed; they were beginning to close fast. She carried on walking, the dim flicker of her torch shining down on the glistening pavement.

Then, she heard a noise, an all-too-familiar metallic click. She'd heard it before, and instinctively knew it was a handgun being cocked. In a split second, Caro turned, almost reluctantly, and in the pale moonlight, she could make out the silhouette of a man. He was standing stock still now, and wearing what looked like a belted raincoat, with a jauntily angled trilby hat. In the soft glimmer, it looked as if he had a handgun resting on his crooked arm, as he took aim.

A combination of training and instinct kicked in. Caro flicked off her high heels and started to run. A shot rang out; it missed, but the bullet sent sparks flying off the wall in front of her. Zigzag, that's what her instructors in Scotland had told her, over and over again. Whatever you do, don't ever run in a straight line. So, she zigzagged. *Christ would it make any difference?* It might give her a fighting chance, but then, she heard another shot ring out. It fell short this time, but only just. He was coming after her, his footsteps approaching rapidly.

Caro's breath came fast through her mouth; the will to live, to flee, flooded her mind. She ran faster than she'd

161

ever done in her entire life, fuelled by a mix of adrenaline and a deeply rooted instinct for survival. As she fled for her life down the narrow side street, it was clear her attacker was a professional. The way they had cradled the pistol over their arm to take aim spoke volumes; they'd been trained either by the Military or the Police. *But why would anyone want to kill her? What in God's name had she done, or more importantly what had she inadvertently stumbled across? What had she missed? There was something, something she should have picked up on. Had her relationship with Burdis perhaps blindsided her?*

She desperately crossed the road again. By now, Caro's lungs felt as if they were burning up. She was running hard, and didn't know what to do. She was still some way from her uncle's flat in Lincoln Inn Fields. She needed to take cover, and get out of the road. At some point, her attacker would strike lucky.

With tears streaming from her eyes, Caro knew her only real hope of surviving was if she could make it to the Three Bells pub; it wasn't that far ahead, but as another shot rang out, it was far enough. The searing pain of running barefoot seemed a small price to pay. She knew the publican, Charlie, but more importantly, she guessed her attacker probably wouldn't chance following her inside. It was a risk she had to take. Another shot rang out. It was close, too close for comfort. The sparks flew off the wall. She couldn't afford to miss a beat, and kept running until she stumbled into the doorway of the Three Bells. Caro collapsed against the wall, and fought hard to catch her breath, but there was no time to waste. Her would-be assassin was still hard on her heels.

Taking a deep breath, she pushed the door open, and as she stepped inside, half of her pain and fear began to subside. It was a place Caro knew well, and loved. It wasn't only a haven, but had always struck her as akin to taking a step back in time to the 17th century, warm and friendly, with a

162

multitude of rooms, stairs, nooks and crannies. It was all higgledy-piggledy, a baffling labyrinth of passageways and rooms; more importantly, it was her one and only chance of escaping her attacker. There were two rooms on the ground floor. To her right was a small dark-panelled bar with a fireplace and uneven floorboards, and to the left, a slightly larger area, with a scattering of circular tables and wooden booths. The place oozed atmosphere, all narrow corridors and staircases leading to bars on different floors.

She needed to find the landlord and make a phone call. From the smaller of the two rooms, she caught his voice. He was laughing and joking with a customer. On moving into the bar, she managed to catch his eye.

A look of unadulterated alarm crossed his face. 'Caro, are you okay?' he asked.

'Do you have a phone I can use?' she gasped, still fighting for breath.

'Yes, of course, I have. It's in the back,' he said, ushering her around the bar. 'Christ, what's happened? Where are your shoes?'

'Please, Charlie, not right now. I just need to make a call.'

He showed her into a tiny back room; it was furnished sparsely with a small bookcase and various ledgers spread out on a desk.

'The phone's over there,' he said, pointing to the sideboard.

'Thank you,' she murmured breathlessly.

Charlie hesitated, but as Caro glanced back over her shoulder, he sensed she wanted to be alone. She waited until the door closed, before lifting the receiver. Her hands were shaking so much she had some difficulty in dialling the number, St. James's 1219. Caro closed her eyes despairingly, and whispered, "Please God let him be there." She waited anxiously. It seemed like an age but, in reality, it wasn't. The phone rang a couple of times, before there was a click, and someone answered.

'Major Hall,' she heard him say.

'I'm in trouble, Spence,' Caro sobbed tremulously down the phone.

'What kind of trouble?'

As always, his voice sounded calm; it seemed to help. 'Someone's just tried to shoot me!'

'Where are you now?'

'At the Three Bells off Kingsway.'

'Are you calling from the bar?'

'No, I'm in one of the landlord's private rooms.'

'Whatever you do don't move. Just stay put, do you hear me!'

'I'm frightened, Spence,' she whispered.

'I'm sure you are,' he said smoothly. 'Don't worry, Caro. I'll bring Garvan along with me. We should be there in about ten minutes.'

Caro shakily replaced the receiver, and sat herself down in a rickety old chair across the room. The door from the bar gently clicked open again; she panned around, half in dread, but it was only Charlie bringing a large gin and tonic.

'There, love, get that down your throat. Do you want me to call the police?'

She smiled up at him gratefully. 'It won't be necessary, Charlie. I've taken care of everything, friends of mine, a major and a superintendent, are on their way over here, but thank you all the same.' Caro grasped the tumbler glass tightly between her hands and raised it to her lips; she swallowed before taking a deep breath. 'Do you mind if I stay here, until they arrive?'

'Why should I.' He smiled, and added gently, 'You're in a hell of a state, girl. Did someone attack you?'

'Sort of, Charlie,' she murmured, 'sort of.'

'Did you manage to see who it was?'

164

She shook her head. 'It was too dark.'

'Will you be okay sitting here by yourself?'

'Yes, I'll be fine,' she reassured him.

*

Spencer set the receiver down in the cradle, and called across the office to Garvan. 'Do you still have a handgun on issue?'

He looked up from his desk. 'Yes, why? What's happened?' he shot back at him.

'Someone's just tried to murder Caro Tait; she's hiding out at the Three Bells in Kingsway.'

By the time Garvan had reached into the bottom drawer of his desk for the gun holster, Spencer was already halfway out of the door.

A quarter of an hour later, they were pulling up outside the pub. Garvan peered curiously through the windscreen; he couldn't recall ever having visited the place before.

'Just remember to duck as you go through the doorway. It's really low,' Spencer said, turning off the ignition.

He followed him inside; the pervasive dark panelling and the rather ineffective lighting made it a little difficult trying to accustom their eyes to the gloom. There were a few customers in each of the downstairs bars having a quiet drink, but it certainly wasn't overly busy.

Spencer moved over to the main bar, and said to the tall, lean figure behind the bar, 'Would you be Charlie, by any chance?'

'Who's asking?' he replied bluntly.

Spencer introduced himself and Garvan, but Charlie still continued to eye them warily. He'd never forgive himself if anything happened to Caro. He demanded to see some form of identification. Once he was satisfied he then showed them into the backroom, where Caro was still nursing the gin and tonic.

'Thank god you're here,' she gasped, with undisguised relief.

Spencer waited until the landlord had left them alone, before introducing Garvan to her. 'So, come on. What's happened?'

Caro shakily set the glass down on the floor beside the chair, and briefly closed her eyes, before recalling how she'd heard the tell-tale metallic clunk of a handgun as it was engaged, to the moment, she frantically kicked off her high heels, and of zig-zagging back and forth across the road in a desperate bid to escape as bullets ricocheted all around her.

'It sounds as if you've been bloody lucky,' Spencer said evenly.

'Lucky isn't the word; it's a miracle I'm still alive!'

'They obviously knew what they were doing.

'They were certainly professional.'

Spencer thoughtfully compressed his lips together. Professional maybe, but it ran through his mind if he'd been ordered to take Caro out, she'd certainly never have reached the Three Bells alive. Now was not the time to argue the toss. He kept his thoughts to himself, although judging by the look in Garvan's eyes, he was probably thinking along much the same lines.

'We need to get you out of here,' Spencer said, dredging up a half smile. 'We're sitting ducks in this place.'

'But, where can we go to?' she inquired tentatively.

'You know the drill, Caro.'

'You mean, a safe house?'

'There's no other way.'

'But, my clothes…I mean, look at me,' she whimpered, staring forlornly down at her torn stockings.

'No exceptions, Caro, not even for you. We'll have someone drop by your flat tomorrow morning to pick up a few things.'

The set expression on his face said it all; he was in no mood to start arguing with her. His mind was made up, and no matter how much she might want to collect a night bag, realistically, she knew without their help, she certainly wouldn't be able to make it out of the pub, at least not alive. Whoever tried to kill her was probably still loitering in the vicinity, and hadn't given up all hope of finally sealing the deal.

Spencer asked the landlord to re-join them; he wanted to know if there was a rear exit to the pub. Charlie explained there was a turning directly behind the Three Bells, called Chamber Mews, although it was even narrower than Court Lane. He assured them it was just wide enough to drive a car down.

'Good,' Spencer said briskly. 'I'll meet you round the back.'

'I'll keep the delivery door bolted, until you pull up,' Charlie suggested.

'Thank you.'

Spencer passed through the bar, and back out into Court Lane; he'd already taken the precaution of loosening his PPK from its holster, and checking to see there was a round in the chamber. As he was unlocking the car, he caught a sharp movement out of the corner of his eye, as if he'd taken someone by surprise. He could only assume it was Caro's attacker. Spencer didn't react; there was no point. He didn't doubt whoever it was may well have been professionally trained, but they certainly weren't in the first division, otherwise he'd have been dead as soon as he'd stepped back outside the pub. That, in itself, was curious, but also significant. Whoever was lurking in the shadows had already had ample opportunity to take a pot shot at him. If they were going to do it, they'd have done so by now. Even so he had no intention of releasing his grip on the PPK, until he'd started the car.

He pressed the ignition and slammed his foot to the floor, speeding off out of Court Lane and taking a sharp right into Chambers Mews. The landlord hadn't been joking about how narrow the Mews was. It was a fairly tight squeeze.

Not wanting to overshoot the rear of the pub, he started to slow down. He could just make out the silhouetted shape of a beer barrel up ahead. He headed down the mews, and drew up beside it, keeping the engine turning over. True to his word on hearing the car outside, the landlord hurriedly unbolted the back door to let Garvan and Caro out of the pub.

'Thank you,' she mouthed to Charlie.

'My pleasure, love,' he called after her, in a muted voice.

'Get a move on,' Garvan said urgently. He opened the rear door, and almost bundled her inside.

Once Garvan was safely beside him, Spencer slammed the accelerator pedal to the floor again, and shot out of the Mews toward the relative safety of Kingsway. With its large tram terminus and tube station, he figured from here on in there was little chance of being intercepted.

A quarter of an hour later, they were entering a smart Edwardian red brick apartment block in Chelsea. From behind the reception desk, the middle-aged concierge sprang to his feet. His demeanour and ramrod straight bearing reeked of his being ex-military. The block contained several apartments leased permanently to British Intelligence via a faux holding company, and as a precautionary measure, the concierge staff was to a man in the pay of the security services. It was quite a lucrative deal, as they were also in receipt of a separate salary from the landlord.

'Good evening, sir,' the concierge barked at Spencer.

'Long time no see, Ralph. How's the wife?'

'She's in fine fettle.'

Spencer allowed a slow bemused smile to cross his face; Ralph's marriage had been volatile from day one. In fact, throughout their time together serving in the Commandos, the state of Ralph's marital problems had been something of a running joke. After being invalided out, Spencer had recommended him when a post became available at the apartment block.

'I'd like the keys to No 15,' he said.

Ralph reached beneath the reception desk, and handed over the keys. 'Are we expecting a long stay, sir?'

'Hard to say, Ralph, but if you could arrange for the flat to be serviced until the end of the week, that should about cover it.'

'Yes, sir.'

'If we need it any longer, the office will let you know.'

The elegantly furnished flat was situated on the first floor, and overlooked the street above the main entrance. Spencer flicked on the light switch, leaving Garvan to shut the heavy blackout curtains. Caro promptly excused herself, and headed off in search of the bathroom to remove her tattered stockings, and bathe her bruised and bloodied feet.

Over the last year, or so, a girlfriend of Caro's had managed to secure a steady supply of nylons from her American GI boyfriend, but since Operation Overlord, the handsome young man had found himself battling his way across occupied Europe, and sadly, their treasured supply of stockings had all but dried up. Caro found herself staring thoughtfully at her reflection in the bathroom mirror. She began to smile almost wistfully. *Had she really become so fatuous she was more worried about a stockpile of nylons than the young man who was serving with the 82nd Airborne in France?* God knew if he was still alive.

169

It was a reality check, and Caro needed to get a grip and think fast. *Somewhere, she'd crossed the line, but what line? Had she perhaps unwittingly stumbled across Toniolo's identity?* It was possible, of course, or maybe, there had been another motive for tonight's attack.

As Burdis's diary secretary, she'd been dubbed "the keeper of the secrets," but from Caro's perspective that was down to his sordid personal life, rather than any threat to National Security. Either way, there was no escaping the fact she'd inadvertently come across something important. She wasn't a fool, far from it. Perhaps Spencer was right. Her close relationship with Burdis had possibly clouded her professional judgment. Spencer thought it had; she was treading water almost to the point of drowning. Becoming romantically entangled with Burdis, whose reputation was mired in controversy, had placed her in an untenable position with her ex-intelligence colleagues.

Spencer phoned the duty officer at St. James's, Captain Eldridge. 'When do you get off duty?'

'Twelve-thirty.'

'I need you over at the Chelsea block by one.'

There was a pause. 'Sir, I've only had two hours sleep in the last twenty-four hours.'

Spencer cut him dead. 'Then count yourself bloody lucky!

'I'm sorry, sir?' he answered.

Spencer had a short fuse, but Eldridge's response hadn't exactly helped his mood any. He'd missed the point. 'There are thousands of men like you in France right now, who consider themselves lucky just to be alive, let alone the luxury of waking up in their own bed.'

Spencer slammed the phone down.

When Caro returned to the drawing room, she knew the questions would begin. Almost reluctantly, she padded barefoot across the thickly carpeted floor, and settled herself

170

down in an armchair beside a large mock Georgian fireplace. By now, Spencer had discovered a fully stocked drinks cabinet, and was rubbing his hands together in anticipation. He poured two bourbons and soda, before glancing over his shoulder toward Caro.

'I presume you'll have your usual?'

She smiled; it was answer enough she rarely drank anything other than gin.

He dispensed the drinks, and sat on the small sofa beside Garvan. 'I've asked Captain Eldridge to drop by after he comes off duty at St. James's.' Spencer announced.

She looked at him questioningly.

'As a stop gap, I've asked him to stay overnight, until we can arrange around the clock cover.'

For some reason, the sudden enormity of her situation began to dawn on Caro. She had a strong comprehension of the intelligence game, but, in the past, the boot had always been on the other foot. She'd always been tasked with providing cover for other people, but this was getting personal, and serious.

It kept playing on her mind she'd missed something; perhaps her once renowned skills as an agent were beginning to slip. She'd been out of the system for a little while now; maybe she was becoming a little rusty. The only thing Caro knew definitively was Spencer had been disappointed by her decision to turn her back on the intelligence community; it still hurt her he hadn't found it in himself to forgive her. She needed his approval and his affirmation far more than she cared to admit, but it wasn't forthcoming.

She feared there was more chance of hell freezing over before he ever forgave her. A large part of her regretted leaving. If you wanted excitement, Spencer was your man. There was always something going on; it had never been dull.

Caro could understand his anger, but at the time, she'd desperately wanted to distance herself from the almost

171

claustrophobic atmosphere, and the intolerable pressures of working for British Intelligence. The only saving grace was although she was no longer current, they still used her services on an ad hoc basis, even if sometimes that involved her spying upon Jamie Burdis. She fully accepted her reputation had been tarnished irrevocably by having a sexual relationship with Burdis. Things could never be quite the same again, and there'd always remain an element of doubt regarding her ultimate reliability and loyalty to the Service.

The only unknown quantity in the mix this evening was Garvan. On first impressions, he seemed very constrained and somewhat taciturn in his approach. His eyes were watchful, but it was near nigh impossible to read his face. Caro knew Spencer and Robertson highly regarded him; he certainly came with quite a formidable reputation from Scotland Yard.

She calmly looked at each of them in turn and decided to break the ice. 'I still can't quite fathom out why anyone would want me dead.'

'I think you probably do,' Garvan said evenly. 'It's just you haven't figured it out yet.'

Caro blinked at him. She watched him as he took his time slipping a pack of cigarettes out of his hip pocket; he then offered one to Spencer, before slipping a cigarette between his lips.

'I know you didn't get much of a chance, but are you able to describe your attacker?' he asked.

Caro took a deep breath. 'No, not really, I suppose, looking back, he didn't seem overly tall,' she decided, 'and slim, yes, very slim.' She made a face. 'I'm sorry, that's about it. I didn't exactly hang around long enough to get a good look at him.'

'Has anything out of the ordinary happened lately, either at your flat or work?' he said, flicking on his lighter.

'Not that I can think of. Nothing springs to mind.'

'Tell me something,' he said, blowing out a cloud of grey smoke, 'did Jamie Burdis know before becoming his secretary you worked for British Intelligence?'

'I didn't think it was relevant. It's not something you exactly go around advertising, is it?'

'That's not what I asked.'

Caro considered her reply carefully, and reluctantly admitted when Burdis was serving as a junior Minister at the Foreign Office, Jeremy Haining had once asked him if he wasn't a little concerned his secretary might be spying on him. Jamie hadn't known what the hell he was talking about, and so, Haining had taken some pleasure in enlightening him.

'Did that happen before, or after, you became lovers?' Garvan queried.

It was a sensitive subject with her, and she seemed disinclined to give him a straight answer, but Spencer intervened, and said to her sharply, 'Well, Caro, was it?'

As she looked at him, her eyes were stormy. 'What's that got to do with anything?'

'Just answer the question,' he said curtly.

'If you must know, it was before.'

'And how long after was it you started sleeping with him?' Garvan asked.

'I don't know what you're driving at.'

Garvan gave her a little, bitter smile. 'I should imagine, at the time, it must have been a bit of a body blow for him. One way or another, his time at the FO wasn't exactly crowned in glory; he managed to upset most of the staff, including Haining, who was agitating to have him removed from office. On top of everything else, it must have come as quite a shock to discover his secretary, of all people, the one person he'd hoped was on his side, might well be a part of the problem, and feeding his enemies with information.'

She gave an indifferent shrug. 'I can't deny it wasn't tricky for a while. There was a week, or so, when he actively

173

started looking for someone else to fill my shoes.' She thoughtfully sucked in her lower lip, before saying, 'But that's all in the past now. Eventually, I managed to convince him I was no longer an active member of the Service.'

'I guess sleeping with him must have helped.'

She shot Garvan a withering look, and said candidly, 'Let's just say, it didn't do my cause any harm.'

'No, I don't suppose it did, but the fact remains, you were spying on him.'

Caro fixed him with a hard-eyed stare. 'Unlike Jeremy Haining, Jamie, fortunately, doesn't realise you can never entirely divorce yourself from the intelligence community. I was simply doing General Menzies a favour by keeping an eye on Jamie.'

'Is that why you reported the break-in at your office to Menzies. Rather than going through the usual channels?'

'In my experience, Superintendent, cutting out the middleman tends to get better results. It was evident someone had deliberately taken the one piece of correspondence I was bound to miss.' She shot Spencer a rather quizzical look. 'I don't suppose that was your idea, was it?'

He smirked. 'If your political career is in freefall, a summons to have lunch from the Chief Whip's office is almost as rare as hen's teeth.'

'You've always been a clever *bastard*!'

'It's what I'm paid for.'

She didn't respond.

'I take it you've told Burdis about the break-in?' Garvan pressed her.

'I didn't have a choice. The invite had come in late that afternoon, and I hadn't entered it into my diary. I couldn't remember the timings, or anything. So, one way, or another, I reckoned he'd find out eventually, so I called the Chief Whip's office to get another copy.'

'Wouldn't they have covered your back?'

'It's not that easy. Maybe if I worked for someone else other than Jamie, then I could have wangled something, but he's not exactly favourite of the month with either the Chief Whip or his outer office.'

Garvan thought it seemed plausible enough, so he decided to change tact. 'How serious is it between you?'

Caro threw her head back and laughed. 'Whatever else I am, Superintendent, I'm not a bloody fool. I know how things are with him. So, in answer to your question, no, it's not serious at all. Jamie has his own agenda, and I'm not on it.'

Garvan held the cigarette lightly between his fingers, and said almost casually, 'Recently, one of Colonel Robertson's agents was asked to set a honey trap.'

She looked at him with narrow-eyed curiosity, and said, with a certain amount of resignation etched in her voice, 'Do you mean with Jamie?'

He nodded.

She let out a peel of laughter. 'Christ, that wouldn't have been too difficult to set up!'

Despite her apparent amusement, Garvan noticed there was a hint of undisguised annoyance etched across her face. Caro might claim there was nothing serious between them, but her reactions showed she was not being entirely honest with them. Caro didn't need to ask whether Robertson's agent had been successful. She knew her subject; it was a given Burdis had fallen for her, hook, line, and sinker.

'At his flat, they found a letter embossed with the design of a pentagram with the "Lilburne Club" printed beneath it. I've passed a copy of it to Central Registry, but, so far, they've drawn a complete blank about the Club.'

Caro rolled her eyes rather dramatically. 'They must be slipping since my days,' she sniped.

Spencer interrupted sharply. 'Since your days with the Service, Caro, things have moved on a pace.' His eyes bore into her conscience. 'After the invasion, even *you* must realise they've got more than enough on their plates. Looking for some random club isn't exactly their highest priority. In fact, in their eyes, it's probably not a priority at all.'

He met her gaze in an almost expressionless way. She guessed it vaguely masked his disapproval of her leaving the Service, and then ending up with someone of Burdis's somewhat dubious qualities. Ultimately, Caro knew Spencer thought she'd let not only MI6 down, but had also let herself down. He looked at her searchingly; he'd known Caro long enough to sense she was not entirely open with them. He suspected somewhere along the line, her misplaced loyalty toward Burdis had badly clouded her judgment, even to her detriment. Whatever the reason, Caro was holding back about something.

Garvan asked. 'What *do* you know about the Lilburne Club?'

She gave an indifferent shrug. 'From what I can gather, the five points of the pentagram represent its five founding members.'

'Anything else?'

'Not much, really.'

'Go on.'

'When I started working for Jamie, we went over his diary. The first Saturday of June was always ring-fenced for a Club dinner. It was usually, although not exclusively, held at a private dining club in Westminster. I questioned him about it, and asked him what it was all about. He told me he'd joined the Lilburne during his time at Cambridge University. Apparently, at his initiation, he was briefed on the Club's history and tradition, and then signed a leather-bound diary they called, "The Book," which all former members had signed, followed by a vow of secrecy. Jamie described it as a way of making contacts, but I guess that's no different from any other society or club at Oxbridge. To be perfectly honest with you, I think it was primarily a dining club, with some obscure political overtones.' She gave them the impression of being a little unsure of herself.

'Political overtones…what's that supposed to mean?' Garvan queried.

'The Club was named after a Civil War Army officer, John Lilburne. According to Jamie, he was regarded as extreme, even by his own side. He was an agitator, who coined the term, "freeborn rights." She hesitated, uncertainly. 'From what I could gather, the Club's mantra was about equality and suffrage for all, with a twist.'

Garvan raised his eyes questioningly. 'What twist?'

'The twist being the Club's members viewed Lilburne's extremism as being on a par with the organisation of the Soviet Army during the Russian Revolution.'

'So, membership was restricted to students with Soviet sympathies?'

She bit her lip thoughtfully, 'I never asked the question, but I guess so.'

Spencer slowly twisted his glass, and stared at the bourbon. 'I'm beginning to believe it's probably just as well you decided to leave the Intelligence Service when you did.' He raised his eyes, and thoughtfully examined her face. 'Why, in God's name, didn't you mention all this to us before now? You must have realised there might be a connection to our Soviet spy!'

Caro started to grope for the right words; she was on the back foot. 'I thought it was an open secret, as a young man, Jamie had Communist leanings. I believe, at the time, it was almost fashionable amongst his set.'

'But, we didn't know about the Lilburne Club,' Garvan said.

'I wasn't to know that. Besides, it's all in the past now.'

'Is it?' Garvan asked bluntly.

Spencer drained his glass. 'Who else attended these annual get-togethers, beside Burdis?' he asked sharply.

'Lord, I can't remember.'

'Then, you'd better start bloody trying, hadn't you!'

Spencer eased himself off the sofa, and began to pace to and fro. Her gaze followed him around the room. Caro suspected, if she'd been a man, he'd have probably throttled her by now.

'I know the Club keeps a record of all past and present members.'

'Have you seen a copy?'

'I think Jamie has one, but I suppose they all have one.'

Spencer pulled up sharply, and rounded on her. 'Don't lie to me, Caro. Have you seen a copy?' he repeated.

'Yes, yes, I have.'

'Then, stop defending your boyfriend, and tell us the truth!'

'I can't remember all the names, it was ages ago,' she snapped back at him.

'But, did any of the names stand out; was there anyone you knew?' It was less a question than a demand.

She considered her reply. 'There were one, or two, yes.'

He moved toward her, and angrily thumped a clenched fist on the table beside her chair, sending her glass crashing to the floor. Caro almost jumped out of her skin, and instinctively recoiled. 'L-Lucern,' she stammered. 'Frank's name was on it; that's all I remember,' she pleaded with him.

Spencer shot Garvan a look; they hadn't bargained on Lucern having once held Communist sympathies. Maybe it was on his personal file, but Colonel Robertson certainly hadn't brought it to their attention.

'What about Lord Oakways? Was his name on the list?'

She shook her head. 'The Club was created way after his time at Cambridge, but I do recall seeing Simon Paxton was a member.'

They both looked at her blankly.

'Paxton was the maiden name of Oakways's wife, Laura. Simon was her brother.'

'So, there was a connection of sorts,' Spencer said.

There was a knock on the door; it was Captain Eldridge.

'I'm sorry,' he apologised. 'I would have been here earlier, but I've had to walk the...'

Spencer raised his hand to silence him; he wasn't in the mood for excuses. 'Have you met Caro Tait before?' he asked abruptly.

'Yes, sir.'

'Good, then we'll leave you to it.' He turned once more to Caro. 'Whoever tried to kill you tonight, will certainly not give up, until either we track them down, or they succeed in finishing you off.' He cast Caro a cold, probing stare. 'I don't know what kind of game you're playing with us, Caro, but whatever loyalty you may, or may not, feel toward Burdis is misplaced. I think even you know, he'd drop you like a ton of bricks, if he thought there was anything to gain by it.'

Caro didn't respond, but stared at him in mute silence. He still felt Caro held the key to identifying the gunman, and, by default, Agent Toniolo.

As Spencer closed the door to the flat on them, her eyes suddenly began to burn with tears. He was right, of course. Jamie's only real loyalty was to himself, and no one else, not even to his wife or children.

179

Chapter 16

With Caro Tait safely out of harm's way at MI5's flat in Chelsea, questions were bound to be asked about her sudden disappearance, not least from her boss. When she failed to turn up for work, he naturally called her flat in Lincoln's Inn, her friends, in fact, just about anyone he could think of, including, as a last resort, Jeremy Haining. Only then did he finally pick up the phone to the police, and formally report his secretary's disappearance. The matter was transferred immediately to Special Branch, and it was DCI Mackenzie who returned his call.

Fortunately, Spencer had already briefed Mackenzie about the attempt on Caro's life, and that MI5 had forbidden outside contact with anyone, not even with her own family. It was simply too risky, without knowing the identity of Caro's would-be killer. For all they knew, Burdis might well have paid someone to have her murdered.

When Mackenzie returned Burdis's call, he'd sounded concerned, and made all the right noises. Burdis had sounded not only on edge, but was downright rude. He'd played it calmly, but it was obvious, for whatever reason, Burdis had taken an instant dislike to him, but, by all accounts, he was in good company. Their somewhat terse conversation had ended with Burdis shouting the odds down the phone, and demanding action.

Burdis seemed to have convinced himself Caro's sudden disappearance was part of a wider establishment conspiracy against him. It possibly hadn't helped any when Haining advised him to keep a firm lid on his temper, or he'd end up making himself as much of a laughing stock as Oakways had. Even his staunchest allies on the Tory backbenches privately warned him to play it carefully, and not create too many waves. Perhaps, they weren't willing to place their necks on the line, by openly supporting his conspiracy theory. Apart from anything else, it seemed way too far-fetched to be taken seriously. Like Haining, they advised him to tackle the problem with an open mind, and to drop his customary bull in a china shop attitude, especially with the police. Unfortunately, since being dismissed to the backbenches, he'd found himself increasingly isolated, and any real support for him had long since haemorrhaged. Many of his fellow Tory MPs believed, rightly or wrongly, they might end up being tainted by association.

Rumour had it Burdis's wife, Jenny, had arrived unexpectedly from their palatial family home in Kent. Garvan speculated he'd probably had the audacity to ask for her support, while the police searched for his erstwhile mistress. In spite of his endless affairs, the intelligence reports indicated Jenny remained unaccountably loyal to him. There had to be something about the man to inspire such loyalty, but for the life of him, he couldn't see what it was that attracted a legion of women to a man, who was not only egotistical and selfish, but treated them with oafish disdain.

Garvan couldn't help wondering how much of an effect the note from Toniolo had played on Burdis's already tattered nerves. It was a sheer stroke of luck Michelle Rookwood had managed to find it at his flat. Although short on content the fact it had mentioned that "*the hyenas were circling,*" presumably served to increase his growing paranoia about an establishment conspiracy. That Burdis was embroiled in some kind of Soviet spy ring was now generally accepted within MI5.

*

By the time Garvan pulled up outside Bolton's Bank in Mayfair, there were already a number of police cars parked on either side of the road. The local uniformed coppers were in the throes of cordoning off the area. A tall, rather imposing sergeant approached his unmarked vehicle. Garvan wound down the window.

'I'm afraid you can't park there, sir.'

As he flashed a warrant card at him, the sergeant visibly blanched, took a respectful step back from the car, and opened the driver's door. 'I'm sorry, sir. Had I known.'

Garvan raised his hand to silence him. 'It's not a problem. Can you let me know where DCI Mackenzie is?'

'Yes, sir. He's with the bank manager.'

Garvan climbed out of the car, and stood for a while, appraising the scene. In the middle of the road, the lid of a manhole cover had been removed. A plain clothes detective was kneeling beside the circular hole in the road, and was talking to a disembodied voice somewhere in the gloom below. A red post office van was parked to the right of the bank, its back doors were open, and the bodywork was peppered in a zig-zag pattern of bullet holes. It seemed unlikely anyone sitting inside of the van would have survived.

Noting Garvan's interest, the Sergeant explained, 'It's the gang's getaway vehicle.'

Garvan nodded, and said sardonically, 'Only, I take it, they didn't get away?'

'No, sir. Two dead and three in custody.'

He looked at him questioningly.

'The two occupants of the van are dead, sir, but we found the others in the tunnel beneath the manhole.'

'Did any of the gang manage to escape?'

'Yes, sir. We know there was another van on its way to help stash the haul. Whoever it was had a lucky escape. We believe they probably heard the commotion, and sped off before they turned into Davis Street.'

Garvan thanked him, and headed across the road to the Bank. Inside, two female cashiers were being comforted by a male colleague. Across the lobby, he caught the eye of a plain clothes detective, who was hovering anxiously outside the bank manager's office.

'Where's DCI Mackenzie?' he demanded.

The young man gestured toward the door. 'He's interviewing the manager, Mr. Carrington.'

Garvan crossed the lobby.

The Detective stood his ground. 'I'm sorry, sir, but you can't go in.'

Garvan smiled to himself; he really ought to start thinking of getting himself back to Scotland Yard. The trouble was the young, up and coming, wet behind their ears officers didn't recognise him at all, but, then again, there was no reason why they should; he'd joined the Intelligence Service back in 1941. They were relatively new to the Force, and he had no right to be offended, but, even so, his reputation still commanded respect.

'Just tell your Guv'nor Superintendent Garvan's here to see him.'

The colour instantly drained from the young man's face. 'Yes, yes, of course, sir,' he stammered, and knocked on the door.

Hearing Mackenzie answer, Garvan brushed past him. The manager gave every sign of bristling at the interruption, but calmed down somewhat after being introduced to the tall, imposing figure framed in the doorway. In fact, Head Office would be gratified Scotland Yard appeared to be taking the attempted robbery of their Davis Street Branch so seriously, with not only a DCI but a Superintendent in attendance.

'Please excuse us,' Mackenzie said to Carrington.

'Yes of course,' he said expansively.

As they stepped outside into the lobby, Gavan asked, 'What's going on Harry?'

'The gang managed to tunnel their way into the vaults below the bank from the street. It looks as if they weren't only targeting money, but also the safety deposit boxes.'

Garvan looked at him speculatively. 'Why has Special Branch been called in?'

'DCI Venables from West End Central decided to hand it over to us.'

'Why?'

'Up the road at Claridge's, there are many resident exiled royals and wealthy refugees sitting out the war. Most of them apparently use Bolton's Bank for stashing away not only their ready cash but also jewellery and government gilts. By the state of the vault, it's the safety deposit boxes they were targeting. Venables had a tip-off while the raid was going on. Whomever gave him the heads up was spot-on. They must have been tunnelling through to the vault for some time. The manager said there's been a gas van parked near the manhole cover for the last two weeks, or so, and on most days, there were up to half a dozen blokes working there. At the time, he thought nothing of it, why would he? They seemed a pleasant enough bunch, and always made a point of passing the time of day with him and his staff. To make it look good, the buggers even dug up part of the road, and then used the tunnels under the manhole cover to dig their way into the vault. To be honest, it's a pretty classy job.'

'By the look of the Post Office van, I take it they didn't get away with anything?'

'No,' Harry said. 'Thankfully, we pretty much had a clean sweep.'

Garvan smiled slightly. 'Do you know you're almost beginning to make me feel nostalgic? But, I don't understand why you called me in.'

Mac returned his smile. 'I've got something for you in the vault.'

Mac asked the bank manager to join them. They made their way down three flights of stairs into the bowels of the building; one of the local coppers was guarding the entrance to the vault. They passed through two large heavily-plated doors, before reaching the vault itself. Garvan's gaze glided around the surprisingly large area. In the centre of the floor was a hole surrounded by rubble, where the gang had successfully broken in. The entire area was banked with safety deposit boxes, most of which appeared to have been broken into by drilling through the locks.

Carrington explained Bolton Bank's policy was anything could be held in the box; the only stipulation was customers were required to sign a document stating they wouldn't contain anything illegal, such as stolen goods, money, or guns. Garvan arched his brows questioningly. Whatever document the bank required the key holders to sign, didn't exactly guarantee the legality of the contents or the honesty of its clients. It was perhaps naivety on the bank's part, or more likely the vault had proved a lucrative way of making easy money, and they'd deliberately chosen to turn a blind eye and hope for the best by covering themselves with a signed declaration.

Garvan's eyes travelled slowly across the vault. Each of the boxes was numbered, and from past experience, he knew people used them to stash away their jewellery, cash, wills, deeds, confidential papers, and anything they deemed to be important. Carrington explained they also offered a mail receiving service.

Garvan's eyebrows rose in surprise; that was a new one on him. 'How does that work?'

'Since the outbreak of the war, many of our customers have been dispersed.'

'You mean, refugees?'

'Yes, I suppose you could describe it as being like the left luggage service at railway stations, only with us, they pick up their mail, when, and if, they can.'

'No questions asked?' Garvan asked.

'They've paid for the service.'

'Even so, doesn't that leave the bank wide open to criminal activity?'

'We vet our customers,' Carrington said indignantly.

'You mean, if their cheques bounce, you don't accept them. I know how it works,' Garvan said dismissively.

Carrington chose not to respond.

'What about proof of identity?'

'We require sight of a passport or an identity card, in fact, any legal document. We also record their address and occupation, although,' he added proudly, 'most of our customers have a private income.'

Garvan made no comment; a private income was hardly proof of innocence, and in many cases, was likely to have been phoney.

'You have to understand, Superintendent,' Carrington continued in some distress, as he looked round the vault, 'we have some *very* important customers. We go to great lengths at Bolton's to ensure they have unlimited access and privacy during opening hours.' He pointed to a small cubicle in the right-hand corner. 'The room is available to our customers to view the contents of their safety deposit boxes in complete privacy. We only allow one person in the vault at any one time during the visit, so their valuables are always kept private. Discretion is our byword, Superintendent.'

'Only someone else had other ideas,' Garvan observed drily.

He decided to take a closer look, and moved further into the vault, peering into the large hole in the centre of the thick concrete floor; it was surrounded by rubble where the gang had broken through. Strewn across the floor were discarded paperwork and boxes, which had once contained valuable items, presumably the stolen loot was still sitting in the back of the post office van. The sheer scale of the operation was more than slick. To Garvan's mind, there were

186

only two outfits in London capable of mounting such a raid. His gut instinct was it had all the hallmarks of Charlie Price's outfit. Charlie ruled the West End's underworld with a rod of iron, and bribed whoever he needed to employ on high-profile heists, be it architects, surveyors, or even bank employees.

Garvan glanced back over his shoulder, and said to Mackenzie, 'It's got to be Price's gang. What do you think?' he asked Mackenzie.

Mac grinned. 'You haven't lost your touch, Guv; we've already picked up a couple of his boys.'

There was no doubt Charlie would have a cast iron alibi; he always did, and if past experiences were anything to go by, his gang to a man would keep their mouths sealed, for he inspired more fear and loyalty than any other gangland leader in London. If they squealed to the police, retribution would be swift and unforgiving. They knew it was far safer to keep your mouth shut and do your time in Dartmoor.

Garvan stared down into the dark void in the floor, and announced, 'It's got to be an inside job.'

Carrington nervously cleared his throat. 'I'm sorry, what do you mean, an inside job?'

'Do I have to spell it out for you?'

'Are you seriously accusing a member of *my* staff?'

Garvan pointed toward the rubble surrounding the hole in the floor. 'What do you think? What are the odds of the gang breaking through in the centre of the vault? Without some kind of inside help, it's got to be a million to one! You have to face up to it, Mr. Carrington, somewhere along the line, the gang must have had access to a blueprint of the bank's layout. Either from an employee or a contractor, a surveyor perhaps, but they couldn't have done this without inside help.'

Carrington found himself staring bleakly toward the hole. He folded his arms, not quite defiantly; it was more of a defensive gesture. It suddenly dawned on him the police report would trigger an internal enquiry. Questions would be asked, and heads would roll, and if he was found wanting, he'd undoubtedly end up either without a job, or demoted to some backwater in the suburbs.

Garvan turned to Mackenzie. 'What have you got for me?'

Harry pointed to a safety deposit box, No B121. It had been broken into by the gang, but its contents had been virtually left untouched, aside from some letters. Garvan reached inside and rifled through the correspondence. It didn't take him long to realise Mackenzie had come up trumps. It was obvious the safety deposit box had been used for receiving and distributing mail between Toniolo and not only the Lilburne Club, but, at least one other agent.

Mackenzie joined him at the box, and pointed out one particular letter.

Garvan unfolded the letter. The wording was somewhat cryptic, but there was little doubting the recipient's identity. The Lilburne Club logo headed the paper. It began "Dear J," and beside it had been drawn a well-endowed matchstick figure with a cartoon bubble, and inside it was written in blue ink, "*the Loins of Westminster.*" The figure obviously alluded to Burdis's nickname in Whitehall. Garvan shot Mackenzie a look. Whomever wrote it was either supremely confident they'd never be discovered, or perhaps guilty of becoming over complacent. "From your old colleague in arms. Keep the faith. We will prevail against those who wish to harm us. Everything seems well. The Plebs at MI5 still appear to be floundering. I have deposited the usual amount (£100) directly into your rainy day account. I cannot guarantee when the next payment will be received. Our friends appear to be having something of a cash flow crisis at the moment, but as you're currently in semi-retirement, it strikes me as something of an added bonus they are still happy to continue paying you for the foreseeable future. I suppose in the longer term, they view the payment as a retainer, until such time as you'll be able to lead a somewhat more active life. Kindest regards Toniolo."

There were a couple of other letters referring to enclosed payments. They were all undated, but they could also have been aimed at other Soviet agents. Presumably, the bankrolls had been snatched by the gang, and were now stashed in the back of the Post Office van.

'Is this how you found it?' Garvan asked.

'No,' Mackenzie confessed. 'The Burdis one was inside a sealed envelope. I guess it was waiting to be picked up.'

'What made you open it?'

Mackenzie pointed toward the back of the deposit box, where there was a pile of blank blue headed notepaper bearing the embossed pentagram of the Lilburne Club. 'It was lying beside them.'

'Is a member of staff detailed to accompany customers to the vault?' Garvan questioned the manager.

Carrington explained the boxes were always unlocked in their presence, and it was either his or the deputy manager's responsibility. Customers could also nominate another party to have full access to their safety deposit box.

'Do you hold the original keys at the bank?'

'No, we don't.'

'How many keys are there for each box?'

'Two. They're unique for each deposit box.'

'I don't suppose you happen to know off the top of your head who hired B121?'

'As a matter of fact, I do. Mr. Michael O'Hanlon was one of our more regular clients, a very pleasant man.'

Garvan and Mackenzie exchanged glances; the significance was completely lost on Carrington.

'Was a second key issued to anyone?'

'Yes, yes, there was.'

189

'Do you have a name?' Garvan asked impatiently.

The manager thought for a moment. 'Mr. Shaw Jones. A charming man, he's here quite often, in fact, far more so than Mr. O'Hanlon.'

Garvan rolled his eyes. 'Do you think that's his real name?'

Carrington looked perplexed. 'We, I mean, I had no reason to doubt him, either of them. Their documentation was completely above board. We're very strict about security here, Superintendent.'

'You could drive a bloody double decker bus through your bank's security!'

'You think they had something to do with the robbery?'

Garvan didn't give him a direct answer. 'I guarantee you whatever documents O'Hanlon and Jones showed you, were forged.'

Carrington looked genuinely horrified, and didn't quite know how to counter the accusation. His eyes were hostile, mixed with a degree of uncertainty. 'You didn't answer my question, Superintendent. Do you believe they were behind the robbery?'

'No, Mr. Carrington, I do not. It's far worse than that.'

'Worse, what's worse than this?' he exclaimed. 'But, for the grace of God, they might have made off with the entire contents of the vault!'

'Well, I'm afraid, Mr. Carrington, right now, I think that's probably the least of your problems.'

Carrington looked completely nonplussed.

'I take it you retain a list of your key holders?' Mac asked.

'Yes, of course. It's in my office.'

'I'd be interested to know what information they gave on their declaration forms.'

'Would someone like to tell me what's really going on here?'

'Unfortunately, sir, the contents of Mr. O'Hanlon's safety deposit box have ratcheted up the stakes.'

Carrington was almost afraid to ask, but he did.

'It's a matter of National Security,' Mackenzie said bluntly.

Just when he was on the point of believing his day couldn't get any worse, it just had. 'I don't know what to say,' he rasped.

'We'll need access to the banks records, and a full description of O'Hanlon and Jones.'

'Yes, of course, Chief Inspector.'

Garvan wandered back across the vault, and once again peered into the large dark abyss in the floor; there was a wooden ladder propped up against the side of the tunnel, and a discarded torch amongst the rubble. 'We'll also need access to the remainder of the boxes.'

'You can't do that,' Carrington spluttered in alarm. It's…it's against the bank's policy.'

'I don't particularly care about the bank's policy.'

'You'll need a search warrant.'

'I think it's a bit late for that, don't you?' Garvan said, looking at the unholy mess strewn across the vault's floor. 'Of course, if you insist we can go through the formalities, but, either way, I'll gain access to every last shred.'

'I'll have to let Head Office know.'

'You can do what you like,' he said dismissively. 'But, I'm sure Bolton's Head Office wouldn't wish to impede an investigation of National Security.'

'No, no, of course not, but I'll have to inform them all the same. This has come as a terrible shock to the bank.'

Garvan wasn't interested in Carrington's internal problems with Bolton's Head Office. He made to leave the vault, but as an afterthought, turned back and said to Mackenzie, 'I think it wouldn't hurt releasing this to the Press, you know. A few well-chosen headlines in the morning might help rattle a few cages.'

'What about the bank?' the manager blustered.

'What about it?'

'I don't think you realise our reputation is at stake here; we can't have this splashed all over the headlines.'

'There's more at stake here than the bank's reputation,' he parried dismissively.

Garvan passed Mackenzie a smile and disappeared out of the vault. A few well-placed editorials would serve the double purpose of not only, alerting Toniolo, and his cohorts about the raid, but that Scotland Yard might have discovered their means of communication.

Chapter 17

While Garvan was still inspecting the extent of the robbery at Bolton's Bank. Spencer was being escorted into Jeremy's Haining's impressive office at the Foreign Office. Precious government-owned works of art once lined the walls, but since the outbreak of the war, the priceless paintings, along with the porcelain and silver, had been removed and stored in a deep Welsh mineshaft. Although sparsely decorated, Haining still managed to retain a certain lifestyle. Immediately behind his desk stood a large antique mahogany cabinet; the doors were open, revealing a well-stocked supply of spirits. Spencer's eyes alighted on the booze. There were many quality whiskies and bourbons, no doubt the latter were a perk for his efforts in fostering a working relationship with his American counterparts.

Haining appeared to be on fine form surrounded in a blue haze of cigar smoke. He invited Spencer to sit opposite the desk in a leather upholstered captain's style chair. Haining offered him a drink; it was scarcely eleven o'clock, but it seemed churlish to decline.

'What would you like?'

Spencer's gaze drifted toward the drinks cabinet again. 'I wouldn't say no to a bourbon and soda.'

'Ah, a man after my own heart. I think I'll join you.'

Earlier that morning, Haining's personal private secretary had placed a call to St. James's, and had requested Major Hall visit the minister at the earliest possible convenience. It was an unusual request, if not highly irregular. In the normal run of events, there were certain protocols to observe. Approaches to British Intelligence operatives were usually fielded through a chain-of-command, and it was frowned upon that anyone, including ministers, made contact with an agent directly. But, then again, Haining rarely, if ever, entangled himself in unnecessary red tape.

He handed Spencer a generous glass of bourbon, with just the merest splash of soda.

'What's this all about?' Spencer asked, lighting a cigarette.

Haining eased himself back in his high-backed chair. 'You're a straight-talking bastard like me, Major. I can do business with you.'

Spencer blew out a column of smoke. 'What kind of business Minister?'

Haining reached forward, and picked up his cigar from a large cut glass ashtray. He drew heavily on the cigar, which had an almost woody scent to it. 'The trouble with politicians, Major, is trying to decide their real motives.'

'You'd know more about that than I do.'

'The only time you can be sure they're not lying is when they're not talking.'

Spencer allowed a wry smile to cross his face.

Haining pulled on his cigar. 'The devil's always in the detail trying to decide whether idealism or self-interest has become a politician's main overriding passion.'

Spencer eyed him quizzically, and said noncommittally, 'I'm sure that's all very true, sir.'

'How goes your investigation into your Soviet double agent?'

'You know full well I can't discuss it with you.'

Haining rolled the cigar thoughtfully between his fingers. 'I presume Burdis and I are still prime suspects?'

Haining, with his usual no-nonsense approach, viewed any allegations or suspicion as being unworthy of his contempt; it was water off a duck's back. Whereas Burdis was beginning to kick up a stink why anyone should doubt his loyalty to the Crown.

Spencer met his eyes, and said flatly, 'No-one has been ruled out of the equation.'

'Let's face it. If you had anything of worth by now, you'd have pulled one of us in.'

'You can presume whatever you like, sir.'

'For what it's worth, Major, I may be many things, but I'm not a Soviet spy!'

Spencer gave a slight shrug. 'In my experience, Minister, spies don't usually own up to their guilt, without at least a little gentle persuasion.'

'Touché, Major Hall. As you know, my brief flirtation with Communism is on record, but my misplaced utopian dreams died along with my youth; reality and life got in the way.' He pulled heavily on his cigar again, and added thoughtfully, 'But, even if it hadn't, Stalin's pact with Hitler in 1942 would have certainly given me a final wake-up call and killed my dreams.' He started almost absent-mindedly to finger the knot of his tie. 'I suppose there's a certain irony about it all.'

'Is there, sir?'

'Back in the day, I was considered a left-wing firebrand, but now, most of my fellow Labour MPs view me as something of a social pariah for being on the right wing of the Party.'

Spencer eyed him curiously. 'What's this really all about, Minister?

Haining leaned forward on his desk, and clasped his hands together tightly. The cigar clenched firmly between his teeth, he hesitated for a moment before withdrawing it from his mouth. 'I had a call from Jamie Burdis,' he said.

Spencer's face registered surprise. 'Jamie Burdis called *you*?'

'Don't take me for a ruddy fool, Major; you know damn well why Burdis phoned me. I've no liking for the man, in fact, I can't bloody stand him, but that doesn't mean to say I don't share his concerns for Caro Tait. In fact, I rather liked the woman. I always found she had a good sense of humour.

Well, he snorted, 'I suppose she'd have to working for that bastard! God knows why she ended up taking on the job; everyone warned her against it. Even my wife begged me to do something about it.'

Spencer looked at him speculatively.

'I couldn't get involved,' Haining explained. 'It wasn't my place to start meddling in affairs that didn't concern me.'

'Why did Burdis contact you?'

He rested the cigar down in the ashtray. 'He asked me to touch base with my contacts in MI6.'

'Why was that?'

'Stop playing cat and mouse with me, Major. You know why he called me. To find out if they knew anything about her disappearance. It was a favour. I wouldn't usually have given him the time of day, but for Caro's sake, I put out a few feelers. You see, Burdis assumed as Caro was a former member of MI6, they might have heard a whisper about what had happened to her.'

'And had they?'

A flicker of irritation crossed Haining's face; he knew Spencer was toying with him. 'No,' he grunted. 'That's just it, Major. Caro's disappearance appears to be as much of a mystery to MI6 as it is to Scotland Yard.'

'Why ask to see me?'

'I know how things work, Major. I figured, as Burdis and I are currently under suspicion of being your blessed NKVD mole, we'd both been placed under surveillance, and, therefore, you'd also put Caro under surveillance.'

Spencer blew the cigarette smoke slowly through his lips. 'What makes you think her disappearance is connected to our enquiry?'

Haining drained his bourbon, and shot Spencer a penetrating look. 'I'm not saying it is, I'm just asking the question!'

196

Haining was a wily old bugger; he knew how the land lay between the two intelligence organisations, and more to the point, he also knew how they operated. Spencer considered his reply carefully; it would be a gamble to reveal the truth, but it might just provoke a reaction, or, at least, give both Haining and Burdis a jolt in the right direction and help with their enquiries. To his mind at times Haining seemed a tad too complacent about being under investigation, it probably wouldn't hurt to give him something to chew over.

'You have to understand, Minister,' he said, with the merest flicker of a smile, 'what I'm about to tell you is strictly off the record.'

Haining suddenly perked up, and was interested in what he had to say. 'I perfectly understand, Major.'

'Good, then I can trust whatever I say will go no further than these four walls.'

'You have my word,' he said, as quickly as a flash, and lied with all the accustomed polish of a seasoned politician.

Spencer accepted his assurances with a pinch of salt. He'd never yet managed to meet a politician he would have trusted with either his life, or a secret.

'Someone recently tried to murder Caro.'

Haining's expression dropped. He wasn't quite sure if he'd heard it right. 'Tried to murder her?' he repeated in disbelief.

'Yes, sir.'

'My God, no,' he said. 'Is she all right, was she hurt?'

'She escaped with a few minor cuts and bruises, but, by all accounts, it was a pretty close shave.'

'I don't suppose you're at liberty to tell me what happened?'

'No, sir, but you can rest assured we're looking after her.'

197

'You mean, she's in hiding?'

'We didn't have a choice. She called for help. Let's just say, MI5 took care of the situation.'

'Did you catch them?'

'No, we didn't.'

'But, why the hell didn't you let us know she was safe and well?'

Spencer held his gaze. 'We believe Caro may have inadvertently stumbled across the identity of our mole. Unfortunately, Oakways, and presumably Dunmore, weren't quite so lucky.'

A look of dawning horror clouded Haining's face, not least because the security services might consider him capable of having a hand in the attempt on Caro's life. His initial reaction was one of outrage, but they were only doing their duty, and he needed to keep his emotions in check.

'I feel awful,' he said at last.

'Why?'

'Some time ago Oakways mentioned to me there was a rotten apple in the Department.' He suddenly shot his hands up in despair wafting a trail of cigar smoke. 'I thought he was just stirring up trouble for the sake of it; I never believed him,' he said regretfully. 'I ended up telling the poor old sod he was off his bloody rocker, but, looking back, he was probably the only sane man in the asylum.' Haining hesitated before asking, 'Does the Prime Minister know what's happened to Caro?'

'I believe Colonel Robertson has briefed him.'

'I'd like to have been a fly on that wall.' Haining smirked.

'So would I.' Spencer said, checking his watch. 'I'm sorry, sir, but if it's all the same to you, I ought to start making tracks to St. James's.'

'Yes, of course, Major thank you for your time and also for your frankness.'

'And thank you for the bourbon.'

Haining reached across the desk and shook his hand. When the door closed he picked up his phone and pressed the green button, his diary secretary answered.

'Get Jamie Burdis for me, will you!'

Chapter 18

Colonel Robertson had initially been uneasy about going public so soon after the robbery at Bolton's Bank, but Garvan explained there were two ways of playing the investigation, to stand back and merely wait for something to happen, or to force the pace with a few well-placed editorials to make something happen. Toniolo would immediately be on the back foot, and uncertain how close MI5 was to outing his identity. Robertson could not fault his logic, and after a little persuasion, eventually came around to Garvan's point of view, Toniolo would realise his covert communications with members of the Lilburne Club had been discovered in the Bolton's vault. He gave his consent for the editorials to be published in the Press to see if Garvan's plan might throw some extra light on the investigation.

Robertson had also been keeping a close eye on events with Michelle Rookwood. Since Caro Tait's disappearance, she'd continued to meet Burdis on a somewhat irregular basis, but, by all accounts, his mood had soured considerably; it became equally apparent Jeremy Haining had wasted little time in mentioning the attempt on Caro's life to his one-time colleague.

Burdis had been quite open with her about Caro's plight, and kept blaming himself for what had happened, but without ever going into specific details. Rookwood had reported back to St. James's he seemed depressed and, in her opinion, was close to a nervous breakdown. The fact he'd asked his wife to remain in town for the foreseeable future was testament enough to his current mood. In the ordinary run of events, she was the very last person he'd have wanted around cramping his bachelor lifestyle in London.

*

The sound of a phone ringing woke Garvan up, and he wearily turned on the bedside lamp and picked up the receiver.

'Garvan,' he grunted.

'Sorry it's late, Guv'nor,' Mackenzie apologised.

'Christ, Harry, what time is it?'

'3.30.'

Garvan propped himself up in bed. 'What's wrong?'

'We've got a problem.'

'We've always got a problem, Harry.'

'It's Jamie Burdis.'

'What about him?'

'He's dead.'

'Dead,' he echoed.

Mackenzie told him Jenny Burdis became concerned when he hadn't returned home for a supper party at their flat in Sloane Street. Apparently, the Chief Whip and his wife were guests. Realistically, this was probably his last chance of getting back in the Tory Party's good books, so she knew something must have happened when he didn't turn up. She decided to call his office, his friends, in fact, anywhere she could think of, even the local pub. Eventually, the duty clerk at the Houses of Parliament checked his office, and found Burdis dead, slumped over his desk.'

'Was it a heart attack?'

'No.'

'Was he murdered?'

'The doc says he committed suicide.'

'Good God.' He hadn't seen that coming, Michelle had mentioned about his being depressed, but no-one had suspected things had come to such a pitch he'd take his own life.

'We found a poison phial clasped in his hand; the doc reckoned there was a smell of bitter almonds.'

'Cyanide?'

201

'It looks that way. We'll have to wait for the post-mortem, of course, but the doc thinks it's a pretty foregone conclusion.'

'Did he leave a suicide note?'

'Yes, the usual kind of stuff to his wife that he couldn't see any other way out.'

'Have you contacted St. James's?'

'I left a message, but then called Spencer at home. I didn't want to get too bogged down explaining things to the Duty Officer. Spencer's heading back to the office, and will let Colonel Robertson and No10 know what's happened.'

'Is his wife still at the flat in Sloane Street?'

'Yes, I thought you'd want to be there.'

'Christ, yes.'

'Good, then I'll drop by and pick you up.'

By now, Garvan was out of bed. 'Give me five minutes and I'll be ready.'

Half an hour later, Garvan and Mackenzie were sitting with Jenny Burdis in the elegant drawing room of the Sloane Street flat. The entire room was a reflection of Jenny's taste, a mix of creamy ivory wallpaper and matching hearth rug set on dark wooden floor boards. There was floor to-ceiling blue silk curtains, and above the mantelpiece top was a large gilt frame mirror.

For a woman who had just lost her husband, it had to be said Jenny seemed remarkably composed. She was a slight figure, with faraway eyes and a gentle smile of great warmth. She was rather prim in appearance, dressed in a tweed skirt and plain white blouse, that, to Garvan's mind, seemed more suited to a woman twenty or thirty years older. He couldn't help wondering what on Earth had first attracted Burdis to her. She seemed rather gauche and unsophisticated, not at all like the women he was usually attracted to. Maybe it was for that very reason. She had no interest whatsoever in the gilded world of Westminster.

Mackenzie kicked off proceedings by offering his sincere condolences for her loss, and apologised for needing to see her at such an inappropriate time. He offered to delay things until later, but she refused, and said it was probably better to get things over and done with.

'There's really no need to apologise.' She smiled, absent-mindedly twisting and untwisting the gold chain around her neck. Aware of their interest, she looked at them sharply, and asked, 'How did my husband die, Chief Inspector?'

'We believe he took a cyanide capsule.'

A flicker of surprise crossed her face. 'Cyanide,' she repeated slowly. 'I'd made up my mind he'd shot himself.'

'Had you ever seen him with any drugs or phials?'

'No,' Jenny said, shaking her head. 'But, then again Jamie wasn't exactly an open book, not even to me.' She studied Mackenzie's face warily. 'Where do you think he managed to get his hands on a cyanide capsule? I mean, I really wouldn't know where to start looking.'

Mackenzie looked at her sympathetically, but didn't respond.

'Did he leave a suicide note?' she asked stiffly.

'Yes, he did.'

'When can I see it?'

'Perhaps tomorrow,' Mackenzie answered, 'once the forensic team has completed their tests.'

Jenny nodded. 'Have you read it?'

'Yes, I have.'

'Did he mention me in it?' She sounded almost desperate.

'And your children,' he assured her.

Jenny seemed content, and let the matter rest, but then said, almost as if she was thinking aloud, 'I know Jamie's career was going downhill, but I never suspected things were this bad, at least not enough for him to want to take his own life.'

'It must have come as a terrible shock,' Mackenzie said sympathetically.

'You have to understand I loved my husband dearly, but being married to him was, well,' she smiled slightly, 'let's just say, it wasn't always easy.'

'Why was that?'

'Part of the problem was he constantly fretted about even the smallest of things.'

Burdis had never exactly struck either of them as a worrier, quite the reverse, in fact.

'What kind of things did he fret about?'

She sighed wearily. 'Mainly about his work, but things really came to a head since his demotion to the backbenches. It all started to go terribly wrong, and there was a time when the Tory Party viewed Jamie as the golden boy of the future.' She passed them a rather doleful look. 'Sadly, for Jamie, that ghastly man Jeremy Haining stuck a knife in his back, and ruined everything.'

As he sat listening to her, it began to occur to Garvan what she failed to understand was Jamie had brought his fall from grace entirely down upon himself.

Jenny continued to talk in her gentle, rather breathless voice. 'Jamie organised his political and personal life on the premise he was intellectually and socially superior to everyone around him.' She smiled at them hesitantly. 'He possessed a quick-fire intelligence. I think everyone, even his enemies would agree with me.'

Garvan somehow doubted it.

Mackenzie returned her smile. 'Would it be fair to say he didn't always use his skills wisely?' He looked at her expectantly.

She considered her response. 'I think,' she said, carefully, 'he was misunderstood. Jamie was all bluster, but he was a very caring man, and a good father to our children. Marriage to Jamie was a roller coaster. I won't deny there were difficult times between us,' she conceded, almost reticently. 'But, I learned to cope, and accept both the highs and the lows.'

Jenny looked at each of them appraisingly, and suspected correctly neither of them could quite understand her loyalty to a husband who had betrayed her unswerving loyalty, time and time again.

'I'm not unemotional,' she said, almost defensively, 'and I won't deny Jamie's behaviour was occasionally humiliating. It's just that my feelings are private. I'm fully aware people view me as being cold and unemotional. They're entitled to their opinions, of course, but it's simply not true.'

Her eyes travelled across the room to a photograph, taken some years ago, of Jamie; he was smiling and still passably handsome. For a moment, she seemed lost in thought.

'When did you last see your husband?' Garvan asked her gently.

She held his eyes for a fraction, and answered matter-of-factly. 'It was at breakfast.'

'How did he seem?'

'Absolutely fine. We discussed going down to our house in Kent for the weekend. In fact, everything seemed boringly routine. He also promised to be on time for our dinner party.'

'I don't have a great understanding of politics,' he lied, 'but presumably after your husband's demotion to the backbenches, it was quite a feather in his cap to have the Chief Whip accept an invitation to dinner?'

'Yes, it was. I've known his wife for some years.' She smiled self-effacingly. 'So, you see, Superintendent, even Jamie was occasionally forced to admit I had my uses.'

'I'm sure he must have done, but after all that happened, over the last few months, did Jamie genuinely believe he could still claw his way back into the Party's good books?'

She thoughtfully pressed her lips together. 'To be honest, he was realistic about his chances. It certainly wasn't a given. But, the fact, the Chief Whip was prepared to accept an invitation to dinner was, to his mind, a start in the right direction, and the first rung on the ladder to return from the political wilderness.' Jenny's eyes were watchful and questioning. 'That's the only part I don't understand, Superintendent. If Jamie had committed suicide a fortnight ago, I'd almost have understood, but why would he kill himself, just when things appeared to be getting better?' She took a sharp intake of breath. 'It doesn't add up in my mind.'

'There has to be a reason. Did he seem upset about anything in particular?' Garvan suggested.

Jenny gave the matter some consideration, her thoughts tumbling back over the last few days. 'There was something,' she said quietly, 'but it might be nothing.'

'Go on,' he said encouragingly.

Jenny briefly placed her hands together, as if in prayer. 'Jamie seemed really happy at breakfast this morning. It was almost like old times. He was in good form, laughing and joking.' She shot them a half-hearted smile. 'But, his mood changed, almost as quickly as turning off a light switch.'

'What happened?'

'I pointed out an editorial in the *Times* about some robbery or other at Bolton's Bank in Mayfair. I didn't think anything of it, but he tore the paper out of my hands, read the article, and then flung it across the kitchen. It's not as if we had an account there, or anything,' Jenny said, 'or at least, I wasn't aware we had.'

The glances exchanged between Garvan and Mackenzie were not entirely lost on Jenny. It briefly crossed her mind she ought to press them, and demand to know what was going on. But, she'd been around the system long enough to understand she was merely a bit part player, and they'd never divulge the entire truth about Jamie's past and the real reasons behind his removal from the Foreign Office.

'Didn't you ask why he flung the paper across the kitchen?' Garvan pressed her.

She appeared surprised by the question. 'No, not at the time. He was always doing things like that,' she explained. 'I didn't think anything of it. Besides, he seemed fine again shortly afterwards, and started chatting about our dinner party, and how we needed to pull out all the stops and make an impression. Why would Jamie kill himself, tonight of all nights? So much depended on making it a success.'

Unwittingly, Jenny had provided the answer. Burdis, for all his faults, was an accomplished politician, but the Bolton's Bank robbery had been the final catalyst. He knew Special Branch and MI5 would be able to implicate him in Toniolo's spy ring.

Garvan decided it was probably the right time to call it a day. Jenny was an innocent victim, caught in an endless spiral of her husband's deceit. That she loved him dearly wasn't in question; it was obvious. But, common decency dictated she needed to grieve in private, and they could always interview her at a later date. However, to his surprise, Jenny wasn't quite finished with them yet. She moved over to the sideboard, opened one of the doors, and retrieved a walnut veneer box from inside. She set it down on the top.

'I know they called his secretary, Caro, the keeper of my husband's secrets.' She shot them a smile, with a pinch of mischief written on her face. 'But, I assure you, gentlemen, she was only scratching at the surface. Jamie always said if anything happened to him, I was to open the box.'

Garvan held her gaze, and said jokingly, 'You mean, it's a bit like Pandora's Box?'

She let out a half-throated chuckled. 'It's something like that, yes.'

He began to feel a frisson of compassion for her.

Jenny started to flick through the box. 'It's not easy knowing your husband's nickname amongst his fellow MPs is the "Loins of Westminster."'

'No, I don't suppose it is,' Garvan said, somewhat uneasily.

She cast him a rather world-weary smile. 'You have to understand I endured the slights and the embarrassment for one reason, and one reason only, for the sake of my children.' She looked steadily at each of them in turn; her inherent gentleness had suddenly turned to steel. 'To the outside world, I appear to be nothing more than fatuous, and an unswervingly loyal wife.' She clutched a handful of papers in her hand, before letting them drop back into the box. 'I know everyone calls me "poor Jenny," but I'm neither blind nor stupid. Jamie was incapable of fidelity, and resented my minding about his affairs. In the early days of our marriage, he was often openly rude to me in public. The trouble is, you see, I began to realise he possessed a fatal flaw. An overwhelming arrogance and an unshakable belief he was born to rule. It wasn't his only flaw, of course.' She smiled deprecatingly. 'But, years ago, I saw through all Jamie's faults.'

There was a certain detachment about Jenny as she spoke; her eyes seemed lost in thought.

'The one thing I did command, was his trust.' She slowly closed the lid of the box. 'He always knew I'd keep my mouth shut, and whatever our problems throughout our entire marriage, he always confided his innermost secrets to me.' She looked at them with an expression of almost smug satisfaction. 'I knew he'd come grovelling back to me, full of remorse after his latest affair had blown up in his face. But, whatever you may think of me, I'm certainly not some meek, downtrodden wife. I knew he was afraid one day I'd eventually pull the plug on our marriage, and I'd crucify his career.' She smiled again, in that deceptively gentle way of hers. 'But, you see, gentlemen, knowledge is power, and I had that in abundance. As strange as it may sound, there were times when Jamie's peccadillos were almost a welcome distraction. They allowed me the time and space to run the estate in Kent, and breed my race horses. Don't get me wrong, I loved seeing Jamie, but the sexual side of our relationship was never that important to me,' she said candidly. 'Despite my family's opposition, I stayed with him through thick and thin.'

She stared ruefully at the contents of the box. 'In the early days, he could be very loving. I was naïve, and I wouldn't listen to my father's warnings. I thought there was a side to Jamie no-one else could see. In hindsight, it was me who'd misjudged him. But, for all his selfish arrogance, I still loved him. Jamie was a complex man; irascible, yes, but also extraordinarily generous.' Jenny looked at them searchingly, trying to gauge their reaction, but she guessed they were far too professional to allow their personal feelings to intrude. It wasn't their place to be judgemental. 'I never enjoyed the Westminster hothouse,' she explained, 'and I wasn't exactly cut out to be a compliant wife hanging on my husband's every word. I had my uses, but I found life in London suffocating.' Jenny snapped the lid of the box shut. 'I knew Jamie always had his fingers in lots of pies, and he sailed pretty close to the wind throughout his career.' A flicker of a smile crossed her mouth. 'Why else would he have been demoted to the backbenches?'

Garvan began to realise he had completely underestimated Jenny. She was probably far more politically astute than her husband had ever been.

Quite unexpectedly, she handed the box over to him. 'I was married to Jamie for twenty-five years.' She gave out an involuntary laugh. 'If I'm entirely honest, it seemed a good deal longer.'

Garvan took hold of the box.

'Are you sure about this?' he found himself saying.

She smiled at him quizzically. 'Yes, I am.'

'I was just wondering what your children would think about your handing over their father's personal papers to the police.'

'My eldest son, Superintendent, is God only knows where in France with the Household Division, and my youngest has just received his call-up papers. The boys loved their father, warts and all, but that doesn't mean to say they approved of his behaviour toward me. The papers are mine and mine alone to hand over. In fact, the box only contains a small selection of his diaries. You're more than welcome to the rest of them. As far as I'm concerned, you can do whatever you like with them.'

'Thank you.'

She cast them a tired smile. 'It's strange you can live with someone for all those years, without ever really knowing them,' she said, without rancour, or regret. 'Please take it, Superintendent. I'm sure you'll find something of interest, and who knows, it may even shed some light on why Jamie killed himself.' Jenny took a step away from him. 'Either way, I want nothing to do with it!'

'Have you read the contents?' he asked.

'It was never locked,' she replied. 'Of course I have.'

Garvan looked at her guardedly; there was something about her; an inner steel that had surprised him. The look on Jenny's face spoke volumes. It was obvious she knew its contents were political dynamite. Maybe, at last, this quiet, unassuming woman would finally have the last laugh on the Westminster establishment. This was her chance to fight back and to break even. She could now happily return to her beloved estate in the Kent countryside, with the knowledge its contents could help bring the entire house of cards crashing to the ground.

*

Although it was impossible to achieve a complete news blackout in the aftermath of Burdis's death, Robertson raised the issue with the Director General of MI5. He requested they make an approach to the Home Secretary, Herbert Morrison, with the intention of keeping the details of the suicide under wraps, and it should be reported in the Press as a sudden and unexpected death, hinting Burdis had died from a suspected heart attack.

Initially, the Home Secretary appeared reluctant to any suppression or tampering with the truth. However, Robertson explained it was very much a matter of National Security, and might prejudice their on-going enquiries into the identity of MI6's Soviet mole. Morrison still erred on the side of caution, and passed the matter over to Downing Street for approval.

Three hours later, Robertson was informed Churchill had given the go-ahead. He also gave permission for a security lock down, which would keep both MI6 and Whitehall out of the loop. Garvan's task was to keep Special Branch involved; he needed to batten down the hatches, and ensure Toniolo was no wiser than the general public.

Permission was granted for Mackenzie to approach Jenny Burdis, and explain the reports of her husband's death in the newspapers would omit any mention of suicide. Initially, he wasn't quite sure how she'd react, but much to his relief, Jenny seemed genuinely relieved the sordid details of his death wouldn't end up splashed across the front pages. Jenny wasn't a fool, and knew there was probably a hidden agenda behind their decision, but from a purely personal stance, she didn't much care. It meant the family would be shielded from any unwarranted intrusion. As it was, she explained to Mackenzie, one particular journalist from the *Daily Sketch* had already got wind of Jamie's death, presumably via a contact at Westminster Coroner's Court, and had already been loitering around the front entrance to the flat.

Mackenzie duly reported back to Garvan, and confirmed Jenny was more than happy with the decision not to go public with the details surrounding Jamie's death. Garvan assumed marriage to the man had been difficult enough without having to endure any additional intrusions and never ending speculation into why he had decided to take his own life.

*

Robertson decided Garvan was far better placed to break the news of Jamie's suicide to Caro Tait than Spencer. Robertson knew Garvan had an innate copper's ability to tone down his approach and turn on the charm when required. Diplomacy had never been Spencer's strongest attribute.

Ever since the failed attempt on Caro's life, she had remained under armed protection at the same smart apartment block in Chelsea they'd driven her to on the night of the attack. While Caro readily accepted that until Toniolo was finally tracked down, she'd have to remain at the apartment, she had inevitably felt increasingly frustrated at being cooped up, and effectively under twenty-four-hour surveillance.

Garvan's visit was a welcome distraction. Spencer had visited the flat on several occasions, and had supposedly kept her up to speed about the on-going investigation. But, to Caro's mind, he always appeared somewhat reticent in revealing too much. Spencer had never been one to hide his light under a bushel, and it was blatantly obvious he still didn't entirely trust her. She guessed there remained a nagging element of doubt in his mind whether she was still covering up for her former lover Jamie Burdis.

Garvan thought Caro looked as attractive as ever, dressed in a smart blue tailored suit, her dark hair falling softly to her shoulders. Only perhaps the rather taut expression and watchful grey eyes gave away any hint to Caro's stress at being placed under what was, effectively, house arrest.

She flashed a smile, and extended her hand. 'It's good to see you again, Superintendent.'

He acknowledged her greeting with a flicker of a smile.

'Would you like some tea?'

'No, thank you, I've not long had one.'

She gestured toward a small two-seat sofa. 'Please have a seat.'

Caro moved over toward the large mock Georgian fireplace, and briefly held out her hands toward the spluttering gas fire. 'What brings you here, news of Toniolo?' she asked hopefully.

'I'm afraid not.'

'Then why are you here?'

'I'm afraid I have some bad news for you.'

Caro met his gaze warily. 'Bad news?' she queried.

'It's about Jamie Burdis.'

A look of panic crossed Caro's face. 'What's happened?' Her voice was sharp with anxiety.

'I'm sorry,' he said evenly, 'but there's no easy way of telling you. We've been informed Burdis committed suicide last night.'

Her face registered disbelief; she lowered her eyes, and for a while, she couldn't bring herself to speak. She was badly shaken, but to her credit, at least in front of Garvan, she fought hard to keep a tight grip on her emotions.

'Are you allowed to tell me what happened?'

Garvan explained to her the police physician suspected he had died from cyanide poisoning. Although they'd have to await formal confirmation from the post-mortem, as things stood, there seemed little doubt about the cause of death; a phial had been found clasped in his hand with a distinct smell of bitter almonds.

Caro folded her arms tightly, and moved over toward the window overlooking the street. 'Did he leave a suicide note?' she murmured.

'Yes, yes, he did.'

She twitched the net curtain, as if something had caught her eye outside. 'Did Jamie explain why he wanted to kill himself?'

'Not really.'

She knew there was little point in pressing the issue. Garvan was unlikely to share the contents of Jamie's suicide note with her. There was no reason why he should. Garvan allowed a silence to fall between them. He indulged it for a while, before breaking it.

'I don't suppose you know where he might have got the poison from, do you?' he asked her.

Caro glanced over her shoulder at him, her pale grey eyes glistening with tears. 'I'm sorry, I haven't a clue.'

'Caro,' he said gently.

The sudden softening of his tone made her turn round to face him. 'Yes?' she said hesitantly.

'I was just wondering if there's anything you'd like to tell me.'

She feigned ignorance, and immediately went on the defensive. 'I'm not sure I know what you mean.'

'Have you been totally up front with us?'

Caro's eyes flashed with anger. 'For God's sake, not that again. For the last time, I've told you everything I know, why wouldn't I?'

He smiled tightly. 'Well, I'm not entirely sure. Let's just say, I've always had the distinct impression there was something you were keeping back from us.'

She rolled her eyes. 'Why should I?'

'Precisely,' he replied, 'unless, of course, you were covering up for Jamie Burdis.'

Caro took a sharp intake of breath. 'Why, in God's name, won't either you or Spencer believe me? I've told you everything. I haven't a clue who tried to kill me. If there is some connection to Toniolo, then God only knows what it is.' Her voice was rising now. 'Do you honestly believe I want to stay shut up in this place?'

He lit a cigarette, but didn't respond.

'Well, I don't, and if I knew who Toniolo was, don't you think I'd tell you, like a shot.'

Garvan drew on his freshly lit cigarette, before perching it casually in the corner of his mouth. 'No, I don't think you know who Toniolo is, but I suspect you believed or knew Burdis had somehow become caught up with him.'

Caro didn't quite know how to respond.

Garvan made to leave. As he reached the door, he turned back toward her. 'Was Burdis being blackmailed?'

The look of panic on her face spoke volumes.

'When did he tell you?'

She cupped her hands over her mouth. 'It all came tumbling out one evening. He was drunk,' she confessed, 'and told me someone at the Foreign Office had something on him.' She shook her head in despair. 'I believe it was all to do with removing classified papers from the office.'

'Go on,' Garvan said steadily.

She gave a shrug. 'That's it, really. Yes, I knew he was being blackmailed, but Jamie was way too frightened to tell me who was blackmailing him.' Her eyes again started to burn with tears. 'You see, in his own way, he wanted to protect me.'

'Protect you from Toniolo?'

She nodded.

Garvan grimaced. 'From where I'm sitting, he didn't do too well on that count, did he?'

215

'Maybe not,' she whispered.

'Perhaps,' he continued flatly, 'if you'd been completely upfront with us from the start, and told us he was being blackmailed, we might, just might, have managed to have prevented his death.'

She looked away, no longer able to meet his gaze. He mentioned something about giving her a call, but she wasn't interested, and turned back to face the window. As Garvan closed the door, Caro stared unseeingly out of the rain-splattered window, tears slowly tracing down her cheeks. Her thoughts were in freefall, as she recounted their life together, her very last conversation with Jamie, his loving phone calls, and his maddening mood swings. Jamie's life, and now his death, had shaped her in a profound and sometimes inexplicable way. For all his faults, she'd adored him. It didn't make sense, but then, it never had.

However many romantic gestures he'd made, however many promises he'd made, realistically, there had never been any serious prospect of a future together. Jamie would never have divorced his wife; there was too much at stake. His career was everything to him. At the end of the day, it was the only thing that truly mattered in his life. Caro knew all that, but there'd always been a certain frisson of hope, of expectation, fuelled by Jamie's undoubted charisma, occasional tenderness, and sheer exuberance. The truth of it was, Caro had become infatuated with him, but Jamie had always led a double life; it was what he did. He manipulated people. Looking back at their time together, he never seriously contemplated leaving his wife and starting again.

As Caro stared unseeingly out of the window it still seemed unreal to think of Jamie being dead. He'd always been so full of life. She couldn't help blaming herself for what had happened.

Caro closed her eyes, and began to sob, her whole body convulsed with grief. She'd wanted nothing more than to

216

shield Jamie from British Intelligence knowing Toniolo was blackmailing him, but, in doing so, she'd left him fatally exposed. If only she'd come clean with Spencer and Garvan at the outset, they'd have lifted Burdis out of harm's way. To them, he was never more than a means to an end, to out Toniolo. His career would have been destroyed, but at least, he'd still be alive.

Chapter 19

Following a post-mortem examination, it was determined the cause of death was from cyanide poisoning. No alcohol was found in his stomach, although a glass of brandy was next to the body. The subsequent tests on the brandy had proved not to contain any unknown substance. The autopsy reported that fluid which smelled strongly of bitter almonds was in the stomach. It was also reported there was a trace smell of bitter almonds in the vital organs. The poison phial found clasped in his hand tested positive for cyanide. The autopsy, therefore, concluded the cause of death was asphyxia due to cyanide poisoning, and ruled a verdict of suicide.

While Garvan accepted the findings, there remained a nagging doubt in his mind. *Did Burdis kill himself, or had he been murdered by MI6 or Toniolo?* There was simply no way of knowing. Spencer was dismissive about the idea. There was nothing to be gained by killing off a lame-duck politician. But, the fact the Tory Chief Whip had agreed to attend a supper party on the evening of his death, remained uppermost in his mind. He tended to agree with Jenny Burdis; the timing of his death seemed somewhat questionable. But, perhaps the editorials in the National Press, reporting the raid on Bolton's Bank, had tipped him over the edge. That it was only a matter of time before his involvement with the shadowy Lilburne Club and his connection to Toniolo would fall into the hands of not only Special Branch, but, inevitably, into the clutches of MI5. When that happened, there would have been no clawing his way back from the political wilderness. The Chief Whip and the powerful grandees of the Tory party would have cut him dead. In essence, the ensuing shame of possibly being outed as a Soviet spy would have sent his world into a terminal spiral.

As for "Pandora's Box," as he had suspected, it was evident Jenny had known all along the contents were not only salacious, but also politically explosive. His diaries were witty, sleazy, and ultimately cruel in recording his endless sexual exploits; he'd left a trail of broken marriages, paternity suits, and a growing coterie of the powerful and disaffected in his wake. True to her word, Jenny duly provided them with the rest of her late husband's diaries, including a leather-bound list, containing the names of past and present members of the Lilburne Club.

The suicide note had not contained any real hint of his underlying fears and inner turmoil, but at least, Jenny confirmed her husband had penned it. Thanks to this, they could discount any possibility of forgery and the note being placed in his hand at the time of death.

It soon became apparent, reading through the diaries, Burdis took himself very seriously as a career politician, and it was a matter of disappointment and bitterness Jeremy Haining had been instrumental in helping to thwart his ambitions. He recorded, with some rancour, how Haining had once witheringly announced his ambitions far outweighed his abilities. Haining's condemnation was followed swiftly by Churchill's final summation Burdis believed he was a far better politician than he actually was. If being damned by an eminent Labour Minister wasn't bad enough, it had been the kiss of death from Churchill.

For a man as proud and egotistical as Burdis, the setbacks must have been difficult to accept, but reading between the lines, his innate self-belief, no matter how misguided, was not apparently dampened for long. He soon started to bounce back; both his ambition and political drive undented by his demotion from the Foreign Office. Whether he genuinely believed he could fight his way back into favour was quite another matter. Maybe the sheer arrogance of the man had blindsided him to the reality of his situation. There was simply no way of telling. His deep-rooted ambitions appeared to transcend their condemnation. As Garvan read

219

through the diary, the one thing which became increasingly clear was, over the last few months, he still fervently believed his time would come; he'd prove them all wrong, and he'd ultimately redeem his political career.

Garvan began to suspect Jenny probably viewed her husband's political future rather more pragmatically, and knew his ambitions would never come to fruition. His dreams of rehabilitation in the eyes of the Westminster elite, was just that, a pipe dream.

While Garvan set to work ploughing through Burdis's personal papers, Mackenzie obtained the necessary Home Office clearance to gain access to his private accounts, which included the one at Bolton's Bank. In total, there were three accounts his wife knew nothing at all about. The first two appeared to fund his mistresses and the offspring he was legally bound to support after various proven paternity cases against him. They also came across a meticulously kept ledger covering all three accounts. The balance in the Bolton's account exceeded £500, and as indicated in the note they found from Toniolo in the bank vault, there were regular cash payments of a £100 on a quarterly basis. According to the ledger, the first payment in the vault was deposited almost two months to the day after his promotion as a junior Minister in the Foreign Office, and continued in line with the note from Toniolo, which described them as so-called "loyalty payments."

His early diaries indicated his politics started to veer increasingly toward the right throughout the mid to late 1930s. In fact, there were one or two entries in which he appeared to be alarmingly intrigued by Hitler. It could have been a passing interest, but there were also several references to Aryan supremacy, which went way beyond the pale.

Garvan called for Burdis's security files from Central Registry, and checked to see if anyone had already investigated or raised any concerns about his holding extreme right-wing views. There was nothing of real interest contained in the file. The vetting section had carried out additional checks, but could find nothing out of the ordinary, which might have denied him access to top secret material. Therefore, from a security aspect, his appointment had been a rubber stamp job.

The more Garvan ploughed through the correspondence, the more he began to wonder if somehow Burdis had unwittingly played into Toniolo's hands. The general opinion was, the payments into the Bolton account had emanated from the Soviet NKVD, but at the back of Garvan's mind, he came to the conclusion, for all his faults, and there were many, Burdis had somehow been ruthlessly manoeuvred into a corner, and been blackmailed by Toniolo.

There had to be a hook, a reason Burdis would agree to spy for the Soviets. In many respects, his personal life had been played out on an open stage. Garvan began to wonder if there was another skeleton rattling in the cupboard, but it would have to be something serious enough to make Burdis want to cover his tracks. He just couldn't imagine what it could be.

Garvan began to believe the Lilburne Club was becoming almost something of a side issue. While Oakways, Burdis, and Toniolo might have had tenuous links to both Cambridge University and the Club, he began to doubt whether it was that relevant to the current investigation. *Was Toniolo perhaps a politician, a civil servant, a party official, a well-placed journalist, or, their worst nightmare, someone embedded within the intelligence community itself?* The latter had always been a possibility.

Garvan reported his findings to the so-called "three wise men," Robertson, General Menzies, and the Director General of MI5, Sir David Petrie. In the normal run of events, such an illustrious gathering would have proved intimidating, but Garvan was by now on more certain ground. He had also

221

taken the precaution of running the report by Spencer first; he valued his opinion.

Spencer had read through the brief. It made sense, and he'd picked a couple of holes in it. On the whole, it backed up the premise whoever managed to loop Burdis into the fold, must have had a hook, and enough inside intelligence to gain the leverage to blackmail him. Garvan's conclusion was Burdis was probably no more than an unwitting dupe, a fall guy in Toniolo's end game plan. In his opinion, he didn't possess either the inclination, or the intellect, to be a top-flight spy.

Garvan had meticulously backed up his research by cross-referencing certain important points with MI5's Central Registry. By and large, he hadn't been disappointed, as the disparate strands of intelligence were slowly, but inexorably coming together. The more he delved into the matter, it seemed ever more likely their rogue Soviet mole was probably a member of the intelligence community, and not some disaffected politician or well-placed civil servant. Of course, the one thing he didn't have was concrete proof, and there was always going to be an element of doubt, until they finally managed to bring Toniolo to justice.

Garvan's brief was not only well-researched but was succinct and to the point. However, the ball was very much in the court of the "three wise men," and whether they agreed with his findings was an entirely different matter.

As he suspected, they decided to play for time. They needed longer to confer and to investigate their own intelligence lines of enquiry. Garvan was ordered to re-interview George Rowlands. He was slightly disappointed there hadn't been a more positive reply, but, at least, they hadn't thrown the report back in his face. Spencer assured him it was a good sign, and, at this stage, they were unlikely to commit themselves either way.

After Jamie Burdis's death, they wanted Garvan to see whether Rowlands might come up with any additional nuggets of information. Garvan's initial reaction was he was probably on a fool's errand. For what it was worth, he didn't mince his words. At the end of the day, it was a fait accompli, and Garvan didn't have a say in the matter.

*

Latchmere House was built originally as a private home, before eventually becoming a military hospital for officers during World War I. It was now a sparse detention and interrogation centre, known as Camp 020. Prisoners were not generally held there on a long-term basis, Rowlands being the one exception to the rule, on the explicit orders from his former MI6 boss, General Menzies.

Driving toward the main gates, Garvan couldn't help thinking it would have been a rather pleasant place to live in its heyday. However, since 1939, it had become a fortress, surrounded by vast interlocking piles of barbed wire. Beside the front gate was a large sign stating it was "Home Office Property".

Having negotiated his way through the heavily-armed entrance, a military policeman showed Garvan into a bleak interview room. His gaze glided slowly toward a heavy metal grill covering the window, and then up toward the single bare light bulb hanging from the ceiling. In the centre of the interview room, stood a dilapidated wooden table, smudged with ink stains and tea cup rings.

He lit a cigarette, and waited until two muscle-bound military police NCOs escorted George Rowlands into the interview room. It crossed Garvan's mind they'd probably been hand-picked; they certainly seemed the right type to instil fear in Latchmere's somewhat disparate collection of inmates. He tried his damnedest not to register surprise at Rowlands's

223

appearance, but he did. An ill-fitting drab prison uniform and badly scuffed slippers had replaced the dapper Savile Row suits, the Turnbull & Asser shirts, and bespoke shoes from Lobb in St. James's Street.

How the mighty had fallen. There was a time when Rowlands had been a rising star, a force to be reckoned with, his name once mooted as a possible future successor to General Menzies, but that was all in the past now. He was persona non-grata with British Intelligence, an outcast forever, shamed by his activities as a double agent in Portugal.

Rowlands shot him a flicker of recognition, but it was begrudging all the same. As the guards closed the door on them, he asked, 'To what do I owe the pleasure?'

Garvan pulled up a chair to the table. 'I'm certainly not here by choice.'

'No, I don't suppose you are. Why are you here?'

'I'm under orders.'

'Why not try telling me something I didn't already know.'

'The three wise men asked me to have a word with you.'

He stopped dead in his tracks. 'Did they?' he said, with a faint, almost cynical smile.

Garvan retrieved a hip flask from the inside pocket of his jacket, and set it down on the table in front of him. Rowlands had always been a prodigious drinker, although, in fairness to him, no-one had ever accused him of being an alcoholic. But, he knew his subject, and guessed correctly the prospect of a neat dram of whisky would help lighten his mood.

Rowlands looked into his eyes with a certain amount of suspicion.

'Take it,' Garvan said, pushing it across the table.

He hesitated.

'It's a present.'

224

Rowlands was touched by his thoughtfulness. Whatever Garvan's real motives were, he didn't have to make the gesture. It was way above and beyond his remit; in fact, the three wise men would have castigated him for showing an ounce of compassion. He moved over to the table, picked up the hip flask, and twisted open the lid. It was a malt whisky; he knew instantly from the aroma it was Macallan's, his favourite.

'You didn't have to do this.' He said.

Garvan shrugged. 'I know I didn't.'

He thanked him for his generosity. There had to be a catch, of course, there always was, but he hoped, somewhere along the line, Garvan had acted out of a deep-rooted sense of compassion. He took a swig, and briefly closed his eyes, as he savoured the peaty taste of the single malt, before asking again, 'Why are you here?'

'Jamie Burdis is dead.'

Rowlands looked shocked by the news. 'Dead, what happened?'

'He committed suicide.'

'Why the hell did he want to kill himself?'

'It would appear he was in the pay of Toniolo.'

Rowlands looked at him quizzically; he seemed unconvinced. 'Are you sure?'

Garvan held his gaze. 'We have proof he was.'

'You do surprise me.'

'Why's that?'

'It's just, from all I know about Burdis, I find it difficult to believe he was leading a double life.'

'What's so difficult to believe?'

'He struck me as being incapable of successfully leading a single life, let alone a double one.'

Rowlands opinion was damning, but, to Garvan's mind, was not that far off the mark. 'We believe Toniolo was blackmailing him.'

225

Rowlands gave a shrug. 'It seems reasonable.'

Garvan looked at him curiously. 'And what's that supposed to mean?'

'Let's face it, Burdis was no more than a dupe.'

'Why do you think that?'

'He didn't have the intellect to be a serious player.'

'*You* were a serious player once.'

'Yes, I was, but we were poles apart.'

Garvan looked at him curiously.

'Jamie was a politician, with limited talent. He was never a real contender in the political world; part of the problem was he genuinely thought he was.'

'What did you think of Burdis?'

'He never knowingly over-impressed,' he pronounced witheringly. 'Whereas Jeremy Haining was a different kettle of fish altogether, tough as old boots and a mind like a cut-throat razor. You always had to be on your guard around him; he was always picking holes in the intelligence reports.'

'In what way, do you mean?'

'The odd, slapdash mistake. Say something hadn't been picked up on from the last briefing. He has a prodigious memory, and a deep understanding of not only the political world but also the vagaries of the Intelligence Service. Since being at the FO, he's made it his business to get to know his potential opponents, including MI6.'

'I guess he'd make a deadly enemy?'

Rowlands smiled weakly. 'I think Burdis underestimated him, and, as a result, came unstuck. The way I see it, for an agent of Toniolo's abilities, Jamie was rich for the picking.' He stared thoughtfully through the iron-barred window, and saw in the distance beyond the perimeter fence, a small glimpse of the outside world he missed so much, like a double decker bus heading toward Kingston. In the long silence that followed, he seemed distracted and deep in

226

thought. Garvan was in no immediate rush to break the silence between them.

When he turned to face him, he said at length, 'Maybe I also underestimated Toniolo.'

Garvan shot him a questioning look.

'There's always a hidden layer, and then another, and so on, until at last you find a kernel of the truth. By then, it's sometimes too late. I convinced myself Toniolo was a one-trick pony, but that he would probably try to bag a tame MP or two.'

'You mean someone like Burdis?'

'No, not particularly. I would have thought someone with more overt left wing sympathies. Whatever he had on Burdis must have been pretty damning, but I can't imagine what it was. His life was already a pretty open book, and none of it was particularly edifying.'

Garvan felt inclined to agree, and decided to change tack slightly, 'I understand you were both members of the Lilburne Club.'

Rowlands stopped pacing the room, and sat himself down opposite Garvan. 'Yes, we were. He was a good deal older than me, of course. We never actually met at Cambridge, but once or twice, I came across him at the annual bun fest. To be honest, he was too self-opinionated for my liking, I couldn't stand the bugger. When the powers that be decided to give him a junior ministerial post, it came as quite a shock. Most of us who knew him of old thought it was a train crash waiting to happen, and he'd eventually screw up. It just happened rather sooner than we were expecting.'

'Did you raise your concerns about the appointment with MI6?'

'Of course, I bloody did.'

'What happened?'

227

'It fell on deaf ears, dear boy.' Rowlands smiled tautly. 'I guess that probably seems rather strange coming from *me*, of all people?'

'No, not really,' he replied smoothly.

Rowlands liked Garvan's style; it was understated, but deadly all the same. He took another sip of the Macallan's. 'I'm not going to lie to you, I thought Burdis was an utter shit.'

'A shit, or not, you have to agree there's a certain symmetry to our investigation.'

Rowlands looked faintly bored, but then again, he frequently did. 'Is there?'

'So far, the one common denominator is you and Burdis were members of the Lilburne Club, and that Oakways's brother-in-law, Simon Paxton, was also a member.'

He rolled his eyes. 'Is that a crime?'

'Not in itself, no, it isn't.'

'If you care to check the records, Superintendent, I think you'll find at some time or another, half of the Government and MI6 have all belonged to the Club, even Frank Lucern, for Christ's sake.'

'I've checked,' Garvan assured him.

'I won't deny some people took the Lilburne Club terribly seriously, but for the vast majority of us, it was nothing more than an excuse for a weekly piss-up at University.'

It was obvious Garvan remained unconvinced.

Rowlands fixed him with a narrow-eyed stare. 'If you must know, I joined for no other fatuous reason than the wine was supplied by my friend Eddie Barton's father.'

Garvan looked at him questioningly.

'The Bartons are one of London's leading wine merchants,' he explained.

Knowing Rowlands's love of booze, the prospect of an endless supply of fine wine was probably more than enough of an incentive to lure him into joining any Club, let alone the Lilburne.

Rowlands still continued to eye him warily. 'For what it's worth, if you want my opinion, this whole business doesn't add up.'

'Doesn't it?' Garvan said enigmatically.

'Knowledge, Superintendent, is rarely wasted.'

'I'm afraid you'll have to spell that one out to me.'

'From what I knew about Burdis, his politics were right-wing, extremely right-wing,' he said emphatically.

'But, he was known to have jumped ship more than once,' Garvan suggested.

Rowlands frowned. 'He tended to play to the crowd, and changed tack slightly according to whoever he was trying to impress at the time. Burdis was one of those people who had an almost addictive personality; there were no half measures, it was all or nothing with him. Admittedly, there were times when his politics ebbed and flowed with the tide, but since leaving University, he was either bordering on being a fascist, or pandering to the mainstream centre of the Tory Party. That's partly why I could never take him that seriously. At Cambridge, it was all about Lenin and the great Utopian ideal of the Communist revolution. Then, during the thirties, he became increasingly obsessed by Hitler's rise to power, and, trust me, it was an *obsession*,' Rowlands emphasised. 'But then, of course, you'll already know all about it. There's a whole ruddy annex attached to his security file about his close links to Oswald Mosley and the Fascist Party, not to mention the Right Club.' He stubbed out his cigarette in the ashtray. 'At one point, it was even rumoured he had a signed photograph of Hitler he'd picked up in Germany during the thirties. But, whether it was actually true or not, God only knows.'

229

No, Garvan did not know, and more to the point, the security file had not contained an annex detailing his affiliation to the far right. There had to be a reason he was passed an incomplete security file.

Rowlands detected an unmistakable flicker of irritation on Garvan's face. 'Don't tell me,' he smiled knowingly, 'the Mosley stuff was missing?'

Garvan wouldn't be drawn, but it was answer enough for Rowlands. 'My dear boy, you have to start asking yourself why the papers were missing. If you raise the matter with Central Registry, the official line will be that it's down to a clerical error, and from time to time, the girls in the registry misfile things. You can't disprove it, and they're an easy target.'

'But, it's not that easy.'

'You're learning, Superintendent, you really are.' Rowlands grinned appreciatively. 'As you know, each file has a minute sheet, which meticulously records every confidential and secret document it contains. The annex on Burdis's file was annotated and cross-referenced with the original minute sheet, so by the time you received his file, someone had not only removed the annex, but had gone to a great deal of trouble to weed through it, and presumably remove anything that might shed light on our rogue spy. You have to ask yourself,' he continued smoothly, 'whoever accessed the file, has way more clout than either you or I am ever likely to have.' Rowlands took a last deep swallow, before placing the hip flask down on the table. Aware of Garvan's gaze, he looked candidly at him. 'I'm telling you now, there's no way Burdis volunteered his services to the NKVD. On the other hand, if you'd said he was working for the Abwehr,' he gave a slight shrug, 'well, that's a different matter altogether. I wouldn't have batted an eyelid.'

Garvan looked at him searchingly. For the first time since his arrest, there was a spark of the old Rowlands. He was good, as wily and clever as ever. For some reason, he genuinely seemed to want to help, but again, Garvan wondered why. What had he said to entice him back out of his defensive shell. It turned out he didn't have to ask.

'For all Burdis's faults, he was probably as much a victim of Toniolo as I was.'

'What do you mean by that?'

'When I became deputy head of the Lisbon Station, it was a serious step up for me. I knew I had to keep my nose clean, steer clear of trouble, and keep on the straight and narrow. The world was my oyster; I was well-reported on, and bloody good at what I did. But, somewhere along the line, I believe I was deliberately set up.'

'You were by the Germans; it was a classic honey trap,' Garvan offered flatly.

Rowlands lit another cigarette. 'With a certain twist, yes, it was,' he confessed.

'What was the twist?'

'No-one outside of British Intelligence knew I was homosexual, and certainly not the Germans.' He snorted out a cloud of smoke. 'Initially, there'd been a wall of resistance against my recruitment, but war tends to even out preconceived prejudices. I'm not ashamed to admit I pulled a few strings and a few favours from my old university friends to join the Service. At the end of the day, I proved my worth, and clawed my way up through the ranks.' He closed his eyes briefly, almost in despair. 'But, somewhere along the line, I'm convinced our friend Toniolo informed the Abwehr about…' He hesitated. '… about my preferences.'

Garvan could see where he was coming from; why else would German Intelligence have set him up with a young, good-looking male prostitute rather than a local girl.

Garvan was unable to fault his logic, and he said as much to him. It seemed feasible, but it was still a long shot.

There was an expression of deep regret on Rowlands's face. 'My only failing was I panicked,' he said candidly. 'I lost sight of the bigger picture; my training went out of the window. In fact, everything I was taught paled into insignificance. I was being blackmailed, and that was the only thing that truly mattered to me. There were photos; it was all so hideous. Selfishly, I needed to save my own skin,' he added sadly. 'Well, you know all the sordid truth anyway.' He suddenly looked into Garvan's eyes. While they were not entirely unsympathetic, all the same, he knew there was an element of accusation in them. He said, without prompting, 'I know I handled it all wrong. I should have come clean, but I didn't, and I'll have to live with the consequences of that decision for the rest of my life. Innocent people died because of my mistakes.'

Garvan had no reason to doubt Rowlands's sincerity. Instinctively, through years of experience as a copper, he knew when someone was lying to him, and right now, he felt Rowlands was being completely upfront and honest with him.

Rowlands nudged the empty hip flask across the table. 'Thank you,' he whispered.

Garvan shot him a smile. 'Maybe we can arrange something?'

'Like what?'

'Perhaps the occasional odd refill, what do you think?'

For the first time, Rowlands broke into spontaneous laughter, but there was still a hard edge to it. 'If you can swing it, I certainly won't say no!'

Garvan pushed his chair back and made to leave, but Rowlands hadn't quite finished.

'Whatever you do, Superintendent, don't ever lose sight of the fact there's always a hidden layer,' he said seriously, 'and then another, and so on, until you finally find a small but important kernel of the truth. By then, it's sometimes way too late to do anything. My one failing as a field agent was Toniolo knew far more than I allowed for. It's only now I'm beginning to realise that he probably has rather more than one string to his bow.'

At the end of the day, Garvan was a novice in their world, and still learning the ropes, but traitor or not, Rowlands's views remained insightful.

'The more I think about it,' he explained openly, 'maybe you really should start considering broadening your search.'

'Tell me how?'

'Just don't get too stove-piped into a single strand of investigation. At the moment, it's fixated on the Soviet connection.'

'Well,' Garvan shot back at him, 'I guess, in no small measure, that's very much down to you.'

'Yes, I know,' Rowlands said, almost dismissively, 'but you've been in this game long enough now to realise you rarely get a straight answer, because there usually isn't one.'

'Then, for once, why not give me a straight answer about Toniolo.'

'What's the question?'

'You've obviously given this whole matter a good deal of thought.'

Rowlands gaze glided meaningfully around the spartan interview room. 'To be honest with you, there's very little else to do in this godforsaken place.'

'What's your gut instinct about Toniolo?'

Rowlands considered his reply carefully. 'I'm beginning to believe he might just be your greatest nightmare.'

'And what's that?'

'That he's a triple agent.'

Garvan steadily held his gaze; he was inclined to agree with Rowlands, maybe he'd hit the nail on the head, but without proof, there was very little he could do.

Garvan hadn't immediately dismissed his theory out of hand, and Rowlands, at least, began to feel vindicated maybe Toniolo had not only successfully betrayed him, but had also outwitted British Intelligence as well. He was also pretty sure of his ground. His incarceration at Latchmere had given him more than enough time on his hands to reflect about Lisbon, and his epic fall from grace, not least the unending shame of betraying his colleagues and friends. His duplicity had ultimately led to a trail of bloodshed and destruction. He'd never expected forgiveness, for he couldn't even forgive himself, let alone have expected the Service to extend anything other than condemnation for his treachery.

'Like it, or not, the way I see it, is he's managed so far to run rings around all of us. The one thing you'll probably never be able to discover fully is how much he's managed to divulge to his Russian spymasters. In comparison, I'm a mere minnow to the depth of his betrayal, not only to the Service, but the country at large.'

Garvan studied him speculatively. 'What's your gut feeling, a politician or a member of British Intelligence?'

'Ah, Superintendent, I might be good but not that good. The only thing I know is whoever Toniolo is, they're at the top of their game. More than that, I can't help you!'

Chapter 20

His meeting with George Rowlands was over; Garvan knocked on the door, and was let out by an armed soldier, and escorted back along the green painted corridor. In the guardroom, the senior NCO was on the telephone. He looked up at Garvan, gestured toward him, and mouthed silently to hold on.

'Yes, sir, he's right here. Of course, I will,' the sergeant said, before placing the receiver in the cradle. 'That was Major Hall on the blower. He wants you to meet him at the Cabinet War Rooms.'

'Did he say when?' Garvan asked.

'Right away, sir. He says it's urgent.'

Garvan felt a distinct sinking feeling. 'Thank you, Sergeant,' he said by rote.

'Will you want to see Mr. Rowlands again this week, sir?'

'I'll let you know.'

Within the hour, Garvan was drawing up outside the unprepossessing entrance to Churchill's underground bunker. Spencer was sitting on a low wall, enjoying a few minutes' peace and quiet with a cigarette on the go. Garvan assumed the three wise men were getting impatient for results. In turn, they were no doubt under increasing pressure from the government to provide them with answers, and get to the root of Agent Toniolo's real identity. Time was pressing, for not only was the War Cabinet concerned about the prospect of a Soviet mole in their midst, but it had also placed an unnecessary strain on relations with Washington.

Toniolo was important, but Garvan sensed as far as the Director General and C were concerned, the whole sordid business was an unwelcome distraction. He could hardly blame them. Their main concerns, not unnaturally, were with the day-to-day operation of their respective departments. A constant stream of intelligence data had to be evaluated, decoded, and sent to the various Allied Headquarters on the Continent. Not only were the lives of many thousands of troops at stake, but also the eventual successful outcome of the war itself.

Whatever the bigger picture might be, they were equally aware, with Toniolo still at large, and apparently becoming ever more volatile and ruthless, they needed to eliminate him altogether. The inherent risks of his continued double-dealing were becoming greater with every passing day.

Seeing the approach of Garvan's car along Horse Guards Road, Spencer looked up, and raised his hand in recognition. Garvan switched off the engine of the Austin 12, and somewhat reluctantly climbed out of the car.

'What's this all about?' he called over to Spencer, as he locked the driver's door.

'The three wise men want to see you.'

'But, why here?' he queried.

'They were here earlier for a meeting with the Prime Minister.'

Garvan felt slightly mollified, but only slightly. Unease was written all over his face.

'It seemed sensible while they were still here, under the same roof, they might as well haul you in for a chat,' Spencer explained, waving his hand in the air, and wafting a stream of grey smoke. 'Especially as they knew you'd arranged to meet Rowlands first thing this morning. By the way, how did it go?'

Garvan gave him an indifferent shrug.

'What's that supposed to mean?'

'There's still no denying George is a clever bastard.'

'Did he give you anything?'

'He was more open this time, but there was nothing tangible about Toniolo. Maybe, we just have to accept he simply doesn't know.'

Spencer didn't disagree. 'What *did* he have to say for himself?'

'He believes Toniolo is a triple agent.'

'It's a possibility.'

'I think George probably might have something.'

Spencer eased himself up from the wall. 'Well, rather you than me, trying to sell *that* one to the three wise men.'

Garvan held his gaze. 'I bet you are, but I'm not selling anything, other than the options.'

'Even so, it's a big ask, and I wouldn't want to be in your shoes.'

Spencer smiled slightly, almost apologetically, but noted the steel behind Garvan's eyes. Since his secondment from Scotland Yard, he'd learned to play the game well, very well, and had contented himself with acting like a sponge, soaking up everything there was to learn from his MI5 colleagues. In many ways, it had been a baptism of fire, but Spencer had known all along Garvan was far from being a run of the mill copper. His meteoric rise through the ranks, going from Detective Sergeant to Chief Superintendent in under a decade was entirely unheard of. He was considered a force to be reckoned with, and you underestimated him at your peril. He knew that, but wasn't quite certain whether it had filtered through to the three wise men. Robertson being the only exception, he'd worked closely with Garvan right from the start. He knew him of old, and knew he wouldn't hesitate to face them down and defend his corner, no matter what the odds.

Spencer escorted Garvan to the only public entrance to the War Rooms, not that anyone would have realised the importance of the inconspicuous doorway banked by sandbags; it was certainly no different from any number of entrances to other government buildings.

A Royal Marine, whose sheer bulk seemed to fill the space around them, a man mountain, with a pistol strapped to his hip, met them at the reception. On recognising Spencer, he snapped sharply to attention.

Spencer turned, and gestured toward Garvan. 'I think that you'll find Superintendent Garvan is on your list.'

'Yes, sir!' he barked, and reached for the clipboard resting on the reception desk. He ran his finger down the page, and ticked off his name. 'Gentleman, would you like to follow me.'

They did, down into the bowels of Churchill's wartime bunker. Spencer had been there many times, but for Garvan, this was a first. He was intrigued. He'd heard about it, in meetings, but had never before been allowed access to the hub of the Government's communication centre. The place was dimly lit, and a rabbit warren of dark corridors lined with truncated communication cabling. The bunker was spread over three acres, and it was said to be capable of housing over five hundred staff, including a hospital, canteen, dormitories, and even a shooting range. Apart from the unprepossessing entrance on Horse Guards, which was a designated escape route, the normal access to the extensive underground network was via the numerous tunnels connecting government departments situated on either side of Whitehall.

They negotiated endless flights of stairs toward the inner sanctum, and the further they descended, the air began to become increasingly stale. Their Marine escort came to a halt, and gestured toward a closed door. Garvan guessed it was a meeting room for the great and good.

'They're waiting for you inside,' Spencer explained.

'Aren't you coming in?

'Me? Lord, no!'

His suspicion suddenly grew into alarm. 'What the *hell's* going on here, Spence?'

'Count me out. I've already had one grilling this morning, thank you.' Spencer grimaced. 'Trust me, once was more than enough.'

'Did they mention my brief?'

'Well,' Spencer said, with a slight shrug, 'only in passing.'

'That's it?'

'I'm sorry, mate, but you're on your own from here on in.'

Garvan wasn't entirely surprised. Having written the report, he knew that his neck was very much on the line, but until the so-called three wise men could shoot him down in flames and refute his findings, he felt he was still very much on safe on ground.

On being shown into the room, the first thing he noticed was a series of maps plastering the walls. Various coloured pins randomly dotted their surface. No doubt they meant something to the planners and the operational commanders.

Menzies, Petrie, and Robertson sat side-by-side; the first thing he noticed was they each had a copy of his report sitting in front of them. Robertson invited him to take a seat. He did so.

Garvan had done his homework; he knew Petrie had a reputation as a rugged, and tough-fighting Scot, who had earned his spurs not only as a copper, but also as the Assistant Director of Criminal Intelligence and then as Director of the Intelligence Bureau. It was Churchill's decision in October 1940 to appoint him as the head of MI5.

Since his appointment as DG, he'd gone out of his way to forge closer links with his counterpart, General Menzies. On Petrie's appointment, Churchill had made it clear to him there was simply no place left for their former interdepartmental rivalries. The fact Churchill had personally appointed Menzies ensured he had some measure of control over the sister Intelligence Service.

Spencer had described Petrie to him as being unfailingly courteous, and a firm, but a safe, pair of hands.

239

After Garvan's first encounter with the man, he couldn't entirely fault Spencer's appraisal, but had the distinct feeling the DG was holding back, almost to the point of reticence. By any account, it was a difficult situation, MI5 having been tasked to investigate a traitor, embedded within MI6. Perhaps he didn't want to cross a line with Menzies, at least not in front of Garvan.

It was Petrie who was the first to speak. 'Well, Superintendent Garvan, may I just say you do seem to have a great deal of circumstantial evidence in your report.' He waited for a response, but didn't get one. 'And, if I may add, even more in the way of speculation.'

Petrie's opening gambit was a slight, but Garvan was giving nothing away. If they'd been able to come up with anything to counter his report, they would have done so right way. He knew they were probably still stumbling in the dark, almost as much as he was.

Garvan decided to take his time. He figured the ball was still very much in his court. He wasn't quite sure what they were expecting, but he was good at what he did, and they knew he was. He also knew the best form of defence was to attack.

'Let's face it, gentlemen,' he announced, 'we all have to accept Toniolo has played us like a fiddle.'

As he had suspected, his opening gambit didn't go down too well.

'Did anything come of your meeting with Rowlands?' Petrie shot at him.

'That probably depends on your point of view.'

A flicker or irritation crossed Petrie's face. 'Don't even start to think about playing games with me, Garvan. I know exactly how things stand with Rowlands. Is he still holding out on us, or not?'

'How long is a piece of string?' Garvan said flatly.

'That's not what I *asked*.'

'I know it isn't, but one way or another, I think we've all been probably a little guilty of underestimating Toniolo.'

'Does that include Rowlands?'

'Yes, it does.'

'Really, do you think so?' Petrie said carefully.

'God only knows George has messed up, in his time.'

'I hardly think that's in dispute.'

'But, you can't deny he was good at what he did.'

'The man's a ruddy traitor!' Petrie rasped angrily.

'Yes, he is, but in his day, he was a force to be reckoned with. He was certainly head and shoulders above his peer group. Or have I perhaps missed something?'

'Go on,' Petrie barked at him.

'Whatever we may, or may not, think of him now, he was once considered good enough to be a Head of Station, but in the longer term, he was mooted as a possible Chief of MI6.'

Menzies was impressed. He'd done his homework, but he wasn't quite sure where Garvan was heading. 'Whatever his merits as a field officer, Superintendent, let's not lose sight of the fact the bastard ended up spying for the Germans!' C grunted.

Garvan appeared unruffled by Menzies's intervention. 'If you'd kindly allow me to finish, sir,' he said sharply. 'Faults, or not, I don't think anyone in this room could dispute Rowlands's abilities as a first-rate intelligence officer?' His gaze locked meaningfully onto Menzies.

Albeit reluctantly, C agreed with him Rowlands had once been the golden boy of MI6. His early promotion had been significant in itself. The Portugal post was, and remained pivotal in the Allied intelligence war against the Third Reich. It was also on record, Rowlands had initially been well reported on, up until his fall. But, in C's mind, Rowlands was an also-ran, yesterday's man, and more importantly, a traitor.

He held Garvan's eyes. 'At the end of the day, we all know the man screwed up, he was a bloody fool and should have seen it coming!'

Garvan readily agreed. 'Fool or not, he's still a lost asset to the Service!'

There was an uneasy silence between them. Garvan decided to float Rowlands's theory there was a real possibility Toniolo might have been responsible for revealing his sexuality to the Nazis, for, up until that point, he had believed it wasn't generally known, even amongst his MI6 colleagues.

Although Menzies accepted it wasn't generally known, he'd assumed people might well have guessed for themselves. While he couldn't refute the theory out of hand, he pointed out Rowlands had been a well-known West End theatrical agent before the war, and his personal life wasn't necessarily an entirely closed book to German Intelligence. Within the theatrical community, he had been well regarded, not only for his professionalism, but also for his wit and sense of style.

Robertson said, with characteristic understatement, 'I think what C is really trying to say, is George has always been rather colourful.'

Menzies smiled slightly. 'The problem we have, Superintendent, is although there's a certain logic to it all, the bottom line is we still don't have any proof.'

'What else did Rowlands have to say for himself?' Petrie queried, his voice sounding strangely toneless and almost indifferent.

'Our investigations have been too focussed, up until this point.'

Petrie looked querulous. 'I'm sorry, am I missing something here? I thought we ordered you to interrogate the bastard, not ask for his bloody advice!'

Garvan held his gaze. 'I'm merely telling you what he said, sir.'

242

Petrie shook his head in disgust, and mumbled something or other about it being a complete waste of their time.

'Getting back to the investigation being too focussed, what's that all about?' Robertson asked, as he began packing tobacco into the bowl of his pipe.

'That, so far, we've been concentrating solely on the NKVD connection, he just felt that we might well have missed a trick.'

Robertson struck a match and lit his pipe. 'Really?' he said reflectively. 'And what do you think he meant by that, exactly?'

'Until we know where Toniolo's true loyalties actually lay, he'll always be one step ahead of us. We've always assumed it was to Moscow.'

Robertson cast him a questioning look; he was curious. 'We've headed down this strand of enquiry for no other reason than Rowlands gave us the tip-off in the first place. If we're to believe him, he supposedly overheard his German spymaster discussing Toniolo with a Gestapo officer in Lisbon.' He looked at Garvan sharply. 'You've more experience than us interviewing cunning bastards like Rowlands. Do you think he's still leading us up the garden path again?'

'No, not this time, Colonel. He's rattled, maybe because he's had time on his hands to work things out. But, what he said made sense; therefore, it might just be true.'

'Go on,' Robertson said encouragingly.

'It might be a shot in the dark, but if Rowlands is right, then we need to figure out whether Toniolo's ultimate loyalty is to Berlin, to Moscow, or perhaps, even more simply, to himself.' The fact that they didn't immediately shoot him down in flames was assurance enough he was probably on the right track, even Petrie appeared to have settled down. 'If we don't understand what drives the man, and what motivates

243

him, then that narrows down our real chances of catching him.'

Garvan waited for a response. Robertson finally spoke, accepting they needed to know whether ideological reasons drove Toniolo or financial gain. His best guess was they would probably never get to the root of his motivation to betray his country. Garvan didn't refute it, but as things stood, that was no reason not to pursue their line of enquiry.

Menzies, who had been making notes in his customary green ink, looked up, and sharply cut in. 'Let me get this straight, gentleman, are you both implying that Toniolo might be a *triple agent*?'

'Yes sir, I am,' Garvan said flatly.

It didn't go down too well with either of the chiefs; he wasn't expecting it to. Thankfully Robertson, at least, appeared to be on-side. He needed his support, but even if he hadn't decided to give it, Garvan wouldn't have backed down. 'The one given we have to accept is Toniolo has run rings around all of us!'

He wasn't wrong, and the three wise men knew it.

'Before I can take things forward, I also need more background information about Jeremy Haining.'

Menzies looked at him speculatively. 'What information?'

Garvan examined his face closely. 'Is there something else I ought to know about him?'

A faint smile crossed Robertson's face.

'I'm sorry,' Menzies said evenly. 'What do you want to know about him?'

'Exactly where does he sit in your organisation?'

Robertson was pleased; sometimes, it took an outsider to ask the right questions. There was no side with Garvan, and, more importantly, he wasn't bogged down by the internal wrangling within the Intelligence Service.

Menzies leaned forward on the desk; his hands clasped together. 'There's not that much to know. It's all on record.'

'All the same, General, I'd appreciate it if you could tell me.'

Robertson sucked heavily on his pipe; he'd been dying to ask C about Haining for years, maybe, at last, he'd come clean.

Menzies carefully considered his reply. 'Before Jeremy Haining became an MP, he had, shall I say, several close friendships with MI6.'

'With due respect, sir, what exactly is that supposed to mean?'

C chose his words carefully. 'It was a relationship,' he said, enigmatically.

An expression of incomprehension spread across Garvan's face. 'A relationship?' he repeated.

Menzies unclasped his hands, and grunted. 'If you must know, Superintendent, he worked for MI6 for a while.'

'And is he still on the books?'

'Not as such, no. Our paths cross, from time to time, because of his ministerial work at the Foreign Office, but I assure you, it's no more than that.'

Garvan knew C was being disingenuous. Once a member of the Service, no-one ever quite managed to split themselves from the inner sanctum. It was a given the ties could never be entirely cut asunder from the intelligence fraternity; they became almost family. He didn't question Menzies response; he hadn't expected a straight answer. There was no point, so he moved on.

'If you're permitted, sir, can you at least tell me in what capacity Haining worked for the Service?'

Menzies appeared to adopt a rather world-weary look. 'What you have to remember, Superintendent, is throughout the decade leading up to the declaration of war,

245

from an intelligence perspective, we were fighting a two-pronged attack from both the fascists and the communists.'

'I thought we still were,' Garvan said drily.

'Yes, Superintendent, of course, we are,' Menzies said tartly. 'But at the time, our task wasn't exactly made any easier when Stalin, unfortunately, signed a non-aggression pact with Hitler. Given on a political level, they were meant to be diametrically opposed to one another, it sent shock waves around Westminster. We missed the boat, and didn't see it coming. We were literally stunned by the news. Everything, all our planning, had been sent out of kilter.'

Garvan looked at C speculatively. 'With due respect, sir, you still haven't answered my original question. In what capacity was Haining working for the Service?'

'Don't you see it's all tied up?' he said testily.

Garvan held his ground. 'No, sir, I don't. I think you'll have to spell it out for me.'

'Jeremy Haining was ideally placed to know what was happening on the ground with the communists in this country, and over the years, he'd also fostered a number of valuable contacts in both the Soviet Union and Nazi Germany through several high profile trade delegations. Over a period of time, we made various approaches to Haining, with the view to sounding him out.' Menzies began to toy absent-mindedly with his pen, rolling it between his fingers, and occasionally sketching a doodle on his notepad. 'We needed to see if he was amenable to helping us in the run-up to the war.'

'It can't have been easy.'

'It never is, Superintendent. Some you win, and some you lose. It's the nature of the game, but you have to chance your luck.'

'Didn't the fact he's openly criticised both the Soviets and the German regimes compromise his usefulness to British Intelligence?'

246

'Not really,' Menzies said, with a shrug, 'Haining's a clever so-and-so, and despite his public announcements, his contacts and friends remained second to none. Both sides of the divide believed he was merely playing to his political needs. In fact, it was a veritable masterclass in diplomacy.'

'I daresay you know him better than anyone else sat here round the table, but where, sir, do you believe his political allegiances lay?'

A flicker of irritation crossed Menzies's face, for he sensed it was less a question than a demand. It ran through his mind it was a smart move; this Scotland Yard Detective was certainly no pushover. Somehow, Garvan had skilfully managed to turn completely around what had meant to be a grilling from the three wise men, and it was now *they* who found themselves under his scrutiny. Menzies was just beginning to appreciate why Robertson had always rated him so highly.

For his part, Robertson had retained a rather fixed, if not bemused, smile on his face. Even he hadn't expected Garvan to come out fighting quite so forthrightly against such high-powered opposition. He was pleased, of course, but in his own way, he'd also been guilty of underestimating him. But, Robertson knew Garvan well enough to sense, judging by the unflinching hardness in his eyes, something had set his back up. Perhaps Rowlands loosened up and come clean. If he had, Garvan was keeping it close to his chest.

'Well, sir?' Garvan persisted, without missing a beat, 'do *you* know where Jeremy Haining's loyalty really lies? Is it Moscow, Berlin, or London?'

It was Petrie who intervened. 'I think you'll find, Superintendent, the idea of this meeting was for you to supply *us* with the answers, and not the other way around!'

'I'm quite sure it was, sir,' he said sharply, 'but whether we like it or not, Haining is a prime suspect, he always has been, and right now, we're drastically running out of suspects. Having gone through Burdis's personal paperwork, it's apparent he was never more than a bit-part player.'

'Are you certain about that?' Robertson probed.

'From everything I've read and been told about him, I doubt if he was astute enough to run rings around the Service, let alone someone of Haining's abilities.'

'You may have a point,' Robertson accepted, thoughtfully drawing on his briar.

'We need to consider whether Burdis's links to the far right, and possibly to the Abwehr itself, were used as a hook or a bargaining chip by Toniolo to blackmail him.'

'I'm not entirely sure what you're getting at Superintendent, but as I said before, this is all just pure speculation on your part, and nothing more.'

Garvan allowed a deliberate silence to fall between them, before saying, 'That brings me to another point.'

'Go on, man!' Petrie barked impatiently. 'Just spit out what you mean to say, and get it over and done with!'

'Some time ago, I pulled Jamie Burdis's file from Central Registry.' He again paused, and deliberately took his time to light a cigarette, before slowly exhaling the smoke through his lips. 'Bearing in mind Burdis's somewhat flamboyant lifestyle, I was expecting his file to be bulging at the seams. Even the vetting checks prior to his appointment to the Foreign Office seemed pretty routine and tame, almost to the point of being non-existent.'

Petrie looked to Robertson. 'Is this true?'

'If Superintendent Garvan says it is, then it is,' he said cagily. He had a feeling he knew where Garvan was going with this one, but sat back, and kept his mouth firmly shut.

'You can well imagine my embarrassment this morning, sir,' Garvan continued addressing Petrie, 'when George Rowlands of all people referred to the large annex attached to Jamie Burdis's master security file. The trouble was that I didn't know about it!' He took another long draw on his freshly lit cigarette. 'The annex apparently contained intelligence detailing Burdis's affiliation to the far right, his close links to Oswald Mosley and the British Union of Fascists, not to mention his links to the Right Club.' He allowed his words to slowly sink in. 'The trouble is, where does that take us?'

'I'm sure you're about to tell us,' Petrie said, almost resignedly.

'To the day I die, I'll never completely understand politicians.'

'Join the Club,' Petrie snorted.

'What do Haining and Mosely have in common?'

'If you ask me, they're like chalk and cheese.'

'After the 1929 election, Moseley became a member of the Labour Government. For all his aristocratic pedigree, he sided not with the Tories but with the Labour Party. Burdis likewise flirted with Communism before eventually veering violently toward the far right like Moseley. The trouble is, their politics, like the men themselves, including Haining, seem to be based on shifting sands and on tactical skills, rather than any deep-rooted ideology, and I have a feeling that probably sums up Toniolo to a tee.'

Petrie folded his arms, and eased himself back into his chair. 'So, what about this annex Superintendent? Much of what you've already said is on public record.'

Garvan took an unhurried drag on his cigarette, and calmly looked at each of them in turn. 'The annex on Burdis's file was obviously important. Even George Rowlands had seen the bloody thing, and knew all the sordid details. Actually, to be honest with you, I'm glad he had, otherwise I'd have been none the wiser. At the time when I requested the file from Central Registry, I didn't think to question it. In hindsight, that was my mistake. I took things at face value. I'd always assumed the security files were sacrosanct, and beyond question. But, someone had gone to a great deal of trouble to weed through the paperwork, and remove any incriminating evidence, which may have helped identify Toniolo. Why else would anyone have wanted to tamper with the file?'

'Why indeed,' the DG agreed.

But, just as Rowlands had predicted, Petrie suggested the missing annex might simply have been a case of clerical error. Iit could easily have become detached from the main file, and inadvertently attached to someone else's security documentation.

'The annex wasn't simply removed, sir,' Garvan argued. 'The entire file was tampered, with including the minute sheet.'

'Are you sure Rowlands wasn't lying about the annex?' Petrie persisted.

'No, he wasn't,' Robertson intervened sourly. 'At one point or another, over the last six months, I've requested any number of security files from Central Registry, including Burdis's. It certainly had an attachment when I saw it. If memory serves me, the main file was bursting at the seams with umpteen reports, most of which were either secret or at best confidential. Rowlands isn't lying about it; the annex contained references to Burdis's affiliation to the far right. Some years ago, it was decided for ease of reference to consolidate all the right-wing reports into the annex.'

Menzies looked up from his note taking, and suddenly tossed his pen down. 'Whatever way we look at it, gentlemen, someone has gone to a great deal of trouble to cover their tracks. I don't suppose, for one minute, checking Central Registry's records will help shed any light on the matter. Whoever redacted Burdis's file will have done so by circumventing standard procedure.'

'It wouldn't hurt checking all the same,' Petrie suggested.

250

'No, I guess not. We can go through the motions, of course, but I wouldn't hold out any real hope of finding anything worthwhile.'

'Could Haining have pulled this off?' Garvan hinted.

'Not easily,' Menzies said, 'but it's not entirely impossible. I'll have to sound out things my end, but whoever managed to get hold of the file knows the system inside out. They'd have covered their tracks, and covered them well.'

'Would you like us to have another word with Jeremy Haining?' Garvan asked.

Menzies's expression remained as taciturn as ever. He certainly didn't want to commit himself. In part, that was down to the fact Haining continued to be held in high regard, not only by Churchill, but also by the entire coalition government. In some respects, he was treading on eggshells, and didn't want to create any unnecessary waves. While his natural instinct was to eliminate Haining altogether from the equation, and save himself a great deal of unnecessary trouble, he also had to factor into his decision Haining might well be an innocent party, and the political fallout of insinuating he was working for a foreign government would be seismic. It was a difficult call to make. Menzies needed to play an even hand. Admittedly, it was a fine line to tread. His primary concern was whether Haining was in the pay of the Soviets. Leaving him in-situ at the Foreign Office raised its own inherent risks. Haining had complete access to a broad range of highly-classified material from both sides of the Atlantic. In fact, the Soviets would have given their eye teeth to have someone of Haining's standing under their control.

On the other hand, the Americans might, as a precautionary measure, still demand to pull the plug on Haining, regardless of whether he was innocent or guilty. But, Menzies needed time, and, more importantly, he needed to consult the Prime Minister on the political nuances of the situation. Garvan had worked with British Intelligence long

251

enough to realise C was finding himself increasingly caught between a rock and a hard place.

'Do you have anything else for us?' Petrie asked.

'One or two things, yes, sir.'

'I rather thought you might have, Superintendent.'

'I think we need to sort the wheat from the chaff.'

'I'm sure we do,' he replied drily.

'When Major Hall and I interviewed Jeremy Haining, he told us Lord Oakways believed there was a rotten egg in the Department.'

Petrie held his gaze. 'So which Department are we talking about, the Foreign Office or MI6?'

'I think that's probably still open to conjecture, but either way, we have to face the fact Oakways wasn't that far wrong. Otherwise, he wouldn't have paid with his life.'

Garvan waited, half expecting them to come back at him, but they didn't.

'From the security files, and from those who knew him well, I've no reason to doubt Oakways was eccentric in his ways, but I do think we need to take stock, and not give too much credence to venomous Whitehall tittle-tattle.'

'What's your *point*?' Robertson asked him.

'I think Oakways's enemies played upon his weaknesses, especially Toniolo.' His eyes flicked toward Menzies. 'Perhaps you might be able to clear something up for us, sir?'

'What's that?' C barked gruffly.

'We've still not been able to confirm whether MI6 had Oakways house wired in Lord North Street.'

'Certainly not with my authority!' he came back sharply.

'With due respect, sir, it doesn't mean to say it didn't happen.'

'No,' he conceded,' 'but I can assure you, it wasn't with official sanction.'

For the first time, Garvan had an unequivocal answer, it was progress of sorts.

'I can't help thinking the endless rumours about his paranoia were exaggerated.'

'Exaggerated?' Petrie queried, curiously.

'They were circulated, probably by someone with a vested interest in damaging his reputation.'

'I take it you mean by Toniolo, Superintendent?'

'Like most politicians, he had his enemies. Who else, other than Toniolo, stood to gain by destroying him? By all accounts at the time of his death, he'd almost become something of a laughing stock.'

Petrie pulled a face. 'Then, why go to the bother of killing the man?'

'I think Oakways had somehow stumbled across something important, perhaps Toniolo's identity. Whatever it was, had placed his life in danger. Yesterday's man, or not, Toniolo certainly wouldn't have taken the chance of leaving him alive, which is precisely why he also murdered Len Dunmore.'

The connection to Toniolo, he explained, was staring at them in the face. Petrie accepted it was a point well made. In his experience, if it seemed logical, it was probably correct. Garvan's abilities, he knew, were sharpened by years of skilful detective work, and with it, had come an inherent self-confidence built on a career of outstanding success. That he hadn't been fazed or intimidated in front of them was proof enough Robertson's decision to second him from Scotland Yard had been a shrewd choice.

The fact the three wise men greeted Garvan with a wall of silence was, to his mind, a small, if not significant, victory. At least they hadn't yet shot him down in flames at the first opportunity. That he'd given them food for thought was without question, or, at least, it was for the time being. He might have misread the situation, but as he gazed slowly

253

around their faces, the only given was he'd managed to place the investigation back in their respective courts.

'You know, of course,' Petrie said, at last, 'whatever we discover about Toniolo will have to remain in-house.'

Garvan shot his boss a half-hearted smile. 'I'm well aware, sir, British Intelligence and our political masters like to keep their shit well-shovelled.'

Petrie arched his brows disapprovingly it wasn't quite the analogy he was thinking of, but, all the same, it brought a smile to Robertson's face.

'Well,' Petrie grunted at length, 'that's one way of putting it, Superintendent.'

'Quite,' Menzies smirked, snapping his notebook shut.

The three wise men called an end to the meeting, albeit an uneasy one.

Chapter 21

Her hours were sporadic, Joyce reported for duty at St. James's whenever Spencer ordered her to. It was late afternoon; she knew what she needed to do. He had already provided her with a script to follow, concerning a fictitious military attack on the Pas de Calais. But, to avoid arousing her German controller's suspicions, she needed to slant the missive in her own personalised style. From Leader's perspective, the scraps of information she was asked to send didn't always make sense, but tonight was different. She needed to convince the German High Command the Normandy invasion was just the precursor to the main thrust of the Allied assault.

She met Spencer to discuss the evening's transcript, but, however, important, it wasn't long before there was a knock on the door. Tar Robertson's secretary said it was urgent, and he was needed right away on another matter.

'Can't it wait?' he asked her.

Lil shook her head. 'I'm sorry, Major.'

Spencer hesitated; he was torn, and didn't want to leave Joyce out on a limb. 'Can you give us a minute?'

She nodded and closed the door on them.

'Do we need to go over this again?'

Joyce looked at him searchingly. 'No, I'll be fine,' she lied.

Spencer hesitated. He wanted to stay, but he didn't have a choice. There was always some meeting or other, and yet another flap needing his immediate attention. It was the nature of the beast, but the timing was wrong, and Robertson must have known that. Maybe he had assumed Joyce was more than capable of handling the transmission on her own, but as her Case Officer, Spencer knew now more than ever, she needed his support, a guiding hand, as there were so many lives depending on tonight's report.

255

He pushed back his chair. 'Are you sure?'

She gave him a tight smile. 'Yes.'

'I'll make my excuses as soon as I can.'

He disappeared out of the office, leaving Joyce to re-read the transcript. Shortly after she started to tap out the message to her German Controller Bernard Drescher, there was a knock on the door. She looked up; it was Captain Eldridge.

'John, what are you doing *here*?' she asked.

'Spence asked me to keep an eye on you,' he winked.

'I'm sure he did.'

Eldridge sat beside her in the windowless office, as she continued the transmission to her Abwehr spymaster. In the past, it had been chicken feed, dross in its own way, but there was always just enough tantalising information to keep Drescher and his colleagues in German Intelligence interested.

It was a fine balancing act. The occasional snippet of genuine material was always integrated into the deception plan. The aim was to impress, but without any serious military consequences. With Spencer's help and shrewd imagination, Joyce had invented no end of talkative contacts, both military and political. Fortunately, the Germans still regarded her as being entirely genuine, and an outstanding agent. More to the point, they were totally unaware Joyce had become one of MI5's most valuable active double agents.

Under Eldridge's watchful gaze, she continued to tap out Spencer's typescript. Over the years, she'd grown to like John. He was good looking with a mischievous sense of humour, but his seemingly light-hearted, and sometimes off-hand bonhomie belied his innate toughness and ability as a skilful MI5 Case Officer. She sensed, at times, Eldridge felt slightly stifled by the constraints of working for British Intelligence, and would have returned to his regiment serving with the Guards Armoured Division. Joyce knew his elder brother had served with Bomber Command, but had died early on in the war. Eldridge's mother believed he was holding down some desk job at the War Office. She probably rather naively thought her youngest son was safe from harm, but Joyce knew Eldridge had been on some difficult assignments for British Intelligence, often far more dangerous than anything he would ever likely to have encountered with the Guards Division.

For all its faults, her small cupboard of an office afforded a degree of privacy. Away from the main hub of the operations room, which was constantly filled with the noise from the banks of transmitters, and the clacking machine gun like tat-tat rattle of the cipher machines, and the never-ending signals routed to various far-flung intelligence and military commands. Dominating the wall above her desk was Spencer's large, coloured-coded planner. It detailed meetings, target dates, and times when Joyce was expected to transmit messages to Drescher. But, much to Spencer's frustration, she'd never quite mastered the colour coding; to her mind, it seemed overly complicated. Over the years, it had been a constant source of frustration, as he'd tried in vain to explain it all to her. Joyce would invariably look at him blankly, and was at a complete loss as to how it was meant to make her life easier. It had lately become something of a running joke between them. Joyce wouldn't budge. She either wouldn't, or couldn't, understand it. Spencer remained convinced she was just being bloody-minded.

Joyce ran her finger down Spencer's typescript. Had she missed anything, anything the War Office and the Allied Command would never forgive, if she cocked up. Even now, however, valuable she was to Tar Robertson and the Double Cross System, an agent was only ever as good as their last transmission, and whether their Abwehr spymaster bought their lies. There was no way of knowing if Drescher would bite the bait. Joyce was good at her job, but there was always a chance, a real one, that her world could implode at any given

257

moment. It would take only one mistake, one fatal error, to end her usefulness, and her possibly her life.

Joyce relaxed back in her chair. The message had been sent, and was somewhere in the ether between London and Hamburg. Fortunately, Bernard Drescher responded almost immediately. It was short and sweet; he'd get back to her in a couple of hours. It was enough; she hadn't been expecting too much from him at this stage, other than a holding reply.

Eldridge had not been briefed on the content of her message. But, the fact Spencer had asked him to stay with her was testament enough. Whatever it contained was important. Noticing the expression of unease on her face, he asked, 'Is everything okay?'

Joyce swung her chair around and looked across at him. Her eyes met his; she seemed uncertain. 'I'm not sure.'

'What do you mean?'

'Did Spence tell you about it?'

He shook his head and confessed he hadn't.

She spread her hands out on the desk over the script. 'What do you think the chances are of our convincing Berlin Normandy was just the starter, the opening gambit, and the main Allied thrust is Calais?'

Eldridge let out a low whistle. Whatever he'd been expecting her to say, it certainly wasn't that. Christ, he thought, she was in it up to her neck and drowning. A lot was riding on her skills, and the faith German Intelligence had in her trustworthiness. He wasn't sure how to respond. If it paid off, then the Germans would continue to batten down their elite Das Reich Panzer divisions around Calais, and give the Allies time to consolidate their hard-fought gains. Either way, thousands of lives were at stake. They'd already been delayed, that much he did know, the result of a well-executed plan of sabotage by the French Resistance and the Special Operations Executive.

'God only knows if they'll buy it,' he said to her at last.

'Spencer reckons there's an outside chance they might just fall for it.'

'There's always a chance, Jo, but I wouldn't go holding my breath.' He snapped on his lighter, and lit a cigarette. 'Come on. I think we're both in need of a break, don't you?'

There was no point hanging around cooped up in the office until the cryptanalysts started to intercept something from Hamburg. Joyce knew they had time on their hands, maybe an hour or so, but probably a little longer, before Bernard Drescher was in a position to give her some semblance of a response. His messages always began in the same way, "When can you next use the piano?" It was Drescher's codename for the transmitter; little did he know it was now firmly embedded in MI5's HQ.

She knew Spencer's aim was to force Drescher into asking for more information about the Allies intentions for Pas de Calais. If that happened, it would mean Berlin had taken the bait, but it was by no means a given.

The canteen was situated in the bowels of the building. It was bustling, open twenty-four hours a day to cater for the War Room, which was staffed mainly by a mix of MI5 and MI6 officers, plus an ever increasing contingent from the American OSS intelligence agency.

They grabbed a bite to eat, but she scarcely touched a morsel, idly playing with it on her plate. Joyce seemed unusually nervous, constantly twisting and untwisting her ebony cigarette holder between her fingers. It wasn't like her at all; the transcript was apparently playing on her mind. It seemed as if she was lost in some distant thought, answering, as if by rote, and all the while looking through him, rather than at him, as he tried to engage her in conversation.

259

As far as Eldridge was concerned, she'd always been a closed book; he didn't exactly dislike her, but she was a handful to control, which he guessed was probably one of the reasons why Spencer was her Case Officer.

'Don't you want anything else to eat?' he asked.

'No, I'm fine,' she assured him.

He was on the point of clearing the table, when he noticed Hugh Dickinson enter the canteen. You couldn't exactly miss him; he was a tall, striking man, with a mop of sleek dark hair, and an equally dark moustache, a remnant of his RAF career before his recruitment to the Double Cross team. The women at St. James's loved him; in fact, much to the disgust of his male colleagues, they positively drooled over him. He was effortlessly charming and sexy in equal measure, without ever seeming to try.

Dickinson weaved his way through the canteen, and made straight for their table. 'I'm sorry,' he apologised. 'Am I interrupting anything?'

'No, no, of course not,' Eldridge said. 'Is anything wrong?'

Dickinson instinctively glanced at his watch. It had been just over an hour and a half or so since Leader's transmission to Drescher. 'The Abwehr appear to have taken the bait.'

Eldridge looked at him dubiously. 'It's a bit early, isn't it?' he queried.

'Not judging by the sudden increase in wireless traffic between Hamburg and Berlin, no, it isn't.'

'So what happens now?' Joyce asked.

'How did you leave it with Drescher?'

She shrugged slightly. 'He told me to give him a couple of hours.'

'In which case, you'd better start making tracks back to the office.'

She drained the dregs from her mug, and pushed the chair away from the table. 'Do you know where Spencer is?' she asked Dickinson.

'I'm afraid he's still tied up.'

'Do you know how long he's going to be?'

'I'm not sure he was hauled into a meeting by the DG.'

Dickinson never thought he'd live to see the day when Joyce, of all people, would actually look disappointed. Usually, she seemed far happier when he wasn't around. Their working relationship had always been combustible. Dickinson was curious, and wondered what the hell had brought about Joyce's apparent mellowing toward her Case Officer. Perhaps the pressures of being a double agent were finally beginning to crack the ice maiden, but even so, it seemed unlikely. Joyce had always been totally in control of herself, and more importantly, emotionally impenetrable to those around her, including Spencer.

He'd heard the rumours circulating the team Joyce had become sexually involved with Garvan. Personally, he'd never given them that much credence. To his mind, they were just that, rumours, and nothing more. Spencer was a hard task master, and everyone within the Service knew he simply couldn't imagine Spencer turning a blind eye to a potentially compromising relationship. He'd always been utterly ruthless in his dealings with anyone who dared to step out of line, and endanger the Double Cross System; no quarter was ever given to agents. Dickinson couldn't imagine however valuable Joyce and Garvan might be to MI5; Spencer would ever make an exception to the rule. He was wrong, of course, but like everything else within the Service, it was on a need to know basis, and Dickinson simply didn't need to know.

Eldridge accompanied Joyce back to the office; there was nothing to do but wait. Another hour came and went, and Joyce began to suspect Drescher might not get back to her at

261

all this evening. He was in limbo, until Berlin formulated an official response.

She had almost given up hope, when the transmitter once again sprang into life.

As usual, Drescher's opening gambit was, "*When can you next use the piano?*"

Joyce immediately tapped out a response. "*I've been waiting for you.*"

She held her pen in readiness, and began to write down the encrypted message. Since arriving in England, she'd always used the same method of communication. To reduce the chances of interception, the Abwehr had supplied her with a one-time pad; it was, in essence, a notepad. Drescher retained a duplicate copy, and after each transmission, the top sheet could be easily torn off, and destroyed after use. Whenever she'd been close to running out of supplies, a quick message to her spymaster would ensure a package containing a one-time pad was delivered to London via a diplomatic bag to the Spanish Embassy, and specifically to a member of staff with Fascist leanings. The code pad would then be dropped off at a secure location; it was a different one each time, leaving Joyce free to pick up at a pre-arranged time.

Once Bernard Drescher signed off, Joyce began to decrypt the transmission against the cypher pad to reveal the message. Unsurprisingly, the Pas de Calais figured large in his follow-up questions. Berlin needed verification of troop movements. The transmission had set the ball rolling; in due course, the Abwehr would cross-check Leader's intelligence with their other British-based agents, who would, in turn, under MI5's command back up Leader's message.

'Is everything okay?' Eldridge asked.

She looked up, and passed him a tight smile. 'I think so.'

Joyce continued writing, almost obsessively re-checking the cypher pad to ensure she'd interpreted Drescher's

262

message correctly. Eldridge leaned over her once or twice, but Joyce made it clear the transmission was for Spencer's eyes only. He'd never forgive her, she explained, trying to soften her tone if she allowed him to read the transmission. Eldridge didn't kick up a fuss. There was no point. She was obviously under strict instructions, but, more importantly, he had no great desire to cross Spencer.

Once or twice, she carefully re-read her notes from the decoded transmission, but as she did so, Eldridge couldn't help noticing there was an increasing look of dawning horror etched across her face.

At last, he said in exasperation, 'For Christ's sake, Jo, what's going on?'

She passed him a plaintive look and said urgently, 'I need to speak to Spencer *right away*!'

Eldridge held her gaze, at any other time he might have questioned her, but the look on Leader's face said it all.

'I mean, *now,* John!' she continued pleadingly. 'It can't wait, it really can't!'

As Eldridge reached to pick up the phone, the door opened behind them, never had Joyce been so relieved to see Spencer.

'Everything all right with you two?' he asked breezily.

'I was just about to call you,' Eldridge said.

'Have the Abwehr taken the bait?'

'Yes,' Joyce said quietly, 'but Drescher has come up with something else.'

Spencer looked at her searchingly, the tension written all over her face. In his experience, it took a great deal to unnerve her; whatever it was, was important. With an understated, quiet authority, he said to Eldridge, 'Could you give us a few moments alone, John?'

'Yes, yes, of course, sir.'

263

As the door closed on them, Spencer said, 'What's this all about, Jo?'

She took a sharp intake of breath and blurted out. 'You won't believe this, but I've just been ordered to arrange to kill Frank Lucern!'

A silence followed, as he looked at her. 'Frank,' he repeated in disbelief, 'what in God's name has he ever done to upset Drescher and his henchmen, or at least enough they'd want him dead?'

Joyce shifted uneasily in her chair. Her eyes flicked toward the desk; she hesitated a moment, before nudging the decrypted message toward him. 'I think you'd better read it for yourself,' she offered.

He picked it up, and began to read, it started off well enough, in fact, better than he expected. Leader's original message had been followed up by a series of in-depth questions about the supposed Allied onslaught against the Pas de Calais.

'It's further down,' she said, impatiently gesturing toward her notes.

Spencer flicked his eyes toward her. 'I'm getting there,' he said coolly.

He continued to read on, his gaze drawn to the next passage.

"Reichsfuhrer Himmler has ordered the immediate elimination of Frank Lucern, who has, of late, operated under the Codename Agent Toniolo. Information has been received of his continued links to the NKVD. He has been found guilty of giving away State secrets to the Soviet Union injurious to the security of the Third Reich. Expedite and confirm elimination. Bernard Drescher. Heil Hitler."

If nothing else, it was stark, and to the point.

Deep down, he had never seriously suspected Frank of being capable of spying for the Russians, let alone betraying the Service. The enormity of Drescher's message was still sinking in. In comparison, Lucern's monumental betrayal started to make George Rowlands almost look like a novice. His thoughts were in turmoil; perhaps Lucern had been instrumental in setting Rowlands up. Had he made him a dupe to cover his tracks, and to bring him down? It was all possible. He was certainly the one man who had been closest to him in Portugal, and who was capable of discovering the truth.

'Where do we go from here?' she asked uncertainly.

He glanced down again at the transcript, before folding it in half. 'Give me ten minutes.'

'And then what?'

'I'll meet you downstairs in reception.'

It wasn't up for question.

'I'll get John Eldridge to draw a pistol for you from the armoury.'

'Christ, Spence,' she pleaded. 'You're not actually expecting me to kill Frank, are you? I can't do it; I really can't!'

'I'm not asking you to do anything,' he said enigmatically.

She watched him leave the office, with a growing sense of dread.

Spencer headed back upstairs to a meeting room. He only just made it. General Menzies was on his way out of the building.

'Sir, can I have a quick word with you?'

Menzies somewhat reluctantly stopped dead in his tracks. 'Is something wrong, Major?'

Spencer gestured toward the meeting room. 'Can we speak in private?'

C hesitated, wondering if it was worth his while. He guessed it might be, and retraced his steps back into the now empty meeting room. He set his old leather briefcase down on the large conference table, and sighed wearily. 'Well, what have you got to say for yourself, Major?'

'We've managed to discover Toniolo's identity.'

Menzies's expression suddenly lightened. 'That's the best news I've heard all day; I was on the point of beginning to believe we'd never get our hands on the bugger. So, who is it?' he barked.

Spencer handed him Leader's message from Bernard Drescher. 'I think you'd better read it for yourself, sir.'

On seeing the name of his most senior and trusted Case Officer, Menzies expression didn't falter. He calmly re-folded the transcript, and handed it back to Spencer.

'It's over to you, sir. How do you want us to play it?'

C responded with chilling, professional detachment. 'I can't say I've often agreed with Bernard Drescher, in fact, I don't think I ever have done, but I can't fault his logic. Whatever side of the political fence we're on, be it in London or Berlin, on this occasion, we have a certain common interest, the elimination of Toniolo.' Menzies picked his briefcase up off the table. 'One way or another, he's a dead man walking.' He added matter-of-factly. 'I think it's far better we keep the matter in-house, don't you, Major.'

C's decision wasn't exactly open for discussion; Spencer knew that.

'I will have to inform the Prime Minister immediately,' he continued smoothly. 'I'll leave it to you, of course, to sort out the disposal of our problem.'

'Yes, sir.'

'Let me know when the deed's done, will you?'

It seemed pointless to reply.

Menzies made to leave the meeting room, but swung round and said, 'I think you'll find Frank is probably still at his office with your Superintendent Garvan.'

'Yes, sir.'

C cast him a rather rueful look. 'I do hope to God he doesn't end up getting the better of you, Major?'

Spencer gave Menzies a sharp, short smile. 'I think there's probably more chance of hell freezing over first, sir.'

'Good, good,' he said brusquely. 'We'll credit Joyce Leader, of course, with killing the bugger.'

Spencer arched his brows warily.

'You never know. She might just end up being awarded an Iron Cross.'

'Where can I contact you, sir?'

'I'll either be at the Cabinet War Rooms or back at the office.'

Chapter 22

In blissful ignorance of the unfolding events at MI5, Frank Lucern and Garvan took a slow stroll back to Broadway, after having enjoyed an extended booze-fuelled dinner together at the Eros restaurant near Piccadilly. Garvan had decided to keep the conversation light, by only occasionally referring to the on-going investigation into Agent Toniolo. Lucern was in good form, but then again, he always was after a couple of large glasses of red wine, which was, in part, why Garvan had suggested meeting for a meal in the first place.

Sitting in Lucern's office, Garvan gazed at him, as he opened the large tumbler lock safe. Dressed in a white shirt, a red silk tie, and a pin-striped suit, Lucern seemed even leaner than usual. He moved and talked quickly, brimming with nervous energy, as he retrieved his work trays from the safe, and arranged them neatly on the desk. He repeated the trip back and forth across the office several times, before finally removing a large ink blotter pad. Catching Garvan's somewhat bemused expression, he felt obliged to explain himself. The night duty security staff had repeatedly pulled him up about his habit of doodling and scribbling notes on the pad. In themselves, they seemed harmless enough, but his highly sensitive jottings were considered by security staff to be classified material. He'd already had one or two warnings to lock the pad away, and destroy each leaf in the classified waste bin.

As Lucern set the blotter foursquare on the desk, he asked Garvan, 'Fancy a drink?'

Garvan initially baulked at the idea; he'd probably had enough already, but he needed to keep Lucern on an even keel, and ended up saying he wouldn't mind another.

Lucern flicked off a key hanging on the inside of the safe door, and used it to open a small dark green metal cupboard beside it.

'I need to keep it locked,' he explained, with a frisson of irritation.

'Why's that?'

A look of exasperation clouded Lucern's face. 'It comes to something when you can't even trust your own colleagues. They were helping themselves!' he said, opening the door.

Lucern could have been right, but behind his back, a flicker of amusement crossed Garvan's face, accompanied by a slight sense of unease. Perhaps unwisely, he'd been playing his cards too close to his chest. He guessed old habits die hard, but Garvan knew he was playing with fire, and should have consulted Spencer before setting up the meeting with Lucern. It had been a difficult call; on the one hand, he'd been seconded to provide MI5 with an unbiased opinion, all the same, whenever he'd placed Lucern's name in the mix, the suggestion had always been met by a wall of indifference. But, right now, he was beginning to question his judgement. He was out on a limb, and it could seriously backfire.

Lucern asked what he'd like to drink. Garvan glanced toward the well-stocked cupboard, and asked for a vodka and tonic, with a splash of bitters. Lucern plumped for a Bloody Mary, with a generous dash of Worcester sauce. He then eased himself down at the desk, and immediately swiped his pipe off the ashtray, packing it with fresh tobacco from a personalised engraved silver case. All the while, he continued to look calmly into Garvan's eyes. He seemed genuinely unconcerned, and completely at ease. It was just another day, another meeting. There was no reason to suspect Garvan's business would be anything other than mundane.

'Shall we start getting down to business?' he suggested, taking a sip of the Bloody Mary.

'I received a call yesterday afternoon from DCI Mackenzie.'

Lucern didn't appear to be particularly interested; he was more concerned that his Bloody Mary needed more Worcester sauce. 'Go on,' he said, heading back to the cupboard.

'Mackenzie phoned me about the raid on Bolton's Bank.'

Lucern didn't react; he splashed some more Worcester sauce into his drink, before returning to the desk. 'What about it?' he asked, with an air of complete disinterest.

'It's about notepaper DCI Mackenzie found with the Lilburne Club logo in the deposit box.'

He sat back down at his desk. 'Yes, I read the report from Special Branch. There was quite a lot of incriminating evidence against Jamie Burdis. He must have had one hell of a fright seeing the robbery plastered all over the newspapers. I suppose it's little wonder he decided to top himself.' Lucern calmly struck a match to light his pipe, and discarded the spent match into the ashtray. 'I'm sure there's a point to all this, Luke, but what is it?'

'You see, Frank, at the back of my mind, I needed to discount *you* from the investigation.'

Lucern's watchful eyes turned to steel. 'Me! What the hell are you talking about?'

'Your profile fits the bill,' he said bluntly.

'Good God, man, have you taken leave of your senses?'

'It was a process of elimination.'

'Was it, really?'

'What did you all have in common?'

'I'm sorry?' Lucern said blankly.

'What did you have in common with Oakways and Burdis?'

270

He shrugged indifferently. 'I haven't a bloody clue; you tell me.'

'For a start, you all studied at Cambridge.'

Lucern was obviously unimpressed by his analogy. 'Since when was that a crime?'

'It isn't, to my knowledge,' Garvan said, his voice edged with sarcasm. 'But, even you've got to admit, there's an undeniable symmetry to the case.

'Really? You're the Detective. You tell me.'

'And you're the smart-arsed spy. I'd have thought the facts would have leapt off the page.'

'Well, they *obviously* didn't.'

'I understand you're a member of the Lilburne Club?'

'Past tense. I *was* a member!'

'From all accounts, it's a left-wing fraternity.'

Lucern rolled his eyes. 'For some of us, it was, but in the main, we joined because it threw the best parties. It wasn't about the politics, but about getting pissed and enjoying ourselves.'

'Funny. George Rowlands said much the same thing.'

In the silence that fell between them, Lucern looked across into Garvan's eyes. 'I'd be lying to you if I didn't admit I was an idealist. At that age, you have such hope and expectation for the future. Sadly, reality and life tend to get in the way and shatter your dreams.' He shrugged slightly. 'There's no denying it sets you back.'

'So, at heart, were you a communist?'

Lucern pulled a face. 'A communist one day, a liberal the next. I was a learning curve. For Christ's sake, I was still growing up,' he protested. 'It was of its time.'

'Yes, that's what Jamie Burdis said.'

'Then, he wasn't wrong. We were young. Thought we could make a difference and change the world.'

Garvan decided to steer the conversation back to Bolton's Bank, and explained Mackenzie had passed the contents of the safety deposit box over to the forensic team.

He looked toward Garvan speculatively, but didn't respond.

'They managed to lift a nice set of prints from the box, so Mac ordered them to cross-reference the prints against the records we already held on Oakways and Len Dunmore. We didn't come up with anything, of course, but it was a start in the right direction.'

Lucern let out a deep-throated chuckle. 'Surely, to God. you didn't seriously believe Dunmore had anything to do with this lark?'

'I didn't think he was a Soviet spy.'

'Then, why bother?'

'Once you eliminate the impossible, whatever remains, no matter how improbable, must be the truth. My main concern was we couldn't rule out the possibility Toniolo was blackmailing him.'

'Where does that leave you with Jeremy Haining?' Lucern queried.

'What do you mean?'

'He might not be a Cambridge man, but, all the same, he fits the bill to a Tee. I take it he's still in the frame?'

'Yes, he is,' Garvan conceded. 'He's always been the fly in the ointment, the one real unknown quantity in the whole investigation.' Garvan slipped out a cigarette case from his hip pocket and coolly lit one. He could see Lucern was on edge; it was written all over his face.

'After Jamie Burdis had killed himself, I asked Mac to recheck the forensics from the bank. Only, this time, we struck pure gold.'

'What was that?'

272

'We already knew only two people had access to the safety deposit box. One of the prints we'd lifted from the box belonged to Burdis.'

Lucern kept his pipe on the go, and either fidgeted with the match box, or carefully inspected how well the tobacco was burning in the bowl. He was listening, but gave the impression Garvan had failed to capture his interest, or merit a justifiable reason for calling the meeting.

'Now we had two distinctively separate sets of fingerprints,' Garvan went on doggedly, 'the obvious conclusion was the other set of prints belonged to Toniolo.'

Lucern tended to agree with him, unless of course, he suggested, they belonged to the manager or some other member of the bank staff. Garvan explained they were all discounted from the enquiry. He leant down to reach for his briefcase, and retrieved a small notebook, with lined paper, and a pen from the inside pocket of his suit jacket, before setting the briefcase back down on the floor beside the chair. He flicked open the pad, and took his time searching through the well-thumbed pages. Lucern glanced at his watch. There were a number of files sitting in his in-tray needing his urgent attention. A booze-fuelled extended dinner was one thing, but if he didn't crack on soon, C would come down on him like a ton of bricks.

'Ah, here it is,' Garvan said, tapping an entry in the notebook. 'Last week, Frank, I believe you attended a meeting at the Home Office.'

Lucern shifted slightly in his chair. 'Yes, yes, I did.'

Garvan arched his brows, as he carefully re-read his notes. 'The Home Secretary chaired a security meeting with representatives of the Service and Special Branch.' He flicked his eyes up toward Lucern, and waited for an answer.

Lucern returned his gaze questioningly; Garvan was up to something. He was a clever bastard, that much he did know, but for the life him, he couldn't imagine why he was interested in a meeting at the Home Office.

'Why not just cut to the chase, Luke. What's this really all about?'

'After the meeting was over, Mac held back. If you remember, the Home Secretary was hosting a lunch for the attendees.'

'He certainly wasn't there, that much I do remember.'

'He was under orders.'

'What orders?'

'I asked him to hang back, to take his time.'

'Why?'

'I asked him to pick something up.'

'Like what?'

'Something you'd handled during the meeting, a pen, or a civil service hand-out. It didn't much matter what it was.' Garvan paused, inhaled on his cigarette, and blew out a plume of smoke.

Lucern didn't respond.

Garvan continued. 'Mac didn't fancy taking any chances, so, for good measure, decided to swipe your cup and saucer. The trouble was the young clerk clearing the meeting room wasn't exactly impressed with Mac pilfering the Home Office crockery.'

'I don't suppose they were!' Lucern sniffed.

'After a while, Mac managed to sweet talk her around. I'm still not sure whether he convinced her or not, but you never know. On the plus side, he hasn't received an official complaint, at least not yet.'

Lucern drew deeply on his pipe, his eyes remaining direct and unwavering.

'Yesterday afternoon,' Garvan said flatly, 'the Yard's forensic team passed their findings to Special Branch. The prints found on the cup and saucer were a perfect match to those we found in the bank vault.'

Garvan eased himself back in his chair; he needed to see Lucern squirm. He wasn't disappointed, as a look of dawning horror slowly, but inevitably, enveloped his face. In the ensuing, uneasy silence, Lucern leaned forward, and carefully placed his pipe in the ashtray.

Garvan had a copper's analytical brain, which was why Robertson had employed him in the first place, but, more importantly, he had no underlying loyalty whatsoever to the Service, or any familial ties. His job was to apply an unbiased opinion, but Frank assumed he'd kept Spencer out of the loop.

He flicked his eyes up toward Garvan. 'You haven't mentioned any of this to Spencer, have you?'

'What makes you say that?'

Lucern shot him a cold, hard, calculating look, and said sneering, 'Because, if you *had*, with or without C's orders, I'd have been dead by now, that's why. I'm impressed, Luke, I really am. I didn't see that one coming at all. In hindsight, it was probably a combination of sloppiness and sheer bloody arrogance on my part. I thought I'd covered my tracks well enough, but I guess I hadn't bargained on dogged detective work.'

'There was nothing simple about it!' Garvan assured him.

'You struck lucky, Luke, that's all. If it hadn't been for that bloody bank raid, you'd be no closer to finding out the truth than you were at the beginning.'

'Maybe,' he said, diffidently, 'but I guess we'll never know, *will we*?'

'I suppose not.'

Garvan decided to turn the screw another notch; he was playing with fire, but there was nothing to lose. 'So Frank, *I am* talking to Toniolo, aren't I?'

Lucern's silence was answer enough.

'George had it in mind you might be a triple agent.'

275

He looked aghast at the idea. 'Good God, no. Work for a bunch of bloody fascists, never! You see, Luke, I could never quite give up the dreams of my youth. Whereas others happily moved on, I held on to my beliefs. It's not as if I was feeding Berlin with our secrets.'

'No, instead you're passing it all to Moscow!'

Lucern sighed. 'But, aren't you forgetting something?'

'What's that?'

'The Soviets happen to be on our side. We're Allies, and even with the Americans, we still haven't a cat in hell's chance of defeating the Third Reich without them.'

'That's as maybe, but it certainly doesn't give you the right to betray your country, and to kill anyone who gets in your way.' His gaze locked hard on Lucern. 'It's not just about holding a particular ideology. I can accept all that, but you've systematically betrayed everyone who has come within your radar, even friends, who you feared were getting too close to finding the truth!'

Automatically, he assumed Garvan was still referring to George Rowlands. 'I needed to cover my tracks,' he said candidly. 'If I'd allowed George to stay put as my number two, it would only have been a matter of time before he discovered the truth.'

'So, you set the poor bastard up with the Abwehr.'

'It was necessary,' Lucern said, without an ounce of compassion. 'The spying game, Luke, is never quite what it seems to be.'

'And Lord Oakways…how did he manage to get in your way?'

'We went back a long way,' Lucern said thoughtfully. 'I never knew him at Cambridge, of course. He was some twenty to thirty years older than me, but we occasionally met at the odd University reunion or the annual Lilburne Club bun fight.'

'But, you also met up during his stint at the Foreign Office?'

Garvan already knew the answer. Given the pivotal importance of the Iberian Desk in the Allies planning, Oakways had worked alongside members of MI6 on a daily basis. Lucern decided to side-step answering directly, and launched into an appraisal of Oakways's ministerial qualities, or lack of them, in the coalition government.

Garvan bided his time, before saying, 'What did the poor sod have on you? He must have had some hook or other.'

'A security document landed on his desk. It was one of many, only this one was different.'

'How was it different?'

'It was the first time he'd seen any reference to Agent Toniolo, and that he was suspected of being a Soviet spy.'

Garvan looked at him quizzically. 'But, why on Earth would he have made any connection to you?'

Lucern leaned forward, and scooped up his pipe from the ashtray, the last glowing strands of tobacco in the bowl slowly turning to ash. 'In 1939, before Italy entered the War, Oakways had been a member of a so-called trade delegation which visited Rome.' Lucern sharply tapped out the fading embers from his pipe into the ashtray. 'But, Oakways was always double-hatted. Even before becoming an MP, he was well known for being a diplomat with certain extras.'

'What's that supposed to mean?' Garvan said testily.

'That he's always had links to MI6.'

'What happened in Rome?'

'There was the usual merry-go-round of high powered meetings, coupled with a full diary of lavish entertainment, courtesy of Mussolini and his fascist cohorts. I'd met Oakways socially before, but this was different. It was the first time our paths had crossed professionally. Officially, the British government still wanted Italy on-side against Germany, but anyone with half a brain could see it was never

277

going to happen; the whole visit was no more than a fishing trip for information.' Lucern began to refill his pipe. 'One evening, the Ambassador, Sir Percy Loraine, treated Oakways to a meal at his favourite restaurant.' He shot Garvan a taut smile. 'Quite by chance, I was there, as well, only I was the guest of the Soviet Defence Attaché. Let's put it this way; Oakways was a little surprised to see me,' he added, striking a match, 'or should I say, he was surprised by the company I was keeping.' He puffed on the briar to get it going. 'The significance of our chance meeting was the name of the restaurant was Toniolo's.'

Lucern explained his codename was forever linked to the swish Italian restaurant, for it was on that warm sultry summer evening, he finally agreed to spy for the Soviet Union. At the time, Oakways had passed it off. The security services were always playing one another off against each other; after all, it was no more than their political masters demanded of them. It was when the security file referring to Toniolo landed on his desk at the Foreign Office he finally managed to make the connection. The more he read, it was only a matter of time before Oakways started to piece everything together There was nothing concrete to go on, but it was just enough for him to make the fatal connection.

'He started calling me,' Lucern explained, 'saying he knew what I was up to.'

'Why didn't he report you?'

'For a start, no-one would have given him the time of day, at least not without proof.'

'So, it was you who had his house wired?'

'Unofficially, yes, I did.'

'Meaning you didn't have C's approval?'

'It happens all the time,' Lucern said breezily.

'But, if things went wrong, you wouldn't have any top cover.'

'It's the name of the game.'

278

'You were playing with fire.'

'Oh, come on, Luke. It's not as if you haven't played the system before, a different system, but all the same, at Scotland Yard, you must have bent the rules. It's what makes us good at what we do.'

Garvan wouldn't be drawn.

'I was on to a winner. The beauty of it was, Oakways had started to become so paranoid he was under surveillance, no-one took him seriously, he'd become a complete bloody laughing stock.'

Garvan held himself in check, and answered evenly, 'And, I guess, behind the scenes, you helped stir up trouble?'

'I needed to cover my back.'

'But, you messed up.'

Lucern looked affronted. 'I'm sorry, how did I mess up?'

'I'll be honest. I looked like a bodged job.'

'It was meant to,' he said glibly.

Garvan wasn't convinced.

'If I'd made it look like a professional hit, you'd have put two-and-two together, and might have given his ranting's some credence. I lifted a few things; it was all a bit random, but it was just enough to make you wonder whether it was a run-of-the-mill robbery.'

'You really are a cold-hearted bastard, aren't you?'

'I did what I needed to do.'

'And the attempt on Caro Tait's life.'

'What about it?'

'I'm not an expert, so don't quote me if I'm wrong, but Spencer reckons it was a bodged job, and whoever had carried it out had lost their edge.'

Lucern bristled, as Garvan knew he would. His answer, when it came, was stilted. 'I've always been a desk man, and not some bloody gung-ho thug.'

'Why did you want to kill her?'

279

'Burdis was all over the place about spying for the NKVD. As far as I was concerned, he'd always been the weak link in the chain. Looking back, I should never have approached him in the first place.'

'So, why did you?'

'At the time, it seemed like a good idea.'

Garvan looked at him speculatively.

'I knew he was close to Caro, and I had a hook over both of them.'

'What went wrong?'

'Burdis had always been pretty slapdash about his official correspondence. I'd pulled him up once or twice. After Caro became his secretary things, became a little more complicated.'

'Did they?'

'I knew she'd been blabbing to Spencer about Burdis. Back in the day, Caro was regarded as a safe pair of hands in the Service, someone you could trust. I was concerned if she seriously started sniffing around, she'd end up piecing everything together. I couldn't take the chance. I was afraid she'd come across something important.' He drained his Bloody Mary, and set the empty glass down on the desk. Reluctantly, he admitted, 'I guess Spencer has a point. It probably wasn't exactly my finest hour.' He then shot Garvan a half smile. 'So how is Caro?'

'How do you think?'

'It wasn't personal.'

'Not personal? You tried to kill her!'

Lucern didn't respond.

Garvan stubbed out his cigarette. 'What I don't understand is, how you ever managed to persuade Burdis to spy for the NKVD?'

Lucern shrugged indifferently. 'It wasn't *that* difficult. He'd always sailed pretty close to the wind.'

'But, even so.'

'He only ever believed in one thing, himself!'

'At Cambridge, Burdis flirted with the idea of Communism,' Garvan said, thoughtfully nursing the vodka between his hands. 'Was his conversion to the far right just a ruse, or did he simply manage to fool everyone by concealing his allegiance to the Kremlin?'

'Good God, no. He reverted to kind. Burdis didn't exactly hide his light under a bushel, like his father. He was a bloody *fascist* in all but name.'

'Then, how the hell did you end up getting him to spy for the NKVD?' Garvan took another sip of the vodka.

Lucern wasn't forthcoming.

'I take it you blackmailed him?'

'It was something like that, yes,' he answered, and took a sharp intake of breath. 'It was more a case of divide and rule.'

Lucern explained how it hadn't taken him very long to realise relations between Burdis and Jeremy Haining at the FO were, at best, volatile. The astute Labour politician had little time for his newly-appointed junior Tory Minister, and considered him to be a political lightweight. They clashed constantly, and in the end, it came to a point something had to give. Haining had the ear of the Prime Minister, and was out for blood. His initial objections about Burdis's appointment to the Foreign Office proved to be well-founded; Haining reported he simply wasn't up to the job, and behind the arrogant bluster, there was very little substance. Haining's voice alone had not been quite enough to bring him down, but he was backed up by not only his colleagues across the political divide, but also a growing number of senior civil servants.

Lucern explained how he'd seized the opportunity of honing in on Haining's antagonism toward his colleague; it was a weakness on which he could capitalise. Behind the scenes, he began to discreetly foster and elaborate on the rumours surrounding Burdis, but the one real hook he had over him was his on-going cavalier attitude to document security. To Burdis, it seemed like an unnecessary layer of red tape. It was bureaucracy gone mad, or, at least, that's what he told the girls in charge of the registry. Gossip in government always departments spread like wildfire, especially if it was aimed at high-ranking officials. For Lucern, it was an opportunity to make a move on him, but he decided to bide his time. Burdis was always a train crash waiting to happen.

Quite by chance, he'd heard from a friend of Caro Tait Burdis had taken to having his suit jackets designed with specially styled poacher's pockets in the lining, apparently for the sole purpose of covertly removing classified documents from the office, and bypass the usual authorised channels. It was just another example of his ingrained arrogance. He didn't have any ulterior motive by side-stepping the system. He simply wanted to work on them at home, but couldn't be bothered with having to sign them out. It provided Lucern with a golden opportunity; he finally had Burdis just where he wanted him.

Lucern decided to take the bull by the horns, and confront Burdis about how it had come to his notice certain classified material had been removed from the Foreign Office, without the necessary authority. To start with, Burdis had fiercely denied any wrongdoing, but by this time, he'd done his homework. Long before either Spencer or Garvan had been ordered to break into his flat, Lucern had decided he might as well take a look around, and, by luck, had found some incriminating secret documents in an unlocked desk drawer.

When confronted, Burdis had assumed, at that point, he'd lose not only his security clearance, but also his ministerial post, to boot. Having crossed the line, he also knew, without the correct level of sanctioned clearance from British Intelligence he'd never again hold down another high-profile government post.

It was at this point Lucern had suggested a possible way out, a way of covering his tracks, and that the official report about his transgressions might not have to see the light of day. When he told Burdis his only means of redemption was spying for the Soviets, he was genuinely horrified, not just from a personal level, but also someone whom he considered a close friend, was, in fact, a double agent. His gut instinct was to report Lucern's approach to General Menzies immediately, but by doing so, he'd also open himself up to an investigation by the security services.

In disgust, Burdis had ordered him out of his office; Lucern openly admitted he was afraid he'd entirely misjudged the situation, and, more importantly, Jamie Burdis. He heard nothing until later that day; it was an anxious time, wondering which way Burdis would decide, either to report him for being a double agent, or roll over and accept his offer.

In the cold light of day, Burdis had known full well if he didn't play the game, Lucern would present Jeremy Haining a security report detailing how unauthorised top secret documents had been discovered in his flat, no doubt with the inference he was, in all probability, spying for a foreign government. It wasn't true, of course, but no-one would believe in his innocence, least of all his old sparring partner, Haining.

Self-preservation and overriding personal ambition finally won the day, but not without a cost. Three hours later, he had picked up the phone and reluctantly accepted Lucern's offer. It was to prove a Faustian pact, which would eventually lead to Burdis taking his own life, rather than endure the prospect of exposure as a Soviet spy and the ensuing public humiliation.

Unfortunately, for Lucern, things didn't go quite according to plan. Six months later, Haining had successfully forced his annoying colleague out of the Foreign Office. For a while, Burdis had been afraid Lucern might dispense with his services altogether. He was out on a limb, but, as it turned out, the risks of dropping him was deemed to be far too risky by the Soviets. Burdis still had his uses, maybe not on the same scale as before, but as an MP, his contacts across the various ministries straddling Whitehall meant they still continued to regard him as a valuable asset.

Garvan observed Lucern carefully, as he rolled out the full litany of his treachery and the ensuing fallout on those around him. He spoke without the slightest sense of remorse, and Garvan guessed Lucern did not really consider spying on behalf of the Soviet Union to be a crime. Lucern spoke passionately about how they were all simply allies, fighting against a common enemy, the tyranny of Nazi Germany. What harm was there in passing a few under the counter-intelligence reports which might help shorten the war. The one fundamental error in his reasoning he appeared to have overlooked was neither the British or American governments shared his views. As the war progressed, and an Allied victory seemed assured, the consensus on both sides of the Atlantic was they fully expected a post-war stand-off with the Soviet Union. Garvan started to believe Lucern had become so wrapped up in his spiral of deceit, the unwitting victims of his betrayal seemed to have become an almost secondary issue to him.

'I pulled Burdis's file from Central Registry, before he died.'

'It doesn't make for a pleasant read, does it?'

'I wouldn't know.'

Lucern expressed his surprise.

'It had been tampered with.'

'Tampered with?' he repeated.

Garvan's expression turned to one of resignation. 'As you know, the annex containing the stuff about his association to the far right was missing. In fact, the whole sodding file had been doctored. Someone, Frank, and I guess it was you, had gone to a great deal of time and effort to remove anything which might assist our enquiries. There had to be something on there you were afraid might connect Burdis to you.'

Lucern took his time answering. 'There were a couple of reports on there I'd written, questioning his reliability. Nothing too obvious, but I figured out a clever bastard like you might just work out how I'd secured his services, and put the pieces together. It was a pain, but I couldn't take a chance.'

There was just one more question Garvan needed to ask. He'd saved it until last. 'Why the hell did you murder Len Dunmore?'

Lucern looked searching into his eyes. 'Ah, yes, you were friends, I believe.'

'Just answer the question.'

'I feared him,' he said candidly. 'Dunmore was a top-flight journalist. He'd been around the block so many times, he'd become a permanent fixture on the scene. He knew every politician worth their salt, and, what's more, they listened to him. He knew where *all* the skeletons were hanging; he had something on nearly everyone. But, my greatest fear was Oakways had already revealed my identity to him. But, as it happened, I struck lucky. If I hadn't acted when I did.'

Garvan cut in. 'You mean, you killed him?'

'If I'd left it until the 27th, when he was due to meet Oakways for lunch at the Savoy, it would have been too late. However, at the time, I wasn't to know that.' He looked across the desk at Garvan. 'I take it you came across the entry in Oakways's diary?'

'Yes, of course, we did.'

'I couldn't take the chance of leaving Dunmore alive. He'd known Oakways for years; they often had lunch together. For all I knew, the old bugger might well have given Dunmore his acclaimed scoop. Oakways wanted to be vindicated, and have the last laugh on all of us who had, at one time or

285

another, accused him of chasing his tail and fighting shadows. He'd already threatened me with exposure, and so,' he said with a sigh, 'I didn't have any choice.'

'And I take it the scoop would also have outed you?'

Lucern smiled tautly. He could see Dunmore's murder was personal to him; there was an indefinable intensity in his expression, which hadn't been there before. 'Even without Oakways threatening to blab,' he felt obliged to explain, 'it was already getting complicated. You see, your journalist friend and Burdis were always sinking one too many at the Damaris bar. One false slip, one drunken conversation too far, and Burdis could have accidentally spilled the beans, and destroyed not only my cover, but his, for that matter.'

'It wasn't that simple, though, was it?'

'I'm sorry?'

'Len was running scared. Someone had got to him, someone, in the Service. I got the impression he didn't particularly want to run with the article about Oakways's alcoholism. Did you put pressure on Len to write it?'

'What do you think?'

It was answer enough. Garvan stared at him speculatively. 'The editorial would have destroyed Oakways, but it was never published.'

'No, it wasn't.'

'Why was that?'

'Because Oakways was going to spill the beans about me being a double agent to Dunmore. There wasn't time to pussyfoot around. I needed to silence both of them.'

'How did you manage to persuade Len to meet you outside the Adelphi Building?'

'I asked Burdis to make the arrangements; he gave him a promise of some inside information.

Garvan smiled lamely. 'He didn't think you'd be there?'

'Why do you ask?'

'Because Len had a nose for trouble, and always tried to avoid tipping his toe into the security world. Politicians were fair game, but he knew his limitations, which was why he was running scared about the editorial on Oakways.'

'Actually, it wasn't that hard persuading him. We'd bumped into one another, once or twice. Let's just say, he was aware I was not a nine-to-five civil servant at the FO. I'm sorry,' Lucern said, 'I know you were good friends.'

Garvan looked through him rather than at him, and said coldly, 'Whichever way you look at it, the game's up, Frank. There's no going back now.'

Chapter 23

Seeing Spencer striding purposely across the reception toward her, Joyce gave him a careful appraising glance.

'Did Eldridge sign a weapon out for you?' he snapped.

'Yes, he did.'

'Good, let's get a move on then!'

'Where are we going?'

'We're off to Broadway.'

'You mean to MI6?' she said uneasily.

He cast a bemused smile. 'Do you know there are times, Jo, when I seriously start to question how you ever managed to end up being our top double agent?'

She bristled immediately at the inference. 'But, why not meet up somewhere of our choosing, rather than at MI6?' she pressed.

'Precisely why we're going to Broadway. It's the last place on Earth Frank won't be expecting any trouble.'

Spencer made it clear the discussion was over, and so, Joyce followed him out of the building, toward his beloved racing green Jaguar, which was parked a short distance up the road. The rain was sweeping along the street in stair rods; forcing the gutters on either side of the road to overflow with fast-flowing rivulets, as the drains became increasingly unable to cope with the sudden torrential downpour. Joyce pulled the collar of her jacket up against the heavy driving rain, and teetered after Spencer on her high heels, trying desperately to keep pace, as he strode toward the car.

They drove out of St. James's, across the Mall, and down into Bird Cage Walk. The Jaguar's windscreen wipers began struggling against the incessant deluge. With the Blackout in full force, the weather conditions were making driving all the more treacherous.

Spencer suddenly took a sharp right through Queen Anne's Gate, and into Broadway, before pulling up outside MI6's Headquarters. He flung open the driver's door, and without bothering to lock the car, headed straight toward the heavily sand-banked entrance, leaving Joyce trailing in his wake.

On seeing Spencer, the smartly uniformed military policeman manning the reception desk immediately sprang to attention.

'Good evening, sir.'

Spencer breezed up toward him and smiled in greeting. 'Hello, Sergeant Nightingale. It's good to see you again. How are you?'

'Well, sir, very well.'

'I was just wondering if Mr. Lucern's still here.'

'I believe so,' he said, checking against a list of names registered in a large foolscap book on the desk. Everyone entering or leaving Broadway was required to report to the duty NCO. 'I've just come on duty, sir, but I believe he's not long returned to the building.'

Patiently, Spencer waited until Nightingale confirmed Lucern had booked himself back in, before twisting the book around to check for himself. Joyce kept a respectful distance, but judging by the expression on the Duty Sergeant's face, she assumed Spencer was a regular visitor, and, more importantly, someone who wasn't to be questioned.

Spencer leaned on the desk and slowly traced his right index finger down the length of the page, until he reached the entry he'd been looking for.

He flicked his eyes up toward the NCO, and said, tapping the page, 'Do you know if Superintendent Garvan is still with Mr Lucern?'

'I believe so, Major, unless, of course, he's been called to another meeting.'

289

'Can you book Miss Leader into the building? She's a member of my staff,' Spencer said, gesturing vaguely in her direction.

The Sergeant's gaze glided appreciatively toward Joyce. She was bloody attractive, that much he did know, and began wondering if he might not be in the wrong job. It ran through his mind maybe he ought to consider asking for a transfer to St. James's.

'Whatever you say, sir. May I have the lady's details?'

Joyce stepped forward, and produced an identity card; it was phoney, of course, but looked official. After her recruitment to MI5, the documentation had been forged by the Home Office, so was, in its own way, an entirely legal document. Nightingale glanced at it. If he harboured any suspicions, he wasn't about to quibble. She was well known to Major Hall, and that fact was authority enough. He dutifully copied her name into the notebook, checked his watch, and entered the time.

'May I have your signature, ma'am?' he asked, pointing to the entry with his pen.

She flashed him a smile, and signed her name. As she handed him back the pen, Joyce glanced round to see Spencer heading off toward the lift. It was an old metal-style contraption resembling an oversized bird cage. He dragged open the creaking door, which concertinaed back on itself, and waited for her to join him.

'Is this thing safe?' she asked him warily.

'To my knowledge, it hasn't killed anyone. At least, not yet. Come on. Get in!' he added impatiently.

Nightingale reached for a phone. 'I'll just let Mr. Lucern know you're on your way up, sir.'

'Thank you, but that won't be necessary,' Spencer called back to him.

Nightingale hesitated, but did as ordered, and set down the receiver.

Spencer pulled the door shut, and pressed the button for the fifth floor; they waited, nothing happened. Joyce swore under her breath; she'd much rather have taken the stairs. Spencer pressed the button again, only more forcibly this time, the ancient lift responded to his command, and slowly juddered into life.

He looked into her eyes. 'Did Eldridge give you a silencer?'

'Yes,' she said blankly.

Spencer slipped his PPK out of its holster, and momentarily cradled it in his hands, before screwing on the silencer into the muzzle. Her eyes flicked warily toward him. There was a cold, calculating intensity about him. While she didn't care a fig if he took out Frank Lucern. She just hoped to God Garvan didn't inadvertently get in his way.

The lift finally juddered to a halt at the fifth floor; Spencer heaved back the metal trellis gate, and headed off along the corridor. It was all brown linoleum and dully painted walls. Joyce's heart was in her mouth. She wasn't quite sure why he'd asked her to tag along; maybe he felt her report to Bernard Drescher would have an added air of authenticity to it, if she actually witnessed Lucern's execution. She knew Spencer must have spoken to C for permission to close Lucern down, but, even so, she was scared. It was inevitable, of course. If British Intelligence didn't take him out, then it was only a matter of time before the Abwehr, or possibly even the Soviets, eliminated him. Lucern had been playing a dangerous game, and in wartime, all bets were off.

Spencer stopped a little way ahead, and turned around to wait; once she'd caught up, without saying a word, he inclined his head toward the door. Her gaze drifted to the brass nameplate with Frank's name written in black lettering.

'Are you ready?' he mouthed at her.

291

She nodded, and loosened the catch on her handbag. She checked on the handgun, and then half closed it again. Without further preamble, Spencer flung open the door with such force, it ricocheted off the metal cabinet behind it. If nothing else, his entrance guaranteed their immediate attention; both Garvan and Lucern turned toward the door, each of them registering varying degrees of surprise, even more so when they noticed Joyce Leader standing behind him. She was the last person either of them had expected to see at Broadway. As good as Joyce was, she was very much an asset of MI5. Spencer had either completely taken all leave of his senses, or, for some reason, had been given authority. Lucern's expression was uneasy.

'I was under the impression Luke had been keeping everything under wraps,' Lucern blurted out. It was the only thing he could think of saying.

'Close the door,' Spencer said, quietly to her. 'I'm sorry.' He looked back to Lucern, and continued, 'I'm sorry, what's he been keeping under wraps?'

Lucern began to shift nervously in his chair. How could he begin to admit to Spencer, of all people, he was Toniolo, and had betrayed everything they had worked together for and he'd divulged countless high-grade intelligence to his Soviet spymasters over the years, leaving a bloody trail of death and destruction in his wake. Spencer was not only a friend, but also a force within British Intelligence; someone whose name was spoken openly as a future Director General of MI5. Garvan's forensic evidence was damning enough, but Spencer's unexpected appearance had suddenly put the fear of God into him.

'Luke said he hadn't told you.' He found himself saying, as if by rote.

'What the hell are you going on about?'

Fortunately, Garvan intervened, and saved him the trouble. He explained how, with the help of DCI Mackenzie and Scotland Yard's forensic team, they'd managed to match Lucern's fingerprints to those found not only in Bolton's Bank vault, but also from several items Mackenzie had removed after Lucern had attended a recent meeting at the Home Office.

'The prints were a perfect match,' he said matter-of-factly.

Spencer hid his feelings well; Garvan had played this one rather too close to his chest. Maybe he just hadn't wanted to break ranks, until he had concrete proof, or maybe he thought his position might have become untenable, accusing a senior member of the Service of being a Russian spy. Although Garvan had expressed his somewhat guarded thoughts about Frank in the past, his suggestions had always been met by a degree of unwillingness to listen, or take seriously. Whatever his motives for keeping everything under wraps, now was not the time to raise it. There would be time enough to thrash things out back at St. James's.

Once Garvan had finished, Spencer calmly lit a cigarette, and moved over toward the window. He stared out through the heavy net curtains to the street below. The rain was still falling heavily. He swung around suddenly to face Lucern; his expression was difficult to read.

'The trouble is, Frank, I'm here on C's orders.'

He raised his brows questioningly; even Garvan's face registered surprise.

'You see, earlier this evening, Jo received a message from her controller in Hamburg.' He took his time, and blew out a plume of smoke. 'And just when you thought it couldn't get any worse, it has.' He allowed himself a slight smile. 'You see, Frank, even if Garvie and DCI Mackenzie hadn't managed to swipe your fingerprints, I'm afraid the writing was already on the wall.'

'What do you mean?'

'Somehow, you seem to have upset Reichsführer Himmler.' Spencer glanced over his shoulder at Joyce, who was still near the door. 'I think that's a fair interpretation of the message, *don't you*?'

'More than fair,' she said bleakly.

His words hung menacingly in the air, and in the silence that followed, Lucern wondered how it was possible his world had not only imploded, it was in freefall, in the space of half an hour.

'H-Himmler,' he managed to stammer out. 'What are you talking about?'

'Reichsführer Himmler has ordered your elimination with…with…' He pretended to search for the right words. 'Now, let me get it straight. Yes, the message said, "with immediate effect." Spencer started to pace the office in a slow, deliberate manner, occasionally stopping to emphasise a particular point. 'In my experience, upsetting the Reichsführer tends to result in an unhappy outcome.' He smiled tightly at Lucern. 'But, of course, you would already know that, Frank.' The cigarette was perched casually in the corner of his mouth. His gaze set on his past colleague, without a trace of emotion. 'There's no two ways about it, Frank. They are out for your blood.'

'But, why are they?' Lucern pressed him.

'The message was clear enough,' Spencer explained. 'German Intelligence has managed to intercept information about Toniolo's links to the NKVD, and, in their words, not mine, is now guilty of giving away State secrets to the Soviet Union. You've been playing with fire, Frank, and juggling so many balls in the air at any one time, that, eventually, something had to give.'

He looked, half defensively and half pleadingly, at Spencer. 'But, how did they link me to Toniolo?'

Spencer shrugged indifferently. 'We don't know,' he answered truthfully. 'At least, not just yet. It's still early days.'

Lucern nodded.

'Just how much money have you been raking in from the Soviets?'

'I'm sorry?'

'It's an easy enough question.'

'It wasn't about the money,' Lucern blustered.

'Then, what was it about?'

'I did it for reasons you'd never begin to understand,' he said almost bitterly.

'Maybe not, but, the way I see it, Stalin's Kremlin and the Nazis appear to have a great deal in common,' Spencer said coldly.

'You're mad!' Lucern said contemptuously.

'Both regimes have complete contempt for individual liberty and freedom of thought.' Spencer looked at him searchingly. 'Why can't you see that, Frank? How could you stand by a regime that once made a pact with Hitler?'

It was like a red rag to a bull, Lucern bristled. There was nothing to lose, or so he thought; there was nowhere else to hide. The truth was out, so why not try and defend his corner, and in, some small measure, justify his actions. He tried explaining his political and ideological beliefs in Communism and social justice, but it was evident the die was cast. There could be no justification for his monumental deception and the betrayal of his colleagues and friends.

There remained only one question on Spencer's mind, how had the NKVD paid him. The answer, when it came, was simple; the money and instructions were dropped in a safety deposit box at Selfridges on Oxford Street. All formal communications between the NKVD in Moscow and London were passed routinely via diplomatic bags. That, in itself, was important. Unbeknown to the foreign delegations in London, or their closest Allies, diplomatic bags were routinely, albeit covertly, broken into and searched. But, something had been missed, and something important. It was a failure of the system, but, at least, they might be able to close the loop, and limit any further damage.

Lucern knew full well how the Abwehr would play it from now on in; they'd deliberately leak to their contacts Agent Toniolo was a busted flush, and so, in turn, his Soviet spymasters would eventually realise his cover was blown. He didn't even bother asking Spencer why C had sent him. With three intelligence agencies closing in for the kill, he was a dead man walking. If the Abwehr or NKVD didn't take him out, then British Intelligence would certainly finish the job off for them.

'Do I have a choice?' he asked.

'What do you think?'

Lucern shot him a half-hearted smile. 'I take it C would prefer to keep everything in-house?'

The look on Spencer's face was answer enough.

'Just as I thought,' he said.

On seeing Lucern opening his desk drawer, Spencer slipped the PPK out of its holster. 'Keep your hands where I can see them!'

Lucern raised his hand. 'There's no need,' he said flatly. 'I can't do this to you, I really can't,' he whispered, his eyes filling with tears.

Spencer glanced round at Joyce. 'You can put your pistol away, Jo,' he said to her.

'I'm sorry. I'm so sorry,' Lucern said, the tears freely trickling down his face.

Spencer held his gaze briefly; they both knew what had to be done, but he was eternally grateful Frank had given him a way out. Spencer made for the door, and gestured to both Garvan and Joyce to join him in the corridor outside. They followed, and waited for the inevitable sound of a gunshot. The gunshot was muffled; Spencer smiled to himself. It was obvious Frank had considerately screwed a silencer into the muzzle before taking his life.

Spencer paused a moment then turned the door handle before slipping back into the office. Lucern was dead, slumped back in his chair. Joyce instinctively recoiled from the doorway; the last thing she wanted to see was a body, least of all someone who had blown their brains out.

Lucern had placed the revolver in his mouth and fired. It certainly wasn't a pleasant sight. They stood in silence for a moment or two, taking in the blood-splattered scene. The only saving grace was his death had been mercifully quick. In Spencer's mind, his death was not only justified, but testament to his treachery and consistent betrayal, finally been underscored in his own blood.

Garvan wasn't quite sure how to break the silence between them. During the early days of the War, he knew Spencer and Lucern had worked together on a daily basis. They were not only friends in the literal sense, but in their cloak and dagger world, it had a far wider meaning. It was a relationship borne not only out of mutual trust, but they'd also lived by an unwritten creed, they wouldn't only watch each other's backs in a time of trouble, but, if necessary, lay down their life.

'This can't have been easy for you.' Garvan found himself saying mechanically.

'It never is,' Spencer said flatly.

'But, at least, we've closed down the leaks from MI6 to the Kremlin.'

Spencer stared almost unseeingly at Lucern's body. 'But, have we, Luke? That's the problem. I'm not so sure that we have.'

Garvan shot him a questioning look.

Spencer had a gut feeling it wasn't quite as clear cut as Garvan hoped for. 'Just when you've caught one bugger, another comes out of the woodwork.'

Spencer had once believed he knew Frank Lucern better than anyone else in the Service, but he was fooled, taken in, as he had been with George Rowlands. He suspected Lucern probably wasn't acting entirely on his own, and the Soviets would certainly have targeted not only other members of the Service, but also politicians. It was unthinkable that they hadn't. There were others, just like Frank, who had the right profile, and who, in spite of their cut-glass Oxbridge accents, were seduced in their youth by the idea of a utopian society, both classless and stateless. To Spencer's mind, in its way, Communism was as much a pipe dream as Hitler's deadly plans for an Aryan Third Reich. But, there were other people, like Frank, who could never quite see beyond their youthful fervour and blind belief in a regime, that, under Stalin, squashed political opponents as ruthlessly and brutally as the Nazis.

Spencer calmly wiped the phone receiver with his handkerchief, before throwing the blood-stained cloth into the wastepaper basket. He dialled zero, then waited for the duty telephonist to answer. At the back of his mind, he feared the worse that, somehow, a spy ring, a Soviet one, had skilfully managed to penetrate the heart of MI6. It was all sheer speculation, until he had proof. Like Garvan, it was probably sometimes safer to play your cards close to your chest.

'Can you put me through to C at the Cabinet War Rooms?'

There was a slight hesitation on the other end of the line. The telephonist had naturally expected to hear Frank Lucern's voice. 'Yes, yes, sir,' she stammered. 'And who shall I say is calling?'

'Major Spencer Hall.'

'Please hold.'

A series of clicks followed, as she connected the line to the War Rooms.

'I have C on the phone for you, sir,' she came back to him.

'Thank you.'

'Well, Major Hall,' Menzies grunted down the phone, 'have you managed to clear up our little mess?'

'Yes, sir.'

'Were there any problems?'

'No, there wasn't.'

'Good, then I'll let the PM know we've shut everything down.' Menzies hesitated. 'I take it you'll let our *friends* across the water know what's happened.'

Spencer knew he was referring to Berlin. 'It's all in hand, sir.'

'I'll call you first thing in the morning.'

Conversations with C were invariably short, and to the point.

'What do we do now?' Garvan queried.

'We return to St. James's.'

Garvan eyes flicked toward Lucern's body. 'But, what about Frank? Do we just leave him here, like this?'

Spencer shrugged. 'We can't do much for him, can we?'

'That's not what I meant.'

'I know it wasn't.'

'Well?'

'I think you'll find MI6 will want to sort out its dirty laundry.'

*

In the early hours of the morning, with Spencer at her side, Joyce Leader sent a short reply to Bernard Drescher in Hamburg.

"Confirmation, repeat confirmation, Agent Toniolo has been eliminated.
Await further instructions. Heil Hitler"

Spencer looked up at Garvan, who was hovering behind her chair, and said, with a wink, 'Why don't you two get yourselves off home to bed?'

Joyce's startled eyes met his. It was almost as if he was granting them tacit approval for their budding relationship, a relationship which had been on hold, ever since Spencer had confronted them both about it. That didn't mean to say he approved, but he was prepared to give them some slack, and to turn a blind eye, just as long as they remained discreet. If word ever got out, and came to official notice about their affair, then he'd no longer be able, or willing, to shield them from the consequences.

'Thank you,' she whispered.

As Joyce stood up, Garvan gently slipped his arm round her waist. 'Aren't you going to call it a day?' he asked Spencer.

'No, I need to clear up a few things in the office.' He watched them leave before slowly making his way back along the corridor. The door to his office was locked; his secretary was expecting him back, and hadn't bothered to pack away the paperwork. He felt in his trouser pocket for the key, and then let himself in. He flicked on the light switch, and slumped down at the desk, pulling open the drawer and grabbing hold of a pack of cigarettes. He slipped one between his lips, and flipped on his lighter, but it was out of fuel. He rummaged in the drawer, and under a pile of discarded pens and sweet wrappers, found a box of matches; he struck one, and then tossed it into the overflowing ashtray.

As he settled back in the chair, his eyes wearily glided across the desk. There was the usual pile of cipher stuff to deal with, but placed neatly on the inkpad in front of him was a file. There was a note attached to it. He instantly recognised Tar Robertson's copperplate handwriting. "For your immediate attention." it read. He pulled off the note, his gaze setting on the file. It was top secret, with a caveat of UK and US EYES ONLY, and titled, "Mission to Berlin." Spencer wearily flicked the file open; he had a feeling that he had a long night ahead of him.

If you liked this book you may also wish to read the other books by the same author:-

Codename Nicolette
Review from Amazon UK

A really absorbing story which screams out to be made into a BBC produced series or British produced film (to catch the atmosphere of the like of Tinker, Tailor). The author gives the real feel of how we were "up against it" and that the strategies of the intelligence services, when needed most, played a critical part. It looks as though DCI Garvan is in the position to provide further adventures into the doings of the cloak and dagger brigade and I look forward to reading them.

Mission Lisbon the V-1 Double Cross
Review from Amazon UK

This is a very well researched wartime novel with believable characters and a twisting storyline. It is a gripping story of espionage during World War II, and I hope there will be another book in the series as it leaves the reader on a cliff-hanger.

Made in the USA
Columbia, SC
04 August 2017